THE TAMARISK TREE

SEEDS OF HOPE & WAR.

ROBERT W CELY

THE TAMARISK TREE

SEEDS OF HOPE & WAR

ROBERT W CELY

Published by

The Tamarisk Tree
by Robert W. Cely

Published by Bard and Book Publishing.

ISBN 978-1-947844-52-0

To my wife, Liz,
who has faithfully
wandered beside me.

Chapter One
Hiram's Well

Dust rose up as the magi traced figures in the sand. The villagers crowded around, curiosity etched on their sunburned faces, wondering what the cryptic symbols meant. They didn't understand anything the magi traced in the dust, but they understood the dust.

The dust was everywhere. As far as the eye could see and as long as any man had ever walked, all they ever saw was dust and sand and rock and sun-baked wasteland. Sometimes they would cross over canyons of deep red rock and clay, or hear a rumor about scrub grass or a cactus that somehow managed to cling to life. Anyone of any learning at all knew these were only rumors. The only true fact of life was the sand and dust.

The magi leaned back to look at his figures again before bending back to his work. He carefully moved the roughly-hewn wand, the charred end tracing the sibylline characters. Around him he could feel the anticipation of the villagers, almost hear them wondering if this would work. The magi had done it a thousand times. A simple spell like this he could have cast in his sleep. At the same time he understood how a simple thing could mean so much to a village like Hiram's Well.

"I require payment now before I can finish," the magi looked up and spoke to one of the villagers.

The man addressed quickly fumbled in his worn and faded trousers. Held up by a nearly dry-rotted rope, the pants threatened to fall off the thin figure as hands groped through a secret pocket to ceremoniously pull out two copper pieces.

The magi motioned with his head towards the burly guard that stood over him. Compared to the villagers, Bannus looked fat. But any who ever tested the man's strength quickly found that the bulk was almost all muscle. Still, size like that attracted attention, especially when everyone else struggled to stay alive. Fat meant food and food meant wealth. Not that anybody who lived in the interior cared about wealth. Or at least their care extended as far as wealth's ability to buy food.

Bannus looked at the copper pieces handed to him and frowned before slipping them into a pouch at his side. He shrugged his shoulders and gave a slight nod to the magi. There was something about the copper he didn't like. Probably too small, perhaps an outlawed minting, or the coins might have showed signs of shaving or diluting. Whatever the reason, Bannus decided to take it and the magi really didn't care what the guard's hesitation was about.

"What's your name?" the magi asked his newest customer.

"Thom," the man answered. He patted the shoulders of a boy beside him who stood just over waist high. "And this is my boy, Frederick."

"You should address the magi properly," Bannus reminded with a threat gleaming in his eye.

"And what do you do?" the magi asked, trying to ignore the over-bearing Bannus.

"My father was a farmer, Sire," Thom was careful to add the honorific. "The last independent around here. It was him that taught me how to dry seeds."

"Yes, he must have been very good at what he did," the magi mused.

As the magi leaned in to his work a shadow fell over the characters drawn in the sand. The day was too bright to be dimmed, but the shadow seemed to cast a deep darkness over the magi. Something stirred in the magician as the shadow fell over him, a remembrance, a hint, something that tugged at his memory which he could not lay hold of.

The magi looked up at the figure who had stood over him and cast the shadow upon the sand. He could not make out the features of the stranger because of the sun that blazed just behind. The magi even had to squint as the bright light formed a halo around the head of the stranger.

"You're in the magi's light," Bannus spat, pointing a beefy finger at the stranger.

"My apologies, honored one," the stranger said as he bowed and stepped away, taking his shadow with him.

Something in the voice stirred that vague sense of familiarity in the magician. He let his eyes follow the stranger. For a moment their eyes locked. Something about the stranger's deep blue eyes reminded the magician of a thunderstorm. Not just any storm, but one in particular, a storm not just of weather. One that shook the whole world.

The magician turned away from the stranger's arrogant smile.

"Well, Sir Thom, son of the last independent farmer," the magi said as he drew the finishing touches on his casting. "I give you a cucumber plant."

The magi stepped back as the crowd of villagers drew around the cryptic drawings in the sand. For a moment, the drawings sparkled, but only briefly. It was so subtle that one could easily think it was the sunlight dancing on the sand.

From three different spots on the earth three sprouts broke free of the sand and began twisting towards the sun. The crowd gave an ah of approval, watching the vines branch out, and even as they watched, sprout broad, green leaves and bloomed yellow flowers.

Thom rubbed his hands eagerly together, a broad smile across his dirty face. He put an arm around his skinny, underfed son, both anticipating a rare feast, even if it was only cucumber.

"You'll see boy," Thom promised. "I'm telling the truth. These are the most delicious things you've ever tasted."

The crowd waited as tensely as Thom. They continued to stare at the cucumber plant, anticipating the growth of fruit along its vines.

"Where are the cucumbers?" Thom asked after a few moments of nervous waiting with no appearance of vegetables.

"Well, you paid me for three cucumber plants," the magician answered, pointing to the three flawless specimens that had sprouted magically from the earth.

"Yeah, and cucumber plants have cucumbers on them," Thom countered.

"Eventually," the magician said. "But you only paid for the plant. You didn't pay for the plant to fruit."

Thom looked at the magician, confused. All the anticipation had gone out of the crowd. Their energy suddenly diffused to disappointment.

"How much do I have to pay for fruit?" Thom asked with a quivering voice.

"Half copper per plant," Bannus interjected without the slightest trace of sympathy in his voice.

The crowd murmured as Thom let his head fall. He looked down at his son and fought back tears.

"There ain't no way you could get me some fruit," Thom pled. "You don't know what I had to do to get you that money. If I'd have known that the money wouldn't have given me fruit I would have waited."

"You could have had one plant with fruit for the two copper pieces," the magician told him.

"Why didn't you tell me that then?!" Thom shot back angrily as the crowd began to voice their disapproval. "What am I supposed to do with this?"

"Just water the plants and they will probably begin to fruit," the magician suggested.

"Where am I supposed to get water?"

"This place is called Hiram's Well, right? Get it from the well"

"The well's been dry for years. No water around here except what's doled."

The magician looked down at the three cucumber plants. He truly felt sorry for the man. There was no doubt that the plants would never fruit. Even if there was water the heat would likely kill the plants without magical aid to sustain them.

"You can't help me out and I pay you back later," Thom bargained. "I promise I can get you the money."

"Guild rules," Bannus spat. "Sorry, the Guild sets prices and terms."

"Come on now, that's just low down and dirty!"

The crowd agreed noisily. A stir ran through them that threatened to break open with violence. The magician wasn't sure he didn't blame them. He locked eyes with the stranger again and felt something pass in that glance. The smirk came back to the stranger's face and the magician turned away.

"You will address the magician appropriately," Bannus warned again as he stepped toward the crowd. He reached behind him and placed a hand on the massive sword that was strapped to his back.

This was all the threat the crowd needed to be subdued. They quieted instantly and stepped back from the overbearing guard. For too long they had been starved and oppressed. There was no fight in their hearts.

"Please, Sire," Thom begged as tears pooled in his eyes. "Is there some mercy you can show me? My boy's never had cucumbers. I been promising him for months now."

The magician looked down at Frederick. The boy, who couldn't have been more than eight years old, also had tears pooling in his eyes. He looked up at his father and took his hand reassuringly.

"Maybe I can get you a few cucumbers to hold you over until the rest come in," the magician suggested.

"Guild rules," Bannus reminded.

"A few cucumbers wouldn't hurt," the magician said.

"Guild rules," Bannus repeated without any sign of weakening.

"Have a heart, Bannus. I'm going to give them a few cucumbers."

"I would be forced to report this infraction to guild authorities," Bannus said, staring down the magi.

The magician fumed inside. Bannus and his stupid guild rules. He was reminded how much he loathed the guard's presence.

"Is that the way to address a magi?" the magician shot back at his guard.

"I would be forced to report this infraction to guild authorities, Sire," Bannus repeated properly, an edge of resentment sharpened his voice.

The magician forced himself to look at Thom. He gave a slight shake to his head and looked quickly at the ground. He could feel the crowd deflate, the excitement leak out of them. Slowly, they dispersed until there was no one left but Thom, Frederick, the magician and Bannus. The stranger lingered for a moment, staring hard at the magi before filing away with the crowd.

"I'm sorry," the magician said. He stretched a hand out towards the man and his son, but let it drop.

"Keep an eye on the plant," the magician told Thom as a way of advice. He turned and walked back towards town. Bannus eyed the man up and down for good measure then followed the magician.

Man and son stood for a while over the cucumber plants. Disappointment couldn't begin to describe what they felt. Defeated perhaps? Torn down? No different from the rest of their lives. In fact, the three cucumber plants could be a representation of their entire lives. Promise, potential, but eventually dashed hopes and disappointment. For decades, magic had been promising to deliver a future of bounty and promise. Like these plants, it was only the appearance, a show of plenty without substance.

The boy eventually pulled out from under his father's hand and made his way back to town. He was hungry, and there was sympathy he saw in the magi's eyes. Perhaps that sympathy would end in a heel of bread or some water.

The father didn't move. Thom stared at the plant with no intention of moving. He didn't believe the plants would ever fruit. But the plants were all he had. He had given so much to see them through and he would stick with them, watching every leaf wither and fall if he had to.

All the way into town the magi fumed at Bannus. He deliberately walked ahead of the guard, not being able to tolerate the presence of the despicable man. Thom and his son wouldn't leave his mind, stoking his fury at Bannus and his own impotence.

He could feel the guard's eyes boring into his back. Without even looking he could see perfectly that insipid, dull glare, full of officious stupidity.

The magi couldn't help but turn and look behind him. Just as he imagined, Bannus had those empty, grey eyes focused on him. Beefy jowls finished the freckled face, sitting atop a ridiculously over-muscled shoulders. The thin, sandy blonde hair, receding more everyday, finished the effect. All of it, including the artificially muscled figure (the magi was convinced that Bannus owed much of his bulk to magical enhancement) made Bannus into the perfect oaf.

It would have been better if Bannus was a total idiot, the magi concluded. He wasn't bright by any standard, instead possessing just enough intelligence to be dangerous. Not enough to know what he didn't know, Bannus was one of those rare creatures too smart to be stupid but far too stupid to be smart.

The magi sighed and kept towards the town. It wasn't fair to blame Bannus. The guard was simply following guild rules. Those damn guild rules. Bannus would follow them until death.

The magi pushed the thought out of his head and trudged into the dusty town of Hiram's Well.

As a town went, Hiram's Well was nothing short of pathetic. Most of the dried and rotted buildings were vacant except for the squatters that might huddle there at night. A few collections of these hungry people milled about the unpaved streets. There was literally nothing to do but stand around and wait for the dole to arrive.

And by the looks of things, the dole was late. The ragged faces of the people were a little more worn and haggard than usual. The sovereign guards watching over the water store looked around a little more warily, wore a little more tension than usual.

The magi headed towards one of the few decent buildings in town, a pub built of wooden slabs called Hiram's Dowser. He stepped onto the porch and stamped what dust he could off of his light, leather boots before stepping inside. He was careful not to meet eyes with any of the men or women who gathered just off the porch. All of them, no doubt, waited for anyone rich enough to buy beer and merciful enough to share. The magi did notice the seal of the Enclave of Kilgaro over the door.

Inside, the pub was mostly empty. A pair of soldiers sat on the far side, one sleeping, the other quickly nodding off in his beer. Another pair of men dressed in silks looked over a ledger, arguing quietly with one another. A lone figure sat at the bar and four women huddled on the end away from the door, their eyes afraid and desperate, willing to go to any length to survive.

The magi took a seat at one of the many vacant tables as the thin bartender hurried towards him. Bannus followed close behind, surveying the mostly empty establishment before taking another table near the soldiers. He exchanged a nod with the soldier who had yet to fall asleep. Neither spoke a word.

"Honored Sire, honored Sire," the thin bartender greeted, rubbing his hands together as he approached.

"Welcome, the Hiram's Dowser welcomes you to its humble abode. We would be most pleased to serve you, Honored Sire. Of course, we love to serve the magicians who keep this fine land alive. May the grace and blessings of the gods shed their light on you."

"What do you have in the way of wine?" the magi asked, not expecting much at all, just something that would slake his thirst and dull the annoyance that had settled in his chest like an itch he couldn't reach.

"Oh yes, we have several bottles of fine Alderan that would suit a man of your obvious refinement," the bartender gushed.

"Something lighter," the magi waved off the suggestion. "A Galen or Vitoria would be splendid about right now."

"Nothing like that, sire, I am afraid to report."

"Any chilled whites?"

"Well," the bartender chuckled nervously. "We have several bottles of a New Seton."

"Rubbish"

"Or perhaps a Melan would be more to your taste," the barkeep suggested.

"That tastes like sand."

"Oh, we could not have that for the honored magi," the bartender said, growing more nervous, his hand wringing increasing in intensity. "Certainly there is something here that would please the Sire."

"What about beer?" the magi asked.

"Of course! Why didn't I suggest that?" the barkeep exclaimed, growing artificially excited. "I expect either a Pale Neuman or the Wheat Reiser for a taste that is distinguished as yours."

7

"You have a Pale Neuman?" the magi asked with obvious interest, amazed how a fine beer like that would make it as far inland as Hiram's Well.

"Yes we do, sire," the bartender gushed with self-satisfaction. "We pride ourselves on meeting the needs of the magi who brave these wild and desolate places to serve us, and will go to any end to offer the comforts that they may require."

"Just make it cold as you can," the magi dismissed the barkeep with a wave of his hand.

Under a flurry of bows and hand-wringing the barkeep backed away before turning and hurrying down the cellar. The magi found his annoyance stoked by the pitiful man's eagerness to please. Even the sounds of his footsteps retreating down into the cellar grated on his nerves.

The magi looked around the bar again, searching for some distraction, another human being to engage with. The businessmen on the far side were engrossed in their figures. One good look at the women discouraged any notion he may have entertained with them. They would have gladly welcomed his money, but the desperation with which they offered themselves made any enjoyment the magi would seek from them all but impossible. Of course, he would rather eat sand than speak with Bannus or the soldiers. And to try and converse with any of the dusty men who peered inside from the porch would defeat the purpose of seeking solace from the sweaty masses. This left the figure at the bar as the only source of diversion available.

At the moment, the figure had his back turned towards the magi, huddled over something hidden from view, most likely a drink. The magi stared at the man's back, willing him to turn around so their eyes would meet and a conversation could begin naturally.

Amazingly, the man did turn around. No sooner had the magi fixed his eyes upon him, than the man spun around on his stool.

A pair of distant, blue eyes fixed on the magi. He recognized them immediately. The stranger who had stepped into his sunlight.

"Honored Sire," the stranger said mockingly as he lifted a glass in toast.

That sense of recognition flowed again in the magi, a certainty that he knew the man from somewhere, but could not remember where. Lightning struck in his mind, tearing open the darkness that howled around. Rain fell in unforgiving torrents. He felt cold iron beneath his hands, the taste of blood in his mouth.

A storm.

A storm that shook the world, the magi thought to himself.

As soon as he thought it, the image fled his mind. The magi was almost surprised to find himself in the dusty public house. The stranger still stared at him with an arrogant grin and tempestuous blue eyes.

"It's you," the magi said to the stranger. "You were standing in my light."

"A thousand apologies most honored one," the stranger piled on sarcastically with a grand wave of his hand and a bow.

The stranger slid off his bar stool and walked over to the magi's table without being invited. As he approached the magi took the opportunity to appraise him.

The stranger didn't wear the same look of starved neglect common to men of the interior. Even a modestly healthy frame was considered fat in a place like Hiram's Well. The stranger, however, seemed the picture of health, even down to his light brown hair and finely, almost perfectly proportioned face, easily handsome by any reckoning. Yet there was something about the stranger that was decidedly unattractive.

It was nothing the magi could put his finger on. At first, he thought it might be the stranger's pale blue eyes, the ones he couldn't look at without hearing thunder in his mind. But no, it was something else.

For certain, the stranger stood out, for reasons other than his obvious health and lack of privation. Instead of the white linens that most people wore who could afford it, like the magi himself, the stranger wore a dark green shirt. Upon the front was stitched a brown tree that branched up the arms and around the back. His brown pants were plain enough, though still not white or rags. On his feet were sturdy leather boots that showed the sign of many rugged miles upon them. He didn't carry a pack, only a pouch on his belt. A long knife was the only weapon visibly upon him, though conspicuous because of its black handle covered in silver scrollwork.

The magi finally decided there was nothing about the stranger that made him look alien. It was only a vague sense, but the magi couldn't help but feel it. The stranger seemed... artificial, he decided. There was an air about the man that reeked of falsehood, as if everything about him was contrived and fake.

The magi decided he didn't like the man at all.

"So why would an illustrious magician such as yourself grace the dusty backwater of Hiram's Well?" the stranger asked as he lowered himself into a seat across from the magi.

"Just spreading the hope of magic," the magi answered with a shrug.

"Well that much is obvious," the stranger laughed artificially. "You certainly filled poor Thom with hope. Does the Enclave's charity know no bounds?"

The stranger laughed again at his own wit. He drank from his clay cup, oblivious to the magi's challenging stare.

Strangely though, the magi did not feel insulted at the exposure of his own hypocrisy. After all, it wasn't his hypocrisy. It was forced onto him by the Enclave and its brainless policies. Perhaps the stranger wasn't as bad as he looked, perhaps he might even be sympathetic to his plight.

"That's how we love," the magi replied with a forced grin, feeling a little self-conscious.

"Ahh, my Lord Sire," the bartender cooed as he returned with a mug of ale. He presented it to the magi with a flourish.

"My every confidence it will be to the Sire's pleasure," the bartender gushed and backed away.

The magi took up the mug, glad for the distraction. He drank deeply, savoring the rich, malty beer, though it wasn't nearly as cold as it should have been. Still, the taste relieved him for a moment of the dusty world outside.

"Pitiful excuse for a Pale Neuman," he muttered over the rim of his mug.

The magi glanced out the door and saw the boy - what was his name? Frederick? - looking at him from the porch outside. He stared at the magi with wide and hungry eyes, unashamed in their plea. The boy could have been one of a million in the dry and starving world they inhabited. They all wore the same look, held the same tired plea in their eyes.

He turned away from the accusation in that stare, in all the crowd that gathered outside the pub, waiting for someone to help them. The stranger had his gaze fixed firmly upon the magi. He stared at him in a way that only people who didn't understand the subtle, unspoken rules of society would stare. The stranger didn't speak, just stared, as if expecting the magi to carry the burden of conversation.

"Do you live here?" the magi asked, just to have something to say.

"Oh by Hell and all her dirty princes, no," the stranger answered, sounding offended. "Just passing through."

"So where you headed?"

"Don't know," the stranger shrugged and downed his drink. "Somewhere else."

The stranger lifted his hand for another round. The bartender hurried over and filled his cup with a clear liquid, then topped off the magi's beer. Silence fell over the table again with more of the stranger's insistent staring.

"My name's Elias," the magi introduced. "Elias Whitsun."

"I didn't ask your name," the stranger pointed out.

The magi thought he heard a taunt in the voice. Annoyance itched deeper in him.

"Well, I thought that if we were going to sit here and stare at each other like a pair of love-sick children we may as well be on a first name basis," the magi said, making no attempt to hide his irritation.

The stranger smiled and lifted his glass.

"Elias Whitsun then," he said. "I'm Thoran."

"Do you have a last name?"

"Never bothered with one." Thoran answered.

"Where are you from?"

"All over."

"What do you do?"

"Wander. Drift about from place to place. Looking for...just looking."

"What are you looking for?" Elias asked, feeling increasingly frustrated by the stranger.

"Something...else," Thoran gave as a meager answer.

"Okay then, Thoran Wanderer, searching for something else," Elias summed up.

Thoran shrugged and the two men fell to their glasses. Elias looked around the room again. Nothing had changed. The boy still stared at him from outside, squatting on his haunches now. Bannus had his gaze fixed on Thoran and Elias, suspicion etched on his face. This, more than anything else, warmed Elias towards the stranger. If Bannus didn't like him, then maybe Elias should.

"So how long have you been wandering, Thoran?" Elias turned back to the stranger and asked.

"All my life," Thoran answered.

"And how long is that?"

"Not as long as you might think."

"Are you any closer to finding what you're looking for?" Elias asked, digging for something that would endear him to the stranger.

"Very close," Thoran said, leaning in. "In fact, I'm so close I have to ask myself if I really want to find it."

Elias had no idea what the stranger possibly meant by these words. A vague sense of dread came over him, completely without warning. Something about the stranger made him wary, set off the alarm cry in his head.

"What about you?" Thoran asked, leaning back in his chair. "How long have you wandered?"

"A long time," Elias sighed. "Too long."

"Aren't you a little too old to still be wandering about?" Thoran asked with a sly grin. "Don't recall ever seeing a Walker your age."

"My situation is..." Elias searched for the right word. "Complicated."

"I'll say," Thoran agreed. "You have a personal bodyguard as well."

Both men looked towards Bannus. The guard still had a glare fixed on the stranger. His look of suspicion had narrowed to mild hostility.

"I don't think your friend likes me," Thoran said, lifting his glass to Bannus.

"He's not my friend," Elias muttered, regretting the comment immediately. He knew for certain his emotions had been made too plain.

"Ahh, I note some resentment," Thoran said with clear enjoyment. "Does that mean he isn't here to guard you? What then? Babysit?"

"Like I said, my situation is complicated," Elias stressed. He lifted his empty glass, signaling the bartender for a refill.

"That would explain the little tiff about the cucumbers," Thoran pressed in. "You obviously wanted to help the man. But him over there with his 'guild rules' wouldn't let up. Yes, I think he's there to watch you. Make sure you're behaving.

"Have you been a bad boy?"

"Something like that," Elias admitted. "I probably pissed somebody off."

He downed his beer in a few quick gulps and slammed his mug on the table. The bartender hastened to refill it. A welcome, numbing sensation ran through Elias, the pleasant relaxation brought about by the alcohol. He found himself warming to the stranger despite his conscious misgivings. He downed half the mug quickly again.

"So you believe in your quest then?" Thoran asked him, rapping his own glass against the table. "Sharing the hope of magic?"

"Why not?" Elias answered. "What else is there to do? The soil has degraded too much and the seeds have lost their potency. Look around. There isn't a crop that can grow out there without the help of magic. What hope is there outside of magic?"

"True," the stranger agreed. "No one can grow food without the help of magic. However, rumor has it this problem was caused by magic."

"Now who says that?" Elias challenged, but without hostility.

"No one you would know," Thoran chided.

"You mean no one who knows anything at all about magic believes that magic is responsible for the present famine?"

"So you admit it's a famine," Thoran said, jabbing a finger at Elias. "Is that the official stance of the Enclave or just what you magi whisper to each other when no one else can hear?"

"Of course," Elias conceded. "No matter what the Enclave says, it's a famine. Hell, it's more than a famine. I don't know what it is, but it makes a famine look like a party. I think most people these days would sell their soul for a famine.

"But that's besides the point. Anybody who knows anything about magic knows that magic didn't cause this."

"You mean anybody with a vested interest in magic won't admit that magic caused The Blight," Thoran argued.

"If you say so," Elias waved the stranger off.

"Okay, consider this," Thoran proposed. "A hundred-fifty years ago nobody grew food with magic, and there was no problem with the soil, no problem with the seed, no major food shortages. A famine here, a blight there, but nothing we couldn't recover from. Not to mention you could see green everywhere and trees and forests, life everywhere."

"Certainly some of that is embellishment," Elias contended. "People tend to remember things a bit idealistically."

"All that aside," Thoran brushed away the objection. "It wasn't until people started using magic to grow food that all this trouble started."

"I think you have a selective memory," Elias countered. "Magic ushered in an era of unprecedented prosperity. Not long after we discovered how to apply magic to food production crop yields quintupled. Starvation was essentially abolished. In fact, food was so abundant that Kings could give it away to whoever couldn't afford it. Wealth increased across the board, innovation and invention exploded. So much of the labor that had gone into food production was freed up for hundreds of other pursuits. There was a marked increase in the appearance of new universities and theaters and copy houses. Learning, art and culture flourished with the increased abundance. Hell, even a war was hardly fought for nearly thirty years. Hardly anything to disparage magic over."

"Ah yes, the great Golden Age of Magic," Thoran mused as he jabbed his empty cup at Elias.

The bartended discreetly filled both glasses without either man noticing or asking. They had become too engrossed in their debate.

"But consider what happened after that. About forty years into this supposed Golden Age there were some who quietly noticed that land yields were actually decreasing. Very subtle at first, so that it was many years until others started to notice. Some began to wonder whether it was the interference of magic that was causing the problem. In another twenty years yields had gone down to their pre-magic numbers. Of course, by this point the only farms in operation were those operated by magic, strictly run by Enclave policy. They had long ago put any private farms out of business. Not to mention, the Enclave were the sole owners of any viable seed. Any whispers of damage due to magic was quickly and harshly suppressed. The Enclave controlled the food supply and were able to keep the secret well kept.

"Then it got nasty. People noticed it was taking more and more magic to produce less and less food. The soil got depleted, seed potency fell. Then, it was the forests that began to shrink, weather patterns changed, wild grasses withered and almost every animal that wasn't domesticated all but disappeared. Eventually, no one could grow food without magical assistance. Until here we are now, children of The Golden Age of Magic. Only magic can grow anything at all. And even then with great difficulty."

Elias shrugged and shook his head at Thoran. The stranger held his arms out defensively, begging the magi to explain his doubt.

"You haven't said anything that hasn't been said before," Elias pointed out. "But you left out something crucial."

"What would that be?"

"You have failed to demonstrate that magic was responsible for The Blight. All you've done is outline what happened. You've given me no proof."

"No proof?" Thoran asked incredulously. "Is it just coincidence that the increase in the use of magic in agriculture coincides with the dying of the soil and the ruin of the land's food supply."

"It might be," Elias contended. "Don't forget that when magic was first used there was a marked increase in food production. You didn't account for that. Why did food production increase so much if magic was bad."

"Short term result, long term consequence," Thoran said. "Magic worked at first growing more food but it was slowly damaging both seed and soil. Over time the depletion became complete and perhaps irreversible."

"It could easily be some other cause that led us here."

"Like what?"

"The Flash," Elias suggested. "At about the same time it was noticed that land yields were decreasing the first Flash Rains began to appear on a regular basis. It's entirely possible that the heavy downpour of rain washes away the topsoil too quickly, hence explaining the depletion of the soil."

"What about seed potency?" Thoran asked. "How does the Flash explain the seed losing its ability to produce?"

"A weaker soil produces weaker seed," Elias theorized.

"You believe that?"

"It makes sense," Elias shrugged, sounding unconvinced. "Seed is harvested from whatever is grown. It follows logically that a weaker soil will produce a less potent seed."

"And what caused the Flash?" Thoran asked suspiciously. "Why did we experience, all of a sudden, sporadic, torrential downpours that can flood an area in seconds."

"I assume you are suggesting that magic is responsible for the Flash Rains as well," Elias incredulously challenged. "There's no magic powerful enough to create storms like that."

"Can't think of anything else that would."

"You obviously haven't a clue about magic," Elias chided. "It takes such incredible power to influence even a minor change in the weather. Something as systemic and widespread as the Flash is far beyond the power of all known magic."

"So maybe unknown magic then?" Thoran countered. "Something vast and secret. Something that never should have been dabbled in because of its inability to be controlled. A wisdom acquired too late."

"And so begins the steady spiral into total paranoia," Elias smiled. He reached out and clinked his glass to Thoran's.

"Secret weapons, vast conspiracies, destructive power unleashed upon the world. Have I left anything out?"

"You've forgotten the cover-up that naturally follows," Thoran reminded him. "The Enclave has to hide their blunder if they want to hang on to power. Too late to reverse course without taking blame for The Blight. If people lost their faith in magic it would all be over."

Elias winked and tipped back his glass. Intoxication was quickly becoming a possibility for the day. How else could he tolerate the company he was forced into?

"So what's your theory?" Thoran asked him. "What do you think caused all these problems?"

"I gave up on theories," Elias told him. "It is what it is. What good does it do us to waste so much energy on arguing about what caused this?"

Thoran furrowed his brow and stared queerly at the magi. Elias felt like a foreign specimen under that gaze, or that something was hanging out of his nose.

"What?" he asked, disquieted by that expression.

"Just didn't expect to hear that from you," Thoran said with disappointment.

"Why would you expect anything from me?" Elias wondered aloud.

Thoran held his stare for a moment, boring into Elias with his stare. A flash of lightning flared in Elias' mind again, as blue as Thoran's eyes. The magi jerked his fingers to his head to stop the thunder that wasn't far behind. Dark seemed to fall over the public room. Or perhaps it was the light that was being drained from his eyes. That surreal sense of recognition came over him. The room was fading.

"Do I know you?" Elias asked, overcome by a haunting certainty that he did know the stranger. Perhaps knew him quite well.

"I just didn't expect that answer from an educated man," Thoran clarified. "You know you can't fix a problem if you don't know what's wrong. Am I right?"

"Yeah, sure," Elias agreed, squeezing his hand to his temples.

Slowly, the light filtered back into his eyes. A sense of normalcy returned. That certainty that he recognized Thoran faded with the return of the ordinary.

"Sorry," he said sheepishly, embarrassed as much by his certainty that he knew Thoran as his question. It was that damn gap in his head. The lost years.

"I had an accident a few years back," he said by way of explanation. Even as he spoke the words he wondered why he was justifying himself to the stranger. He resented Thoran even more for it.

"There's a few missing spots in my memory," Elias continued, tapping his temples. "Sometimes I come across people I think I know."

Thoran smiled broadly at this, almost laughed. He didn't say why, but obviously found what Elias said to be highly amusing. It was as if there were a private joke between them but only Thoran knew what it was.

The amusement goaded Elias' irritation. The alcohol had all but subdued him, doused his annoyance in a haze of mellow contentment. But looking at Thoran's wide, stupid grin, almost giddy, all the goodwill purchased by the beer dissipated and his earlier irritation crackled back to life.

"You find that funny?" Elias asked with tightness in his voice.

"How bad is it?" Thoran asked, ignoring Elias' curt query.

"What does it matter?" Elias shot back.

"How much memory did you lose?" Thoran pressed, still grinning. "A day? Two? A month?"

Elias didn't dare tell the stranger how long his memory gap was. He could hardly bear to think of it himself. So much was lost, so much he didn't know. So much of himself was lost. He had become a stranger in is own body. And now, this man spoke with near giddiness of Elias's deepest pain.

"Why do you find this funny?" he asked. "Is this comical to you?"

"Maybe a little," Thoran said, the smile dropping from his face. "Or maybe it just feels like divine justice."

"Go to Hell," Elias spat.

He rose from the table, holding up his empty glass to signal for a refill. He plopped down at an empty table and turned away from Thoran.

"I didn't mean to be rude," Thoran said, walking over to Elias' new table and sitting down across from the magi. "It's just that I don't like you."

"Then why do you follow me?"

"Unfortunately, you're the best company in here," Thoran wryly observed. "I mean, who have we got? Fat head soldiers? Boring businessmen? Whores? As bad as you might be, you're the only man of interest."

"Why do you hate me?" Elias asked. "What do you have against me?"

"It's not you personally," Thoran pointed out. "I kind of hate magicians in general."

"Because we are at fault for the state of the world today?" Elias expressed the thought for him.

"Something like that," Thoran agreed. "Not very fond of a broad abuse of power, short-sighted goals of greed and lust, toying with nature like its your personal play thing, oblivious or totally unconcerned about consequence. Yeah, guess I'm aggravated with that for some reason."

Elias chuckled despite himself. All his irritation and fight dissipated for a moment at the stranger's amusing ways. He even leaned his glass forward in a mock toast to Thoran.

"Whine all you want," Elias told him. "Magic is here to stay. You'll have to get over it or remain petulant. But I gather you will remain petulant."

"I prefer to resist in agony rather than rest in complacency," Thoran answered tipping his glass in return.

"Suit yourself," Elias said. "I don't find it worth the effort anymore."

"Wasn't always like that, was it?"

"What makes you say that?"

"Look at you," Thoran observed wagging a finger towards Elias, pointing him up and down. "You've got this cynical, world-weary thing down pat. You really do. But I bet it came about from a serious streak of rebelliousness. You still have the swagger. It screams out from you. Hell, I can even tell by the way you walk that there was a day when you didn't take mouth from anybody, powerful or not. I bet you would have told your guard there where he could have shoved it, wouldn't you? Five years ago? Ten? When did you lose all your fight?"

Thoran nodded over at Bannus. Elias looked back to see his guard glare menacingly at the stranger. Thoran didn't seem the slightest bit disturbed.

"I'm talking about you tough guy," he said and winked at Bannus.

The guard only stared back. Elias couldn't decide whether it was shock, stupidity, or the fact that Thoran was so brazenly unafraid that kept Bannus from responding. Either way, it made Elias feel a bit giddy to see his guard, for once, without a response.

"I stopped caring when I realized it didn't matter," Elias lied.

Honestly, Elias didn't know when he stopped caring. He really didn't know if he ever did care. He remembered a sense of concern, for sure. He recalled getting in trouble from time to time as a student, and sometimes as a young Walker for his attitude towards authority. He even remembered talking with other magicians about the possibility that magic really was the source of the world's current problem. But care? He didn't remember anything like passion for a cause. Maybe he did feel strongly about challenging the policies of the Enclave at one point. But that was....

No. There was no point in going there. Elias pushed away the gnawing in the back of his head, that insistence to try and remember. It never amounted to anything.

Elias felt eyes on him and looked up. The boy still stared at him from outside, squatting down on the porch outside. How he could maintain that pleading look on his face for so long was beyond Elias. Must have had plenty of practice.

A sensation stirred up in Elias, a sudden surge of contempt for all the order of the civilized world. He motioned the boy to him. The boy leapt up from his haunches and ran over to Elias.

Digging in a pouch beneath his shirt Elias held up two silver pieces and held them up to the boy.

"I want you to run an errand for me," Elias told him. "Can you do that?"

The boy nodded eagerly, his eyes fixed on the silver.

"There's a message I want you to deliver," Elias said, pressing the silver pieces into the boy's hand. "It's very important, you understand."

The magician leaned in and whispered into the boy's ear. As the boy listened he nodded at first, then his face lit up in a broad and ebullient grin. He flashed a smile at the magi then tore out of the bar at a sprint. Somewhere down the dusty road Elias could hear him give a laugh of pure joy.

"What the hell was that?" Bannus angrily asked.

"Enclave business," Elias said nonchalantly. "Nothing to concern yourself with."

"You gave him more money than his father gave us," Bannus angrily pointed out. "Those were Enclave mints."

"So they were," Elias shrugged. "Couldn't be avoided."

"What was so important you had to pay him two silvers?" Bannus asked.

"A very important errand. Enclave business."

"In Hiram's Well?"

"Magicians have business everywhere," Elias offered by way of explanation. "Nothing you would understand."

Bannus fumed silently, knowing there was nothing he could do. Still, he could make trouble for the boy and his father. Elias thought for a moment, struggling within himself over whether he wanted to go through with it at all. Part of him wanted dearly to engage in some disobedience, no matter how trivial. But another part of him, the tired part, just wanted to be left alone.

"Why don't you enjoy yourself," Elias said to his guard, his mind made up. He gestured over to the thin and pitiful women gathered at the far end of the bar.

"It's on me," he offered.

Bannus sniffed and shook his head. He stole a look over at the women, a hungry desire in his eyes. He tried to cover it with a look of disdain, and Elias knew why.

Reaching into another pocket Elias pulled a small vial of pale, red liquid. He tossed it over to the guard who caught it in surprise. Eyes narrowed suspiciously towards Elias as Bannus held the vial in his beefy hand.

"It's not hard to make," Elias pointed out.

Conflict froze Bannus' features. Elias knew he wanted to relent, but his pride held him in check.

"Everyone uses it," Elias tried to assure him. "For recreation."

Bannus nodded, convinced enough to save face. He walked over to the women and looked them over for a minute. After some inner deliberation he nodded at one to follow him.

"Nothing rough," Elias called out to the Bannus. "Gregor would not pleased."

"Gregor would not be pleased if I wasn't as rough as he is," Bannus laughed.

"Bannus, I mean it," Elias threatened, showing uncharacteristic menace towards his guard.

"Fine," Bannus conceded. He turned up the stairs with the

prostitute close behind him.

"Well done," Thoran gushed ostentatiously. "Way to spread the hope the hope of magic to everyone."

Elias stood up and emptied his beer. He pressed a handful of coins into the bartenders hand.

"What are the chances of getting a bottle of the liquor my companion here is drinking?" Elias asked.

"Ah, that would be the Raison Nectar, Sire," the bartender announced proudly. "And I have several bottles left. Very rare. In fact, the two of you were the only ones to request that in many, many years."

Elias didn't hear what the bartender was saying. He stared down at Thoran in disbelief. Certainly, this could be no coincidence.

"You're drinking Raison Nectar?" Elias asked. "How do you even know about that?"

"It's my favorite drink," Thoran smiled and answered.

"It's extremely rare," Elias whispered, still in disbelief. "Hardly anyone even knows it exists."

"You mean, it's not made anymore," Thoran corrected. "In fact, the only place that it can be found is an out of the way cellar like this one. At the height of its popularity a town like Hiram's Well would have never appreciated the Raison. The few bottles they had collected dust while the world's supply quickly disappeared."

"Thank you," Elias muttered as the bartender handed him the dusty bottle.

Elias looked down at the rare liquor, savoring the feel of the old bottle in his hands. The excitement he normally would have felt was tempered by Thoran's uncanny presence. The quicker he got away from him the better.

"Thoran Wanderer," Elias said. "I hope I never see you again."

Still in disbelief, Elias walked out of the public house and into the insistent glare of the sun. He pushed Thoran and his strangeness out of his mind. Bannus would only be distracted for a little while and Elias had something important to do.

As he made his way to the pilgrim train Elias relaxed his mind and let his lumen drift out. Hoping he hadn't drunk too much he tried to concentrate on the point of light within him, the source of his power and control and to focus it on the little plant outside the city.

It didn't take but a second to find it. Sometimes a few drinks actually helped. Of course, any plant that a magician himself evokes should be easy to find again.

Just when he reached the crowd of pilgrims Elias was firmly attached to all three cucumber plants. He found an empty wagon and sat down on the back. Closing his eyes he focused the strength of his lumen, reaching into the plant. He breathed deep and began to release.

* * *

The cucumber plant had already begun to wither. Hardly an hour since it had been grown and the green leaves drooped and their edges had lost what original luster they possessed, even browning slightly. The plant would be lucky to last the day.

Still Thom kept vigil over his plants. He knew they wouldn't last. How could they? No water, blasting hot wind and dust, no shelter from the sun.

That damn sun. Would it ever leave them alone?

Still Thom watched his plant. He could see it wither before his eyes, and with it all his hope died one scorching second at a time. It was for Frederick more than for himself that he was sad. Just once, he wanted the boy to taste something clean and pure, something that wasn't gritty bread and stringy meat and lukewarm water with dust floating in it. Just once, he thought, a father should be able to give his son something really good.

And oh, had he built it up to the boy. Ever since he had gotten that second copper piece he talked on and on about how good these cucumbers would be. Many a night when hunger and thirst deprived them of sleep Thom would tell Frederick about cucumbers and how good they were gonna taste and how when you bit into them it was all wet and crisp. And for a little while they wouldn't be hungry. Hope would feed them a little bit now and then.

But now hope was gone. Hope had been tied up in this little cucumber plant, and just as it wilted under the dust and sun so did Thom's hope wither. It was still for the boy that he was sad. He was sad that Frederick would probably never know what a cucumber tasted like.

So wrapped up in his thoughts, Thom didn't hear Frederick's excited cries until they were very close. Still, he didn't pay them much mind.

"Dad! Dad! Daaaaaad!!!" the boy cried out as he ran to his father and the cucumber plant.

"Dad!" he yelled out again breathlessly as he finally reached his

22

father. "You won't believe what the magician told me."

Thom resisted at first. He didn't want his hopes dashed again. But then the boy showed him the two silver pieces the magician had given him. Not like the old, bitten pieces that he had paid the magician with, these were a new mint, heavy and glinting in the sun.

Laughter finally took over Thom. He danced around the cucumber plant with Frederick, full of the exuberance of good fortune. Breathless, he stopped and watched the cucumber plant again, this time with anticipation.

It took a few moments, and even in that time the plant wilted even more. Then, it moved, slightly at first, a nudge. The leaves seemed to sparkle for an instant and green life blazed in them again.

Bannus heard a commotion outside his window. He looked out and saw a crowd moving towards the edge of town, out where the magician had grown the cucumber plant. Realization dawned on him. This was Elias' doing.

For a moment Bannus considered going downstairs and tearing that stupid cucumber plant out the ground. What could they do to stop him? The thought gave him pleasure, to think about his strength and the helplessness of an entire village, albeit a small one, to stop him.

Even this pleasure failed to stir him like he wanted to be stirred. He looked at the skinny whore lying across the bed in a pathetic attempt at being seductive, and then at the little vial in his hands. He decided to let the matter go and he downed the liquid.

Almost instantly he could feel the potion work. Warmth began in his stomach and slowly worked its way down until it reached his thighs. He sighed as life tingled back into his dead member. That magician wasn't totally worthless.

Ignoring the growing stir of excitement outside Bannus unbuckled his belt and turned to the bed. Who knew how long the potion would last. Better not to lose a moment.

Chapter Two
Forgotten Memories

The sun burned half way across the sky before the pilgrim train left. Elias waited with the mingled pilgrims and the dozens of others who hovered nearby, hoping to be included with the other transfers. Not as many villagers waited by the train as they normally would. An excitement still stirred at the edge of town around the cucumber plants. More than one person ran by with a healthy, green cucumber, showing it off to stunned friends or biting into it without ceremony.

Elias looked up at the sun and reminded himself what season it was. The distinction had long since ceased to matter. Everyday was hot and dusty. Some were just longer than others. Still, he almost religiously kept touch of what season it was supposed to be. It mattered somehow, in a way he could not even begin to articulate. But it mattered.

It was spring, Elias thought to himself. They were in the second cycle of the spring. Of course, he shouldn't have to think about it so much, shouldn't have to remind himself. The evidence of spring should be all around him. There should be trees full of foliage, carpets of wild grass decorated with flowers, a flurry of insects and birds about their industrious, behind-the-scenes work of nature's great displays.

Instead, there were none of these. Whatever was causing the slow, drawn out death of the world, and despite what he said to Thoran, he was more than suspicious that magic had something to do with it. It was somehow destroying all the budding life of spring. All the other seasons were as equally featureless, Elias reminded himself. More than spring had been ruined.

Bannus finally stumbled out of the public house an hour later. He squinted in the sudden flare of light and shielded his eyes as he looked around. Finally spotting Elias he tousled his own hair, yawned, and made his way over.

A smile crossed Elias' lips. He had added a sleep inducement to the elixir, subtle, so as not to be noticed. Considering the situation it would be used in he didn't think it would take much. Now, seeing Bannus freshly woken from an unintended slumber, Elias figured he had used just the right amount.

"Lot of cucumbers round here," Bannus attempted to growl as he approached Elias, not sounding near as intimidating as he wanted to.

It's not like the gruff guard was in a pleasant mood, Elias thought. Some of his edge had definitely been taken off. It was more that he appeared a little less ornery and hateful than usual.

"Dole must have come in," Elias shrugged, perhaps trying too hard to sound nonchalant. Part of him didn't care if Bannus knew.

"Don't remember cucumbers ever being in the dole," Bannus pointed out.

"Things must be looking up," Elias said with a fake grin. "Maybe it's a sign of good times ahead."

Bannus grunted but offered no further argument. Undoubtedly, he was mellowed. Elias stored that bit of information away for later use. A subdued and mellowed Bannus, even if slightly so, could certainly be useful.

"Passports! Passports!" a town guard yelled out, strutting through the mingled crowd. "Passports at the ready!"

There was a general fumbling as people readied their documents for inspection. Elias shook his head at the miserable state that the situation had decayed to. Things hadn't been so bad that long ago. Now, passports and royal permission to travel from one town to the next.

"Death is upon us!" a man in ragged, black robes cried out as he walked by the line of assembled pilgrims.

Elias watched him pass by. A long scar on his drawn face, running from one corner of his mouth to the jaw bone, gave him a twisted frown to match the wild eyes that searched the people as he screamed doomed prophecies. On the front of his faded robes was stitched a yellow, crescent moon, itself fraying on the edges.

"The dark god comes!" the man continued to cry out. He stretched out his arms wide and gestured to the blasted sands around them. "He waits on the edge of night! Behold! Death is upon us!"

Another change, Elias thought to himself. He had never seen one before his memory loss. Now, the Prophets of Thanatos were everywhere, foretelling the death of the world and praying for the ascension of the dark god of death. It was a poignant reminder of how lost he felt in the world.

As the robed man walked on, prophesying doom, Elias' thoughts rolled back to that empty place in his mind. He didn't do it willfully, usually wanting to avoid the frustration. Sometimes, he just got pulled back in without realizing it.

Memories played before his mind automatically. Early days at the

25

Enclave started them. He remembered his studies there, the breathless thrill when he first felt magic course through him, when he first touched the power that pulsed in all things.

He remembered fondly the accolades and praises that were heaped upon him. "He is the best evoker since Heriod," they would say. The Masters would struggle to hold their faces still as they watched him perform with ease displays of power that seasoned magicians struggled with. The other students murmured in amazement as his instructors shook their heads.

Still, he had to finish the seven years required for magician's training. There was no bitterness as he remembered the wait to be elevated to Perigrinator, even when he knew he was ready. He loved life at the Enclave. When it became clear he had outstripped all of the students and most of the teachers, Elias was allowed to experiment and explore, and dabble in areas normally forbidden to students.

Images of the catacombs and dark recesses of the restricted library flared in his memory. He had pored over ancient texts, even finagling access to scrolls that were forbidden to more than students. The years at the Enclave were years of discovery and excitement and realization of potential, of a time as magical and wondrous as the art he was uncovering.

Unlike most of the other students, Elias didn't take to his wandering with eagerness. He enjoyed life at the Enclave too much. He felt so at home among the robed and venerable Masters, the arcane knowledge, the permeation of secret things that filled the dark and mysterious corridors. Everyday he felt he uncovered something new, and discovery brought with it that particular thrill that accompanies expansion of being.

As expected, Elias' wandering didn't last long. Quickly, his talent was discovered, and he took his first employ with a merchant named Earnest Ulman.

It turned out to be a favorable appointment, as Ulman, a major farmer and salt trader, had several magicians in his employ. Elias stood out in no time, easily outstripping the more experienced magi in the merchant's employ. And while this made Ulman more than pleased with his hire, it only stoked the indignation of the other magician's who, for the most part, had only enough talent to do a merchant's work.

With a little jealous prodding from the others, Elias was only with the merchant a year. His reputation spread quickly, probably by those eager to see him move along, and word reached a nearby lord. So after a brief employ with Ulman, Elias left to serve Mobrey, Lord of the East Step, a coastal holding that was, in fact, in the west. However, since there was another Step farther west, Mobrey's land was named, East Step.

Being on the coast, the East Step did not suffer the same deprivation of its inland sisters. Whatever was draining the land into worthless dust had not yet afflicted the sea. Though fishing boats had to sail further out for full catches, all the coastal cities were still well fed.

Elias remembered his time with Lord Mobrey as fair and nothing less than satisfactory. But he always found himself missing the thrill that had made him feel so vibrantly alive while he was a student at the Enclave. He found the practical applications of his art fell fall short of the glory of discovering that art. A feeling of listlessness and even boredom overtook him more and more as he went through the rote and uninspired demands of practical living. If it weren't for the ten year requirement between student and instructor, Elias would not have hesitated to seek out the Mastership.

He remembered the problems with food production getting worse and worse. As the interior grew more barren, Lord Mobrey's coastal cities swelled with immigrants and grew too quickly for good management. Food riots became common in the inland territories. Fields were yielding less and less for more work.

Elias could himself detect a subtle change when he reached out to touch the power that lay in the earth and seed. It felt more distant, fainter, than it had before. He knew the power inside was still as potent as ever, but it had become harder to reach, harder to draw into action. It was as if magic itself was becoming less responsive to magicians.

Exactly how long he was in the service of Lord Mobrey, Elias could never quite piece together. His last memory was riding in Mobrey's travel train. They were in the interior, on the way to see the Archon of Dubres. He remembered that the Archon was a wealthy and powerful man, prosperous even though his territory was landlocked, deep in the interior. Most of this wealth could be attributed to the abundant gem mines in his holding. This did not explain it all. Mobrey and most of the other rulers were convinced that the Archon, Peter Illich, harbored some dark secret for his uncanny success.

Elias clearly remembered riding in the desert sunset. Strange red and orange hues cast their descending light over the sands and clay hills. He remembered looking over the famous mesas of Dubres, like high tables carved out by wind and rain in red rock. He spurred his horse forward for something, for... He couldn't remember why he wanted to get to the front of the train.

"Passports!" a dusty guard yelled at Elias, shaking the magi from his reverie.

Elias looked at the soldier, confused. For a moment, as he stared at the haggard, unshaven face, at the narrow, bleary eyes of the guard, he couldn't recall where he was. The image of Dubres, its distant mesas and red rock still framed his mind as vividly as if he were standing there.

"Passports!" the soldier yelled again in growing impatience, poking the magi with the butt of his spear.

"Hey!" Bannus yelled back. "We're Enclave dumb ass!"

The soldier glanced down at Elias' hand and his eyes fell upon the magi's ring. His face suddenly took on a look of abashment.

"Pardon, Sire," he said with a half-bow and hurried away.

"Were you sleeping?" Bannus asked with an uncomprehending look on his face.

Elias shook his head and did not answer his guard. He pulled together his few belongings, all fitting in the leather pack he slung on, and gathered to join the other milling pilgrims.

A civil servant, dressed in the faded green robes of office, came hurrying towards the pilgrims pulling in tow an old mare. He looked frantically around, spotted Elias, then made his way over to the magi. Elias groaned quietly and tried not to let the servant see the grimace on his face.

"Honored Sire, the town of Hiram's Well would like to offer you the use of this mare to your esteemed person as a sign of gratitude towards the Enclave for all the invaluable service they provide to the needy and wanting of the interior, to be used as long as the Sire is in the territory of our proud town."

The servant bowed again after his obviously scripted presentation and handed the reins to Elias. The magi took them with an inclination of his head, dreading such officious moments as these. Especially considering how a town like Hiram's Well was virtually ignored by the Enclave. He wondered if the cucumbers had made it back to whatever feeble power structure existed in the town.

"The Enclave certainly notices such generosity," Elias answered. He was sure to put on what he thought of as his impressive voice, adding an artificial Helvic accent.

"The guards will return the horse when they leave the train," the servant told him. "So you may enjoy without the bother of returning until you are ready to privilege us again."

"May the gods bless and shelter the giver of such a gift," Elias responded.

The servant bowed again and hurried away, leaving Elias with the temporary use of the ragged horse.

"How long will we be in the town's jurisdiction?" Elias asked, wondering how long he would have to burden the pitiful animal.

"Day. Day and a half," Bannus guessed.

Elias sighed and pulled himself up in the saddle. The mare skittered under the magi's moderate weight, and for a moment he was scared the horse would collapse. But the mare held up and calmed beneath Elias' soothing hand. He hated to hurt the old animal that he could tell already limped a little. Refusal, though, was out of the question. He would have to ride as far as the horse was offered. Otherwise, word would come back with the guards that returned the animal, and his refusal would be an insult. Ever aware of their sometimes precarious position, the Enclave forbid the magi from delivering such insults.

"Will she last that long?" Elias wondered aloud in genuine concern.

Bannus shrugged, showing no more concern for the horse than he would an insect under his boot.

"Serves them right if she doesn't," he said. "Giving the Enclave such a piece of crap gift."

"Look around, Bannus," Elias pointed out. "They don't have anything. Probably the only horse in town."

"Still, they could do better," Bannus observed. "Start with getting off their ass and working. Look at 'em, mostly stand around all day. Don't think I've seen a full day's work since we got here."

"Always the humanitarian, Bannus," Elias observed as he scanned the crowds of the hopeless who had acquired the privilege of leaving Hiram's Well. So many others clamored nearby and pressed at the crowd. Some saying goodbye to loved ones forever, others scratching at a last chance to be included among the deportees.

"It's true," the burly guard shrugged. "The whole town sits on its ass all day."

Elias shook his head but didn't answer, didn't point out the obvious - that there was no work to do. In a town like Hiram's Well work had long dried up, like the parched and thirsty ground. He reminded himself of how deservedly his guard had earned the moniker, "Bannus the anus". The thought brought a smile to his face.

"Moving ahead!" a guard at the front of the pilgrim train yelled out.

The gathered refugees began to shuffle forward. Elias turned his horse north and waited for the movement to reach him. Something unexpectedly pulled inside of him, a preternatural shiver that drew his attention.

Elias looked around and saw a boy staring up at him. Large, curious eyes fixed on him in that total lack of self-consciousness that only children can manage. Curiosity mixed with awe were written in the boy's dark, brooding eyes. Something else lingered there also, something the magician couldn't place. Did the boy have the touch? Probably. He had practically pulled Elias with his stare. But that wasn't it. Something else, written on the sunburned, dusty face, buried but staring plainly out.

"You're a magician." the boy said in a matter-of-fact tone.

"I am," Elias nodded.

"Do you have a wand?" the boy asked next.

In reply, Elias let the wooden wand fall out of his sleeve and appear suddenly in his hand - as if by magic. He flicked the rough-hewn wood with the charred tip. A little cloud appeared before the magi, and it morphed into the shape of a horse. Elias blew gently on the cloud horse and it galloped towards the boy. The evocation dissipated when it reached the boy's nose, disappearing in a puff of mist.

The boy touched his nose, rubbing the fresh dew on his fingers, and smiled weakly at the magi. The smile made Elias sad. For the weakness of the boy's smile was not made of restraint, but rather to Elias it seemed that it did not have enough joy to make itself complete. To even think what sadness could have caused such a loss of wonder in one so young made sorrow well in Elias so powerfully that it threatened to burst forth in tears.

"Silas! Come now!" a woman's voice called out.

The boy did not break his stare as a woman came and took him by the shoulders. She gently tried to pull him away. The boy shrugged her off and pointed up at Elias.

"He's a magician mama," the boy said. "He made a horse out of fog."

"I know he is," the woman managed to say gently and contemptuously all at once. "What did I tell you about these men? They killed your father. They're the destroyers of the world."

The woman fixed on Elias a look of such unmasked hatred that the magi nearly recoiled in his saddle. Her green eyes blazed at him with that pure spite that only justified anger could supply.

Even then, Elias couldn't help but notice how beautiful she was, even if in a coarse and violent way. This despite the ragged and faded dress she wore, frayed so badly on the skirt that he could see the patched leggings underneath. Her dusty and matted strawberry blonde hair couldn't make her unattractive either. Perhaps it was the flush on her angry face, a crimson pool on her lightly freckled cheeks, that made her stand out despite her obvious poverty.

She pulled at the boy again and he complied this time. As Elias watched her retreat he noticed the black band wrapped around her upper arm. A wheat widow, he told himself. Something significant, he knew that, but he couldn't remember what. Whatever it was probably lay at the heart of her vivid spite. Elias was almost certain it was justified.

The pilgrim train began to move slowly. Elias nudged the old mare gently. The beast obeyed and plodded forward, and like everyone else, followed the rootless crowd that searched the ever-stretching sands for something they weren't even sure existed.

"The age of the dark god is upon us!" the prophet called out hoarsely to the slow moving pilgrims. "The age of Death is here! Behold! Thanatos rises! His darkness will conquer the light!"

Chapter Three
The Garden of the Prefect

As Elias traveled the pilgrim train, feeling sorry every step for the old mare that struggled beneath his weight, Gregor Valdell, Lord Prefect of the Anjibar Enclave, sipped chilled wine in his garden.

Secretly, Gregor was deeply pleased with himself, so pleased he stood on the edge of giddiness, though he was careful not to let this show. For he was not pleased with himself for anything that he had actually done, but for what he was planning to do. And as marvelous as the plan was, even imagining how it would play out sent shivers of thrill through him, the problem was that his plan was far from being carried out. In fact, the major players in his plan had yet to even be informed of their role. This was soon to be remedied. He could hardly wait to begin, and only restrained himself by the constant reminder that he must not show too much eagerness. Let Prince Stefano wait a little longer.

Besides formulating such a masterful plan, Gregor had more reasons to be pleased with himself.

For one, Gregor did occupy that exalted position of Lord Prefect of Anjibar, arguably the most powerful position in the world. Unlike the other Lord Prefects, Anjibar did not lie in a kingdom, and so did not have to consider the whims of an ignorant king. The Enclave, and the city of Anjibar, was a free city-state, under the rule of Anjibar, which was effectively ruled by the Enclave, a source of power and independence not enjoyed by any of the other schools of magic. As a result, his Enclave was the most influential in all the world. Gregor ruled Anjibar, Anjibar ruled magic, magic ruled the world.

And then there was the garden itself. In a world of sweltering heat and endless brown sand, the garden stood out as a cool and green oasis, like an emerald set in featureless rock. Of all the grand features of Anjibar, Gregor liked this the best.

The garden of Anjibar sprawled out for thirty acres in the heart of the city. Built up beside the great Enclave itself, the garden was a famous tourist attraction, and under Gregor's care had become a much needed balm for the Enclave's wounded public image. As visitors walked under the arched gateway, covered in twisting and purple wisteria that always bloomed, signs announced such messages like, "What Magic Can Do for You," and "Spreading the Hope of Magic." Inside, twisting through the garden, they were directed along paths through exotic flowers and shrubs wafting delicious aromas into the air, trees always heavy with fruit from which all could pick freely, and clear streams of water that trickled along the interior wall, sending out a symphony of nature's most soothing music. Flowering vines hung down from marble pillars while delicately carved statues of past heroes watched over the visitors mingling with the smells of flower and earth. It was hard to walk through this public garden and not believe that magic really was good for everyone.

Behind the wall that ran along the inside of the public garden grew the private garden of the Enclave. Here, the young acolytes practiced their craft with mixed results. Not nearly the impressive display that greeted tourists, this inner garden bashfully produced misshapen limbs, stunted trees, branches breaking with grotesquely large fruit and some stranger results from wayward magic that defied explanation. Every so often a wind would assault the nostrils with a flowering aroma that was anything but pleasant, or carry on it the smell of corn that began to rot the moment it sprouted from the ground.

Such were the necessary casualties of learning magic. These, of course, were strictly hidden from the public. No one needed to see a magician's mistakes as he learned. And he would never be let out to practice in the world until he mastered his errors.

Inside even this garden, protected by its own encircling wall, lay the private garden of the Lord Prefect. Every bit as wonderful as the outer garden of the public, the Lord Prefect kept an oasis for himself full of even more rare and exotic plants. The burdens of his office almost demanded such a retreat where he could lounge in solitary comfort and pull any fruit he desired and expect it to be at the perfection of ripeness. Of course he needed the crystalline spring to be always fresh and cool, and to hear the gurgling of the stream no matter where he walked in his personal haven.

Gregor frowned to himself, momentarily torn down from his giddy heights, as he spied a partly withered leaf on the fig tree that shaded him. He rose and tore the leaf off, mentally noting to reprimand the Master of the Garden for the mistake. Such imperfection could not be allowed in Anjibar.

Of course, Gregor could have repaired the leaf himself, just as he could have chilled the glass of White Vitoria he sipped at, but such an expenditure of magic was far beneath the Lord Prefect. All of his effort must be reserved for more important matters. So it was left to the army of magi that was required to keep the gardens green and blooming to repair browned leaves and chill the refreshment of the Lord Prefect.

"Your Grace," a slave's whispered voice barely interrupted the Lord Prefect's thought. "Prince Stefano still awaits your pleasure."

Gregor surveyed their surroundings, wanting to be sure everything was perfect. Not a flaw should alight upon the Prince's eyes. Too much depended on the image Gregor wanted to portray.

"Yes Renner, send him in," the Lord Prefect instructed.

The slave bowed and hurried away, his simple, white tunic, signifying his status as slave, not making the slightest rustle as he faded back into the garden.

In a moment the slave returned and this time knelt before Gregor, seated on his stone bench beneath the fig tree, heavy with ripe fruit. A young man trailed behind him, dusty and dripping brown sweat down his temples. His faded silks were frayed and even his royal keffiyeh was worn far too much for a Prince.

Gregor allowed himself an inward smile as the young man attempted a contemptuous look. But his awe at the garden was obvious, and Gregor knew that his plans for the young man would be obeyed before a word passed between them. It was only a matter of details now.

"Your Grace, Prince Stefano of Raulia," the slave said with his face turned to the ground.

"Some refreshment for our guest," Gregor solemnly intoned.

The slave hurried away again, leaving the two men alone in the sumptuous garden. Gregor allowed Stefano to drink in the ample bounty of his garden before speaking.

"Your majesty, please, join me in the shade," Gregor invited, indicating another stone bench beside his own.

Across from the two men a small water fall flowed down over rocks, spilling down sweet music. From nearby, the scent of honeysuckles softened the air, filling the garden with the aroma of beauty.

Stefano took his seat as the slave returned with two others, females dressed as he was, who went immediately to work on the Prince. They fell to their knees and removed his sandals. Pouring water from a silver pitcher into a silver bowl, they soaked dazzling white towels into the cool water and washed his feet, his hands, his face, cleaning away every trace of heat and dust. They even removed his keffiyeh and massaged perfumed oil into his hair. Renner presented him with a bottle of chilled wine, poured it into a crystal glass set in silver and placed it in the Prince's hand. Soundlessly, the slaves gathered themselves away and left the men alone again. Gregor, pleased with his slaves, could see the tension melt out of the young man. Indeed, he looked like a different person, nothing like the desperate royal whose kingdom sat on the edge of collapse.

"I apologize for the rustic accommodations I have to offer," Gregor intoned, knowing how much he underestimated. "A magician as myself has not the refinement to offer the pleasures that a royal person as yourself is no doubt accustomed to."

Stefano did not dare answer, only inclined his head, not wanting to give away the fact that he had never been treated so luxuriously. Gregor knew this and smiled to himself again.

"So how fares the great Kingdom of Raulia these days?" Gregor asked politely, knowing full well from his network of spies exactly how things fared in Raulia.

"We still war with the northern provinces," Stefano told him. "Bringing them back under control has proved difficult."

Gregor fought to contain the smile, marveling that Stefano was able to propagate the obvious lie with such ease.

Raulia's aggression towards the northern tribes was barely tolerated by the other kingdoms. No one went so far as to interfere, but this was more a lack of concern than a certainty in Raulia's flimsy justification. For sure, no one wanted another kingdom to gain access to the sea, and with it the world's only reliable food source, upsetting the delicate power balance carved out dearly by wars and treaties and arranged marriages. At the same time, who would commit precious men and resources for a few distant, frozen villages worth no more than fish?

"For a strategist and warrior such as your father, it will only be a matter of time before peace is restored," Gregor assured the prince, confident that the young royal was unaware of his clever double meaning.

"Last I heard, two important cities were back under Raulian control," Stefano told him. "If we can hold these through the year then the rest of the north should open up to us."

"Yes," Gregor hummed. "I pray all goes well."

"And your mother?"

"Cecilia fares well," Stefano answered coldly, obviously irked that

Gregor has referred to his father's third wife as his mother.

"But with Cecilia who can tell? She certainly has no lack of temper."

Gregor nodded and did not needle the point. The young woman's marriage to the king of Raulia still obviously embarrassed the young man. No royal match was offered when the king announced his search, so a lesser - a far lesser - match had to be made. A disgraced duke finally consented, and the headstrong and resentful Cecilia married King Harold of Raulia, thirty-five years her senior. Of course, after two wives Raulia didn't have to marry, but rumor had it the older man did grow awful lonely.

"Well, here is a toast to the prosperity of Raulia and all her children," Gregor said as he tipped his glass and spilled a portion of the costly wine on the ground as a libation.

Stefano followed the Lord Prefect's example, though allowing a considerably smaller portion to spill out of his glass.

"What do you think of the gardens?" Gregor asked after a moment.

"Quite wonderful. A rare privilege to enjoy."

"But does it have to be that way?" Gregor asked plaintively. "Why shouldn't there be many more like this?"

"I should think you could answer that question better than I," Stefano returned. "I can't imagine the amount of magic it takes to maintain a place like this."

A note of irritation could be heard in the prince's voice. Perhaps a slight condemnation there too. Gregor had heard it before in others when they spoke of his gardens. The implication of, why waste so much magic, and thus magicians, maintaining such a gratuitous display of power when the world at large slowly withered and died.

Gregor didn't waste a thought upon it. They would understand eventually.

"Yes, it does take a lot of magic," Gregor agreed. "And many would question why I would waste so much when the magicians could be used elsewhere. They fail to see how important, how crucial it is to keep these gardens in the pristine condition they are in. Do you know why they must be kept my prince? Do you know why it is so important that these gardens be maintained?"

"I'm sure I have no idea," the Prince answered with a note of exasperation.

"I keep this because this is my vision of the world," Gregor told him. "The world I see is full of green and vibrant health. I can hear cool streams gurgling, feel a cool breeze on my face. I see trees so heavy with fruit their branches almost break. I see terraced gardens and pleasure parks in every city of the interior. I see fields full of grain and people fat and happy.

"It's a world much like this little garden. And if I were to let it lapse and become as dry and dusty as the rest of the world, what would become of my vision? If I were not to keep the gardens that I open to the public then the people, I fear, would forget. They would forget what the world should look like, what it could look like. Let it go for a generation and people wouldn't remember at all what green is. I keep this garden to remember. Is it an indulgence? Perhaps. But I, above all men, cannot afford to forget. I must keep this vision always before me, of what the world can look like.

"Because I am the only one that can make this a reality. As I represent Anjibar and as Anjibar represents magic, it is my burden, but also my privilege to bring the world out of the prolonged famine that plagues us. So you see, this garden is not just my vision, it is the seed that will bring life again to the world. Do you understand now?"

"That's all fine and good," the Prince said. "Except that..."

Stefano trailed off. He caught himself before he finished the thought, knowing what an insult it would be.

The Lord Prefect knew exactly what the unfinished thought was. Normally, it would have sent him into a fury. Today he wanted to hear it.

"Except what?" he leaned forward and asked. "Go on. Say it"

"I mis-spoke," Stefano said stiffly. "I meant nothing at all."

"Come now," Gregor encouraged slyly. "We both know what you were going to say. I said I wanted to deliver the world from its languish, and you answered with... Speak up! Say it. Except... Except what?"

"Except that its being said that magic is the problem in the first place." Stefano said straightening up in defiance. "You propose to save us by magic when magic might be the problem."

"Magic might be the problem," Gregor repeated, easing back again. "Yes, I've heard that many times, as no doubt you have. What I have yet to hear though is how magic caused this problem. What exactly did magic do to destroy the world?

"You don't have an answer, do you? Tell me, how did magic cause our present crisis?"

"I wouldn't presume to know," Stefano answered. "I can only

repeat what I have heard."

"Which is?"

"By tampering with the forces of nature magic has depleted them of their potency," Stefano repeated the common, but only whispered, rumor. "Magic has tampered with things they don't understand, and somehow destroyed them by their ignorance and by an abuse of power."

Gregor forced a smile on his face. Of course, he had heard all this and more. He had debated with men in fine detail and with supposed evidence of such tampering and their damaging results. But they were fools. Antiquated fools with outdated and superstitious ideas. They were heretics now to boot, Gregor had seen to that. Their days were hopefully numbered. Still, those rumblings from some of the other Enclaves, especially Osengar, continued.

"As logical as that may sound," Gregor countered. "Even if through flawed logic, I can assure you that magic is not the problem."

"Then what is?" Stefano asked the obvious. "If not by magic tampering then how did this all come about?"

"There are a few theories that are much more plausible than the idea that our feeble abilities could alter the quality of seed and soil," Gregor told him. "It could be the result of minute geological changes over time. It could be a cycle that is quite natural, though disturbing to us. Personally, I believe it is those who insisted on not using magic to grow their crops that caused this problem. Most likely a blight or disease was introduced to the food and soil, one which magic would have quickly identified and eradicated. Had everyone used conventional growing methods approved by magic this never would have happened. But once introduced into the soil, it spread over the entire land. There is much good evidence for this, many of the details too complicated and dull to keep you interested, so I will spare you them.

"But what really matters to us is not the problem. For even if we knew for sure what caused this it wouldn't change our situation. Unlike some people, I prefer not to dwell on problems. I prefer to look for solutions.

"It will get us nowhere arguing and debating over whose fault this might be. It is fairly certain that magic had nothing to do with the present problem. But what we can be sure of is that magic is the only way to lead us out.

"Believe this, magic is all that can save us."

Gregor finished his mini speech, quite proud of himself so far. He watched Stefano nod in a sort of agreement as he drained his cup. A wave of Gregor's hand sent a slave scurrying over to refill the Prince's glass.

"What does all this have to do with me?" Stefano finally asked. "Sounds like an Enclave issue to me. I am no magician."

"No, but as of the present you are still a power player," Gregor told him. "Raulia is the only interior kingdom worth even noticing."

"What about Dubres?" Stefano pointed out. "He may have lost a little of his flash, but he still prospers. Much better off than Raulia."

For the first time that day Gregor allowed his emotions to show uncontrolled on his face. A scowl darkened his features at the mention of that hateful name.

"Dubres is dead," Gregor spat. "Even if he doesn't know it yet. Trust me, in a few years Dubres will be rotting in that vulgar pile of bricks."

Gregor quickly recovered with a wave of his hand. He breathed deep to regain control of his annoyance. He really did hate to lose his composure, even if so slightly.

"No, Stefano, you will see. Raulia is really the only interior kingdom left. But for how long?"

"Raulia isn't going anywhere," Stefano insisted, perhaps a bit too boldly. "Once we've reclaimed the north we will no longer be an interior kingdom."

"And what of the cost? And how long will you hold it? Can you keep a supply line through the old moor forever? You would eventually have to become a northern kingdom. Even if you could take and hold even most of the Reach you would eventually have to abandon your ancestral seat."

"We will never abandon Coswell," Stefano said with deflated conviction. Apparently that very suggestion had circulated through the royal household.

"Regardless, you and I both know this northern war is a desperate gamble," Gregor told him. "Raulia's only options are to move or perish."

"So what then? You brought me all the way here to dispense with some fatherly advice?" Stefano huffed contemptuously. "You waste your breath. Raulia will not be guided by fear."

"I wouldn't presume to instruct a prince," Gregor assured the young man. "No doubt your royal person had been tutored in the ways of statecraft by men more capable than me."

"Then what do you want of me?"

"I've already told you. I have a vision to bring the world into prosperity again. The way I see it Raulia is in the best position to prosper from it. In fact, it wouldn't be far-fetched to see Raulia one day rivaling the Lorian Empire."

It was preposterous even to suggest such a thing. In fact, the only response to what Gregor suggested was laughter. Stefano laughed then, certainly wondering whether Gregor mocked him or if he had truly lost his mind. The very idea that poor, dying Raulia could even dream to rival the great empire of old was beyond ridiculous.

"Raulia in comparison to Loria?" Stefano continued to laugh. "Your flattery goes too far. I think you are insulting me."

Gregor's face showed no signs of amusement. Stefano's laughter died suddenly regarding the Lord Prefect's perfectly serious face.

"You can't really mean that?" Stefano insisted.

"What if Raulia took over the entirety of the interior?" Gregor suggested.

"Ha! So what if we did?" Stefano laughed again. "We could probably do it today, but who would care? We would be taking over dry, desolate and abandoned lands, full of starvation and rebellion. Hell, we might even talk the kingdoms into paying us to take them off their hands."

"But what if it wasn't that way?" Gregor posited. "What if it was as I see it, the interior full of green life?"

"What if I was born a god instead of a man?" Stefano asked dismissively. "What if doesn't really help us."

"But let's say I did find a way to restore the land," Gregor pushed on. "Some kingdom should be able to prosper from it. One led by a man of true vision."

"Why not Anjibar?"

"Oh yes, why not Anjibar," Gregor mused aloud. "You seem to get right to the heart of my difficulty.

"You see, Anjibar occupies a very special place among all the Enclaves, but also the most precarious. We are the only ones that occupy our own, independent territory. While all the others owe allegiance to a king, even though they exert incredible influence over the land's governance, and no doubt occupy a favorable position, they are still vassals to a king. Anjibar is not. And while this is a position of privilege, it is also one of envy.

40

"As you know, all the kings and rulers fear an Enclave taking power for itself. To wield both magic and the sword would make any such kingdom unstoppable. And of all Enclaves, Anjibar is in the best position to do such a thing. So it is important that we make extra effort to show that we have no such aspirations."

"Why not do it anyway?" Stefano suggested. "Like you said, fielding a large army of magicians and soldiers. You would be unstoppable."

"Except there are four other Enclaves who fear that very thing as much as the kingdoms do," Gregor reminded the Prince. "The rest of the world would rise up against us as soon as Anjibar even hinted at such a move. So we have to be careful, stay in the shadows, but remain present."

"Must be frustrating. Having all that power and can't use it?"

"We are content to train magicians and oversee their activity," Gregor shrugged. "We don't have the same aspirations as kings."

"But you need us?"

"For magic to be able to reach its full potential it must operate in a free environment," Gregor pointed out. "This is why Anjibar is chief among all the Enclaves. We have no king breathing down our necks. No offense to your royal self. But we cannot be hampered by men who do not understand what we do."

"I still don't see where I or Raulia come in here," Stefano said. "There is no Enclave in our borders."

A tight smile forced its way onto Gregor's face. He stood up and held his wine cup out to be refilled. The slave hurried over to comply.

"Walk with me," Gregor invited, and turned away without waiting.

Stefano hurried to catch up to the Lord Prefect and fell in beside him.

"We live in dark times," Gregor began. "No generation of men has had to face the difficulties that we now face. Despite whatever wars or plagues or disasters of the past, even the Reign of the Shadow, if that even existed, doesn't compare to what confronts us today."

Gregor stopped and turned to face Stefano. He gestured fiercely in front of the Prince's face.

"Do you understand how dire the situation is?" Gregor implored. "The life of the whole world is at stake."

"I have no pleasure garden to retreat to," Stefano answered coldly. "I listen to the pleas of starving children everyday. I wake up with sand in my mouth and I drink dust in my water. How could I fail to understand what a dire situation we are in?"

Gregor smiled indulgently and chose to ignore the verbal jab. He patted Stefano on the arm and continued to walk.

"Then you understand," the Lord Prefect continued. "You understand what we face."

"Of course I understand," Stefano answered, the chill still in his voice. "I don't see why you would think otherwise."

"Then why hasn't something been done about it?" Gregor asked. "Why has the situation been allowed to fester this long without reprieve?"

"I'm sure I cannot answer that, Your Grace. I am not a man of magic, and this is a magic problem. Is it not?"

"But here is my problem," Gregor exclaimed, punctuating with his fist. "Everyone thinks that magic has been idle, either causing the problem or doing nothing to stymie the disaster. Whereas in truth we have done much. We have studied and searched and experimented diligently to find a way out of this, to restore the land to its former bounty."

"To no result," Stefano assumed.

A frown creased Gregor's features. He turned away and plucked at a nearby gardenia. Crushing the blossom he held it up to his nose and inhaled its beautiful scent. Even here, he noticed. Even here in his magical garden the scent of the flower was weakening, the essence that gave it beauty and power and aroma was fading from his flowers. Quite soon, he feared, there would be no scent at all from the blossoms and his garden would have the same dead, dry smell as the rest of the world.

"What if I had found something," Gregor conjectured, his back still to the Prince. "What if I had found a cure for the Blight?"

"Then you cannot hesitate in sharing it with the world," Stefano answered. "Why wouldn't you use it immediately."

"Suppose there was opposition to the cure," Gregor shrugged. "Suppose the other Enclaves found the solution....objectionable."

"Objectionable? Why would they?"

"An objection of ethics," Gregor clarified.

"Are we speaking hypothetically?" Stefano asked.

Gregor shrugged in response.

"Why would the cure for the Blight raise any ethical objections?" Stefano asked.

"Unpopular methods," was all Gregor offered in explanation.

"How unpopular?"

"It may present a certain danger that will probably result in the loss of life."

"How many?"

"Very few, at most."

"Are we speaking hypothetically?"

Gregor turned slowly around and looked the Prince in the eye. He leveled a dark and serious stare, letting it rest on the young man for a moment. A hush fell over the garden, amplifying the sounds of the waterfalls and bustling insects.

"I am speaking truth," Gregor whispered.

Stefano looked back at the Lord Prefect for a moment without speaking. He swallowed hard. Gregor could see the implications falling into place within the Prince's mind.

Then, "How certain are you it will work?"

"I grow more certain everyday," Gregor said, resuming his walk and more casual tone. "My experiments so far have been quite promising, but there are still a few crucial elements that I am feverishly trying to work out. Success comes closer everyday."

"Is it not dangerous?" Stefano asked with a touch of awe in his voice. "If it might cause the loss of life."

"Oh no, nothing like that at this point," Gregor brushed aside the comment. "The work is still early in development. No risk is present now. It is only the implementation of the solution that could be dangerous."

"How so?"

"It requires working some extremely powerful magic," Gregor explained. "Such an unleashing of power is bound to be dangerous."

Gregor watched Stefano out of the corner of his eye as the ideas rattled around his head. Twice he opened his mouth to ask something, then thought better of it.

"So by the time your solution is implemented we will know for certain it works," Stefano clarified.

"Of course," Gregor reassured him. "I would never expose the world to such danger without being completely certain of success."

"Very good," Stefano nodded. "Then why would the other Enclaves object?"

"They are weak-willed and foolish men," Gregor sneered. "They lack the conviction to take the difficult steps necessary to save the world. Many men are like that, I am afraid, lacking that special courage, that daring, to do what is needed. They are too squeamish for bold steps.

"I hope you don't share that weakness."

"Sometimes a few must be sacrificed for the good of the many," Stefano answered in agreement.

"Ah, you have been trained by the Gerstene philosophers," Gregor gushed, stroking the Prince's flattered ego. "As a Prince should."

Stefano nodded proudly and Gregor could see the self-satisfaction spreading across his face. He found it difficult not to laugh. Every fool with a year of mediocre tutoring knew that insipid Gerstene quote, horribly out of context though it was. He knew Stefano was no more proficient in Gerstene than he was in necromancy. Still, he had the Prince exactly where he wanted him.

"You see why I have chosen you," the Lord Prefect continued with the flattery. "Most of these royal houses have abandoned the traditional training of their sons. Raulia, I see, stays true to her roots."

"It's in our blood," Stefano concurred. "Father says most of the other houses are watered down and addled from all that salt water."

Gregor forced himself to laugh.

"Too true, too true," he agreed. "Then you shouldn't be surprised that I have come to you with this."

"I'm still not sure what this has to do with Raulia," Stefano confessed. "It seems like a magic issue. You can certainly count on Raulia's open support of Anjibar. We implicitly trust your wisdom in these matters."

"As you have already noticed, we lack teeth," Gregor explained. "We lack the military might to defend ourselves if our enemies were to become too aggressive."

Gregor wheeled around to face Stefano again. He allowed exaggerated animation into his features, to paint his situation more desperate than it actually was.

"Imagine what the reaction will be when this method is perfected and the other nations learn of it. They will hate Anjibar and at the same time they will stop at nothing to possess what we have. Oh they might cry that Anjibar must be stopped because what we do is too dangerous. But you and I know that when I perfect this method of healing the land it will become a weapon of power. Whoever has it will rule the land. Chaos will erupt and all might well be lost before we can even start to make a difference."

"I'm not sure Raulia alone could defend you," Stefano pointed out.

"Especially with the other Enclaves involved."

"Then we must avoid the situation in which we are faced with that sort of opposition."

"I don't see how we can."

"Let's keep it with Raulia," Gregor suggested as he resumed his stroll of the gardens. "Instead of letting everyone know and having total anarchy ensue, we quietly begin to implement the solution in Raulia. With a little diplomacy and luck your kingdom will be green and fertile before anyone else knows what's going on."

A smile spread across Stefano's face as Gregor watched the implications sink in. If Gregor's method even slightly worked then all of Raulia's inland territories would see a dramatic increase. Population would grow, money would pour in, the army would bristle with might.

The smile suddenly fell away.

"I am not so foolish to think you would lay this gift at my feet without something in return," Stefano said.

Gregor spread his arms wide in mock offense. Then he smiled, forced and feral.

"You have been trained well," Gregor subtly mocked. "There is something I would need from you. Raulia would have to play a crucial role if my plan were to have a chance of success."

"Such as..."

"First of all your utter secrecy," Gregor told him. "No one must know about this outside of the royal household."

Stefano nodded his assent.

"Then there will be some errands," Gregor explained. "Some delicate operations may have to be executed with discretion. I, nor Anjibar can have any part in them. They would have to be carried out solely by your initiative."

"That may prove difficult," Stefano sighed. "Our resources are stretched thin with the northern war. I could never convince father to pull them away with no assurance that this plan of yours would even work."

"Believe me, it will work," Gregor insisted. "And I will show you how confident I am."

"Show me?"

"A token of my good faith," Gregor told the Prince. "And I will start by winning this war for you. By the end of the month Raulia will be a coastal kingdom."

Chapter Four
Pilgrims

Elias and Bannus, reluctant travel companions that they were, spent the night with the pilgrim train. They camped on the edge of Hiram's Well jurisdiction so the guards remained and all the pilgrim's huddled together for safety. Although most bandits had long abandoned the interior along with anyone else who had the money or clout, the force of habit remained strong. Stories still passed around in horrified retelling of the unspeakable things done in those early desperate days of The Blight. Tales of cannibalism and cruelty, pilgrims burned, villagers slaughtered and eaten, still whispered among frightened travelers. Most were certainly embellished, but the imagination of the common man ruled over him more than his reason, and to him the wilderness was a chasm of horrors.

So they huddled together in the desert night, all at once frightened and hopeful. Hardly any of them could conceive that life could be any worse than from where they came. Distant places always seemed better off. Over that next hill there must surely be a chance for a better life. They can't possibly have it as bad as us. Or so the thought went.

Elias had been with the trains before. Safety wasn't as much a concern for him, with his magic and Bannus' steel. It hadn't even been a subject the two of them had discussed. If a pilgrim train was on the move then Elias and Bannus usually traveled with it for some way. Usually no more than a day or two, then their paths would diverge and Elias' wanderings would take him elsewhere, and the few days shared with the hopeful strangers would fade like runes scratched in the sand. A few times they traveled a week or more, though rarely.

Neither Elias nor Bannus could articulate why they preferred to travel with the pilgrims. It could have been the natural aversion they held towards one another. More likely, it was the tendency for humans to gather into groups. The gravity of other human souls simply pulled them in.

Elias had journeyed with enough of the desperate pilgrims to know what the fate of this one from Hiram's Well would be. They would push through endless miles of dust and blighted wasteland until they stumbled into a village as desperate as the one they left. Or maybe they would end up at a larger town or city, mostly abandoned, as haunted as its people behind unguarded walls. If they were lucky, they would keep moving eastward and end up in a coastal city, one fed from the sea, still hungry and poor but fed just enough to suppress the increasing riots. What they wouldn't find was food, at least not enough of it. In fact, food had become so scarce that the rich and powerful debated among themselves whether or not the common man would be better off dead. They couldn't work, so why continue to support them? They were just a rebellion waiting to happen. At least that's what the latest rumor said, confirmed by the infamous "they".

Maybe it was something deeper that drew Elias towards those desperate people. Like them, there was no place for him in the world. With ten years missing from his memory, no place to call his own - for even the Enclave was effectively shut off from him - why not take up with the searching and hungry tracking the endless blast and drought for anything that resembled hope?

Elias leaned back and looked at the dark and lonely night. That same feeling of loneliness, reflected in the sky and stars, crept into him and infected his heart with its quiet sadness. He was just like these pilgrims, he decided. He too searched for something he didn't even know existed.

A moment of rare self-pity admitted itself into Elias' consciousness. Of all creatures, I alone am without a home, he quoted to himself from the famous poem. If I could just remember, he thought. But no, that was not the road of sanity. Unless he had a way of opening those memories up again, that pointless moaning about what was lost would only drive him mad.

He pulled his thoughts away from himself and back to the night around him. It was the only time the wasteland looked anything but bleak. The air was clean and cool, the moonlight blazing proudly, casting an eerie, blue light over the sands. He could almost imagine he was someplace else beside this blighted world.

Rare moments like this allowed Elias to hope. And though he knew how dangerous that hope was, how pointless were its promises, he could not help but entertain that happy notion. It just felt too good not to hope. The lightness that came with hope, compared to the unbearable weight of dread, was reason enough to seek it. Only if it didn't build you up before crashing to disappointment.

Elias sighed and finished straightening out his bedroll. As soon as he laid down he felt a presence tug at him.

Elias looked up and saw the boy staring at him again, the one he had seen earlier. What had his mother called him?

"Silas?" the magi spoke to the dark and curious eyes that fixed on him.

The boy nodded and moved closer. He looked down at the embers of Elias' dying fire.

"I don't think your mother wants you to talk to me," Elias told the boy.

Silas shrugged and didn't immediately answer. He continued to stare deeply into the fire, as if mesmerized by the flickering heat.

"She's sleeping," he finally said. "I waited for her to fall asleep."

He made no mention of why he waited, though to Elias that much was obvious. The magi answered with a thoughtful grunt.

"Can you show me some more magic?" the boy asked, not timidly, but also without the irrepressible enthusiasm usually prevalent in children.

"I guess I can," Elias said, straightening up and moving to the dying fire. "Would you like to be my assistant?"

Silas nodded soberly and looked up at Elias with that almost dead stare.

What could have happened to this child, Elias asked himself. The blank stare that was fixed on him from across the embers almost frightened him. Something had died in the boy, or was quickly dying.

"Well build the fire up for me then," Elias instructed the boy. "And I will show you something truly magnificent."

Another nod from Silas and the boy turned and made a short survey of the area, searching the ground. Elias smiled, knowing what the child searched for and also knowing he would not find it. He watched intently, studying how the boy would react.

"You've burned all your fuel," the boy simply stated. He stared expectantly at Elias.

"Try sand," Elias suggested. He pointed a stack of sand blocks beside the fire.

The boy never wavered in his fixed stare.

"Sand will smother the coals," he said.

"You can't be my assistant if you can't get the fire going," Elias teased. He believed the broad smile on his face made it obvious it was harmless fun.

Instead of bantering the boy turned around and walked away from Elias and the fire.

"Where are you going?" Elias called after him.

"I can't start the fire," the boy stated. "That means I can't be your assistant."

Both the lack of emotion and the ease with which the boy gave up seized Elias with sadness. Apathy didn't belong in anything that young. What was happening to the world?

"No. Come back, come back," Elias insisted.

The boy stopped and obediently returned to the dying fire.

"It's part of the magic," Elias explained. "You were supposed to try sand. It's a surprise. Just try it. Here, use this sand here, the one in blocks."

If the boy was relieved he didn't give any sign. He did bend down and pick up one the brown bricks that crumbled when he picked it up. He looked up doubtfully at Elias who gave him a reassuring gesture, and tossed the sand on the shimmering coals.

Flames exploded out of the embers. A great whoosh sounded and a ball of fire rose up, disappearing in a shimmer of black smoke. Smaller flames sprung up and brought the fire to life again.

The boy's eyes widened in surprise as his head rocked back. In the bright burst of flame Elias flicked out his wand and threw his arms out wide in a dramatic flourish. An almost imperceptible turn of the mouth was all Silas offered by way of showing enjoyment. It would have to do.

"How did you do that?" he asked with just the barest hint of emotion.

"I didn't do that, you did," Elias told him.

Puzzled, Silas looked down at his own hands. That serious look he had perfected darkened his features again.

"But I didn't do anything," the boy said.

"You threw the sand on the fire."

"You could have thrown the sand on," the boy replied after a thoughtful moment.

"But I didn't," Elias argued. "You did. You helped me create magic."

Elias watched the boy ponder these things. He couldn't begin to process what sort of thoughts ran through Silas' head, but the boy must have reached some agreement within himself because he argued no further.

"Can I do more?" he asked.

"You could help me tell a story," Elias told him. "Do you like stories?"

The boy nodded, again without enthusiasm.

"Do you know the story of Leopold the Rider?" Elias asked as he threw more blocks of sand on the fire, drawing up the flames.

For the first time a genuine and deep smile cracked over the boy's face. His eyes lit up with joy as his whole face brightened. The tension that seemed to be coiled up in him released in an instant. For now, for the brief moment, he looked like any normal boy excited to hear a story.

"That's my dad's name," Silas beamed. "He was called Leopold."

"Well no doubt your father is as every bit as noble and courageous as the Leopold of legend," Elias began. "Did your father ever tell you the story of Leopold the Rider?"

"He died before I knew him." Silas said, losing none of his new-found happiness. He told Elias about the death of his father as matter-of-factly as he would recount the day's weather or what he had for lunch.

"He was killed by magicians."

It took a moment for what the child said to sink into Elias. The magi was thankful for the boy's youth and lack of social experience. Otherwise, both would be feeling as awkward as he did. Awkward and a little guilty. He tried to console himself with the knowledge that he had nothing to do with the man's death. But another voice reminded him he could be sure of nothing. What he had done or not done in those missing years was impossible to tell.

"Well, if you have never heard the story of Leopold you are in for quite the treat," Elias recovered, though for the moment he could not look Silas in the eyes.

"Now I want you to imagine a crown," Elias instructed as he drew a ball of flame out of the fire. "Can you do that for me? A king's crown, golden and beautiful to behold."

Silas nodded as Elias continued to draw fire from the embers and into the ball that hovered just above. He made slow circles with his wand, pulling out small tendrils of orange flame that rose and joined the burning sphere. The ball of fire grew larger and brighter until it looked like a little sun hovering in the dark. Elias stopped pulling the flames in. A small string of fire still connected the burning globe to the coals below.

"Now this fire is like clay," Elias said. "We can shape it into whatever we want. But you need to breathe life into it. That's how you shape fire. So I want you to keep thinking of a crown, the kind a good king would wear. And as you think, hold the image in your mind as sharply as you can, and then blow on the fire."

Silas nodded and closed his eyes in concentration. He stood very still and serious, his brow furrowed in concentration, before opening his eyes. Leaning forward he stole a timid look at Elias, then blew on the fire.

The flames shifted and circled, spinning themselves into the shape of a crown. Fully fashioned of fire the circlet turned slowly, displaying itself. At several points the fire collected in white-hot intensity, appearing like decorative jewels.

The smile across Silas' face widened. Elias couldn't help but feel a bit of satisfaction in that. In many ways, widening the girth of that grin was more difficult to conjure than magic.

"Very good," Elias beamed. "You see, there is magic in you. You will make quite the assistant."

Elias could see the crown of fire reflected in the boy's eyes. Perhaps behind that, the smallest hint of self-satisfaction. Usually not a trait Elias admired, but the boy could certainly use some.

"Long ago there was a good king that fell very ill," Elias began. "No one knew what could possibly have made him so sick, for the king was a robust and healthy man, in the prime of his life. All of the doctors and seers and learned men gathered and couldn't find out what plagued him. Even the magi with all their wisdom could not figure out why the king was so sick. All of their efforts were to no avail.

"Now, I need you to think of a beautiful princess. Can you do that?"

Silas closed his eyes again in concentration. This time when he blew on the fire the sphere transformed into the face a young girl. Silas regarded his creation with obvious satisfaction and even Elias watched impressed as the image turned in front of him.

"Now the king had a daughter, a beautiful princess who loved her father very much. When all of the magi and doctors could find nothing to help him, the princess resolved to find herself a cure for her father's illness. Late one night, on a new moon, when all the castle had nodded off to sleep, the foolish princess snuck up to the old barrows to consult the ghosts that walk under the moonless sky."

As Elias wove his tale the young boy shaped the fire into figures from the story. He proved quit adept at the task, and eventually Elias didn't have to tell him what figures to make. Instead, the boy's imagination shaped fire into figure as Elias spoke, breathing into flame a semblance of living things.

When Elias told him about the ghosts that rose up out of the haunted barrows Silas blew onto the flames to shape them into a long and shimmering specter. He kept the ghost as the story moved to the princess' desperate bargain. For the king's soul was locked away, which was the cause of his illness, and could not be released without the trade of another soul.

Silas blew the fire into a horseman when Elias told him of Leopold, the young stableboy who had loved the princess from afar for many years. That night he had secretly followed her to the barrows. As Leopold watched the soul of the princess being carried away to the land of the Erl King, he followed her there too.

Over three days Leopold rode after the soul of the princess, through darkness and noon, desert and forest. He rode until he and his horse almost collapsed from exhaustion, fueled only by his love for the princess and his horse's love for him. Just when his strength failed and his horse was on the edge of death, Leopold cried out in sorrow of his weakness. But some nearby spirits, in awe of his resolution, took pity on the young lover, filling him and his steed with supernatural strength.

For three more days Leopold rode, this time over mountain and seas, following the soul of his beloved. The spirits of the ocean, impressed by the intensity of his love, held Leopold's horse up as he pounded the mighty waves. On the far end of the ocean he rode into the fabled and deadly realm of the Erl King.

Silas shaped the fire into snarling monsters that set out to destroy Leopold. Then he shaped in the fire the benign face of the moon, who likewise moved by Leopold's courage, sent her aid to him as well, surrounding him with a protective light that kept all the evil creatures of the night at bay.

When Elias told of Leopold riding into the vast keep of the Erl King, Silas shaped a tall fortress, full of towers and high pinions. Elias marveled at the detail emerging from the boy's creations. He even thought he saw guards walking along one of the walls.

The grim face of the Erl King emerged from the fire as Elias spoke of Leopold riding into the dark king's court. Uncaring eyes stared out as Leopold laid out his plea for the life of his love. Even as the whole court wept, the Erl King remained resolute. The soul of the princess was his by right.

Finally, the face in the fire softened when Leopold offered his own soul in exchange for the princess'. Why, the Erl King asked, would a stableboy give his soul for a foolish princess who didn't even know he existed. The poor Leopold could only reply that without his love he would have no reason to live.

Silas shaped the flames back into the rider, now carrying a box in his arms, which held the soul of his princess. So moved was the Erl King by Leopold's love, that he granted him the soul he so desired. After placing the soul in an enchanted box, the Erl King gave Leopold strict warnings not to open the box until he returned to the body of the princess.

So Leopold returned, back over desert and sea, mountain and forest, faithfully carrying with him the soul of his princess. And just before he arrived where her body lay sick and failing, just a day's ride away, his doubts overtook him. Perhaps she will not love me after all, he thought to himself. Just one peak at her beautiful soul, just in case she wants nothing more to do with me. She was a princess after all and he a mere stableboy.

So under the night and moon he took out the box and opened the lid just the tiniest amount. But even through this tiny crack the soul of the princess flew out. It darted about feverishly, looking for her body, then flew off deep into the forest.

Grief overcame Leopold. So close to the end and yet he had failed. With sadness, Leopold mounted his faithful steed again and began to search anew for his beloved.

"Leopold rode all over the world," Elias wrapped up his tale. "He still searched for the soul of his princess as the princess searched for her body. For many years men would see a ghost haunting the barrows and the hills, and always, never far behind, rode Leopold chasing after his beloved."

"Did he ever find her?" Silas asked as the figure of Leopold still rode in fire.

"After many trials and adventures, yes. But that is another story."

As the story ended, Silas looked thoughtfully at the shape-shifting fire. He stared at it as if by looking alone he could unlock its secrets.

"How does it work?" he finally asked.

"It works the same way a potter shapes clay or a sculptor shapes rock," Elias explained. "Except fire is a living thing. It cannot be shaped by pressure or force. Instead, a fire lives off of air. Did you know that?"

Silas shook his head.

"You can see for yourself," Elias told him. "Light a candle then put it under a jar or glass. Eventually, the flame will go out. It needs air in order to live."

"But if I blow on a candle it goes out," Silas argued.

Impressed by the boy's astuteness, Elias nodded and pointed to the fire underneath the figure of Leopold cast in flame.

"Very true," he said. "But when you blow on a little candle you blow away all the little bit of heat is has. So the candle goes out. If you were to blow on this fire, then it will increase in heat. It would take a very strong wind to blow away all the heat from this flame."

Silas seemed to ponder these things for a moment, then nodded his agreement.

"So to shape fire requires breath," Elias continued. "Or better yet, air. Now I made this fire special to respond to what is carried on the breath. The air we breathe out has its own special properties, much of which I couldn't begin to explain to you. It is enough to know that what is in your mind, so deep that it is on your soul, is also hidden on your breath. That is why with enough concentration your breath can shape fire into whatever is on your soul."

"Anybody can do this?" Silas asked.

Elias shook his head. "No. Actually very few can. You are quite a special boy."

Silas stared at the enchanted fire with a gaze that Elias could tell looked deep within. He blew on the fire and it shifted into a three-masted ship, complete with sails and a mermaid affixed to the prow. Again he breathed and the fire shimmered into the shape of a sword. Another breath and the fire turned into a hawk soaring proudly.

The boy's brow furrowed in concentration, then his face dropped and he looked sullenly at the ground. All at once the fragile joy that had possessed him was suddenly spent.

"What's the matter?" Elias could not help but ask. "Has something upset you?"

"I don't know what my father looked like," Silas muttered, still looking at the ground. "If I knew, then I could make the fire look like him."

Against his will tears welled up in Elias' eyes. Such a simple sentiment, yet he had never heard anything so sad in his entire life.

"But you can," Elias told him, willing his voice to steady lest the precocious boy see through him. "I told you, the fire can read your soul as it is carried on your breath."

"But what image would I make in my head?" Silas asked looking up.

"It doesn't matter," Elias assured him. "Just think of your father, concentrate on him. Even though you don't know what he looks like, his very being is impressed on your soul. You know him in ways that you will never fully understand."

"Is that true?" the boy asked as the smile crept back into his face.

"Of course," Elias answered, careful to keep the smile on his own face. "Try it, you'll see."

Silas closed his eyes again in concentration. The intensity he exercised seemed to draw up all around him. Even Elias could feel it from across the fire. After several moments of focused concentration he opened his eyes, leaned forward, and gently blew on the fire.

Not even sure what to expect Elias watched the flames shift and turn. Tendrils of fire peeled off as others folded in and shaped the figure. A face slowly emerged from the flames, shaped by mysterious forces that even the learned magi hardly understood.

The boy regarded his creation with an impassive and expressionless face. He looked at the large curls of hair, much like his own. Then his eyes moved to the figure's own deep set eyes, full of compassion, even shaped in flame as they were. The nose was a bit too large, and a crooked turn on the bridge said it had been broken before. Beneath the nose stood a pair of full lips, unusual for a man. They are poet's lips, Elias thought to himself, casting the whole face with a delicate and sensitive aura. He could see how much the boy resembled his father.

Silas leaned close towards the fire-sculpted face of his father. Elias could see him studying every detail of the figure. He even reached out a tentative hand, as if he were going to touch it. Then, remembering it was made of fire, let the hand hover close by, then drop slowly, reluctantly.

"Thank you," Silas said, his habitual lack of emotion returning, his face closed and expressionless.

Without another word he turned and walked alone back to his sleeping mother.

Elias watched the boy retreat into the darkness. It seemed suitable, as if darkness was the boy's rightful environment. It couldn't be that way by nature.

Orange heat still pulsed from the figure Silas had shaped into his father. Elias twirled his fingers and the flames rotated until the face looked at him. He pondered the figure, perhaps not as deeply as Silas had, and for different reasons. How much did the boy truly resemble his father? Some? None? Was this image the picture Silas conjured in his mind when he thought of his father, or something deeper?

Well, as long as the boy believed it was his father, Elias thought. Maybe I have done some good today.

Without intention Elias thought of the other boy that day, the one whose father had the cucumber seeds.

"Bringing the hope of magic to the world," Elias muttered to himself and chuckled. Was this the way he brought hope to the world? Giving little boys cucumbers and visions of their dead fathers.

A passing notion stirred in him that he might reach out to the boy. He almost certainly possessed the spark. It made sense, the intuitive way he understood magic, the interest that went beyond mere childhood fascination, the way he could shape the fire. And then there was the way in which he could project himself so that Elias always felt it when the boy looked at him. He most certainly had the gift, powerful too.

There was little doubt about how much Elias could change the boy's life. If his mother could get over her aversion to it, magic would afford them a life they couldn't dream of without it. Sure, it would take some convincing, but it wouldn't be hard to get the boy to an Enclave. They were so hungry for new talent that things would move on their own from there.

Elias lifted a hand and waved it toward the fire. Instantly, the flames died and the total reach of night covered him. Stars slowly started fading into his vision.

Let someone else do it, Elias decided. That other part of himself won out over concern for the boy. That part of him that was full of ennui, of apathy, full of the certainty that anything he ever did was a ripple against a tidal wave; that part of him won out over his concern as it usually did.

Cucumbers and dead fathers. That would be Elias' contribution to the healing of the world. Let someone else save it. It was just too much damn work.

* * *

An old, familiar dream settled into Elias' mind as sleep took over him. He stood outside his father's house, the home he had known as a boy. Just beyond where he stood his father bowled on the village green.

Green.

The color struck him in his dream like jagged metal in his eyes. There was so much of it. Green everywhere. Green covered every tree, carpeted the ground in a gratuitous display of color. People trod all over the green without a single thought as to what a blessing that vibrant color truly was.

An irresistible sense of power emanated from all around Elias. As he watched his father crouching down, turning the ball over in his hand in concentration on his bowl, Elias could feel every detail of the moment, acutely magnified through the latent power he felt trembling through the whole world.

He saw it all, felt it all in that moment: the laughing face of his father, always on the cusp of a grin, the sweat that dripped from his brow, the other men watching intently with the calculating minds of competitors. He heard conversations all around him. One lady complained of her husband while another moaned about the taste of corn. Kids played frog leap nearby while one girl cried alone. Elias could taste the salt of her tears and even hear in her mind how much she hated Alice who always kept her out of the games. The buzz of industrious bees hummed in the background. A hawk circled overhead watching the village below. And he could even feel the barley ripening, there in the first field, filling itself with fruitfulness.

All these things Elias perceived in a moment along with the ineffable power that moved behind them all. And he also knew that no one else could sense them, that he was different. He knew that deep power, and that deep power knew him. He felt the draw of that terrible and beautiful thing. It was the most joyful and fearful moment of his life.

Despite the happiness of the moment, the happiness of his childhood and the happiness of his first discovery of magic, a bubbling dread began to fill Elias in his dream. For even in the dream he knew what came next. For five years the same nightmare plagued him. For five years it terrified and tantalized him.

The vividness of the dream was made more awful by what followed. The sky over the village green darkened but Elias was the only one who saw. A black storm cloud swirled down and churned angry. The boy tried to cry out a warning, and even the dreamer screamed to the villagers and little boy.

This was the storm that shook the world.

A flash rain fell and darkened the village with streaks of water. No one even saw the rain. The boy cried out to his father as the rain fell, but his father paid him no heed, nor did he notice the deluge as he pulled back his arm to bowl. The men still laughed and watched on as water fell down their faces.

The water rose with alarming speed and flooded the village. Waves of water came roaring down the green and washed all the men and the children, and even his father away. Elias was torn away by a powerful tide of water that struck him and carried him away.

Images began to bombard his mind. In quick succession, even as the dreamer moaned and stirred, gripped in his hidden agony.

Elias tasted the sharp tang of blood in his mouth. Thunder roared and lightning flashed. His whole body shook with reverberations. Cold shook him with every pelt of rain that beat down on his shivering body. Somewhere his hands gripped cold steel.

Then he felt himself stretched out, his hands bound by cold metal biting into his hands. The dark sky rained down upon him. In a flash of lightning he saw robed figures gathered around him, their faces hidden in shadow.

Gregor's face hovered angrily in front of his. The Lord Prefect's eyes bulged in wrath and spit flew from his mouth as he screamed.

"Where is the tree?!" he yelled, his face inches from Elias.

Then he smelled fire. The storm was gone, replaced by a dry day. Screams cried out in smoke. Someone on horseback, a man with a long drooping moustache, looked at the fire and laughed at the screams below. He laughed and looked at Elias, yelling something he couldn't hear. Nausea swept over, sick at the smell of burning flesh.

The smell of charred bone and burning hair changed into the perfumed aroma of incense. He lounged on silk cushions. Two women reclined by him, the stem of houka pipes passed between them. Elias watched himself as he noticed their clothing was transparent. Another face hovered in front of his, one dark from the sun, with a black, oiled beard and black curls hanging down from his head. He was vaguely aware of the garden around him.

"This is what we live for Elias," the man breathed as smoke plumed from his mouth. "This is our garden of earthly delights."

He heard a child crying. When he looked he saw a boy weeping among a burning charnel of bones. Fire and black smoke swirled around. It was always the same. Elias would reach out to him but the boy would refuse to show him his face.

Except this time the boy looked up at Elias and it was Silas. Around him the fire swirled and the flames formed into the face of Silas' father. The sensitive features of the poet contorted in anger, mouth opened, roaring and accusatory.

"Why did you do this to me?" Silas wept. "Why Elias? Why did you make me this way?"

The fire face grew and the head moved forward to swallow Elias. Elias turned to run and leapt onto Leopold's horse. All night long the magi fled, terrified and haunted, chased by the fiery head of Silas' father.

Elias tossed and sweat in his sleep and found no rest.

As the tortured magi thrashed in his sleep, held in thrall by the irresistible dream, Thoran watched the pilgrim camp from a distance.

High on a hill above the camp, he could only make out vague details through the darkness and distance, but Thoran knew exactly where Elias lay plagued by nightmares. He knew as well as if a beacon of light were flashing over the magi's prone figure. He knew it as certainly as he knew Elias was having a nightmare. He could pretty much guess its content.

Thoran knew these things because just over five years ago Elias had made certain he would know these things, despite Elias not possessing the slightest memory as to why.

A deep sigh filled Thoran and eased out of him again. Conflict ran deep inside him, a conflict few men in the history of the world had ever known.

Thoran reached down and touched the brown, leather pouch that hung from his belt, the one that held something more valuable than all the money in the world. He knew he should take it to Elias. The time might not be the best with that idiot Bannus still hanging around, but the world was dying quickly and soon there might not be anything left to save.

He looked down at the pouch and wondered how so little a thing could mean so much. But that was often the way of things.

For inside that little pouch lay the hope of the world. Inside was the salvation of all that lay dead and dying around him. Inside the pouch was the one thing that could stave off the Blight.

But Thoran hesitated. He paused. And he didn't hesitate out of any callousness or lack of care for the world. Most of these things were beyond him. There was only one reason that Thoran did not want to give that pouch to Elias.

Thoran knew that once the pouch was turned over to its rightful owner and its secrets revealed, he would have to die.

First Interlude
The Fate of Pilgrims

Minutes from the 140th Session of the Council of Nobles, commissioned by his Esteemed Highness, Marco Marosso, Lord Protector of Kairos.

[Excerpt begins as Count Lornan takes the floor to address the August assembly]

My fellow countryman, nobles and lords, servants of the will of the gods, children of the great and unmatched Kairon, the father of us all, I beg you to allow your hearts to be human today as I tell you of a most terrible plight, and a tragedy that I believe could have been prevented if we, the leaders of this great land, would but look up and see the misery that afflicts the people of the interior.

As you know, for those wretched souls that are stuck in the interior, the only hope they possess is to join one of the many pilgrim trains that wind from city to city. We say that it is to allow them to seek a better life. We offer these passports as a sign of our supposed kindness, as if we are offering hope.

At the same time we bar the gates of the coastal cities, even as the desperate numbers swell outside, scorched and starving. And why? We say there is no room here. The seas are being overfished. The commoners riot already and clamber for a greater share of these dwindling, few resources. The streets swell with the stinking masses and their filthy brood. Already, children are employed to thievery, and young girls hawk their flesh in the sweltering ghettos and docks.

So we cannot take anymore in, you say. Instead, we offer the poor stuck in the interior passports, permission to travel from their own town to seek a better life elsewhere. And we congratulate ourselves on our kindness, as if we have done a great favor to the wretched inland man and his thin, starved wife. We sigh at our own magnanimity and count ourselves charitable that we would offer the simple liberty of movement, as if movement alone could relieve the suffering of the poor masses. And in offering them a freedom as simple as movement, are we not only restoring a liberty that should belong to men anyway? Are we giving them anything they shouldn't already have?

The interior suffers from a lack of food and water, this we all know. As food production dwindles the problem will likely increase. To relieve the people there, we give them a simple dole, one that dwindles every month. And we offer them passports to seek opportunities in the next town. Then we consider the problem solved, the matter at an end. We return to our parties and palaces and sleep the deep slumber of men who are both well fed and at peace with their own conscience.

But my fellow lords, if I may dare disturb the tranquility of your conscience. Not with wild tales of the interior told by bards to frighten the delicate ladies of the salons do I bring you. Nor do I seek to disturb your inner peace by exaggerations and melodrama fostered by rebels and agitators who breed rebellion and discontent.

No, I simply relay to you the fate of these pilgrims, so poignantly illustrated to us by the events of the last ten days. It is the fate of your own people, whom you so generously offer passports to, that I lay out to as a plea for reform. And remember, these pilgrims and their state are not only the reasons we need reforms, but also remember these pilgrims, and their miserable fate, exists because of our direct actions. In attempting to relieve the burden of the poor and trapped within the interior, we have only heaped greater horrors upon them.

Earlier this season, a group of pilgrims left the dusty and luckless town known as Hiram's Well. For the first few days things fared quite well. The guards from the town traveled with the people and even a magi and his guard joined the group, we are told. But once the group traveled out of the jurisdiction of Hiram's Well, and the magi took his own course, this search for a better life took a deadly turn.

In only a few days time this unlucky group would wander far off course. Roads are not trusted by the pilgrims, as nightmarish accounts of brutal and cannibalistic bandits haunt the popular imagination. So these pilgrims took to the wastelands off the common roads, something difficult for even a knowledgeable person to navigate.

These were not knowledgeable men, and soon they wandered horribly off course. What little food and water they possessed was quickly used up. Starving and thirsty they attacked a small caravan that carried ore from the east. The meager provisions acquired were immediately devoured.

Two days later, still thirsty and sunburned, the pilgrims stumbled upon a granary owned by Duke Denison, a report that came to this very council at our last meeting. Driven to desperation as they could almost smell the grain inside, they attacked without hesitation or the slightest sense of order. The small garrison easily defended the granary and most of the men were slaughtered along with the children.

The few women deemed worthwhile after repeated rapes were sold into slavery or kept as concubines. Of these, all but two died within the month. The remaining pair barely survived on rations tossed their way.

Most of those not killed in the attack on the granary, those wise enough to flee, died of dehydration in the wilderness. Twelve made it to a nearby village but were denied entrance. They starved to death waiting outside the village gates for some show of mercy.

Two men discovered an abandoned manor and lived for three weeks eating old cloth and leather left behind. After another fortnight one killed the other, cannibalized his corpse, and lived for another few weeks before also dying.

Then, just ten days ago, a boy from this doomed pilgrim train miraculously wandered into the coastal town of Pelemont. His thin and sunburned figure, and the tattered remnants of his clothes hanging loosely from him, shocked the inhabitants, who though hungry themselves, rarely encountered such desperate scarcity. A merchants wife, the kindly Miss Ranon took pity on the boy and had him carried to her own house. There she nursed him with a tenderness he had never known and fed him with an abundance he didn't think possible. Despite all these ministrations he died two days ago of fever.

Miss Ranon has had the boy buried in a temple plot. She came to me after the boy's death, just two nights ago, to tell me his awful story. With tears and a pity I have never known she pleaded with me to do something. I have been entrusted with this heart wrenching story, and in hearing have been endowed with a divine obligation to act on behalf of those who have been subject to such misery. And as I give the story to you, you also will be obligated to act.

For this, my noble brethren, is not their story, it is our story. This is our sovereign holding, not for own enrichment, but for the betterment of all people. I lay before you with the agony of a tortured heart, a plea of my own. Let us not allow another pilgrim train to be dispersed upon the winds of indifference again, or be ground up in the cruelty of our angry world. Noble brethren, let us not be idle, rather we should earn the title we bear of guardians of our people. Let us not concern ourselves with anything else until some measure is put into motion to relieve the plight of our fellow countrymen. If even I myself must ride out and gather these wretched poor myself, then so be it. But I, for one, vow not to rest until we have behaved like the guardians we are supposed to be.

May the gods spare us in mercy.

[At this point, the proceedings of the Council of Nobles was interrupted by word that the Count of Estew was going to divorce his fourth wife. It was voted by a near-majority that all issues should be tabled for the time being. Count Lornan voiced strenuous objections over this, but the vote proceeded nonetheless. It has been agreed that until the balance of power disrupted by the sudden change in dynastic arrangement is resolved, the Council should not seek to resolve any other matters.]

Chapter Five
Flash Rains

The next morning as the sun rose, offering another hot and dusty day, the guards from Hiram's Well left the pilgrims and returned to their own dusty corner of the world. Not to waste the prospect of a free ride, the burliest of the guards leapt cruelly upon the back of the old mare that Elias had ridden the day before.

The guards laughed as they watched the poor animal shudder and struggle beneath the massive weight of the guard. Elias knew for sure the horse would collapse, seeing her hind legs buckle and kick up dust as she fought to remain upright under her burden.

With a snort she rose up straight and carried her charge, if a bit unsteadily. Elias couldn't help the anger that rose in him, watching the old, malnourished animal struggle.

He and Bannus parted with the pilgrims. Their business carried them north while the pilgrims were headed for another village to the west. Elias watched them go with the special curiosity that ponders on future things. It was that way with all the trains they traveled with. He always hoped better things for the tired and haggard fugitives, but couldn't crawl out from under the certainty of doom that covered everything.

Earlier that morning he had looked for Silas, intending to at least plant the idea in his head that he should enroll at an Enclave. He had felt a connection with the boy, however tenuous, and actually surprised himself at feeling a touch of sadness at their parting. He hadn't been able to find him though, and it was most likely on account of the boy that Elias pondered with deeper curiosity what the fate of these pilgrims might come to.

Elias and Bannus trudged north together. Between them a silence settled, the kind that descends upon married couples who no longer like each other but stay together out of spite. They were forced to tolerate one another, but they certainly didn't like it.

Most of the morning passed by in this silence. The two trekked over the never-ending wilderness of sand. Just before noon, when the heat of the day began to rise in full fury, they crested a hill and looked out over a massive rift-bed that spread out across the horizon.

Elias marveled at the structure, as he always did when he came across them, holding equal parts adoration and fear. Even though he understood what made them, they still confounded him as they did everyone. He let his eyes drift over the series of canyons, twisting and snaking through the ground, the ridges above the canyons, following their course like a bank follows a river.

Flash rains is what he had been told caused them. The intense deluge of water in those aberrant storms cut into the soil, devoid of any protection like roots and grass, causing massive erosion in a short period of time. The result were these rift-beds - vast arrays of canyons that twisted and intersected like a maze. Elias understood the explanation. It still amazed him.

The two men paused as they looked out over the rift-bed. Elias considered their options. These structures always presented special dangers. To walk through meant plunging into a labyrinth that may not have an exit. Dead-ends, back-tracks, meandering routes were common in the rifts. It was easy to lose your bearings in the canyons, and a journey of several days through the tortuous rifts was not uncommon. And while most experts would agree that to travel along the ridges was obviously better, there was never a guarantee that once upon a ridge you would be able to get down.

Like most travelers, what worried Elias most were the flash rains. Because rift-beds were caused by flash rains, traveling into one essentially meant walking into a river whose source had been temporarily cut off. Rift-beds were made because there were frequent targets of the storms. And if you happened to be in the canyons when the rains returned, you had only seconds to get out of the rising water. It was a bitter irony, Elias thought to himself, that many people who spent their lives desperate for water died from drowning in a desert.

"What do you think?" Bannus asked, the first words he had spoken in hours.

Elias shook his head, uncertain. This rift-bed appeared larger than most. Its width stretched further than the horizon on either side. He thought he could discern the far end in front of them, and the rifts ran in the direction they traveled.

"Probably should go through," Elias suggested. "No idea how long it would take to go around."

"Would probably help if we knew which one it was," Bannus grunted. "Thought you guys were supposed to know things like this."

"Leaky noggin, remember?" Elias rapped his skull.

Bannus grunted again and returned his gaze out to the rift beyond.

"Any rain coming?" the guard asked.

"Nothing natural," Elias answered. "A flash could show up at any moment. They are impossible to predict."

Bannus squinted in the high sun.

"How is that possible?"

"Wish I knew," Elias shrugged. "It's one of the crazy things about them. They defy all explanation. There's no indication that one is coming so it makes them extremely difficult to study. It's as if until they appear, fully formed, they don't exist at all. No pre-phase or build up or anything like that. Usually with weather there are smaller events that contribute to a larger one, a building up of conditions. With flash rains you don't get..."

Elias trailed off remembering his audience. Bannus, still staring out over the rift, didn't seem to notice.

"Doesn't seem to go that far across," the burly guard observed. "Damn if I want to walk around. We could lose three days."

"Not like we have anywhere pressing to be."

Bannus shrugged and shook his head dismissively. Elias found himself sharing the sentiment. Even with no particular goal in mind he didn't relish wasting a day or two walking around the rift-bed. However, he also hated the idea of agreeing with Bannus about anything. A childish tendency, he knew, but one he found irresistible. Any opportunity to frustrate his bodyguard he found worth some extra effort.

Movement caught Elias' eye out over the rift. Up on a ridge, about halfway through the network of canyons, he spied two figures making their way over. Squinting his eyes he could just make out one of them look around as if regaining his bearings, then the pair turned and disappeared down into the canyons.

Elias thought he could see the route they had taken. Whoever it was out there, he had a good eye and was apparently clever. It looked as if one long rift twisted halfway through the entire bed. Then he could see a low-lying ridge give access to another long canyon that went close to the far edge. If they followed the same route they might be through in an hour.

"I guess you're right," Elias grudgingly consented. "Let's get on with it."

With a shrug Elias shouldered his pack and stepped carefully down the slope leading into the rift-bed. The banks rose up steadily as the two men navigated the steep drop.

As soon as they stepped into the canyon, the afternoon sun was blocked out and the lingering cool of the prior evening swept over them. Thankful for the respite from the heat and sun, Elias was able to look up and marvel at the amazing, if unnatural, structure.

The canyon wall rose quickly as they walked deeper into the rift-bed. Towering on either side, the canyon walls easily stood over a hundred feet. Layers of soil could be observed in the striated ridge. Bits of old, buried debris stood out: planks of wood, sections of an old wall, dried-up roots, litter and detritus from uncounted ages of men losing and throwing away. Elias remembered hearing of one rift-bed that cut through an ancient cemetery. Skulls and bones, stacked on top of each other rose up on each side, like some sort of wall built of sacrificed remains. Every once and a while a story would come back of gold found jutting out of the canyon walls or old weapons forged by lost civilizations.

This rift held no such terror or treasure. Elias searched the wall as he walked, enjoying the shade and even the possibility of coming across something rare. He marveled at the different layers of silt, looking almost as if it were deliberately laid out, one atop the other.

He had just reached out his hand to touch what looked like a seashell in the canyon wall. His fingers ran lazily over the fossilized spiral, following the perfectly symmetrical path to its center, when he felt something shift.

His hand froze as that instinctive awareness he possessed, the very substance of his magic, screamed out to him without warning.

This was not something he saw, for there was nothing to see. Bannus wandered on unaware as Elias stood frozen in fear. That deep sense of his, touching the primal powers that moved through all things; this sense told him that something vast and powerful had just appeared close by. He didn't even have to reach out to it to know exactly what it was.

"Flash rains!" he yelled to Bannus.

They both tore off down the canyon. As they ran they searched frantically for some opening, some rise that would allow them to climb a ridge and get above the rift.

The sense of the flash filled Elias; a storm that grew within him as it formed above him. Black clouds billowed out from the blue sky and blocked out the sun, plunging everything into premature night.

The first drops of rain struck Elias as he and Bannus ran into an intersection of canyon. The ridge they had spotted from afar was right in front of them. They raced up the slope, feeling the rains begin in earnest just as they reached the safety of the top.

Out in the open the full power and terror of the flash stretched out before them. The clouds swirled overhead, a black, angry mass. They billowed low, so close that Elias thought that they might bear down upon him. A rumble sounded from within the storm clouds, like thunder, but constant and unbroken, shaking even the bones of the two men who cowered beneath it.

Even without his innate ability Elias would be able to feel the intense and wild power of the storm. But with it, the magi shuddered in awe. There was a wildness he sensed within that filled him with terror. This was not like other storms, though wild in their own right, which had a sense of form about them.

This thing, this mass of power and black clouds, had no such form. It swirled and broiled unshackled, released full under its own raw power. Elias didn't even dare probe the clouds, fearing his lumen would be overwhelmed if he touched the massive thing. All he could do, like everyone else in this frightened world, was watch and hope he would not get swept away.

The rain that unleashed itself from the cloud fell in a torrential pour. Sheets of rain fell down. Incalculable gallons of water let loose, soaking Elias and Bannus in mere seconds. The downpour fell so thick that the magi could hardly see his guard who stood only two feet away. The world became lost in a gray haze of rain.

From the safety of the ridge the two men distantly made out the water rising. Like everything else about the flash, the display was swift and massive. Below, the canyon turned into a river, cutting deeper grooves into the soft, unprotected ground. The water rose nearly halfway to their ridge, swelling and turbulent. It churned in angry, white froth.

Almost as quickly as it had begun, the display was done. Above, the black clouds shrank and drew in upon itself, dissipating on the wind and retreating to whatever strange place from which it had come. The sun reappeared and the world resorted to its usual sand and desert wasteland. If it weren't for the river of water still running in the rift below, and the saturated clothes that hung from them, it would be hard to conceive that any of it had actually happened.

"That was fast," Bannus observed, a stunned expression on his face.

It gave Elias more than a little satisfaction to see the big man so frightened. Usually, he was the one that intimidated others. A little humbling now and then never hurt.

Elias opened his mouth to reply when another sound broke in. A scream, desperate and pleading, ripped through the air. He couldn't make out the words as it sounded again, though the fear and desperation were clearly carried.

A woman came running over the ridge, soaked and bedraggled. Her strawberry blonde hair was dripping and matted to her face. Wild, green eyes stared out fearfully as she charged Elias. She stumbled and caught herself, hurtling towards the magi. Recognition dawned on him.

The woman from the pilgrim train.

The mother of....

"Silassss!" the woman screamed in naked fear.

She ran up to Elias and grabbed him roughly.

"Do something you bastard!" she screamed, shaking him by his collar.

Bannus grabbed her from behind and pulled her off of the magi. She screamed and kicked and flailed, thrashing wildly to no avail.

"Let her go!" Elias commanded.

Bannus dropped the woman who ran over to Elias and shook him again.

"Please! You have to do something!" she wept fear and with wrath all at once.

"What? What happened?" Elias asked, though he felt he already knew the answer.

"Silas. He's going to drown," she cried. "He just got swept away! I couldn't hold him!"

The boy was in the river.

Elias tore away from the woman and stepped toward the churning current below. He could see nothing but frothing water. So he reached out with his lumen.

Finding the boy was easy. Being the only living thing in the churn of water made him almost glow to Elias' magical sense. Helping was another matter. Immediately upon sensing the boy Elias could tell his air was low and he was on the verge of passing out. Once that happened, there was nothing to stop him from inhaling water.

Elias' mind raced as he felt the boy's air dwindle. He closed his eyes and focused on the water around him. There was little he could do about that. Water was all but impossible to move. It could kill a man if it filled his lungs, but it was also full of air. That, he could do something about.

* * *

To Silas, everything was a churn of dark water. One moment, he and his mother were walking through the cool shade of the canyon, about to come to the next ridge. Last one, she had said.

Then the sky grew black, the heavens opened up and sheets of water began to fall. They ran for the ridge but he didn't make it. He saw his mother step onto the rise of higher ground as she turned and grabbed his hand.

Then the wall of water hit him and yanked him out of her grasp.

It knocked the breath out of him, but the water was still shallow. He struggled to his feet and was able to stand as he leaned on the canyon wall. He looked around but couldn't find his mother, didn't even recognize where he was. Hadn't they just walked through here minutes ago? He cried out but could hardly hear his own voice over the roar and rain.

Another churn of water struck him and Silas was knocked off his feet again. This time his hands and feet touched nothing but water as he flailed to regain the ground. The deluge hurled him around so effortlessly, like his resistance meant nothing at all.

He was slammed up against another canyon wall and managed to get his mouth over the surface of the water. A quick gasp of breath then the current pulled him under.

A vague sense of fear began to prick at him. He tried to swim up. Vainly. The current battered him around.

A tension began to build in his lungs, a hunger for breath. Panic set in and he flailed his arms wildly, reaching for something, anything. Nothing but churning water all around him. His lungs burned and ached.

Suddenly, his face moved away from the water. He was still under water. He was still being carried away by the current. But somehow, miraculously, there was a gap of air between his face and the water. It was as if he were caught in a bubble that hovered around his head. He took a timid breath and found the air good, though it was thick and humid.

Silas had no time to wonder at this strange occurrence. A violent burst slammed into him, knocking the new breath out his lungs as it hurled him against the canyon wall. The bubble around him fell in.

Something else hit him from below. But it wasn't water. Bubbles churned around him. Millions of bubbles, like boiling water, roiled around him. They lifted him, carried him up upon the water. He rose and broke the surface of the river. Cool air hit his face.

A rough hand took hold of his arm and lifted him up. Silas looked dead into a pair of dangerous, grey eyes.

"Ain't got enough sense to make high ground when the rain comes boy?!" the face yelled at him.

The arm tossed him unceremoniously to the ground. Just as he thumped down another face bent down over his. He looked up at the same fiery, green eyes he had known his whole life. This time they were wide with panic and relief.

"Oh Silas," his mother moaned as she embraced him. Sobs shook her body as she held him tight.

Over her shoulder Silas looked at the man who had pulled him out of the river. The hulking figure stared down hard at him, looking more annoyed than anything else. A man of his size was easily recognizable.

His mother held him for what seemed like hours, sobbing quietly into his shoulder. He enjoyed the warmth of her closeness and the rare shower of affection.

"O Silas," she muttered over and over as she rocked him. "O Silas, what would I do if I lost you too?"

She finally composed herself and straightened up, pulling Silas with her. She wiped her eyes and turned to the big man who continued to stare at them blankly.

"I guess thanks are in order," she said meekly.

Then, pulling back her shoulders and regaining her natural feistiness, "Though you didn't have to toss him around like a dead fish."

"Where's your boss?" she asked.

The burly man stared at her for a moment then pointed up the ridge.

His mother took him by the sleeve and led him up the slope. They trudged up the wet sand, his mind still reeling from the most harrowing few minutes of his short life. He hardly grasped what was happening when it all came to an abrupt end.

Everything made more sense when they reached the top of the ridge and saw Elias there. The magi knelt on the ground and drew quick, deep breaths. He looked paler than any man Silas had ever seen.

Chapter Six
Companions for a Night

It began as a vague sense of dizziness. Then his head began to swim as nausea took over and the world tilted to one side. Still, Elias held on, his lumen working furiously around the boy.

It wasn't until he heard Bannus cry out that Elias finally let go. Full exhaustion washed over him and he fell to his knees. Blood drained from his face. Spots danced in front of his vision.

When he saw Silas and his mother come over the ridge the chills hit him. Being soaked through by the rains didn't help and Elias found himself shivering uncontrollably. His legs gave out and he collapsed to the ground.

Surprisingly, it was the boy who came to his aid. Elias rolled onto his back and saw Silas kneeling over him. He still wore that expressionless face, but Elias thought he could see concern behind his eyes.

"Are you okay?" Silas asked.

Elias nodded weakly. He knew he would be okay despite never feeling this weak before. But then again, he had never cast magic like that before. It may have been his greatest magic to date, and no one around to truly appreciate it.

"Are you cold?" he heard the woman ask, her voice as chilly as he felt.

"Just got to get my core temperature up," Elias chattered.

"What can we do?" the boy asked.

"He needs a fire," Bannus answered from behind.

The big man dug in his pack and pulled out an oiled bag. The petroleum smell was thick and quickly permeated the air as Bannus dug out three coils of fuel. He stacked the coils together and set a spark to them with flint. The permeated bundles caught easily. Flames spread and soon flared into a full fire.

"You owe me three coils," Bannus said as he repacked his bag.

"I'll owe you six by the time I warm up," Elias spoke through his shivers.

Bannus shook his head and dug out three more coils. He threw them to the ground and roiled the oil sack up. As he stuffed them into his pack he muttered to himself.

"That leaves us just two," he said aloud. "You better hope we find some soon."

"I'll take care of it," Elias said impatiently through gritted teeth.

A fit of shivers washed over him and Elias had to force himself to draw nearer the fire. Silas held him by the arm in a show of aid. Elias appreciated the gesture more than benefitted from it.

Nearer the flames he absorbed the fire's welcome warmth. On his back he could feel the sun returning to its full power and heat. With luck he could warm back up in a few hours.

"How long we gonna stop?" Bannus asked, visibly annoyed.

"Not going any further today," Elias told him. The way he felt, even the thought of walking made him sick.

"Lost a whole day anyway," Bannus complained, throwing his arms out. He shook his head and reluctantly began to set camp.

"Well...I guess we'll get out of your way," the woman said.

Elias could hear the eagerness in her voice to put some distance between them.

"We can't leave him," the boy spoke up. "Not like this."

"I'll be fine," Elias said. "Just need to warm up."

"See, he's fine," the boy's mother huffed.

"But he's weak, he can't protect himself," Silas protested.

"He's got a guard."

"I'm not leaving him."

"Damn it Silas, they don't want us around," the woman insisted.

"I'll be fine," Elias told him again. "You better do as your mother says."

"But you're weak," the boy pointed out.

"Bannus is with me. He'll look out for me."

Silas leaned in with a grave expression on his face.

"I don't trust him," he whispered. "I really don't think he's a friend."

Elias chuckled at the boy's precociousness. True, he would be of little real help if there was danger, but the magi found the offer too kind to refuse. Rarely was he offered a gift of such selfless depth. It mattered little what its practical worth might be.

"Okay then," Elias agreed. "I could use a friend to look out for me."

"We're not staying," the boy's mother firmly insisted. "That's final."

"I'm not leaving him," Silas countered without his mother's emotion but equally as firm.

"Damn it Silas..." his mother began to press the argument further but trailed off. An unspoken conflict passed between them, an invisible battle of wills. Finally, the boy's mother huffed out loud and stalked to the edge of the ridge. She sat down with her back to them, saying with her body, I can't make you go, but I won't participate.

"Don't worry," Silas whispered. "She knows this is right."

For a moment Elias had to wonder who was the parent and who the child. The mother sat sullenly, pouting, undone by the will of her child. While the child, showing a maturity beyond his years, watched Elias protectively as the magi shivered between a blazing fire and a hot, noonday sun.

The boy was right. Eventually, the mother did come around. As night began to fall, the worst of the shivers left the magi. Cold air quickly flowed in behind the hot day. And despite hours by the fire, Elias found the cold too much to bear.

It didn't help that Bannus refused to sacrifice his last two coils of fuel. So Elias had to use his supply of charwood to keep the fire going, an expense of power he could ill afford. But they all needed the fire. So Elias wrapped himself tightly in his bedroll and sat as close to the fire as he dared.

Making the whole camp colder was the chill anger of Silas' mother and the pure ice of Bannus' heart. The woman had only reluctantly joined the others, though she made it clear that she barely preferred their company to freezing. Elias couldn't think of any company more uncomfortable than those gathered around him. He thought of Thoran, back at Hiram's Well, and wondered if he had become a magnet for unhappy people.

As the four sat around the fire, only Elias seemed to be bothered by the silence that reigned awkwardly around them. The woman was tight-lipped and sullen, arms crossed firmly across her chest. Bannus didn't seem to care one whit for any of them. Not that conversation from him was any real threat. The empty stare that Bannus fixed on the fire all but guaranteed there was little going on beneath.

Of all of them, only Silas owned the silence honestly. Elias could tell the boy was genuinely lost in his own thoughts. His thoughts were the only ones that sparked curiosity in Elias. He would have loved to know what stirred behind those thoughtful, brown eyes.

"So...do I call you mom?" Elias finally asked, breaking the silence.

The woman leveled a stare of such naked irritation that Elias had to chuckle. His mother had given him those very same looks when he wasn't necessarily being bad, just trampling on her very last nerve.

"I prefer you don't call me anything at all," she told him flatly.

"Her name is Kyrie," Silas chimed in.

It was Silas' turn to get the annoyed look.

"Seriously boy, did you have to do that?" she asked him.

"He just wanted your name," Silas shrugged.

"Fine. If you have to call me something, Kyrie will have to do," the woman consented. "Besides, hearing you say mom makes me want to burn my ears off."

The chill around the fire grew deeper and Elias pulled the bedroll tighter about him. He didn't know why he cared. Nothing they said would interest him anyway.

Except he did care. Ever since he had woken with a gap in his memory, an emptiness that spanned ten years, an awful loneliness seemed to follow him everywhere. It didn't matter if he was around people or not, among friendly or indifferent faces. He just felt lonely.

He couldn't remember ever being like that before. In fact, solitude was his tendency. Solitude was thought and contemplation and discovery.

Except now, solitude only offered darkness, as if the weight of his lost years fell heavily upon him every time he was left with the quiet of his own thoughts. Maybe that was why he craved the company of the pilgrims. He couldn't stand his own silence anymore. And that frightened him as much as the loneliness did.

"What are those stars called?" Silas finally spoke up, offering an escape from the silence.

Elias followed the boys pointing finger to the night sky, right at the familiar constellation with its distinctive row of three stars. At the end of the row another series curved down, like a sword hanging from a belt.

"That's the warrior," Elias answered, remembering his first lesson in astronomy from a Perigrinator like himself.

"You see those three stars there," Elias pointed out. Silas nodded.

"That's his belt. And hanging down from his belt, those stars that curve down, that's his sword. And from there it's easy to see the shoulders, feet, and that one star there is his head.

"As always, by the warrior is his faithful dog. He's there in that square of stars. That one there that makes his shoulder is the brightest star in the sky. We call it the Dog Star."

"Did they teach you that at the Enclave?" Silas asked.

"No, I learned that from a magi named Uriel. He came to visit my village when I was a boy, about your age. He showed me the stars, the names of all the local herbs and their uses. He knew diseases and their cures and just about every story you've ever heard of. And then he taught me things I thought to be impossible. I was hooked immediately."

A stab of guilt pierced Elias as he remembered his old mentor. Uriel had done so much for him, had gone through such great efforts to get him educated when his own father couldn't afford it. He had sponsored Elias' entrance to the Enclave. Uriel had even interceded for him once when he was almost expelled.

"You don't want to let this one go," Uriel had pled before the prefects. "You won't find another one like this and you know it."

The Prefects relented and Elias did not disappoint. Except now he probably did. How much had Uriel done for him and he couldn't even dump this boy on the Enclave steps?

Elias pushed the guilt aside, cursing the whole of life for the hassle that it was. Instead, he pointed out more constellations to Silas, telling of their stories and lore. He told the boy what all the stars meant and what signs they gave you for the time of year and what could be learned from them.

For his part, Silas absorbed everything with the enthusiasm of an intelligent mind starved for stimulation. Elias could feel the boy's growing eagerness as his initial aloofness fell away to be replaced by the unassuming excitement of wonder. And he could tell the boy understood by the questions he asked.

"But I though Majorus was the main star?....Was that the same Baen that fought the Dagda?....How does it rotate the earth and the sun?....How does the planet move backwards?....Does it show up every spring?....That's why I never saw that one move," but a few of the endless comments and inquiries Silas spoke as he hung on every word that Elias uttered.

Sometime into their exchange Elias noticed Kyrie looking intently at him as well. Unlike Silas, it wasn't curiosity or the excitement at learning that formed her expression. Instead, she looked at him in a way he could not identify. There was almost a wistfulness to her features. Regret maybe. Sadness? Perhaps the ghostly traces of what might have been.

He lost track of time as he talked with Silas. Eventually, he forgot his weakness and the chill that had sapped his strength. More charwood was thrown on the fire, providing light to their discussion.

This too evoked questions.

"How do you make rocks burn?" Silas asked. "And sand too? You made sand burn too?"

"Very good question," Elias repeated for perhaps the hundredth time. "But these aren't actually rocks. This is something called charwood. It's made of coal, which, incidentally, is a rock that can burn, along with compressed flakes of wood, some petroleum, and a little magical intervention. They're made to burn slow and hot. If a magi is burning them, they can last even longer."

"What about the sand? The other night with the pilgrim train you were burning sand."

"That was actually turf," Elias explained. "It used to be dark, like black soil. It's made of old, dead trees and plants, so it can burn. Of course, most of it is dried out so it looks like sand. But if you can find it then it burns pretty well."

Silas nodded in understanding. He opened his mouth to ask another question when his mother interrupted him.

"I have a question for the wise and all-knowing magi," Kyrie said, surprising Elias with the note of playful humor he heard behind the jab.

"Can you tell what time it is by looking at the stars?" she asked.

"Actually, I can," Elias nodded and looked up at the stars. "Although it's not the most precise method, checking the progression of certain constellations called marker stars can give you a relative time. And judging by what I see right here I would say it's almost the start of the third watch."

"Oh my, the third watch, how late it is," Kyrie exclaimed with a grand touch of melodrama. "Much too late for a young boy to be still awake."

"Stop it, mom," Silas huffed, sounding in that moment like a normal boy embarrassed by his mother. "She knows how to mark the night hours too."

"Does she?" Elias asked, genuinely surprised. The thought struck him that perhaps he had underestimated her somewhat.

"Yes she does," Kyrie replied. "That means I know it's way past time for bed. We have a lot of lost ground to cover tomorrow."

"But I'm not even tired," the boy complained as Elias could see exhaustion rimming his eyes.

"In that case, just go lay down," his mother insisted. "I'm sure you've exhausted the magi as well, especially with all he's been through today."

"I'm actually feeling pretty good," Elias interjected, surprised at his own energy. "It's been a long time since I've had an intelligent conversation. It kind of energizes..."

Elias let the rest of the words dangle when he noticed Kyrie glaring at him. Without uttering a single word she was able to communicate, "Hey idiot, you're not helping here."

"But, we also have a long day ahead of us," Elias changed directions. "Got to get up early and all."

"Fine. Can we talk in the morning some more?" the boy asked through a yawn.

"Sure. Of course we can. We'll breakfast together," Elias assured.

"Yes. Now go to bed," his mother enforced.

With another yawn Silas got up and set out an old and torn bedroll. It looked too thin to keep out a breeze, much less the frigid cold that would frequently settle over the wasted sands.

The boy didn't seem to notice the poverty of his accommodation. A warmth and contentedness spread over his face. He opened his eyes to smile up at Elias then fell quickly asleep.

"Quite a remarkable boy you've got there," Elias remarked as he and Kyrie sat alone by the fire. Bannus snored nearby.

"Yes. He takes after his grandfather."

"Not his mother or father?" Elias asked.

"Not even close," Kyrie laughed. She stopped abruptly as the sound escaped her lips, as if she were both alarmed and ashamed at the sound. Her hand shot up to her mouth. The smile that had suddenly broken over her face gave way to her usual, austere demeanor.

"Leopold was very smart," she continued. "But he didn't care for intellectual pursuits. It wasn't really the life for me either. My father, though, was brilliant. Is brilliant. Growing up I thought he knew everything. And he damn near does."

Kyrie stared into the fire thoughtfully, her mind withdrawn into distant memories. She smiled at something unspoken and shook her head. To Elias, she appeared a young girl, wide open and full of life. For a moment, whatever anger she harbored and nursed had been laid down, and she allowed herself to forget.

"You know, for a moment there, you reminded me of him," she said with a light tease in her voice. "My father, that is. He would get in these real... I don't know... expansive moods. He would talk and talk and everybody would hang on every word he said even though we had heard a lot of it before. People would ask him questions - he was always mentoring some young man, he loved to mentor - and he would sit there in his library, puffing on his pipe, beer in hand, talking away while he pulled at that ridiculous beard of his. He couldn't really grow one, but he thought it made him look distinguished, so he tried. All he got was this wild, scraggly thing that had holes all in it."

She smiled again and looked as if she wanted to laugh, but refused to allow herself.

"He always came up with something we hadn't heard before," she continued. "No matter how many times we heard him, or how many times you watched him hold court, he would always surprise us. He was always learning. Of course that's what made the bastard so dangerous."

The remembered happiness fell suddenly away from Kyrie's face. Heartache and bitterness rose up and hardened her expression. If the transformation hadn't taken place right before Elias's eyes he wouldn't have believed it was the same woman.

"What happened to him?" Elias prodded, trying to be gentle.

"Nothing," she shrugged. "At least nothing good."

"Could you and Silas not live there?" Elias asked. "If his fortunes still hold."

"Oh, his fortunes are as good as ever. At least as good as they can be in this broken world. Dad could find a way to flourish on a barren rock."

"Why don't you live with him, then?"

"There's still work to be done," Kyrie said, staring hard into the fire. "Not to mention he stands for everything we stand against. I couldn't bear to be in his presence."

"Still, it has to be better than this," Elias argued, somewhat at a loss at figuring Kyrie out. He couldn't imagine why someone would drag a child through all the dangers of the wilds if a better home was an option.

"The fight still goes on," Kyrie insisted. "And if I have any say Silas will be a part of it too. So why not start him out young?"

"Is it worth it? Exposing him to all this danger?"

Elias felt a surge of protection for the boy, a sentiment he thought his mother should have. Perhaps it was because of the boys potential ability, a talent he would hate to see unused, or destroyed, in the desert because of a fanatical mother.

Kyrie leaned across the fire and stared at Elias intently. He could see the zealous devotion emanate from the green eyes that widened at him.

"I would sacrifice everything to avenge Covenant," she swore.

Covenant.

Elias knew he should recognize the name, should know what it meant. There was an inland city of Covenant, wasted and abandoned along with the deep interior. He remembered the city when it thrived; the largest city by the Caliban, a major eastern financial center, once known as the hub of the wool trade. It was said that the best sheep pastured in the land around Covenant.

After he woke up from his lost memory, Covenant was no longer spoken of. Not just forgotten, deliberately ignored, like it never existed. Elias had mentioned it once in passing at a public house a few years back. The fearful silence that settled over the place even scared him. Eyes darted back and forth across the tables, as if expecting a predator nearby. Elias didn't mention it again, but the name seemed to hang everywhere, just outside the edge of conversation. Something that everyone thought of, but no one dared utter.

Covenant.

"Covenant is more important than your son?" Elias asked.

Kyrie threw her head back and laughed incredulously. It was not a joyful sound, not remotely. It was angry and hateful and spiced with malice, bordering on the madness of the fanatic.

"He has no father because of Covenant," she spat back at Elias, pointing at the sleeping Silas who slumbered unaware.

"You people disgust me," she continued to rant, leveling her hatred at Elias. "You live so cut off from what real people are going through. You hide in your palaces and pleasure gardens and distantly wonder why everybody is so upset. You've got no clue. Do you have any idea what we lost at Covenant? Do you even care? As long as you have your cheap tricks and your precious magic you're content to keep your head in the sand and pretend this is all just some passing famine, and next spring were gonna wake up and the trees are going to be back and the grass will grow again and we won't have to put armed guards around cornfields or fight for a place on the coast or pass out special papers just so people can search for a better life. You have no clue. You have no idea what it's like. We lost everything, damn you! But for all of you, life goes on! The splendid balls and the dances, your intrigues and power struggles! How dare you even question me about my son? None of this would even be necessary if it weren't for people like you!"

"I didn't mean that at all," Elias tried to explain. Kyrie would have none of it.

"No, I know what you meant," she shot back. "I should just crawl back to daddy's house and keep quiet like a good girl, raise my son to be an obedient, little slave while you and your kind continue to rape the world.

"How about this instead? I'll go back to my father's house if you put the world back the way it was and give me back everyone you killed at Covenant! Deal?!"

Kyrie fell silent but the anger still coiled within her. She continued to stare at Elias, as if daring him to challenge her.

"It's not what you think," was all Elias could say.

"Oh yeah?" Kyrie flared. "Because I've heard exactly what you people think. Quit being so fanatical. Calm down. Be reasonable. Go back to your home and do as you're told and it will all get better. You're making the situation worse. Trust us, we have this under control.

"How long do we wait? Until all our children starve to death? You've taken our land, our livelihood, even our freedom of movement. What else do you want? What else can we give you?"

"That's not what I was thinking," Elias muttered.

"Fine then, what magnanimous thoughts were you thinking? Bigger dole? Free corn? More magic?"

The intensity of her words forced itself on Elias with a pressure that would not be denied. It stirred something within him that aroused his curiosity and guilt all at once. He felt the need to give her satisfaction, to give her justice. At the same time, he knew he had to keep some distance from her. He couldn't get absorbed in her mad quest, or lose himself in the currents of her anger. It threatened to rob him of the little bit of identity he still had left.

"I have amnesia," Elias told her, wondering to himself why he made that confession again.

The look on Kyrie's face was a mix of shock and surprise, clearly caught off guard by Elias' strange admission.

"What the hell is that supposed to mean?" she asked, if anything, more angry at Elias's apparent obliviousness to her righteous anger.

"I don't remember," Elias clarified.

"I know what amnesia is," Kyrie shot back. "What does that have to do with anything? What does that have to do with all you nobles and magicians - power mongers all - robbing life from the people and then condemning us for wanting to grab it back?"

"I don't know," Elias allowed his voice to rise, not matching hers, but pushing back ever so slightly. He couldn't resist the urge for the fight.

"I don't know what it means. I don't know what anything means. I don't know what's so important about Covenant or anything that happened there. I've got a gap in my head that makes me a stranger everywhere I go. I'm a wanderer in every sense of the word. So, no, I can't understand why you would drag your son through the Blight when a good home waited for him somewhere, because I've got no damn clue as to what is going on. Overnight, the world fell apart and I'm lost in it."

The fire popped in the silence that settled over the camp. Elias reached down and grabbed another small piece of charwood and placed it on the fire. Light flared as the flames sprang back to life. In the orange glow Elias could see a softer expression on Kyrie's face. It wasn't pity he saw there, just a concession to some common suffering. The deep furrows of her brow had smoothed out and her jaw unclenched. Beneath that, the same immovable sternness remained, the iron resolve that would die before shifting the slightest.

"You don't remember anything?" she asked.

"I remember some," Elias confessed, pushing at the rim of the fire with his foot.

"There's about a ten year gap, pretty specific. I remember everything that happened before, all that happened after. But for those ten years it's just..."

Elias opened his hands and spread them out indicate the great, empty expanse that was his mind. That great emptiness he carried around with him everywhere he went. Its shadow never left him and cast its persistent darkness on everything around him.

"What happened?" Kyrie asked, not tender or concerned, but purely curious.

Elias laughed. What happened? For five years that question had burned a scar in his mind.

"Wish I knew," he shrugged. "Whatever happened is actually part of the memory loss. Last thing I remember is traveling with my employer, Lord Mobrey at the time, right outside Dubres. Next thing I know I'm back at the Enclave with Gregory screaming in my face."

"Gregory?" Kyrie asked. Her eyes twitched in surprise. "The Lord Prefect of Anjibar?"

"That's the one. Let me tell you, not a man you want yelling at you."

"Dubres? Gregory? Mobrey? You run with a pretty high crowd," she observed. Suspicion and a touch of fear crept into her voice.

"Run with, or from?" Elias clarified. "I don't remember ever meeting Dubres, though. Not to say I didn't. Can't say what I did for an entire decade."

"What's that like? Losing all that life?"

"Pretty disorienting at first," Elias answered. "You get used to that part. After a while it fades into the background, though the emptiness never leaves you. Of course, the biggest problem is running into people you're supposed to know."

"No one would ever tell you what happened?" Kyrie continued to inquire.

"They told me it was an experiment gone bad," he said as he pulled a tendril of flame out of the fire and let it dance over his fingers. He stared into it as he spoke, allowing himself to remember those awful days when he first woke up.

"I was apparently dabbling with some dangerous stuff, opened up avenues of power that men have no business peering into. They tell me there was an explosion. I woke up with the Lord Prefect screaming at me. He was asking me all these things I didn't understand. Where is the tree? Who is the Restoration?"

"What does that mean?"

"He never said. Nothing I said or did could get them to tell me either. There was a large inquest and investigation, nothing I was privy to. I assume those questions have something to do with why I lost my memory."

"You believe him?" Kyrie asked. "You think you lost your memory in a magical accident? Sounds like he's hiding a few things to me."

"There are some problems with the official story," Elias agreed. He closed his hands and the dancing flame went out.

"Like?"

"Well, for one, I supposedly was experimenting with some powerful magic. That is likely enough. I kind of have a reputation for doing that. But they never reacted quite like that before."

"Maybe they were concerned for your well-being," Kyrie

suggested.

Elias chuckled and shook his head. "Remember who we're talking about here," he reminded her. "Gregory isn't concerned for anyone's well-being."

"Point taken," Kyrie agreed.

"Besides, they treated me like a criminal, not a little boy who had misbehaved. I was kept in the High Tower for six months. No one but the Grand Inquisitor or the Lord Prefect were allowed to talk to me. Another year before I could go outside. It was three years after it happened until I was allowed to leave the Enclave. And even then I am stuck as a Perigrinator, not allowed to take an oath of service or work in any one place more than a few weeks. To top it all off I have to drag Bannus the Anus around to keep an eye on me, who I am certain reports directly back to Gregor on all that I do or say."

"Hmmm, that explains all the warm love I feel between you two," Kyrie joked.

"Yeah, right," Elias scoffed.

"I see what you mean though. Why give you all that attention if you had just been dabbling in some forbidden magic? Is that even a crime?"

"Only if you kill somebody with it. Almost all magic at one point or another was forbidden. The Enclave has to disavow all the unsavory aspects of magic, but at the same time they know that the exploration into forbidden arts is how we learn more. It's like, we say you can't do it, and slap you on the wrist when you're caught, but we turn our backs and pretend not to see it go on right under our nose."

"So, not the reaction you would expect from dabbling in forbidden magic?"

"Exactly."

Elias's mind went back to those awful months after he had woken up. The confusion, the disorientation, the dreams of rain and thunder conjured back into his mind. Locked alone in the High Tower, a place reserved for the most dangerous criminals, he felt that emptiness groan and pull at him. He was so completely alone and afraid, and no one was allowed to see him except Gregor and Artherus.

And they always came with questions and accusations. The Grand Inquisitor would apply his probing magics that would send jolts of pain through his mind. He would clamp on him all manner of strange devices, some painful, attached to his head and made him feel like his brain was being pulled apart. Probes would dig into his brain, peeling back memory and emotion. It would tear and rip at his mind until Elias lay in tattered exhaustion. And all the while Artherus would scream questions as he worked.

"What were you doing?!"

"How are you hiding the memories?!"

"Who is the Restoration?! Are you one of them?! What are your plans?!"

"Where is the tree?!"

Of course, Elias couldn't answer any of the questions. Over and over Artherus would apply his cruel techniques. His long, stern face accused and harassed until Elias felt as if he were nothing but a whimpering mound of flesh. Only then, broken over and over again would Artherus finally be done, leaving Elias on the floor of the austere room, with only the cold quiet and the black, stone walls for company.

Gregor would always come in afterwards. The Lord Prefect would pick Elias up off the floor. He would bring in food and wine and speak soft words to him. If Elias was bleeding or bruised Gregor would personally dress his wounds. All the while he would beg Elias to tell him the truth so all this cruelty could stop.

"Just tell us, Elias. Tell us about the memories. Tell us about the Restoration. What is this tree you were talking about?"

As before, Elias couldn't answer the questions. He wanted to, badly he wanted to. He wanted it all to stop. He would've given Gregor anything if he had it. But he didn't remember anything.

Gregor would grow furious then. He would yell and curse at Elias.

"I am so disappointed in you Elias," Gregor would say with a sad shake of his head. "After all the Enclave has given you, and you can't give us this one thing. Why do you make us do these things to you? I suppose Artherus will have to come back after all."

Pleas for mercy would come streaming out of Elias, sometimes with tears. But Gregor was implacable. The thick, wooden door would boom shut again, leaving Elias alone in the darkness until the Grand Inquisitor returned. Long, lonely hours full of tears, an aching deep in his soul from the pain that had no source or cure; these were the months Elias spent in the tower.

Finally, they relented. They let them out of the tower, confining him instead to the main building of the Enclave. He was watched all the time even though he was allowed into a room of his own, and given a few personal effects.

No one at the Enclave would speak to him. Masters whom he had studied long hours with would hurry by when their paths crossed. Old friends would shake their heads when he tried to approach. Faces he didn't know, young acolytes, newly raised Magi, whispered and gawked as he tread the cold flagstones alone.

Alone.

Always alone.

Even sitting at the fire with others, he was still alone. Kyrie held no real company for him. Maybe gratitude, but that didn't compare with the hatred she felt for him.

There was something else missing. A something that he couldn't even name. He was without it, and the absence made him lonely. It was something others seemed to share. Even the disparate pilgrims with no home, they had each other. But Elias, he had no one. He had nothing.

"And these memories, you weren't able to get them back?" Kyrie asked, shaking Elias out of his reverie.

"That's actually the strangest turn of the whole affair," Elias told her. "The way that the memories disappeared. It wasn't normal."

"Is there a normal way to lose memory?"

"Have you ever heard of the Cathedral of the Mind?" Elias asked in response.

"Have I ever," Kyrie answered. "My father was obsessed with it. Talked about it all the time."

"Have you ever used it?"

"Made me and my brother memorize every variation of Kelmer's Algorithm. We use the Cathedral."

"That would be a perfect use of it," Elias said, deeply impressed. Few people could memorize something so complex. There was much more to this woman than appearances, or first impressions, admitted.

"You know the concept then," he continued. "You imagine the mind as a vast and complex cathedral. Each wing holds different functions."

"And you have rooms that organize different memories," Kyrie added.

"Exactly. Every memory is stored in a room with similar memories. But the associations can vary. Usually it's linear. Memories that happened around the same time are stored in a room together. But it can also be organized by subject. Math in one room, literature in another, and so on. Those that are practiced in the art of the Cathedral divide the rooms with more distinction, something I'm sure you know."

"Father made us construct a whole wing for the algorithms."

"Right. So usually, when someone loses a memory you find something missing in the room. Sometimes it has moved to a deeper place in the Cathedral. Sometimes it's in the room but damaged. You can even hide memories by putting them in different rooms. They can all be found. Broken ones put back together, hidden ones uncovered. Magic has become very subtle and discerning about finding lost and hidden memories."

"So why couldn't they find yours?" Kyrie asked the obvious. "Why couldn't you find them?"

"That's just it," Elias shrugged. "They weren't there."

"So they're somewhere else," she pointed out. "Maybe you hid them better than you thought. They have to be somewhere."

"Not the memories," Elias told her. "It's the rooms. The rooms are missing."

A heavy silence fell over them as Kyrie grasped the weight of what Elias said. It should have been impossible. It was impossible. As far as anyone knew.

"I didn't know that could happen," Kyrie expressed her incredulity. "Are you sure?"

"Yes, I'm sure," Elias sighed, the weight of the loss in his long search for answers, the burden of wandering around only a partial man, fell upon him again.

"I can't even begin to explain how much I've looked into this," he said. "Or how much I was looked into. Every expert on mind, on inquisition, retrieval, the world's most knowledgeable men on sention magic, the most talented diviners in the world; and none could find the memories or explain how they disappeared. I can go to the room myself. There's a door. I open it. But there's nothing there. Only darkness."

"Well, they said you were messing with forbidden magic," Kyrie said. "What if it was some magic that could take rooms out like that, remove memories completely?"

"Magic can't cause memory loss like that," Elias explained.

"But if it was forbidden magic..."

"Magic can't do everything," Elias said. "I know it seems like that, but there are some things that are simply impossible. And it's impossible to lose an entire room in the mind."

"Except it happened," Kyrie reminded him.

"Yeah, I guess it did," he huffed.

"So, that means there is some way it can happen."

"I suppose," Elias shrugged. "Not that I'll ever know what it is."

"You found it once. You can find it again."

"I wouldn't know where to start. And that's assuming that a magical accident is what really happened anyway."

Kyrie had no immediate response. She stared at him so intently that Elias could feel her eyes on him as he looked into the fire. He couldn't begin to imagine what might be going through her head.

"I want to thank you for what you did," she spoke softly. "What you did for Silas."

"Just bringing the hope of magic to the world," Elias shrugged.

"Let's not ruin the moment," she said.

"You're welcome then," Elias told her. "He's a good kid. Wish there was more I could do for him."

"I'm already in your debt," Kyrie groaned. "I can't stand to owe anyone. Least of all one of the magi."

"Don't worry about it," Elias tried to brush the idea way.

He looked up to see her staring at him with a different kind of intensity. Her green eyes still flared with a fire of their own, but Elias did not see hatred in them. Her lips were slightly parted and a light flush touched her cheeks. Maybe she was too close to the fire, he thought. The stare made him uncomfortable. He hoped it was the fire. Or maybe he didn't.

"I want to repay you," Kyrie said, her eyes still locked on his. "I need to repay you."

"Whatever you have, keep it," Elias insisted. "Trust me, you'll need it."

Elias could feel himself being drawn in by her stare. It was like a magic of its own, a deep and primitive magic that went back further than all the knowledge and learning of man. There was no doubting the pull he felt, or the deep warmth that spread through him.

Kyrie stood up and moved over to Elias. Kneeling down, she put her hands on his thighs and looked up at him. Elias froze, unable to move or turn away.

"This may be something you can never understand," she said. "But I can't be in debt to you. Everything that I've fought for, all that I stand for, all that I've lost; if I'm in your debt in the smallest way it's all a sham. It means nothing."

"Don't be so..." Elias began, but she covered his mouth with her hand. He couldn't help but notice the softness of her fingers on his lips.

"You will never understand," she reiterated firmly but quietly. "You must let me. Unless you really don't want me to."

There was not a single part of Elias that wanted to refuse. Perhaps some distant whisper told him that this woman was desperate, vulnerable, and to take the offer of her body would be to take advantage of someone in a weak place.

That whisper hardly reached Elias's mind. He noted what it said, then allowed it to be drowned out in the roar of his passion. There was but one other part of him that still resisted. His pride did not want this. It asked if he would allow himself to be paid in this manner because she loathed the magi so much. Would he allow her to do this because she hated him? Would he be swept away by her strange and fanatical logic?

"Are we really all that bad?" Elias mumbled through her fingers.

"Yes, you are," she said.

Kyrie moved her fingers from his mouth and replaced it with her own.

And his pride was silenced too.

Elias allowed himself to be carried by the magic of Kyrie's warmth. It was a warmth hotter than the fire, one he felt completely as she pressed her body next to his. She pulled him down to the sand and drew him into her embrace, covered him with the softness of her body, and the taut, sweet taste of her flesh. Elias felt all the joys of her pleasure, and beneath them he felt something more profound and fulfilling.

For a moment, Elias was not alone.

Chapter Seven
An Unexpected Detour

Elias woke from a dreamless sleep to the soft light of early morning. The chill of the night seeped in through the top of his bedroll and danced over his naked flesh. He shivered as the ripple of cold sent goose bumps down his chest and stomach to the hairs of his thigh. A pull at the blanket kept the warmth in and chased off the chills. After the heat of the night before, the cold morning seemed more austere than usual, and more than a little lonely.

A booted foot nudged him in the ribs.

"Wake up loverboy," Bannus grunted. "Time to get moving."

Elias smiled and reached for his clothes. There was a bitter edge in Bannus' voice. The man was undoubtedly jealous. While Elias didn't know if it was because he hadn't gotten the girl or that Elias didn't need help doing so, it hardly mattered. Another way to needle Bannus the Anus was enough.

"Where did Kyrie go?" Elias asked as he pulled the white linen shirt over his head. Only a depression remained where Silas had laid out his own bedroll the night before.

"Must've left early," Bannus observed. "Guess she was eager to get away from you."

The jab rolled unnoticed off of Elias. A jealous barb was always a harmless one. He gathered the rest of his stuff together: stool, wand, felt in his pack to make sure his few books were there.

A vague disappointment pricked Elias. He would have liked to talk to the boy again. And even Kyrie's company wasn't so bad when she wasn't pissed off. She couldn't even hate him as much as she claimed, he mused. Not really. If she had truly loathed him she never would have been able to...

The thought broke off as Elias picked up his pouch and tied it to the inside of his belt. It was decidedly light. He pulled it open and saw only a handful of chipped coppers where the night before the sack bulged with silver and gold. Throwing down the pouch he felt in his pack, searching for the bulge at the bottom where he carried the bulk of his gold coin.

"That bitch," he cursed.

* * *

Kyrie hurried through the rift, pulling Silas behind. She whipped sharply around the corner and down a long stretch of shadowed canyon that jerked back and forth in an erratic course. A wall of high earth loomed in front of her.

"Damn," she muttered, stopping short. "Wrong turn."

She jerked Silas and hurried the other way, praying to whatever gods might listen. Stopping at a fork, she took a moment to decide then tore off down the opposite path. Time was short, she knew, and every second wasted sent failure hurtling their way.

The weight of gold and silver pulled her faster rather than slowed her down. It meant so much, the opportunity so rare. It wasn't just gold she carried. It wasn't even food for her and her son.

The gold was weapons. It was provisions for raiding parties. It was badly needed intelligence that could make all the difference. Perhaps it was very little compared to what they needed, but that little money could do a lot for the resistance.

"Why do we have to leave so fast?" Silas whined as she pulled him. "I wanted to talk to Elias."

"Something came up," she huffed as she picked up the pace. "We have something important to do."

Silas took the disappointment in silence. Just as he always did, he closed up and became as impenetrable as rock.

That withdrawal nagged at Kyrie sometimes. Feeling more than a little guilty she wondered if she was responsible for it. Maybe she had exposed the boy to too much. Maybe all those hate speeches, that distrust of the establishment she always spewed; maybe all those desperate and angry people she was constantly around might have caused her son to be the way he was. Maybe through all the clandestine meetings and her constant reminding him of the need for secrecy had built a wall up around him.

Not your fault girl, she told herself. You didn't destroy the world. You didn't order the slaughter at Covenant. If Silas was a bit odd it was the fault of the magi and the nobles and all those other bastards that let the earth wither away.

"Come on, pick up your feet boy," she tugged at him and hissed. At least he shouldn't slow her down, she thought.

She stopped short again, unsure of herself as she lost her bearings again. Cursing the low light of morning and the shade of the rifts, she pulled Silas down another corridor, hoping beyond hope that this was the path she was looking for. If they could make it out of the rift before the men woke up she would feel a lot better about their chances of getting away.

When Kyrie whipped around another corner she stopped dead in her tracks. Silas bumped into her. Kyrie's heart dropped.

"Hello there," Thoran said with a smile.

* * *

Elias cursed himself again as he and Bannus hurried in pursuit. He wasn't worried about the money. Catching Kyrie would be a simple matter. Even if he hadn't already made contact with Silas the day before, finding them would still be simple. Any living thing stood out in the barren rifts, and Silas blazed to Elias' enhanced sight.

Using the bond with Silas, Elias traced the retreat of his mother, certain she dragged him behind. They stopped and changed direction, hurrying down another avenue of churned out earth. Elias tapped Bannus on the arm and the two followed through the serpentine caverns.

The loss of money didn't bother Elias, even if it was gone for good. What stung the most was the fool he had become under her seduction. For a moment, he admired her cleverness, for playing her advance in just the way she had, even mixing in her contempt to make it feel real.

"I can't be in the debt of a magi," she had sworn. "It goes against everything I believe."

Bitter memory rose like bile as Elias remembered the details of the night. It had all been a lie. The hatred, perhaps, was real, the rest a ploy. The tenderness, the warmth, the shared pleasures, they had all been a lie. And he had fallen as willful prey, even eager prey, not suspecting for a moment how dishonest she really acted.

"Your girlfriend went that way," Bannus smirked, pointing out the fresh tracks in the sand.

That Bannus took such smug satisfaction in it stung even more. The burly guard looked almost to burst with giddiness. A vindictive smirk played over his face as they closed in pursuit.

"That was an expensive whore," Bannus continued to needle. "She must have charged by the second."

"She's stopped," Elias said, relieved to have something to say. "Down that fork. She hasn't moved for a few minutes."

"Hah! Bitch ran into a dead end," Bannus growled.

The two men hurried in pursuit. The route curved around drawing them in the opposite direction before terminating in a wall of rock and sand.

"You've got to be kidding," Elias exclaimed in surprise and irritation.

Waiting for them at the foot of the rock wall stood Kyrie, pale but still defiant. With her head thrust out she faced them, holding Silas behind her. The boy observed his pursuers with the same inquisitive indifference with which he regarded the world at large.

It was the other figure waiting for them that caused Elias' exasperation. Staring back at them with that same annoying grin stood Thoran Wanderer.

"Lookie, lookie we cornered the nookie," Bannus chimed, fully relishing his role as captor. The words oozed out of his mouth.

"I gotta say, you ain't the worst piece of tail we've come across. But you're the priciest."

"Give me the money," Elias demanded, feeling his face flush with rage and embarrassment.

"I don't have it," she spat, taking a step back from them.

"We'll see about that," Bannus grinned.

With speed surprising for his size Bannus closed the gap between them and grabbed Kyrie with rough hands. The woman only had time to cry out before she was wrapped up in his thick arms. She kicked and struggled violently, fueled by rage, bucking against the grasp that pinned her.

"Let go you bastard!" she yelled, teeth snapping and head jerking back. "Let me go! Let me go!"

The struggle was pitiful. Bannus laughed at Kyrie's resistance, hardly forcing a sweat from the effort. He held her tight with one arm as his free hand moved roughly over her body.

"Oooh yeah, give me a good fight," he said with his mouth to her ear. "You know how I like it, don't you? Come on, give it to me good."

A scream tore out of Kyrie's mouth as Bannus' hand reached under her skirt and felt their way up her legs. She kicked out and arched her back, trying to jerk out of his grasp. Bannus laughed as she fought, his enjoyment growing with each resisting spasm of her body.

"That's enough, Bannus," Elias finally said, sick of the display.

The guard ignored him, his hands continuing to reach deeper under Kyrie's skirts. Her screams grew wilder and more desperate. Silas watched with widening eyes, though his face grew more impassive by the moment.

"Dammit! That's enough!" Elias yelled.

Bannus stopped groping the woman. He pulled her tight in his rough embrace, pressed his face against hers and inhaled deeply. As if to show that he could do as he pleased, he held her there a moment, her body frozen in fear and revulsion, eyes wide and nostrils flared, panting deep and desperate breaths. With a grunt he threw her to the ground.

Dust billowed up as Kyrie scrambled away from Bannus. He crossed his arms and looked down at her in triumph, daring her to rise from the ground. Defiance still flared in the woman's eyes, etched her face in a firm grimace. But her fear and helplessness kept her pinned to the ground.

"She doesn't have it," Bannus said. "Must've dumped it somewhere."

"Just give us the money," Elias said again.

No answer came from Kyrie. Her gaze still held the threatening figure of Bannus.

"Just give us the money, and we'll leave you alone," Elias implored. "We'll go our way, and you go yours. We'll forget we ever met."

"The hell we will," Bannus interjected. "She's gonna give us the money and depending on how fast she does it will determine how many lashes she gets."

"We're not lashing anybody," Elias insisted. "We're not magistrates."

"Out here we are," Bannus said. "Besides, I've been deputized."

"For Anjibar," Elias argued. "We aren't anywhere near that jurisdiction."

"This is empty jurisdiction. No magistrate has any authority out here. We have to be the justice."

"You're not lashing anyone. Kyrie, just give us back the money and I swear we'll leave you alone."

"We're not leaving her alone." Bannus said.

"You'll never leave us alone," Kyrie spat.

"Yes, we will leave you alone. We will. Bannus."

"Are you going to quit destroying the land?" Kyrie asked, still sitting on the ground where Bannus had dumped her. "Are you going to repeal those ridiculous Citizen Safety Laws? Are you going to quit oppressing the people? Are you going to quit starving them and slaughtering them and ruining their lives? Are you going to quit killing children? You'll never leave us alone."

"I don't believe this," Elias shook his head in exasperation.

Still, the defiance was admirable, though now it was bordering on insanity. Elias sighed at his own predicament. Stuck between Bannus's morbid eagerness to execute justice and Kyrie's fanatical defiance, he felt like the only one with the slightest grasp on sanity.

"Just tell us where the money is," Elias groaned.

"Oh, she's gonna tell us," Bannus guaranteed.

A ring of metal echoed through the caverns as the guard drew out the long sword strapped to his back. He held it out for Kyrie to see. A whirr sounded as the blade slashed the air in quick motions. Bannus twirled and slashed at the air, spinning the sword so fast it was but a silver blur in the shadowed rift.

"If you kill me you'll never find the money," Kyrie promised. A quiver disturbed the conviction in her voice.

"Bannus," Elias warned, feeling the situation spiraling quickly out of control.

"Who said I was going to kill you?" Bannus asked calmly, leveling the sword at Silas who had watched all these things in silence.

If the boy was afraid, he didn't show it. He looked at the blade, then up at the large man that held it. Was it truly indifference, Elias wondered, or did he accept whatever fate life happened to throw at him?

Whatever fear the boy didn't display, Kyrie did. Her lips trembled as she looked from the sword to Elias, pleading and conflicted.

"Dammit! Just tell us where it is," Elias begged. "Don't be stupid."

Kyrie jerked her head towards Thoran who said nothing at the unfolding events. The stranger gave her an imperceptible nod, sealing some silent agreement.

"I appeal..." Kyrie stammered, looking back at Thoran again, then Silas. Her fear and indecision tortured her so much her arms trembled, barely holding her up.

"I appeal my case to the Enclave of Latrea," she finished as tears began to fall down her dusty face, the first release of a pressure that had grown too great for her to bear.

Bannus didn't move, clearly unsure of how to respond. His sword still leveled at Silas, the point not wavering from its deadly threat.

"I appeal to the justice of the Enclave of Latrea," she managed with more confidence.

"What in all the nine Hells does that mean?" Bannus asked, cocking his head toward Elias.

The tension flowed out of the magi as he understood what had just happened. Of course, this created a whole new host of problems. But at least this crisis would be averted.

"It means we can't do anything until Latrea hears her case," Elias told the burly guard.

"I'll be damned if that's so," Bannus growled. "We're getting that money."

"We can't, Bannus," Elias growled back. "It's a law of all the Enclaves. If someone appeals to the justice of an Enclave then they are under the protection of that Enclave until their case can be fully heard. We can't touch her."

"Let Latrea protect her then," Bannus shook his head, sword still hovering menacingly at Silas. "You're Anjibar."

"Doesn't matter," Thoran spoke up for the first time. He left his point of observation from the outskirts of the conflict and walked up to stand between Silas and the sword. With his thumbs hooked in his belt he looked over to address Elias.

"The magi are sworn to uphold the justice of all the Enclaves," Thoran pointed out. "You may have been educated and commissioned at Anjibar, but the work of magic is done through all the Enclaves. Same with the justice. Because this matter involves an offense against a magi, it can appropriately fall under the courts of the Enclave. This woman has just appealed to the justice of Latrea. As a magi you must uphold that justice, and see that the accused is taken safely to Latrea for her case to be heard. Of course, by submitting to Latrea she also agrees to abide by the outcome of the case."

"But I'm not a magi," Bannus insisted.

"This law applies even more so to deputies of the Enclaves," Thoran said, turning his gaze to Bannus. "As an officer of one of the Enclaves, you are most responsible for seeing this woman safely to Latrea."

"Is this true?" Bannus asked with clear annoyance.

"It is," Elias agreed, regarding Thoran with even deeper suspicion. "What does it mean?"

"It means we're going to Latrea. They have to sort this out."

"Damn it, I don't want to go there," Bannus huffed. "It's already sorted out. She stole your money and I'm getting it back."

"You could just let the whole matter drop then," Thoran suggested. "Go about your way."

"That's not gonna happen."

"Then you're headed to Latrea."

"Or I could just kill you all and we'll head on our merry way," Bannus threatened. He leveled all his twisted hatred at Thoran.

"Bannus, we don't have a choice," Elias said.

A moment of tense indecision gripped the unlikely group. Bannus still held his sword out, threatening, coiled, ready to orchestrate death at any moment. Kyrie still sat on the ground, rigid and fearful, her breath coming in quick gasps. Elias let his wand drop into his hand as he reached for his lumen. He knew how fast Bannus was and hoped he could be faster.

Strangely, only Silas and Thoran seemed free of tension. The boy silently watching as he always did. The stranger calmly faced Bannus's sword, thumbs tucked into his belt. His expression betrayed nothing out of the ordinary. He could have been staring at a ball of tumbleweed instead of a blade hovering inches from his eyes, held by a violent man who could easily snap him in two.

Finally, Bannus let the sword drop. He plunged it back into its sheath, shaking his head in disgust.

"Your head roles first if this turns out to be some kind of joke," Bannus said, jabbing a beefy finger at Elias.

The tension dropped away from Kyrie as the guard resheathed his sword. Her shoulders dropped and she exhaled a billowing sigh, the breath trembling with tension.

Elias didn't bother answering the threat. He knew it was empty bluster. Besides, he had more pressing concerns. How in the world this all happened he couldn't guess.

As soon as it was clear the crisis had passed, Silas walked over to his mother to help her up. She rose shakily to her feet and brushed the dust from her dress. Reaching out she tussled her sons hair before leaning down to kiss his forehead. A tight smile, bashful and apologetic, touched her own face.

"Thank you for your help," Elias nodded to Thoran. "Looks like we're headed to Latrea. Maybe we'll meet again under more fortunate circumstances."

"I can't leave you yet," Thoran smiled. "We still have a lot to do. It's a good ways to Latrea."

"We'll be traveling without you, I'm afraid," Elias said. "This is Enclave business. And besides, we wouldn't make the brightest road companions."

"But I'm a witness," Thoran reminded him. "I have to go."

"That won't be necessary."

"I have to insist. After all, I'm the only uninterested party in all of this. My testimony will be key."

What have I done to deserve this, Elias groaned to himself. He couldn't think of stranger, more uncomfortable company to be stuck with. A fanatical woman that hated him, a sadistic guard that spied on him, and a stranger that gave him the creeps. The odd boy was the most agreeable member of them all.

It was going to be a long journey to Latrea.

Chapter Eight
Walking a Wasteland

The journey to Latrea began every bit as awful as Elias envisioned. Bannus insisted on binding Kyrie, either to prevent her escape or to indulge his sick whimsy. Elias figured a bit of both.

Surprisingly, Kyrie did not resist her arrest. She held out her hands while Bannus bound her wrists, silently enduring the treatment. A part of her even seemed to relish in the light martyrdom.

Bannus held the other end of the rope, tugging hard now and again to jerk Kyrie along. This too she endured in silence. Clearly annoyed by her lack of reaction, Bannus yanked her to the ground.

Kyrie sprawled amid a cloud of dust, barely able to catch herself with her wrists tied together. As she pulled herself up to her hands and knees, one of Bannus' heavy boots thumped on her back, keeping her from rising any further.

"I think I like you like this," Bannus lorded over her. "You actually look useful for change."

"I'm not surprised you like things on four legs," Kyrie shot back. "Although I'm probably not hairy enough for you."

This brought a roar of laughter from both Thoran and Elias. Dark clouds scarred Bannus's face. He could muster no come back. Instead, he grunted and kicked Kyrie to the ground.

Elias took up the tether after that.

The unlikely group made their way westward into the surrounding wasteland. A day away from the rift bed and the land became flat and cracked. Dried mud peeled off in layers of irregular shape. For miles in either direction they could see the mark of the same fissures and fractures in the withered soil. It looked like a vast puzzle made of small, earthen pieces.

"This used to be the Correlin Swamp," Thoran pointed out as the group traipsed over the cracked flats. "Home to thousands of species of insect, bird and aquatic life. Tupelo and cypress trees used to grow here so tall and thick they formed a canopy that kept the swamp in perpetual shade. This place was known for Pompelo fruit. It was mushy and sweet and full of juice. It made a fantastic wine, very difficult to make but coveted by the nobility. Deer, wild hog, even some alligators roamed in number where today is nothing but a flat and cracked plane of dried mud. But I'm sure this will all pass. The gators will be back any day now."

Elias ignored the jab, knowing the stranger was blaming magic for the parched swamp. He was right, after all. Elias vaguely remembered the swamp, and in remembering felt a tug of grief for what once was, and what most likely would never be again. He could even make out a few dried out stumps and some of the characteristic knees of the old trees, poking through the mud as shriveling knobs of crumbling wood.

These soliloquies from Thoran became common as the group journeyed. Kyrie tortured Elias in her own ways. Usually, this consisted of nothing more than glaring at him. A few times she would goad him with words, to try and make him extra miserable.

"I guess you really enjoy this," she jabbed at him during the second day's travel. The sun had faded to a gray dusk, and the first welcome cool of evening settled after a hot day of walking.

"You get to tie me up and act like the high and mighty lord of the land you pretend yourself to be."

"I wouldn't try to take the moral high ground on this one," Elias returned, regretting that he rose to the challenge as soon as the words came out of his mouth.

"There is nothing you could do that would put you in the right," she returned with heat in her words.

"You stole from me! Remember that? You are bound because you are a thief."

"I am not a thief."

"That was my money you took," Elias reminded her. "It was rightfully mine. You took it. Now, you're under arrest. You don't like it? Quit stealing."

"Rightfully yours?" she asked as the indignation rose fierce in her eyes. "Nothing you have is rightfully yours. If you want to talk about thieves I'll tell you about thieves.

"What about taxes? They got higher and higher as the Blight got worse until there was nothing left to tax. What about inflation? What about exploited labor? Women and children slaving in fields and beaten if they are caught putting a single kernel of corn in their mouths. And at the end of the day getting paid in coin so devalued it couldn't buy a days worth of food. What about the land stolen by your Lords who squeezed out the small farmers, or passed laws to cripple anyone who didn't grow with magic? Or your precious Enclave secrets? How many men have you hunted down for using wild magic? For our own good, you say. I say it's so you can continue to take and take and take, any and everything that doesn't belong to you.

"I'm not a thief. I didn't steal from you. That money had been stolen already. I was just taking it back."

Kyrie gestured wildly as she hurled her accusations at Elias. With her wrist bound this left her pumping her hands up and down and slinging them back and forth.

Most of their exchanges ended in much the same way.

By far, Kyrie's favorite way to torment Elias was to stop without warning as they traveled. All of a sudden the rope would pull tight in Elias's hand. He would look back and see Kyrie glaring defiantly at him. She might hold up her bound hands in a gesture of displayed oppression, daring Elias to jerk at the rope and force her along brutally as Bannus had done.

This provocation Elias resisted. He would sigh and shake his head, staring off into the distance until Kyrie grew tired of the game and started forward again. She did it several times a day until Thoran slapped her on the backside once.

"Get moving sweet cheeks," Thoran winked and smiled.

Kyrie was too aghast to deliver her trademark glare.

Most of the days passed in silence. Bannus brooded in his borderline stupidity, quietly and patiently nursing his anger. Silas remained lost in his own thoughts during the day, withdrawn and mysterious. At night, around the small campfire, he opened up, transforming into a different child altogether. He would question Elias endlessly, asking and wondering on a meandering and variety of subjects.

Thoran was the only one that talked during the day. Long periods of silence were punctuated by rambling lectures about topography and wildlife of the near past. It seemed he possessed an inexhaustible knowledge of what the land used to look like. And he never tired of reminding Elias of life before the Blight. Sometimes he would bring up their initial argument about the Blight's cause.

"Do you remember what place this is?" Thoran asked as they walked down a dry and empty bank. Half-exposed and wind-eroded rock ran in a band across their path, twisting back and forth in a broad, looping pattern.

Something tugged at Elias, something before the loss of his memory. He should know this, where they were. It was something he knew, but it seemed like a fact from ancient history.

"Was this...the Meridon?" Elias hesitantly suggested.

"The Mighty Meridon!" Thoran echoed grandly. "Looks like you haven't forgotten everything."

"What's the Meridon?" Silas asked, his curiosity defeating his daytime silence.

"Let Thoran teach you for once," the stranger said. "The Meridon was nothing less than the very lifeblood of the interior. This dry, dusty bank full of old rocks is all that is left of the longest, widest, most important river in the land. It ran from the Calaban all the way to the sea. It used to carry all the most important commerce in the land on its back. And not only that, it's regular flooding soaked the planes with the most fertile soil man has ever seen. All around us in a band running parallel to the river lay rich farmland that provided nearly sixty percent of the land's food. Of course, the yield increased with the advent of magic, finally resulting in the paradise you see before you today."

Kyrie clapped her hands as best she could with her wrists bound together. Bannus stared, knowing some attack had been made at his institution, but couldn't understand enough to answer. For his part, Elias didn't rise to the challenge. Not even sure he believed his own arguments, he knew he lacked conviction. Besides, being goaded by Kyrie was enough.

Thoran pointed out yesterday's glories almost everywhere they went.

"This was once a swath of ancient forest growth," the stranger pointed out as they walked through rolling, but otherwise featureless land, brown and sandy like the rest. If anything, the sand was looser and harder to walk in than normal.

"There were trees here before the written record of man," he continued. "As long as there have been stories told there has stood a forest in this place. Many of the trees were several hundred years old. When the Blight struck scholars were still discovering new species of plant that proliferated here. It was even speculated that it would be impossible to catalog them all. We should be walking in cool shade right now, climbing over mossy logs and chasing small game. But here we are, sweating and baked, all brought to you by the hope of magic."

A few days later they traveled over harder soil. An orange tint colored the sand, and the dust seemed finer when it rose up as their feet passed over the firmer ground.

"What you see here was the first of the mass incorporated farms. The landless third son of a minor baron name Jacob Guignard teamed up with magicians at the Anjibar Enclave and sold magically enhanced seeds. He sold them dirt cheap to select farmers, and when their competitors couldn't keep up he quickly bought their land at sharply depreciated prices. Once he had gotten a large chunk of land for himself he quit selling to those first farmers and started to out compete them himself. When they couldn't keep up, mostly because of the outrageous sums they still owed for the now-inflated seed prices, he happily relieved them of their land as well. He soon owned enough land to be a small kingdom, and wealthier than most. The model he shamelessly employed was so successful it was repeated by magic–noble alliances all over. Within fifty years, the small, family-owned farm, which had been a feature of life for centuries, and the staple of our land, had almost completely disappeared. The independent freeholder vanished, swallowed up by the insatiable maw of mega–farms and magic."

He sounded like a tour guide for the morbid, a historian of dead places while they walked over their bones. What made it even worse was that he was right. Over the last one hundred years the land had been destroyed beyond recognition. What had been reliable features for possibly thousands of years of life had now eroded to the featureless expanse of dust and sand, distinguishable only by the subtle nuance that marks desert and wasteland apart.

All these annoyances seemed petty to the real problem that quickly presented itself. The party possessed dangerously scant provisions. Bannus and Elias carried only enough food and water for themselves: dried meat, hardtack, a tiny store of dried fruit, the bottle he had bought at Hiram's Well, a few spices, a small bag of almonds and a jar of mostly crystallized honey. Thoran had a personal supply he ate from, while Kyrie and Silas only had a pouch of corn flour and a few old biscuits.

Bannus had predictably objected to feeding the woman and her child. The thought of losing food showed visibly on the burly guard's face as they argued the matter, perhaps hurting him more than the loss of the gold. It had resulted in a day's worth of argument, but Elias eventually convinced him as prisoners of the Enclave they had to feed them both.

By the time they realized how low their rations were, the closest place where the party could resupply was a solid three days travel away. This meant half rations, and by Elias' best guess that would barely get them to the supply point.

It took only a day of reduced food for the results to show. While Kyrie and Silas seem not to mind, Bannus and Elias felt the pain of loss acutely. Bannus grew more ornery than usual, while Elias fought off waves of weakness and dehydration that shook him during the heat of the day. A vague sense of guilt touched him along with a slight faint feeling, as he thought of how many went through the same thing every day. Something deeper tugged at him too, a discontent that boiled into urgency, an anger that burned too brightly for having no particular object. These mixtures of old feelings left him with an unsettling certainty that there was something very important he had to remember.

It always came back to memory.

The provisions, though an immediate problem, wasn't Elias's main concern. He felt certain they would make it to a supply post. What he didn't know was how they would buy anything once they got there. He had considerable money, but all he carried with him had been stolen by Kyrie, and she stood firm in her recalcitrant insistence that the money was hers by right. So it remained hidden, probably beyond recovery.

Elias couldn't imagine what Kyrie hoped would happen in her appeal to Latrea. Perhaps she hoped for leniency, or even entertained the insane notion that Latrea would agree with her claim. Most likely, she was buying for time, or simply acting out of raw defiance.

Against his will, Elias couldn't help but admire the courage and genius Kyrie displayed. Even if Latrea found her guilty and forced her to turn over the money, she would have ample time to get word to a friend, letting them know where the money was hidden long before Elias could recover it. The more he thought about it, the more the magi resigned himself to the fact that he would never see that coin again.

As the days wore on, and hunger became a more real possibility, Elias thought he would've gladly given her the money if only she would hand over enough to buy provisions. This was not a likely option, as his gold was probably hidden somewhere in the rift bed, at least five days worth of backtracking away. The heat and fatigue made him feel desperate, and allowed a sense of doom to creep into his thoughts. He struggled over the merciless sand, a slight tremor to his limbs and felt as if the sun were trying to strip the flesh from his bones.

Elias feared what might happen at the supply post. He feared he wouldn't be able convince the merchants that his credit was good, even as a magi. He feared his forged letters of credit would be detected, and they would have to rely on intimidation. All the same, he found himself glad he had the option.

All these fears and precautions turned out needless in the long run. Even his money, had Elias had it, would have been worthless.

At the end of six days hard travel, dealing with hunger, heat, and thirst on top of Kyrie's and Thoran's antagonism; with Bannus's temper simmering on the edge, and Elias's own growing weakness, he led the group over a final rise in the near dusk light with the supply post now in sight. They found the old road earlier that day, still paved with stone despite being ravaged and cracked by the heat. The gray blocks and mortar had been bleached by the sun, so the road stood out in stark contrast to the brown sands it cut through. A jagged piece of broken post leaned over the road, whatever it marked having been torn away long ago. Bannus pulled it the rest of the way out of the sand, promising himself a wood fire later that night.

Before the supply post came into view they could smell the burning. Not just wood, but some other substance, a mix of different smokes drifted on the wind. There was no discernible plume on the horizon ahead. Just the smell, the undeniable scent of destruction that told the party what they would find long before they witnessed with their eyes.

The supply post was made mostly of stone, the same gray material as the road. Small wisps of smoke rose up as the party approached. No flames could be seen. From a distance, the fire and destruction appeared minor. But as they drew closer they could see the door torn from its hinges, shutters splintered out, and all manner of supplies strewn about the dusty ground. The sound of metal rang out as Bannus bared his sword. He held a hand out to keep the others back as he cautiously approached the building. Elias sent his lumen out into the stone structure.

"It's empty," he told Bannus after he felt no life inside.

Bannus nodded but still approached with caution, his steps silent as he rounded the building. Both men knew there were ways to mask your presence from a magi.

Elias let his wand drop into his hand. Following at a safe distance from his guard, he watched in his own way, using his magical sense to see what eyes alone could not.

Bannus disappeared through the torn door. Moments later Elias followed, reaching deep into one of his pouches and producing a polished, clear stone.

Darkness swallowed Elias as he stepped through the doorway. He waited a moment for his eyes to adjust to the dim light that filtered through the small, broken window. He held up the clear stone and activated it with his lumen. A strong burst of light glowed from its center.

The light revealed carnage strewn about the little room. Wreckage of wooden furniture lay scattered amid tattered clothes and burlap. A few pieces of random armor joined the mess.

It was the blood that stood out the most. It seemed to be smeared everywhere. In one corner, a pool still glistened as if someone had lied there bleeding just hours before. A crimson streak brushed over the floor from the puddle, drag marks in blood.

The sickening aroma of putrescence assaulted Elias's nostrils. He gagged and covered his mouth and nose, too late to halt the stench of death that tainted him from the lungs out.

Bannus held out his hand and Elias tossed him the glowing orb. The guard stepped through the only other door in the room and rolled the ball of light down a dark hallway.

As he waited, Elias took more careful stock of the room. Even amid the mess he could tell this was where the supply post did most of its business. There was a stall on the far side, made up of a long counter and iron bars that covered the top portion. Any transaction the storehouse conducted was from behind the safety of those bars. Or, as it turned out, the illusion of safety the bars offered.

Elias stepped up to the counter and peered through the bars at the little station behind. It looked untouched. Whatever violence had occurred didn't happen there.

"Looks clean," Bannus called out from the hallway.

Elias followed and quickly explored the rest of the supply station. It consisted only of the hallway opening up to four other rooms. One went to the stall that Elias had seen behind the bars. It was as untouched as it looked at first. Even the many drawers were still shut and locked which Elias was convinced contained money of some sort. An uneasy thought suddenly struck him. There was something decidedly bizarre about the place.

Down the hallway were two other rooms with beds. The mattresses had been shredded and the furniture smashed and pulled apart. The last room at the far end of the hall was the store room. Predictably, the shelves had been stripped bare. Another set of bars divided the room in half. Behind these were more wooden drawers and two small, iron chests.

That uneasy feeling stirred more urgently in Elias. The sudden stillness of the place unnerved him. It wasn't just smears and smells of blood, the lingering aroma of sweat and fear, or even the unnatural quiet that pervaded the dark hall. There was something more sinister at work than a simple raid.

Elias looked down and saw a severed finger on the floor of the store room. He grimaced and kicked it away in disgust.

"They didn't touch the gold," Elias said, gesturing to the room behind the bars. "There's probably a small fortune in there. Why didn't they take it? Whoever hit this place?"

"Gold is no good to the hungry," Bannus shrugged. "Cared more about the food. They might not even have thought of the gold."

"Everybody thinks about the gold."

"Maybe they got spooked. Didn't have time to get through the locks."

"Yeah, but all they had to do was take the keys," Elias explained as the walls began to feel too close and his unease blossomed into fear.

"This wasn't a regular hit," Elias insisted. "These weren't bandits, or wayward pilgrims."

"Who was it then?"

"I don't know. That's what bothers me."

The rest of the place was empty. More than empty, the storehouse stood eerily bereft, empty of people but full of the lingering reek of fear and evil. Cursed, was the word that came to Elias's mind. The place felt cursed.

"Nothing's on fire," Bannus casually observed as they made their way out. "Where did the smoke come from?"

Around the back of the building they found the source of the fire. Smoke still billowed and circled on the wind. Embers flared weekly as black and gray ashes followed the traces of smoke on the dry air. An odd smell added to the burning that permeated the atmosphere.

A charred piece of burlap fluttered at Elias's feet. He stooped and picked up the litter of brown cloth and turned it over in his hands. Realization suddenly hit him. And at the same time a greater perplexity as he both understood and grew more confused, recognizing the burning smell and feeling abjectly unable to recognize what happened.

"Barley," Elias whispered as the piece of burlap slipped from his fingers and took its appointed place as a pilgrim on the wind.

"What is it?" Kyrie asked breathlessly. Elias hadn't heard her approach. For once, her voice held none of the challenge and defiance that dominated her usual demeanor. She too was frightened, and fear subdued her.

"It's barley," Elias repeated, not believing his own words. "They burned the barley."

He walked over to the fire and kicked at the smoldering pile. Ashes flew up along with charred seeds and blackened strips of wood and remnants of cloth bags.

"Barley, corn, wheat," he said as he identified the burned supplies.

"They burned them all. They burned all the supplies."

"Who would do something like that?" a voice asked. Elias couldn't tell who.

The group stood in quiet amazement and consternation, watching the last few remnants of food consumed by fire. Another wind came up and blew dust and smoke among them. None stirred. Something deep and fearful, terrible and incomprehensible had silenced them.

In an age such as theirs, an age of want and blight, things normally considered insane made perfect sense. Theft made sense. Murder made sense. Brigandage and lawlessness made sense. That a supply post had been raided and stripped of its goods was a perfectly reasonable occurrence. It was a perfectly regular occurrence. Hunger and thirst drove men to extreme lengths. That the hungry and thirsty would do violence made sense, was part of the sane world.

This was insanity. This made no sense.

That someone would raid a supply post, an oasis in the desert, kill its guards, steal its food, then burn it, made no sense at all. Who would burn food? Who would so blatantly destroy the most precious commodity in the world?

"Reservoirs been drained too," Thoran broke the silence as he peered into the tall tank.

"You sure it wasn't already empty?" Elias asked, hoping the insanity wasn't even worse than it already appeared.

"There's mud underneath," Thoran said grimly. He let the top fall with a bang and climbed back down.

It was worse than it appeared. Elias could see the ground under the reservoir still discolored with the copious amount of water that had been unleashed. A single clear drop fell from the spigot on to the insatiably thirsty ground.

"Who would do this?" a voice asked again.

Elias turned to see that it was Silas. For the first time he saw fear etched on the boy's features, his eyes wide and face grown pale. He wore that distant, unfixed air that told Elias the boy was lost in the surreality of the moment.

"I don't know," Elias muttered, barely hearing his own voice.

Madness, he told himself. Only madness would have committed something so incomprehensible. To shed blood only to destroy some scant food, to consign more to hunger, was only madness. The violence was somehow worse than meaningless. This violence had meaning. And its meaning was madness.

"What happened to the guards?" Kyrie asked. "I mean...their bodies. What happened to their bodies?"

Elias shook his head but did not answer her. He dared not utter what was on his mind, what was on all their minds. None of them dared to voice the possibility that human beings could destroy food fit for men in favor of the greatest corruption of humanity. It was a sin against the very appetite.

"And so another pinion of humanity falls," Thoran spoke in hollow benediction, the words of an ancient poet. "Among this rack and ruin, among the scattered leaves where only remnants of men remain, a waste of wraiths and half things, shadows that turn and mourn their glory past, slip yet further into the bowels of a waking hell."

Chapter Nine
Reasons to Celebrate and Fear

When the shock of all they found finally wore off, Elias was able to think of more pressing concerns. More dire than mad bandits who destroyed perfectly good food was the immediate need of their own dwindling supply. Their food had run out that afternoon, and the water in their last skin sloshed around the bottom.

"Our options are limited," Elias addressed the group gathered around the swirling ashes of the burned food.

"There used to be a small farm about two days east of here. I have no idea if it still functions or if they could help us at all. But our only other option is to stay on this road and hope beyond hope it leads somewhere that can help us."

"How far is Latrea?" Kyrie asked, seemingly unconcerned about their predicament.

Elias had to remind himself how familiar this situation must be to her. She was practically in the same position when he had found her. This being new to him, the situation put Elias in near panic.

"Way too far away," Elias answered. "At least three weeks walking. We'll be dead before we make it a quarter of the way."

"We'll be fine," Kyrie told him.

"I doubt that," Elias laughed. "If that farm is still there we might be able to stumble to it, almost dead from exhaustion. And then I'm not sure how we would convince anyone to help us. No, I think we're far from fine."

It was Kyrie's turn to laugh. Her's was more genuine as it lacked the desperation of Elias'. She sounded like she enjoyed the magi's discomfort.

"Now you see what it's like for the less privileged members of your great civilization," she taunted with considerable glee. "Now you see what burden mothers and fathers have been laboring under for decades. The fear. The uncertainty. The possibility that you might not make it to tomorrow."

Elias rolled his eyes and threw up his hands in disgust. "By the hairy balls of hell, do you ever stop?"

"Does your kind ever stop? Does the tyranny and theft and pillage ever stop?"

"This is not the time," Elias raised his voice. "Do you get that? This is not the time."

"You've been fat for so long you've forgotten how to survive," Kyrie continued to taunt. "Your wealth has made you weak."

"Give it a rest."

"You've grown lazy and overfed and unable to adapt."

Elias turned around to storm off. Somewhere. Anywhere. He had to get away from that persistent taunt.

"It could all be okay if you want it to be," Kyrie yelled at his retreating figure.

"Sounds like a wonderful plan," Elias turned to respond. "Let's just want it to be okay. Hell, why did I study magic for all those years when I could want something out of thin air?"

"I will find us food if you want me to," Kyrie said. "But you have to want it."

"Why wouldn't I want it?" Elias asked as he threw his hands up in frustration. Damn, the woman was infuriating, he thought.

"You have to want it bad enough," Kyrie said, holding up her bound wrists.

Elias' sarcasm fell away in an instant. She was serious. At the very least she believed she could find them food and supplies.

"What do you want?" Elias asked.

"I find the supplies and you let me go," she suggested.

Elias narrowed his eyes and tried to think. Certain this was some sort of trick, he tried to work out the angle. Would she run as soon as he cut her loose? That wouldn't get her far. He was certain there was deceit being formulated in her mind, though he couldn't guess what. Ultimately, he had no choice but to negotiate

."You know about a cache around here?" Elias probed.

Kyrie smiled and twisted her bound hands in response.

"We drop the theft charge and let you go, but you return the money," Elias tried to barter.

"That was your first offer," Kyrie reminded him with a wry expression. "Back in the rift bed. Don't like it any better now."

"Damn you," Elias cursed. She was right though.

"We drop the charge of theft and you return half the stolen money," Elias tried to bargain knowing he had little to bargain with. If Kyrie knew where to find food, she held all the cards. He just couldn't let her off without a fight. He owed her that much for all the aggravation and embarrassment she caused him.

"I find you food, you cut me loose and forget we ever met," Kyrie refused to budge.

"What? And lose all those happy memories?"

Kyrie cocked her head to one side and shot Elias a rude gesture.

With a sigh Elias turned to Bannus. As much as he hated to give in to Kyrie, he knew without Bannus's cooperation it was pointless to consider the offer at all. The very fact that he had to negotiate with both these people chafed him sore.

"What about you?" Elias asked the guard. "Would you kick up a fuss if we let her go?"

The strain on Bannus's face was visible. His color had gone pale and his eyes had taken a wide, desperate fix. Hunger and privation had worked harder on him than any of the others. He was unused to not eating his fill. Elias could feel the panic rising in Bannus, and feared what the big man would do if pushed much further.

"I don't care. Let the bitch go," Bannus whined. "What good does it do if we die out here in the flaming desert?"

Kyrie smiled again and presented her bound hands. Elias sighed even deeper and shook his head. At least he would finally be rid of her.

Kyrie delivered her side of the bargain as soon as she was freed. Watching her, Elias wanted to kick himself. It was so simple, so obvious. It almost convinced him of what she had said about his softness. A few days of low rations had certainly dulled his thinking.

"If you want to keep from starving you have to think like a starving man," Kyrie explained as she walked the group back inside the store house.

She went from room to room, eyeing over the place. Her gaze went from roof to floor, looking for something only she knew. To a casual observer, she could have been sizing the place up for some new furniture or to see if her bedroom set fit.

"You see, the people who run the store house work for somebody else," Kyrie said, walking back into one of the bedrooms.

"Help me clean this out," she instructed.

The men went to work moving all the debris from the ransacked room. They threw out the hacked furniture, pieces of table, chair, bed, and what looked like a simple dresser. They gathered up the tattered bed clothes and the feathers from the bedding. Elias grabbed one pile stuck together in congealing blood. He coughed and pushed down the urge to retch as he shook the crimson-soaked feathers from his hands.

With the room cleared all that remained was a dusty rug, faded and multicolored, that covered about half the wooden floor.

"The guards and the quartermaster have to stay for long periods of time. They have to eat and drink as well, and you can better believe in a world where food is more precious than gold, that they will keep plenty aside for themselves."

Kyrie pulled the rug aside, sending up a cloud of dust and dirt. Underneath, a loop of rope wound into the wooden floor. Kyrie grabbed the rope and tugged. A section of the floor lifted up, revealing a set of stairs that descended into a dark passage.

A smell like tar rose up from the opened hatch. Elias waved away the clouds of dust and stepped forward for a better look. Peering down the few steps that descended into the darkness below he could only make out a few barrels at the bottom. The rest was obscured in shadow.

When he moved closer for a cautious look further in he was shouldered out of the way by Bannus who thundered down the stairs. Stopping at the first barrel, he ripped the top off and plunged his hands inside. He scooped a handful of liquid and drink deep. He retched and spit the water out.

"Ah, Hell, that's saltwater," he spat, wiping his mouth.

He moved to the next barrel and tore the top off. This time, he sniffed the surface before scooping out a handful of water.

"Blessed Gaia, that tastes good," he said before dipping in again.

The others took more time inspecting what the extra stores contained. There were a few barrels stacked on either side of the narrow space. Elias saw bundles of rope, bags of flour, and sacks of corn. One corner was filled with coils of fuel, giving the cellar its pitchy smell.

Along the back wall, Elias dug through sacks that mostly held biscuits. Some contain dried meat. One, however, revealed a healthy supply of dried fruit.

"Oh, I have missed you," Elias said as he popped a shriveled slice of lemon into his mouth.

He moaned as the tart taste squeezed out, crushed between his teeth. The others looked over at the unusual display of emotion from the magi. He eagerly passed the fruit around, enjoying the reactions from all of them, even Bannus, as they sampled the rare treat. Silas's eyes went wide in surprise, perhaps never having tasted fruit before in his short life. Kyrie laughed at his reaction, covering her mouth to prevent the precious food from spilling out.

Two of the barrels they discovered contain brine, the rest were filled with water. In one of the brine barrels Elias found pickles buried beneath the saltwater.

Besides the fruit and pickles, they discovered two other rare treasures. One was a large, leather pouch filled with butter. The other, a chest of salt, held four small hams buried within. Bannus laughed as he held up one of the large chunks of pork, waving it like a victorious brute.

An impromptu meal took place in the cellar. Elias mostly ate pickles, dipping again and again into the deep barrel. Silas couldn't get his fill of fruit, and had to be restrained by his mother. Bannus stuffed himself on dried meat while Kyrie smeared butter on biscuits and devoured them with controlled avarice.

The only one who seemed unenthusiastic was Thoran. He picked over the stores, plucking this or that, but did not share in the group's uninhibited excitement. Had not Elias been absorbed in enjoying his new found wealth, he would've thought this behavior exceedingly strange.

"Too bad we can't take it all," Elias remarked. "This would get us to Latrea and back several times."

"We're not going to Latrea," Kyrie pointed out. "Silas and I will carry what we can and head east."

After eating and drinking their fill, the group picked over what was left in the chambers above. Behind the stalls, they forced open the drawers and found a handful of copper coins and some pen, ink and paper. Unable to find the keys, Elias picked the lock on the barred door in the storeroom and pilfered the chest behind it. It too was filled with coin, mostly copper, though a few silver pieces dotted here and there. Another chest, this one small and metal with a harder lock to tackle, held all the gold.

He kept the gold, telling himself it was replacement for his stolen money. He let Kyrie take all the copper and silver she wanted. A brief protest came from her over this, but it was short-lived. Even she knew not to push the magi and his temperamental guard too far.

* * *

With full bellies, a sense of optimism flowed into the group. It was the natural lift to the spirit that comes when one's fortune suddenly change for the better. They had been hungry and poor. Now they had plenty of money and food to last them for a long time.

This sense of goodwill infected everyone, and the natural hostility that had been the mood of the group warmed into a cool affection. They still didn't like each other, but for now, at least, they didn't hate each other.

That night they all decided to forgo the treat of sleeping indoors. The storehouse still reeked of blood and fear. No one wanted to stay in there any longer than they had to. Without speaking of the matter, for no one wanted to ruin the new found goodwill that possessed them, they set up camp outside a comfortable distance away from the storehouse.

They did decide to indulge in a proper fire. Breaking up the furniture left behind, they piled the wood up to a comfortable blaze. The natural, orange flames increased the positive sentiments that stirred within them. Unlike the fuel coils that produce low flames and exuded a dark smoke that smelled thickly of tar and oil, or the magi's fire, burning dried turf or charwood blocks that produced heat but little lasting flame, a wood fire gave just the right color, light and heat. Very few people got to enjoy one. Even Gregor, surrounded in the comfort afforded by magic and power, rarely enjoyed the simple pleasure of a plain, wood fire.

The group feasted as they sat around the fire. Bannus had skewered one of the hams on the spit and set it over to cook. The pork bubbled over the flames, dripping fat onto the coals below, sizzling and rendering a deliciously decadent aroma around the camp. It was impossible not to be happy. Even Bannus smiled as he deeply inhaled the smell of roasting swine.

"Ahhh, you smell that?" he exclaimed for the fifth time in as many minutes. "That's food for a man there."

Kyrie smiled and sipped at a cup of tea. They had found that stashed away in the basement cache with a more thorough search. Along with two jars of molasses, the dried leaves of tea were found hidden inside a sack of ground corn meal. Kyrie had been delighted at the find.

"What do you want the molasses for if you don't have the tea?" Kyrie asked, picking up the negotiations with Elias over the scarcest goods they would split up.

"I'm out of honey, that's why," Elias answered. "It got eaten up with the other supplies. I think it's only fair to replace it. Besides, one jar of molasses is enough to sweeten the little bit of tea that is left."

"I want the fruit," Silas interjected. "I don't care about the other stuff."

"Why should you get the fruit and the tea?" Elias argued.

"Because you took all the gold," Kyrie answered with mock bitterness.

"Let's not get into that again, now. Just when we were starting to get along."

"Oh, I wouldn't call this getting along," Kyrie said, holding up her hands. "Let's just say I tolerate you for the moment."

"Fine then, we'll take the meat and the butter," Elias continued to negotiate.

"Why the meat and butter?" Kyrie asked indignantly.

"You're taking the tea and fruit."

"But tea has no nutrition to it. You can't live off tea."

"It's your choice to insist on a luxury item."

Kyrie pursed her lips. She took a thoughtful sip of her tea and nodded.

"Fine. You take the butter and meat. We'll take the tea and fruit. We split the molasses and the fuel coils."

Elias narrowed his eyes at her. Kyrie laughed at the ridiculous look on his face. This time, she didn't bother to stifle it or cover it up.

"You remembered the fuel coils," Elias said.

"I want the fuel coils," Bannus piped up as he tested the roasting ham with a finger.

"Yeah, but you travel with a guy who can burn sand," Kyrie pointed out. "We can't."

"It's turf. I burn turf," Elias corrected. "Or I have to make charwood. We'll split the fuel coils and the molasses," Elias conceded.

He thought for a moment then took it a step further.

"What say we cook the rest of the hams tonight and split those up too?" he offered, feeling warm and magnanimous.

"Deal," Kyrie agreed softly and held out her hand.

Elias took the hand and held it in his own. The slightness of her fingers startled him. She suddenly appeared to him very fragile and delicate. In the firelight her gaze softened to him, the pupils of her eyes widened just slightly. A protective urge rose in him, a desire to shield her from the dangers of the dying world, to keep this last bit of softness from hardening like the dry and lifeless sands around them.

"Deal," Elias echoed, reluctantly releasing Kyrie's hand. He thought he noticed hers withdraw slower than it needed, but that could have been his imagination.

"What about you?" Silas spoke up, looking at Thoran.

No one had mentioned the stranger or what portion of money or rare goods he should share. Neither had he interjected himself into the negotiations. Ever since they had discovered the hidden stash, Thoran had fallen oddly silent.

The man shrugged his shoulders. His pale, blue eyes continued to stare into the fire.

"I'll be fine with a share of flour and meal," he said.

"You should take something else," Elias encouraged, feeling guilty and more than a bit greedy.

"You can't take my fruit," Silas hastily interjected. Kyrie jabbed her son with an admonishing elbow.

"Nah, I don't need all that," Thoran insisted. "I don't like to indulge in luxuries too much. It makes me soft."

He turned to look Elias in the eye and the magi wondered at the stranger's behavior. Surely a man who would drink anything as rare as Raisen Nectar would enjoy any luxury available. Or maybe he was just being kind.

The blue eyes burned into Elias, evoking that odd sense of familiarity. He felt the fire darken and the thunder rumble on the edge of his mind.

"Take some ham," Elias said, speaking to keep the storm from invading his mind.

"Okay, thank you," Thoran accepted. He turned his gaze back to the fire and his silent reverie.

"So, where are you off to next?" Kyrie asked before an awkward silence could settle over the group. "Now that you aren't going to Latrea?"

"I guess we pick up where we left off," Elias shrugged. "We were going north anyway. We'll keep heading that way. When it gets real hot we'll head over to the coast. Keep looking for work. Interior is getting pretty bleak for opportunities, even for a magi. What about you?"

"It's probably best we didn't talk about that," Kyrie answered, her native defensiveness popping up again. "We're not really on the same side of the war."

"I'm not even fighting," Elias told her.

"I know you're not. But I am."

Elias opened his mouth to reply, then clamped it shut. It was pointless to engage her. Nothing would come of it except stoking her insatiable rage. Instead, he relented to the silence of the desert night, the crackling of the wood fire, the wind that swirled around the rocky crags to the east, and even the rhythmic thump of drums in the distance. For a while, it didn't even strike him as strange.

"What's that?" Silas was the first to ask.

As soon as the question was asked the sounds suddenly became more prominent. It was as if by mere mention, the distant noise became easier to hear.

"Are those drums?" Kyrie asked.

The group fell silent and listened with strained intensity. Elias cocked his head and leaned towards the sound.

It was faint at first. But the more he listened the more he could make out the sound. A rhythmic thump, an echoing boom, sounds falling over each other. Clearly, he could make out the sound of a drumbeat.

Slowly, a rhythm, a method began to emerge from the sounds. The distant boom fell in time, slow, and fast again. The longer the music fell on his ears the louder it grew. The rhythm picked up, faster and faster, shattering the desert night. A voice cried out, in either ecstasy or pain. A chorus of howls answered.

Without even straining, Elias could hear the drums clearly now, as if the source was getting closer. The sound dominated the night. Howls rose and fell in discordant time. Cries of abandoned fervor, thick with the zeal of madmen punctuated the rhythm of the drums. Elias can almost smell the sweat of the drummers and dancers, pulsing and gyrating with the insistent music. It was a command. It was a summons. It was a call to the distant and ancient echoes of the soul: obey the pounding of the drums. It tore the howls and cries from the people who had no words for a sentiment so deep and savage.

Then, all at once the drums pounded in one last percussive explosion. The cries of the people exhaled a final crash of voices, and one lone scream, terrified and full of pain, tore through the night. The sound stabbed into Elias's ear like the steal of a cold knife.

Altogether, the group stopped listening and turned to the source of the scream. In the distance, the glow of a fire danced on the night sky. Another scream fell, then another. Soon, a whole chorus of screams, frightened and tortured, echoed from the distant glow.

"Get rid of the fire," Elias commanded as he gathered up his belongings.

No one had to be encouraged to obey. Thoran kicked sand over the campfire, dowsing the flames in dust. Everyone else scrambled to gather their belongings, goaded by sudden panic.

Without discussion, the group followed Elias. He ran towards the rocky outcropping he had seen in the east. It rose above them like a small mountain, gray rock eroded into crags and fingers of jagged rock.

They scrambled up the side of the crag following Elias as he dropped into a bowl-like depression in the rock. As they landed, they fell silent. In the distance, they still heard the intermittent screams that chilled the night. The sound mixed with their ragged and panicked breath.

They sat still and unspeaking, long after the last screams had died off. Kyrie wore the same wide-eyed expression as her son, who kept looking at Elias for either answers or encouragement. The magi felt he could give him neither, but nodded in his direction when their eyes met.

"We have to get the rest of our stuff," Thoran finally broke the silence with a whisper. "There's a lot we left behind."

Elias stood up and peeked over the rim of rock. From that height he could survey the whole plain below. A fire still burned on a rise from the same direction that the screams had come from. He could hear nothing now, nor discern any movement. Reaching out with his lumen, he could feel no movement of life directly below them.

"It looks clear right now," he said, dropping back down. He let go of the whisper but still spoke low. "I guess one or two of us can go back for the rest of the supplies. Better that we stay here for the night."

The rest nodded their agreement. Silas reached down to the rock floor and picked up a bleached skull. A beak curved down from the head, as white as the full moon. He turned over the tiny skull in his hand, bewildered.

"It's a sparrowhawk," Thoran told him. "This used to be called Sparrowhawk Mountain, even though it's no more than a hill. The soil was always thin here because it's so rocky. Scrub oaks were about all that could grow. But the rest of the land is flat, so the sparrowhawks would gather here with the perfect view of the entire plain. No one has seen a falcon here in a very long time. You might be holding the last one."

Silas peered at the skull with renewed consideration. It suddenly seemed more tragic now, the last vestige of a great race. Closing his hand around it, Silas placed it in his pocket.

Thoran and Bannus returned to camp to gather the rest of the supplies. Upon returning, Bannus found another depression on the opposite side of the mountain and built a fire there. He kept it low, but with just enough heat to cook the rest of the hams.

"I'll be damned if I miss out on wood-cooked meat," he said, determined to enjoy the rare delicacy no matter what the threat.

The others huddled in the depression and tried to sleep. None slept well. Every time Elias closed his eyes and began to nod off he would hear distant sounds echo through the usually still night. Sometimes a drum would pound. Sometimes a scream would rend the night. He would start awake, and find it quiet and dark. It wasn't until he gave up on sleep, when the fire had burned down to simmering, red coals, that Elias finally dozed off.

Chapter Ten
The Galvin Tor

The next morning the group decided to investigate the sounds from the night before. At first, Elias insisted only the men go check the area over.

"We'll check out what was going on," Elias told Kyrie. "You and Silas go on wherever you are heading. We'll take care of whatever we find. It will be safer this way. Just get as far away as you can."

"Like hell we will," Kyrie immediately protested. "You don't know what it is or where they went. For all you know they could be going in the same direction as us."

Elias couldn't argue with the logic. He certainly couldn't argue with the fear he saw in her eyes. Especially considering her usual bravado - her willingness to expose her son to danger and hunger in the service of her cause - the panic that gripped her was potently unsettling. They all seemed to sense an unusual danger in whatever had happened on the distant hill.

A part of Elias felt relieved that she was going further with them, if only a short ways. He couldn't figure out if it was Kyrie or the boy he wanted around. Maybe even both. There was something about their company, despite how strange and hostile it was, that made him feel more normal, more...complete perhaps. The awful ache of emptiness that gnawed at him ever since he had woken up in the Enclave had filled up somewhat ever since he had begun to travel with Kyrie and her son. Even the thought of them separating now made him anxious. It was ridiculous he knew, but it was there all the same.

"Okay, maybe it will be safer if we stick together for now," was all he voiced aloud. "But you have to do what I tell you if it looks like it's going to get dangerous."

Kyrie nodded her agreement with a clenched jaw. Even afraid, Elias knew that had to hurt.

Traveling across the hot sands in broad daylight, Elias found it hard to imagine that what he had heard the night before was real. Morning had cast that almost supernatural quality over him. It made all the fears of night seem foolish and childlike.

At least it started out that way.

Ahead, from where the sounds of drums and screams had echoed, the land rose in a small hill. They could hear the ominous pounding of the drums in their ears, primal and vicious. Screams of pain and terror echoed through their heads, the memory giving them almost as much terror as the real event.

"You feel anything?" Bannus asked when they approached the foot of the tor.

Elias started to shake his head, then stopped. There was something he could feel, but couldn't say what exactly. A latent power thrummed beneath the hill, something ancient and powerful. It had the feel of a sacred place, a place used to increase the power of magic.

Beneath the power a chill followed. Something made him cold, even as the morning sun bore down on him and sweat trickled down his back. It wasn't part of the hill, but a residue that surrounded it. Something clung to the place that left an invisible, cold mist, like a remnant of evil that hovered in the wake of something more terrible.

"Nothing alive," Elias answered.

As they walked under the shadow of the hill, the chill stretched across Elias's skin. His sweat grew cold and he shivered. Looking at the faces around him, he could see they felt at least some of what he could sense. Even Bannus appeared uneasy, his eyes cutting around, looking for a threat he couldn't see.

Silas looked especially afraid. The blood had drained from his face. He looked pale and suddenly thin, almost frail. Instinctively, he had reached out and taken his mother's hand. Kyrie grabbed the hand tight and pulled her son close.

The path that wound around the hill had been eroded to a thin strip of land. They had to walk up single file, carefully treading the worn earth, hugging the hill as they went. In some places, the way had crumbled completely away, enough to require a long step to traverse the gap.

As they neared the top, Bannus unsheathed his sword and pressed his back to the mound of earth. He signaled for the others to wait and crept forward until he could reach his hand up to the top of the hill. In one, quick motion he pulled himself up then crawled to the shelter of a gray rock. He first peaked out cautiously, then more boldly, and gave a longer look.

"By all the sweaty balls of hell," he cursed.

"What is it?" Elias whispered up. "Is it safe?"

Bannus didn't answer. His eyes moved back and forth, taking in the scene. Something had arrested his attention, made the usually stalwart warrior go pale and silent.

"Bannus," Elias whispered again.

"No one up here," Bannus answered without looking at Elias. "At least no one alive."

Elias followed, moving out of the shadow of the hill. He pulled himself onto the flat surface and had to squint in the glare of the bright light. Shielding his eyes from the piercing sun he surveyed the top of the hill. Behind him, he could hear Thoran file past, and distantly perceived Kyrie and Silas follow. He tried to reach out a hand, to keep Silas from looking at what lay sprawled atop the hill. But he hardly felt his hand, and it hung out behind him, forgotten.

A wave of disorientation washed over Elias. He knew what he was looking at. It was all within the realm of comprehension. There was nothing impossible or in violation of the laws of nature. Still, he couldn't comprehend. It was all wrong.

He could tell immediately that the hill was indeed a place of power. Standing stones were arranged in a circular pattern. Some of them had fallen, others were leaning half over. Oghams and simple figures were drawn upon some of the stone faces, whorls and ancient marks of magic.

A pulse went through Elias as he stepped further onto the hilltop. He felt his own power sharpen, his preternatural senses blaze alive. And with it came the chill of wrongness that lingered over the place, that emanated from the tor.

Kyrie drew in a breath of shock as she saw. She pulled Silas near to her, trying to shelter him with her presence.

"What is this?" she managed to whisper.

Bodies littered the hill of standing stones. Human figures splayed out grotesquely, limbs twisted in unnatural positions, faces and eyes wide in silent terror. Everywhere the eye rested, blood and gore and slaughtered human figures lay strewn about.

The bodies, though thoroughly abused, had been laid out ritualistically. Each one had been staked with arms and legs splayed out. They were sliced open from throat to navel. The chest cavity had been pulled open and the interior exposed. Slashes and gouges marked the arms and legs. Some of the arms had been broken completely, bending in impossible angles. From the looks of pain and terror frozen on the faces, it appeared as if all the torture had transpired while the victims were still alive.

The screams made sense now. The sounds of pure terror that had ripped through the night now merged with the awful figures littered on the hilltop. It made sense. In all the insanity of the scene before them, the screams they remembered were the only bit of sanity in it all. The screams were a cry for decency and goodness, the last protest against whatever had gone mad in the world.

"Who would do something like this?" Kyrie found her voice to ask.

"The same people who would burn perfectly good food," Elias answered. Pieces of the puzzle began to settle into place. The answer hovered just on the edge of his consciousness.

Bannus toed the corpse of a young girl, thin and starved, but still in the bloom of youth. What looked like bite marks rose purple and swollen on her cheek. Her dress was old and worn, with a small patch of pink flowers embroidered on the hem. Blood and dust covered the dress now, torn open by a jagged knife. Someone had cared for it once, though. Someone had enough hope in life to mark the humble dress with a touch of beauty. Even Bannus seemed touched by it. The expression on his face was one Elias had never seen there before, a sadness unfamiliar to the normally brutish man.

"The Galvin Tor, a place of legend," Thoran intoned without the accusation and crassness that usually accompanied his tirades about the past. "The standing stones were erected sometime before the memory of history. It is one of the twelve places of power built by the ancients. With knowledge still unknown today they constructed these tors to magnify the power of magic. Today, they go largely unused because they are misunderstood and their capacity to produce wildly unpredictable results. It has been said that if a man sleeps on this particular tor with a piece of his afterbirth, he will have a vision of his destiny. Some see glory. Some see death. Some go mad."

No one acknowledged his words. Each was lost in his own thoughts, reeled by the horror in front of them.

Silas didn't even look at the bodies on the tor. He stood by the edge of the hill, by one of the stones, his finger tracing a figure drawn in the rock.

Elias walked over to the boy with the idea of offering some word of consolation. He couldn't imagine what that word could be. The boy was obviously coping as best as he knew how – to ignore the carnage at his feet and trace a simple figure drawn in the rock, something put there before the memory of any man alive.

As Elias stood over him he looked at the figure Silas was tracing, and he finally understood everything. The drawing wasn't ancient. It was only as old as the night before.

"Prophets of Thanatos," Elias announced as he recognized the red crescent moon drawn in the blood of a sacrifice to the god of death.

Kyrie looked sharply at Elias. She opened her mouth to say something, but shook her head instead. Bannus took the announcement little better. His features did not waver but Elias thought he could see the guard's face pale.

"How many are there?" Kyrie asked. Her eyes darted to the wide plain beyond the tor. Nothing could be seen except clouds of dust being stirred by hot winds.

Elias shook his head. It was impossible to tell how many of the Prophets were wandering the wilds. All told, they counted eighteen bodies on the tor, and including the drummers it suggested a fairly large number. Especially considering the broken defenses of the trading post, no great feat, but requiring some considerable numbers. All together it suggested a large branch of the cult.

Running numbers in his head, Elias calculated how many they could reasonably handle. Bannus could face down half a dozen. If they were weak, then maybe a full twelve. Elias felt confident in being able to disable maybe ten. What about Thoran? He seemed capable, but couldn't handle more than three or four probably. Under no circumstance could they rely on Kyrie. She was feisty, but Elias counted her as protection for Silas.

Under best conditions, the group could defend themselves against no more than twenty-five, Elias decided. And that was being extremely generous. The cult that was roaming nearby could easily be that large. Or larger. And they were known to fight with that strength and courage peculiar to mad men and zealots. Fear was no deterrent. All of them would fight to the death. Even worse, they would enjoy doing so.

Elias ran scenarios through his mind. He could see the mad prophets throwing themselves wildly at the group with no care for injury or death. It was told that they welcomed death. From a distance, his magic would seriously weaken their numbers. But if they closed in he couldn't see how they would get out alive.

Thinking about the situation tied his gut in knots. From the faces of the others, as they surveyed the desiccated corpses on the hill, Elias could tell they felt the same way. Ever since he announced who was responsible, and the realization settled in, a new fear took over them.

"Bloody perfect," Bannus spat. He paced the tor nervously.

"How many do you think there are?" Elias asked, probing the fighters experience.

"Can't tell," Bannus shook his head. "A lot of bodies up here. Can't imagine they would die willingly. Made lots of noise last night. I say a few dozen."

Elias nodded numbly in agreement.

"Thirty," Thoran answered flatly. His tone carried a mark of confidence.

"How can you tell?" Elias asked, curious to know how he had arrived at that number.

"This was a ritual," he told them. "It's called the Ritual of the Gates. See how they opened up the chest cavity? They do it in hopes of making a gateway that Thanatos can step through. When a person dies they move from the world of the living to the world of the dead. If the prophets do things right, or so they believe, it should be possible to hold the door open as the soul slips away. And if you get enough people dying at the same time, you can make the gate big enough for a god to use. I imagine they came here to magnify that power. We can be thankful their theory was less than sound."

Elias nodded thoughtfully. "Okay. What does that have to do with thirty? How do you know there were thirty of them?"

"Thirty is the sacred number of the Prophets," Thoran replied. "Any special ritual they perform is done with thirty members."

"Why thirty?" Silas asked, his back still turned away from the dead bodies, his attention fixed on the standing stones.

"The moon," Thoran explained. "The moon is the mistress of Thanatos, his symbol. Thirty days to the cycle of the moon. Thirty Prophets of Thanatos for all the important rituals. There's at least thirty of them running around out there. And they can't be more than half a day from us."

Second Interlude
The Prophets of Thanatos

The two guards regarded the body at their feet with indecision. The taller of the two poked it with his foot. The arm flopped out, leaving the hand open, but otherwise didn't respond.

The smaller guard, noticing something about the wrist, stooped down for a better look. Angling for some of the torchlight behind him, he turned the hand towards his eyes and squinted in the feeble light. A slash ran down the wrist with streaks of blood caked down the arm. A jagged piece of metal, also stained with blood, still lay clutched in the other hand.

The guard shook his head and stood up. He peered down the dark alley as a breeze carrying salt water and the stink of refuse grazed by him. He couldn't see anything past the few, dark feet in front of him. The sounds of water lapping at the foot of the wharf sounded nearby. The alley must back up to the docks, he figured.

"See anything?" the tall guard asked, not bothering to look himself.

The smaller man shook his head. He adjusted the cudgel in his hands, running his finger absently along the metal studs that glared out of the thick end.

"Looks like he did it to himself," he said, pointing down at the wrist wounds with the club. "Don't know why he would do something like that."

The taller guard, somewhat older by his weathered look, pointed to the figure drawn on the alley wall. A crescent moon, painted in blood, dried on the dirty stone. Crimson streaks dripped down from the crude artwork.

"Prophets," he said by way of explanation.

"Who are they?" the younger, smaller guard asked.

The taller man shook his head. He looked both ways down the cobbled streets, then squinted into the alley for good measure.

"Not out here," he answered. "Let's talk about this somewhere else."

He shivered as an unexpected chill passed over him. Looking around again, as if expecting somebody, he motioned for the younger man to follow.

The two guards hurried through the deserted night streets to the dockside pub with no placard or visible name written on its weathered, wooden planks. They knew it as Buck's place. And only those who already knew of it would want to go there.

Inside, Buck's was mostly dark. A few figures huddled by the bar. One old man lazily drank at a table by himself. Thin light from oil lamps sputtered weakly, barely making shadows of the half-dozen men inside.

The older guard slumped down at an empty table and motioned for the barkeep. His companion took the chair opposite, laying his cudgel on the table.

"So what was up with that?" the younger one asked. "What did that moon mean?"

"They call themselves Prophets of Thanatos," the older guard said with a shake of his head. "They're crazy. You don't want to cross them. Trust me."

"Prophets?" the barkeep asked with a voice as greasy as his hair as he slammed down two mugs of ale. "Have the prophets shown up here?"

"Just one," the guard corrected. "Don't go getting tied up in knots and telling everybody a coven has arrived."

"Where there's one there's more," the barkeep said with a shake of his head, as if that decided the matter. "Everything's goin' to hell."

"Just one," the guard reiterated, focusing the comment on his younger companion, and not at the barkeep shuffling back to the bar.

"Who are they?" the younger guard asked. "Are they a cult or something."

"The worst kind," the older man said. He took a deep drink and wiped foam from his lips.

He leaned in across the table and lowered his voice.

"From what I've heard they are branch of magi that went mad," he tried to say in a low voice though his voice echoed in the quiet room.

The old man at the table by himself looked up from his drink.

"They say they were involved in dark magic," the older guard continued. "Death magic. There were thirteen of them. One night they sacrificed a virgin to Thanatos, the god of Death. They had been trying to summon him for days, to no effect. This time, it worked. Thanatos rose up from the pit, right in front of them. And he stared at each of them, one after another, with his empty eye. And each one of the magi saw the true face of death. And they saw their own death."

"What happened?" the younger one asked. His mug of beer was lifted halfway to his mouth, forgotten under the spell of the story.

"They went mad. One look into the eye of death and they all fell insane. So they started this cult. The leader named himself Al-Azuhr. They worship death. Every month one of them has to kill himself as a sacrifice to Thanatos."

"You got to be fooling me," the younger man said. "Why do they have to kill themselves?"

"It's a sacrifice, I told you. And what's more." The older guard leaned in even closer. "It's this summoning of death that started the Blight. Just think about it. Why is the whole land dying? It's because Thanatos himself has been summoned and he walks the earth, destroying the crops and the forest and everything else."

"Bah," a gravely voice sounded from the old man. He waved a dismissive hand towards the two guards.

"Bunch of trash," he said. "You don't know shit from silver. That ain't how the prophets got started."

"Is too," the guard countered. "I heard from a damn reliable source."

"Who?"

"Buddy of mine used to captain Count Vega's home guard. Sitting right with the count when some high ranking Enclave men came in to tell the Count about it. Heard it with his own ears."

"He's spinning stories to you, boy," the old man cackled.

"What do you know old timer?"

"I'll tell you what I know." The old man's eyes got wide in the dim light. He pointed a bony finger at the two guards.

"I heard this from a magi. A real magi. And I heard it with my own ears. It was demons, I tell you. And it started with a group of rebels, fleeing Covenant as it burned. They were surrounded, just a few of 'em. Haytham Sandlapper himself was with 'em. They got chased all the way to the Calaban. And as they were trapped Haytham cuts himself and summons demons with his blood to save them.

"And save them they did. But the demons took over the body of Haytham and his men. Haytham renames himself Al-Azuhr, and they are the ones that started the cult. Now they find people by searching out the poorest and hungriest of the lot. They promise all their troubles will be over if they let the demons into their bodies. That's all the cult is, ya see. They're all demon possessed men."

"If that's so then why do they all kill themselves?" the older guard asked.

"They do it when they're first possessed. Before the demon has fully taken over. Sudden remorse comes over 'em, and in a last desperate act they take their own lives."

"You've been drinking too much of the rot gut they serve in here," a third voice chimed in from the bar. "It's pickled your brain."

Neither the guards or the old man could see this third speaker's face. One of the oil lamps burned right behind him, casting his whole figure in darkness. All they could tell was that he had turned to face them, and he didn't sound like he belonged. Something about his voice carried a highborn tone to it.

"Oh yeah, I suppose you know a thing or two there," the old man challenged. "Who are you? The Lord Prefect himself I suppose? What do you know?"

"I know the Prophets weren't started by demons or magi," the man at the bar said.

"How was they started, then?"

"Just a man, though one that was just mad enough to be crazy, and sane enough that he could convince others of what he believed."

"I never heard such nonsense," the old man huffed with a dismissive wave. "What kind of man makes a cult out of death?"

"His name was Loren Fulham," the man at the bar continued quietly. If he seemed bothered by the scepticism his voice didn't betray it. Instead, the level way he delivered his story made the account all the more chilling.

"He's the illegitimate son of Baron Geis. Ever since he was a boy he had the falling sickness. Sometimes they would give him visions as well. One night, when he had fallen to a particularly vicious tremor he awoke with one, clear thought in his head. If Thanatos, the god of death, was indeed one of the gods, and if the world was dying, then would that not make this the Age of Thanatos? As he tells it, of course, it's a vision, but the result is the same. This is the Age of Death. The world runs in cycles, each of the four gods enjoying their dawn, and then a twilight. The cycle, you see, is coming to an end and there is nothing we can do about it.

"So he gave himself the name Al-Azuhr, declaring himself a prophet of the death god. He claims that Thanatos gave him the name, but it actually came from a book of old, Sarmas scriptures. Al-Azuhr is the name of one of the destroying angels of heaven. He began to preach his message, and in this cesspool of a world, it made a lot of sense. We don't need to fight death, he said. Embrace it. Welcome it. Hasten it. Become both the harbingers and the catalysts. The quicker we bring Thanatos into his reign, the quicker this will all be over."

131

An eery silence settled over the bar after this third man fell silent. The older guard shifted uncomfortably in his chair, as if he wanted to say something, but couldn't think of how to respond. Finally, the younger guard spoke up.

"How did you find this out?" he asked with a tone of deference in his voice.

The shadowed figure didn't answer at first. They could see him taking a drink, deliberating whether not to speak.

"I used to be one of them," he finally answered.

The older guard shuddered again. His younger companion looked to him, unsure of how to act after such an admission. The silence deepened and the lamps seemed to grow darker.

"Hah!" the old man cried out, banging the table and breaking the spell. "I can tell that ain't true cause no one is ever allowed out of the Prophets. At least not alive. That's a fact everybody knows."

The older guard nodded his agreement and took a long drink to the sentiment. He looked over at the man at the bar, still in shadow, who made no effort to defend his story. After a moment, he turned his back to them again.

Without noticing, the older guard breathed out a sigh of relief. He peered down into his cup, no longer in the mood to tell stories.

Part II

Chapter Eleven
One Morning at Montreux

Morning found Eustace earlier than usual. He blinked at the bright stab of sunlight that pounded relentlessly into his eyes, making his head ache even worse. He picked that same tender head up and looked around the room. Surmising it was much too early for a decent man's rising, Eustace groaned and dropped his head back on the pile of soft, downy pillows.

It was a truly royal bed that Eustace lounged in, though he was far from royalty. Perhaps if he were royalty, or at least highborn, he could fall right back asleep. But with the blood of workingmen in his veins he obeyed an almost irresistible impulse, bred by centuries of farmers waking up with the dawn, to rise with the first touch of light.

Groaning, Eustace turned over in the voluptuous bed, his body tangling in the mound of silk sheets, fine cotton blankets, and the impossibly soft mattress he had recessed in. Somewhere he tangled with another body and wondered which one the foot belong to. The foot withdrew as a female groan sounded from inside the sheets. He turned the other way and felt another body buried there too. This one didn't even flinch.

Eustace smiled as memories from the night before came back to him. Even with the tender head it was well worth it. He just wished he could sleep it off. Damn if he knew how these women could sleep as much as they did.

Giving in to the impulse of the morning, Eustace swung his feet to the floor and sat up in bed. That stab of light jabbed into his eye again, sending a crack of pain to his head. He shielded his eyes and looked toward the window, wondering how his sleep could have been so rudely interrupted.

He squinted and saw the culprit. On the thick and richly designed curtains a slit drew up the surface allowing the morning light to peek through. He must not have drawn them all the way last night. And the open slit was in just the right place for the morning sun to creep in. And he must have been laying in just the right spot for that thin sliver of light to hit his face.

Eustace cocked his head and looked more intently at the curtain. Did this mean something? Was the coincidence incidental or was something important going to happen today? Was he woken up for a reason?

At the Enclave the Masters would certainly scoff at such a notion. Maybe he would have too as a student. He was certainly arrogant enough then. Today he knew more, more than he wanted to know.

Or maybe he knew less. His mother was the one to look for signs everywhere. She puzzled endlessly over every little event that seemed odd or out of place. A broken plate, a simple accident, slow boiling water, a cracked wheel on the wagon; any of these seemingly incongruous events were enough to have her wondering what fate might be cooking up for them that day. It was an attitude considered ignorant by the more educated.

But maybe she was the one that knew more. Eustace certainly was inclined to believe that the older he got. Maybe some of that old wisdom, for all its vague and uncertain nature, had a better grasp on the world than all the precise knowledge of the magi and wise men of their age. Especially when it came to the unknown workings of the world, it seemed a lot of the old wisdom had a better grasp on what was really going on.

"Well at least we managed to screw the whole place up pretty good," Eustace muttered cynically. "At least we're better at that."

Forcing himself out of bed, Eustace felt around for his pants and pulled on the loose-fitting and thin material. A similar shirt went over his head which he didn't bother to lace up. He thought about his gray robe for a second, then opted against it. Maybe fate wanted him up early this morning, but he didn't have to dress up for it.

What he would do was try to make himself feel better. Maybe a touch of that elixir Jax taught him how to make. He usually felt guilty for magically repairing a hangover, but today it was for fate.

A bottle spun off of his foot as he stumbled around the semi-dark room. He cursed the toe that shot up in pain, and then his head as the bottle clanged into another one. Two bottles? It must've been a really good night. He tried to remember the occasion for such excess, and told himself to be careful of his supply. As vast as it was today, it wouldn't last forever.

Eustace made his way across the large and ornate room. No matter how long he lived here, he still felt like an intruder. Carved chairs, plush rugs, antique furniture, stained-glass and gold filigree on almost everything always reminded him he didn't belong. Any day now he expected the Prince to return and reclaim his palace. He would probably have to fumigate out the common stench.

Eustace laughed at the notion, certain many of the nobility felt exactly that way. Part of him even wished he could tell the Prince himself all he had done in one of the royal beds. Just to see the look on his haughty face would be worth it. Not that there was any chance of that happening now. Eustace couldn't imagine any reason why the Prince would want to return this far inland.

In the half-dark Eustace sifted through the drawers of an ornate, mahogany desk. He pushed through a jumble of empty vials until he found the dark blue bottle.

"My little blue angel," he said with a smile and kissed the glass.

Wasting no time he tipped the bottle back, taking a generous sip, but no more of the tangy liquid then he had to. He held it up and shook it around. Just enough for one more dose, he thought, and put it back into the drawer.

Eustace fell back onto the bed with his legs still on the floor. With arms stretched wide he caressed the soft sheets, reveling in their luxury. His hands met a back curled in sleep. He slipped his fingers under the sheets and enjoyed the touch of the smooth flesh. Rousing thoughts stirred in his mind, and if the back and legs he rubbed would stir in the least, show any sign of wakefulness, he might act on those thoughts. But the girl slept with no sign of waking, so he stifled the arousal lest it become uncomfortable to resist.

Returning his hand to the cool sheets, he focused instead on the elixir running through him. With the concentration trained by years at the Enclave, Eustace focused and found his lumen. The fine point of light searched until it met with the potion running through his veins, the one called Blue Angel. Eustace touched it and could feel every drop that was quickly infusing into his bloodstream.

No matter how often he practiced it, at times like this Eustace couldn't help but be awed by the mystery and power of magic. By principles still mostly not understood, Eustace used his lumen to release the latent potential that had been charged into the elixir, also by the power of magic.

A cool glow suffused through his veins. His entire body felt a strange, deep chill, resembling cold. The taste of mint filled his mouth and nose, and even his eyes so that they watered with the sensation.

The effect was almost immediate. His headache disappeared. His exhaustion and even that touch of nausea vanished under the spread of cool comfort. Eustace smiled and enjoyed the return of good feeling. For a moment, he entertained the notion that this is what it must feel like to be royalty.

* * *

Eustace took his breakfast on the balcony. If anything was able to spoil the feelings of royalty, it was this. No one could imagine himself anyone important with what he had to eat for breakfast while he had to look out at the dead world beneath him.

Often Eustace would sit on the balcony and imagine what the view was like before the Blight. Green, rolling hills, nearby forests, a garden below with a gurgling fountain must have been the sight the royal family enjoyed.

Now, the only thing that remained was the fountain. It had been bleached white and filled with sand. The half nude woman tipping out a jug baked in the heat of the endless desert. Sand and hard-packed gray and orange earth were the only sights he enjoyed on the balcony.

A set of figures appeared on the horizon. He hadn't seen them at first, and now they looked just a few hundred yards away. Refugees, he figured, by the way they walked. Desperation and fear harried their steps, burdened also by weariness. It was too common a sight.

Eustace squinted and could make out five figures in all. One was unusually large, another very small, and another looked decidedly female. Quite a fetching figure she had on her as well, if Eustace judged things right. And in situations like this, Eustace always judged them right. He gave her a more careful look, wondering if there were any way he could talk the Squire into letting her stay.

There was no way. Orders were quite strict at the palace. No refugees. They had turned away dozens already. It was by far the worst part about being there, giving no help, no aid, nothing but a sympathetic nod to the desperate and pleading people that begged for any kind of help.

Here, at the Palace of Montreux, they got nothing. Eustace understood all too well why this had to be. Their purpose was too precise, their rations too exactly doled out to allow for any of the starving multitude. He consoled himself with the thought that they might be doing a greater good. And if they took in refugees, that purpose would never materialize.

A sinking feeling in Eustace's gut reminded him that even with the strict way the Commission was run, their vaunted purpose was still not going to materialize. With a sigh, Eustace turned away from the refugees and focused on his meager breakfast and the job at hand. Two biscuits, honey, and a small bite of salted meat was all he had, but he had it every morning.

Breakfast always made him think of the job at hand. His pitiful meal was just like the pitiful crop they would be harvesting soon. Why he thought he could ever accomplish the task with the resources given him he didn't know. Except he did know. When the Squire approached him, Eustace was desperate. He would've volunteered to capture the moon if he had been asked.

All he could do now was make the best of it. In his mind he tried to organize his resources, plan for the day ahead and where they would best be served. Success was seeming a more distant possibility, but maybe they could come close.

His resources were the main problem. There was himself, a barely competent assistant, and three boys who had no business being raised to acolyte much less graduating. Another sign of the times, Eustace figured with a deeper sigh than before.

The corn was his second problem. It made sense to grow it at first. No crop responded better to magic than corn. The problem was that it required a subtlety to grow. Unlike wheat or barley that needed only pure power, corn thrived on a delicate touch. If done right, the yield was amazing. If done wrong, you get a field of useless, wilting stalks.

What Eustace had was two hundred acres of wilting stalks. And no matter how he arranged things, he couldn't imagine how to get it to work.

Another dry biscuit dipped in honey popped into Eustace's mouth as he considered his options. As he saw it, getting all two hundred acres to harvest was all but impossible. That much was obvious. Trying to convince the Squire was another matter altogether. Long ago they should have abandoned one of the fields and focused on the remaining two. He could allocate the three younger magi to the smaller west field while he and Anton took over the east. Or would it be better to split those up and have he and Anton work independently with the younger magi?

That still left a lot to cover. Eustace feared the situation may already be out of hand. But to abandon two of the fields wouldn't sit well with the King. Would that even cover his cost? And that still didn't touch the groves on the palace ground. The expectations for Montreux, no doubt, included considerable yield there also.

Eustace pushed the matter of the palace grounds out of his mind. They would almost certainly get something from those, a few luxury items perhaps. Those could go a long way in pleasing a king. The corn was his main problem.

The damned corn.

Once again, Eustace cursed himself for joining the Commission. Even if he had little choice, there had to be a better option besides complete failure. The King may even be angry enough to kick him out of Celicia for good. That option definitely didn't sound right.

With a shrug, Eustace sat back and tried to enjoy the morning. He plucked up the little bit of sausage, savoring the rare treat. He could think about his strategy later. The Squire was returning in the afternoon, maybe he would bring with him some good fortune.

Below him he heard voices outside the main entrance of the palace. The refugees must have made it to the house. He had become so engrossed in his thoughts that he didn't even notice their approach.

Although he couldn't make out any of the words being spoken, he could tell by the escalating tone what was transpiring. Lieutenant Omar's voice rose up, no doubt insisting on their inability to help. A plea rose up in a female voice, begging for a bit of human decency. The Lieutenant replied, firm and insistent, holding his ground and stealing himself against the impulse for that normal human decency, ignoring the instinct to mercy. Such things did not belong in this world.

Another protest from the refugees came up. This time a male voice that carried a threat laced in his words. Omar responded with more steel. Did he also detect of note of fear in the Lieutenant? These must be powerful people. But even that didn't matter.

Then another voice rose up and shattered the stillness of the morning.

Eustace jumped in surprise, banging his leg on the edge of the table. He only vaguely noted the stab of pain. In this other voice, he could hear power lifting the words up, giving them extra force.

"You will regret not allowing us to shelter!" the voice challenged from below.

But it was neither the volume of the voice or the words that shook Eustace with alarm. It was the magic.

A magi was down there, and by the force emanating from the suggestion he had cast, he was quite powerful. Extremely powerful. If Eustace didn't hurry the poor lieutenant would be quickly overwhelmed – an amazing feat in itself. It was the rare and potent magi who could overcome the resistance of a will on his guard.

Eustace wondered even with his help if he could resist that level of magic. The influence was staggering. The tendrils of the command even crept into Eustace. He could feel the forceful presence tentacle into his mind and prod him with suggestion.

"Let us in," it said. "Let us in."

Realization dawned on Eustace and he immediately thought of the little sliver of light that had woken him up that morning. A curtain not closed all the way, his head in just the right spot, and now here he was, awake much earlier than normal to hear the extraordinary exchange below him.

Eustace thought he could hear the engines of fate grinding in the heavens above. He felt a shift in destiny, and the movement of the world. Something huge was happening right here under him, something so powerful he felt humble and swept away by the tide of power. He felt as if he had gotten a glimpse behind the curtain that separated the secret workings of the world from the normal, waking lives of man. Such a thing was not a sight for mortals to behold.

There was only one magi powerful enough to cast a suggestion that strong.

With trembling hands Eustace grabbed the rail of the balcony and peeked over the edge. He decided immediately that fate indeed was working today.

There below him, stood Elias Whitsun.

Exhaustion pressed in on Elias. The sun, miles of travel, the harried pace they had set; all had taken a toll on him. And if this wasn't enough, the anxiety of knowing the danger that could very well be hunting them over the next rise combined with his lack of sleep made him feel like an empty sack of flesh.

Their hearts all lifted when they saw the palace from afar. Probably abandoned, they all figured, but it was refuge all the same. When they saw movement and signs of occupation, their relief was palpable. It was civilization, people. It was refuge from the madness.

"You don't understand," Elias pressed the bullheaded guard. "At least thirty Prophets are in the wilderness out there, hunting for anything alive."

The guard pressed his lips together and wiped sweat from his eyes. It was more than the heat that was getting to him. Powerful suggestion hammered at his resolve though he had no idea what was making him feel so nervous and uncertain.

Elias marveled at that same resolve. The suggestion he was casting was powerful, though a far cry from what he was capable of. Waking up every hour for the past three days to scan for life had worn him down considerably. Still, this guard was stubborn.

His orders had to be strict for such resistance, Elias surmised. When the subject truly believed he had no alternative, suggestion became almost impossible to succeed. Considering his level of resistance, this one must have received implacable orders from pretty high up.

"I'm sorry," the guard shook his head. "I can't help you. No one is allowed on the grounds."

"You must help us," Elias pushed again, prodding as hard as he thought wise, careful not to expend his dwindling reserves of power. By the looks of things, he might need them soon.

The guard's lip trembled as he struggled with the forces raging inside him. He wiped his eyes again and then ran the same hand through his hair. A groan escaped from his lips as he grabbed a handful of hair and tugged hard on it.

"Please. I can't help you," the guard croaked. Tears began to pool in his bloodshot eyes. A crazed look came over his face.

"Please, don't be mad," he pled. "Please. I can't. I can't. I can't."

Pity quickly replaced Elias's anger. The poor man was about to fall into madness. His orders, which must truly go high up, were butting up against a powerful impulse planted there by Elias. The strain was about to break him.

Cursing his lack of resolve, Elias released the suggestion. The result was immediate. All at once, the tension came out of the guard. His shoulders straightened and the strain fell off his face. He looked curiously at the group of refugees, as if seeing them for the first time.

"I'm sorry," he said with more force. "No outsiders allowed."

The guard eyed Bannus suspiciously. His hand moved carefully to the handle of his sword. A clear, but cautious move.

Out of the corner of his eye, Elias saw Bannus straighten up behind him. He hoped the big man would keep his temper and not get them all killed. Three more guards moved cautiously closer, their eyes fixed on Bannus.

A long, tense silence ensued. Both sides regarded each other with indecision. Neither knew what to do next.

Elias opened his mouth to make one more plea. But before a word came out, the doors of the palace flew open and a haggard figure came charging out. A hand was held up over the face to block out the glare of the light, but Elias recognized him immediately.

"I've either gone mad or that's Elias Whitsun standing in front of my palace," the newcomer exclaimed grandly. The gesture was made more ridiculous by the fact that he was dressed in thin pants and shirt.

"You've always been one for embellishment," Elias answered, trying to hide the relief in his voice.

"Oh, here and there," Eustace answered, allowing the glimmer of a smile to pass across his face.

Eustace threw a congenial arm around the guard who stood his ground.

"This, my brave Lieutenant, is the great and powerful Elias Whitsun," he nodded in Elias's direction.

"They're just refugees," the guard insisted. "Friends or not, you know the rules. No one allowed in the Commission."

"Ah, that's where you're wrong Lieutenant," Eustace said as he took his arm away and went to stand in front of Elias.

"This is not my friend. This is our salvation."

Chapter Twelve
Squire Montford

A brief and intense argument ensued between Eustace and the Lieutenant. The magician must have wielded considerable influence, because after a short exchange he convinced the reluctant guard.

"One day, Omar, that's all I want," Eustace insisted. "The Squire returns tonight and I will take up the matter with him personally. Trust me on this. He will not be pleased if you allow this opportunity to slip by."

The stubborn Omar relented and Elias and his band of refugees were allowed into the grounds of Montreux, one-time palace of the Prince of Celicia. Like most of the interior, Montreux had been abandoned by her royal occupants when the flight to the seas ensued.

Even abandoned, the palace was massive and impressive. Elias felt the cool of the shaded foyer hit him with gratitude. As his eyes adjusted to the dark, he took in the marble all around him.

The floor had been decorated with a mosaic depicting the gods clothed in celestial glory. Sophia stared at them from the floor, serene with light streaming from her head. Gaia stood next to her, dressed in more humble greens and emanating an earthier beauty. Between them stood the male gods: the powerful and stentorian Dunamis, his harsh gaze piercing any passerby, and the dark Thanatos, mostly obscured by a cloak of dark violet.

Flecks of color filled the vast space, filtered through the skylight that soared above them. A grand staircase curled in semicircles to a second floor balcony nearly thirty feet high. Awe was the emotion immediately inspired in Elias. Though just behind that initial reaction came a haunting sense of emptiness. As great as the palace seemed, it felt bereft, devoid. The quiet of the place struck Elias as profoundly as it's grandeur.

"Welcome to my humble home," Eustace welcomed grandly, his arms spread wide. His voice echoed and bounded off the marble walls.

"So are you squatting or do you have some legitimate claim to this place?" Elias ribbed, trying to echo Eustace's humorous mood despite his exhaustion.

"Legitimately, of course," Eustace answered, with mock offense. "Not like the Prince would know anyway if I weren't.

"No, this is the latest brainchild to be hatched from the Kingdom of

Celicia in the mighty mind that sits on the throne. It's an experiment really. We call it the Interior Food Commission. It's run by Squire Montford, an attempt to get something to grow here in this blasted wasteland."

"Not quite original is it?" Thoran piped in, his sarcasm capable of matching Eustace's own. "Isn't that what most of the world has given up on? What makes this different?"

Eustace eyed Thoran up and down for a silent moment. Uncertainty stretched over his awkward face, as if deciding what to do. A forced smile quickly replaced it.

"You don't want to stand here discussing strategy," he said. "A bunch of boring magician stuff anyway. No, let's get you to some rooms, let you wash the dust of the road off. Besides, you all look exhausted. Let's talk over dinner."

* * *

Their rooms looked every bit like those reserved for honored and distinguished guests of the Prince. No one in the group had experienced such luxury.

"No shortage of space here," Eustace informed them as he showed them each to a private room.

Elias was given, by all appearances, the stag room. Three trophies hung on the walls, while horns decorated the posterns of a large bed. On the far wall a tapestry depicting a hunt hung opposite a balcony window overlooking the interior grounds of the palace. Hunting spears crossed each other over the empty fireplace.

Minutes later a servant entered and poured water for a bath.

"The Sire instructed not to heat your water," the servant said sheepishly with a bow.

Elias nodded and dismissed the servant. He would've appreciated the hot water in his tired condition, but respected Eustace's intentions. Old traditions die hard.

Not wanting to expend his dwindled strength, Elias sank into the cold bath. Under the circumstances, the cool water was welcome to his tired skin. It seemed to peel the heat off of the journey as well as wash off the dust.

Relaxation came easy, and twice he almost fell asleep in the bath. After the second nod, he stepped out and found his old clothes replaced by a new set. After checking to make sure all his other possessions remained untouched, he put on the soft, green material that felt a lot like silk. He didn't know if Eustace was showing off or trying to flatter him. It only took a second for him to decide he didn't care.

Without even pulling back the sheets Elias fell onto the bed. Soft, down comforters embraced him as he sunk into the mattress. Sleep came instantly.

* * *

If Elias had seen Squire Montford in a play, he would've thought him a clumsy caricature. The white, handlebar mustache matched the long hair pulled back in a ponytail. The pale face, marked by bushy eyebrows of the same snowy white, was splotched with hues of red. Dark eyes stared out from a face that seemed to appraise everything with exaggerated seriousness.

To complete the almost comic effect, the Squire wore an odd assortment of clothes. A white ruffled collar stuck out from his neck. Below that, he sported a purple, velvet jacket with tails, cut a tad too small which forced him constantly to try to pull it to fit. Crowning the look, or rather founding it, were black doublets, white hose, and shiny black shoes with the heels. All combined, the Squire looked more than a caricature, Elias decided. He looked like a walking museum of court fashions over the last fifty years.

They ate in the small dining room, a table that could seat twenty. At the moment it seemed too ridiculously large with only nine clustered at one end.

Elias had been given the seat of honor, just at the Squire's right, who sat at the table's head. Just across from Elias, on the left of the Squire, sat his wife, Lissa. Elias thought she was able to fit more wrinkles on one face than he thought possible. She stared fixedly at her husband throughout the meal, as if he were the true center of the universe.

But when Kyrie stepped into the room and took her seat beside the Squire's wife, he forgot all about her odd appearance.

As she passed into the dining room, every eye took her in. The dark green dress she had donned hugged and accentuated her form in ways the ragged clothes she owned never could. Her hair had been braided around the crown of her head, clasped by a circlet with an emerald dangling from the center. The green gem matched the green of her eyes. She shined as Elias had never seen her shine before except in moments of animated fury. Now, the glow was soft,

145

sublime. She emanated a warmth that began in her deep eyes, and flowed into her face and through the smile that seemed unusually kind. Elias thought he must be looking at a different woman.

Beside Kyrie, her son stared wordlessly at the opulence that surrounded him. His mask of stoic detachment had given way to wonder. Beside him, Thoran looked bored, and kept his head turned away as if he were avoiding Elias' gaze.

On Elias's side of the table, Eustace sat next to him, followed by Bannus. On the end sat the Captain of the Guard, Dragis, a grim faced man who looked awkward in his fine clothes. He drummed his fingers impatiently on the table. Every so often, he would glare at Elias or one of his company, making obvious his feelings about their presence there and his desire to put the matter to rest as soon as possible.

The Squire would have none of it though. It seemed obvious he relished the opportunity to entertain guests of any distinguishment, and he was going to make the most of the opportunity.

"We have such few honored guests out here in the interior," the Squire explained as the apricot aperitifs were poured. "It is quite a privilege to have you here."

He held up the small, crystal glass and sniffed at the orange liquid. With an experimental sip he nodded his approval of the liqueur and smiled at his guests.

"You probably know already that Montreux is the private residence of Prince Gelen," the Squire expounded. "It has quite a history. Not only has it entertained countless royal figures and been the site of many treaties, it also has its share of scandal as well. The Arch Duke Tabar, was murdered in the Orange Room, I am told. Some even say his ghost can be seen hovering over the bed some nights."

The Squire's wife chuckled silently and covered her mouth. She swiped playfully at her husband.

"Of course, no one is sleeping there," the Squire assured them. "But I would avoid the room if I were you."

The Squire put on a dinner as lavish as his situation would allow. Aperitif was followed by a small salad of only a few green leaves. Soup came next, then souffle, followed by roast duck without gravy. Between courses a sliver of dried lemon was served to clean the pallet. At every serving the Squire apologized for being unable to provide the customary sorbet. Wine flowed freely as the Squire talked about his illustrious family, serving the Kings of Celicia since Noran the First.

"Eustace tells me you enjoyed a bit of adventure but a few days from here," the Squire remarked, turning the conversation away from himself for a moment.

"That's a mild way of putting it," Elias said with a forced laugh. "We just barely missed a group of Prophets. Thankfully, we missed them. But we got to see their handiwork."

The Squire arched an eyebrow in interest. It seemed to say that he wanted to know more but wouldn't push a delicate issue at dinner.

"Some people are just horrid," his wife piped in. Her face shook when we spoke, making her whole face tremble with indignation. "Who wants to worship death? It's so...I don't know what. So ugly, I guess. The whole thing is ugly."

"Irrationality seems to be the motivator behind the Prophets," the Squire wondered aloud as he held up a forkful of souffle, seeming to consider the souffle and the Prophets at the same time. "A total breakdown of reason. It's like they've lost the ability to think and so have embraced the absurd. It's the only way to explain the cult."

"Thanatos is a god," Thoran spoke up.

The Squire let the fork of souffle drop as he looked over at Thoran. An instant dislike passed over his face. He regarded the stranger coldly, as if to let that dislike be evident, before answering.

"What do you mean by that?" he asked.

Thoran shrugged, seemingly unbothered by the Squire's instant dislike of him. "It can't be completely irrational to worship Death. He is one of the gods, after all. We worship all the others. Why not him?"

"The only way to worship death, is with death," the Squire explained. "Are you meaning to suggest to me that because we recognize Death as a god, we should worship him as would fit his nature? Do you approve of slaughter for no other reason than to please the devourer of life?"

"Why is he a god, then?" Thoran asked in return. "I'm not saying I agree with them, or I like them at all. I hate them as much as anyone."

"What are you suggesting, then?"

"You said they were irrational," Thoran pointed out. "That the desire to worship Death comes about because of a failure in reasoning. I'm just saying that it isn't all that irrational. If we recognize Death as a god, it makes perfect sense to worship him."

"Some gods are meant to be feared, rather than worshiped," the Squire said in a note of finality.

Thoran nodded in deference. An awkward silence fell over the table, made worse by the clink of silver on plates. It lasted only a moment as the Squire began another current of conversation. This time, he made sure it stayed light.

It wasn't until after they had all enjoyed their sliver of chocolate for dessert that the Squire allowed the shift of conversation to move in a more serious direction.

"I always enjoy a smoke after dinner," Squire Montford said to Elias after the last course. "Would you and your Enclave friend care to join me?"

Elias accepted and the men rose. All except Thoran. The Squire fixed him with a glare that clearly said the other man was not invited. Thoran didn't let any tension show on his face, but inclined his head subtly. Elias thought he could detect a trace of a smile on his face.

They followed the Squire through the dark halls of the palace into the library. Tall, wooden bookcases rose to ceiling height, which itself stood two stories. A balcony that wrapped around the length of the room allowed access to the higher placed books. Elias eagerly looked over at a portion of the bookcase covered in glass, no doubt protecting the most valuable part of the collection.

As the Squire settled into a plush chair, an aging butler handed him a thin cigar. Seats were not offered to anyone else in the room, leaving Elias, Eustace, Bannus and Dragis standing. The message was clear: the time for polite niceties was over. Now we return to the normal social order. The Squire was nobility and in charge here. At best, everyone else was a servant.

The butler paused after the Squire received his cigar, frozen in place with the box open in his hand. After an imperceptible nod from Montford, the box was offered to Elias as well. Elias took a thin cigar and inclined his own head in gratitude, fully realizing that the Squire wanted him to know that though Elias was not an equal, he would be respected and honored.

The butler held out a lit wick first to the Squire and then to Elias. When the cigars flared and smoked he shook the flame out and quietly stole from the room. The Squire watched him go as he rolled the cigar in his fingers.

"That's the Head Butler, Gareth," the Squire informed him. "He has more right to be here than I do. Do you know why?"

Elias shook his head.

"His family has served the princes at Montreux for over three hundred years," Montford explained. "They have served two different dynasties. His family was Head Butler here when this place was just a fortified tower. Even though the Prince has decided to take up a coastal residence, Gareth has stayed behind. He is as much a part of this place as the stone under our feet.

"What I'm saying is that this isn't my place. You see? If it were, I would gladly take you and your friends in. But it isn't. I occupy the palace because I'm serving my king. This isn't my house. These aren't my rules."

Elias nodded thoughtfully and pulled on his cigar. He let the flavored smoke roll over his tongue and seep from his mouth in lazy tendrils of smoke. It was clear the Squire had more to say. If he were simply kicking Elias out then he would have spared the formality. He had no obligation to reject Elias with dignity.

"What do you know about what we're doing here?" the Squire asked.

"Growing food," Elias shrugged in response. "Obviously, there's something different involved here than your run-of-the-mill farm. What that is I couldn't venture to say."

The Squire smiled and leaned forward in his chair. His eyes glowed with excitement.

"You would be absolutely right in thinking so," he said, pointing at Elias with his cigar.

"What you see around you is called the Interior Food Commission. This is the latest attempt, and one that I might say I had quite a hand in, to mitigate, or even end, the current food crisis."

The Squire stopped talking but continued to lean forward excitedly. By the eagerness in his face Elias could tell he wanted to say more, much more. What he wanted now was the necessary set up to show that Elias's curiosity had been duly piqued.

"And how do you propose that?" Elias asked, complying with the implicit request and careful to put a heavy note of skepticism in his voice.

"Ah, that is the question, isn't it?" the Squire answered. He stood up and paced the library, pulling on the cigar a few times before answering.

"Most people have approached our crisis in a singular manner," the Squire finally spoke up. "They blame the seed, or the soil, or the water, the crop choice, or the magic applied. Some people even blame magic altogether."

He paused and looked straight at Elias, gauging the effect of his last statement. When there was no reaction forthcoming, he continued his pace.

"But what if the problem is not any one of these things," the Squire pondered out loud. "But all of them?

"What if the problem is the wrong crops planted in bad soil with bad seed being destroyed by bad water and maintained by bad magic? What if we approach the solution in a comprehensive manner? Try to tackle all the problems at once?"

"Hence the Interior Food Commission."

"Yes! The Interior Food Commission!" the Squire excitedly exclaimed. "This is our attempt to get the most food with the least resources, all of it meticulously calculated and taking into account all the factors needed to grow food."

"So how does that work?" Elias asked.

"Well the first problem is location," Montford explained. "We had to be far enough from the coastal crowds that it could be defended with a small force, but close enough to keep down transportation costs. A four-day ride from the coast as we are situated here, I believe is perfect. So far it has worked.

"Next, we picked crops that will grow well in hot and relatively dry conditions."

"It's more than relatively dry," Elias interjected. "It's dry as old leather."

"We'll come back to water," the Squire said.

"Crop selection is key. Forty walled acres that used to be the Prince's private garden are planted with dates, figs, olives, a native breed of grape, a variety of vegetables with honeybees all around. Not to mention blueberry and blackberry bushes, and a few fruit trees. That's just flair.

"The real push here is two hundred acres of corn in three fields just under a mile from the palace."

"Why corn?" Elias asked. "It's a nutrient hungry food that needs plenty of water. Not to mention it can be difficult to grow."

"Perhaps, but not if done right. The key is finding complementary foods that can be grown on a rotational basis that also offer high yields and versatility as food sources. This year is corn, next year beans. They're known as good complimentary crops, and both have a variety of uses and can be stored for long periods of time and transported over great distances. And, it's very responsive to magic."

"Okay, theoretically corn could work," Elias conceded. "But what about your water problem? Two hundred acres is a lot of field to water. It's one of the issues that has led to the death of the mega-farm. Especially if you want to use as few magicians as possible, and it maximizes your need for consistent water."

"Ah, yes, the water," Montford spread his arms and said. "What do we do about the water?"

The Squire walked over to a chest on the far wall and reached in a small drawer. Brandishing a section of dark cloth he presented it to Elias with a triumphant smile on his face.

"That is the solution to water," the Squire announced with the cigar in his teeth.

Elias fingered the square of black cloth in his hands. It looked to be made of burlap with a tighter weave. Unlike normal burlap though, the surface had a slick, waxy feel.

"And how does this solve your water problem?"

"It's something I like to call Montford Cloth," the Squire said with obvious pride.

"It took me four years to perfect. You see, I got thinking about the flash rains. Unfortunately, they are our most abundant source of water. But they're inconsistent and do much more damage to crops than they do good.

"Then I did some research and found that the flash often appears in certain places more often than others."

"Wet spots," Elias interjected. "We passed one some time ago that was so bad it had formed a huge rift bed."

"Exactly. And what crop can survive something like that? That sort of intensity can do no one any good. But if we can find a place that experiences say...a moderate appearance of flash rains, maybe they can be used."

"Hence the Montford cloth."

"Yes! Montford Cloth! You see, I designed this cloth with a waxy coat, partially water resistant, but not completely."

The light of understanding flared in Elias's mind.

"So only some of the water gets through, but not enough to damage the crops," the magi surmised.

"Exactly!"

"Pretty clever, but unfortunately you would need a lot more water than what this cloth would admit from a few flash rains."

A triumphant smile was still plastered on the Squire's face. If anything it had become more triumphant.

"All the cornfields are protected with this cloth," Montford explained. "And they are graded before planting to a gentle slope, all around so it is shaped like an amphitheater. Mind you, it's not steep, but the center of the field is its lowest point. At that center is a drain pipe, running to an underground reservoir. The slick cloth causes a good portion of the water to run off towards the middle, drained down the center, and then collected for later use. The crop is protected, water is allowed through, and the excess is not wasted, but saved for later use."

"Have you tried it?" Elias asked, fully intrigued at this point.

"We've only had one flash to date, a very small one. No damage to the crops and we collected close to a thousand gallons of water."

Elias found himself forced to reevaluate his perception of the Squire. All the odd assortment of dress suddenly didn't seem the result of advancing dotage, but the eccentricities of a quixotic genius. There was no doubting his brilliance. He had found a fascinating solution to a problem that had vexed the rest of civilization.

Looking at the Squire again, Elias saw all the traces of the detached, brilliant mind. Beyond his eccentric dress he noted Montford's excited manner of speech, the wild gestures with his hands, the pacing, the intensity written across his face. The man truly loved ideas and inspiration, and Elias felt himself immediately infected with his enthusiasm.

"So the yield has been good so far?" Elias asked, though he thought he knew the answer. He could sense a heaviness in the room that contrasted sharply with the Squire's exuberance.

All at once the excitement fell off the Squire's face. He looked down at the bright end of his cigar, as if the answers were glowing there.

"Show them," the Squire said, looking at Eustace. He turned to the library window.

Eustace produced a stalk of half grown corn and laid it on a writing desk. The edges of the leaves had withered and browning had grown up the stalk itself. Plenty of green still filled the plant, but it looked too thin and undernourished.

Elias took the stalk in his hand and ran his fingers up and down the surface. Probing gently with his lumen he felt into the stalk of corn. Flickers of life touched him, grazed the secret corners of his mind. Throughout the stalk of corn he could hear, feel, almost see the pulse of vitality. It was weak, sick, struggling though strong and fading.

"Divination has never been my thing," Elias said. "Have you had this checked?"

Eustace nodded.

"Who was it?"

"Diogenes."

"Never heard of him," Elias shrugged. "I assume he produced a schemata."

Eustace answered by handing over a single sheet of paper. Elias quickly looked over the complex markings in symbols that communicated the inner workings of a single stalk of corn. To the uninitiated, it was a connected series of random markings. To those so trained, it was believed to be the very language of life.

"How does this match with the seed schemata?" Elias asked after looking over the Diviners work.

The Squire turned sharply around and fixed a hard stare at Eustace. The palace magi looked confused at first, then realization dawned on them. His eyes widened and he took a frustrated swipe at the empty air.

"Stupid, skinny, worthless punk of a magi!" Eustace fumed. "I'm sorry Monty. I should've thought of it."

"The Diviner should have insisted," Elias told them. "He knows that an underperforming plant needs a seed schemata to succeed. It's a basic service for this sort of thing."

"Nothing to be done about it now," the Squire wisely pointed out. "Hopefully it's not too late. Can you draw us a schemata for the seed?"

"Never been good at those," Elias confessed, dropping the schemata to the desktop beside the weathered corn stalk. "I usually work without them. Do you have any seed left?"

The Squire nodded then sent Dragis off to find some seed. He walked over to a glass decanter and poured three glasses of amber liquid into fine crystal glasses. Taking one up for himself the Squire handed the other drinks to the two magi.

The first sip sent a grimace through Elias as the burning liquid went down. A warmth followed quickly afterward and suffused into his whole body. He looked down at the crystal glass and inhaled the deep aroma of sweet vanilla and oak.

"Corn whiskey," the Squire remarked when he noted Elias's appreciation. "This batch is thirty years old. Pretty soon, it will be gone from the world forever."

The Squire held up his glass to the light of the chandelier and swirled the precious liquor. His eyes narrowed, taking in the subtle nuances of color.

"Can you imagine such a frivolous use of food crops?" he mused. "It's hard to imagine having so much corn you can make whiskey out of it. But we did. We had so much we didn't know what to do with it. We used to throw away enough food to feed the entire land."

Sighing, Montford took another long drink from his glass. His thoughtful gaze fell on Elias.

"I had hoped that within a few years we might be able to make whiskey again," the Squire told him.

"I take it your current projections aren't what you'd expected," Elias guessed.

"When I pitched this idea to the King, I told him we could expect twenty-six thousand bushels of corn. Based on our current outlook we will be lucky to get just under half of that. Considering the resources the king has put into this project, he is not pleased with our progress."

Elias allowed a knowing glance to point in Eustace's direction. Based on what he saw in the withered stalk of corn thirteen thousand bushels was an extremely liberal estimate. Even with two hundred acres, if the whole lot was as bad as that one stalk, it wouldn't matter how big the planting was. As it stood, they would be lucky to garner three thousand bushels. Eustace betrayed nothing on his face.

"So you can see my dilemma," the Squire continued. "If this fails, then the Montford Cloth will never be used again, even though it could help so much. But more immediately, unless we can get this to work the King will abandon the interior altogether."

"Looks like you need help," Elias pointed out.

"That brings us to the other horn of my dilemma," the Squire told him. "The great appeal of this project for the King was the limited resources we demanded. Everything was precisely calculated, measured and portioned. All of us here are on strict rations except for what we can forage from the palace. Most of the servants are women, as you will notice, and small ones at that because they can live off less food. There are a few stores for emergencies, but that is a meager supply. And even if we could enlist help, that would drive down the appeal of trying this again."

"You've certainly allowed no room for error," Elias observed. "In fact, you've kind of worked your way into a corner. Where's the room for your unknowns?"

"No! If you calculate correctly there are no unknowns!" The Squire fumed, whiskey sloshing from his glass as he gestured. "There are only bad calculations."

"So where did your calculations go so wrong?"

"Magic," Montford huffed. "Though that's hardly my fault. We have five magicians working which should be adequate for the job."

"You have two magi and three boys who shouldn't even be acolytes," Eustace protested. "That's hardly adequate magic."

"They were approved and released by the Latrean Enclave," Montford argued. "Why wouldn't I think they were adequate?"

"But once you see they aren't, like anything else, you send it back when you find you were sold something other than what you bargained for."

"Enough!" the Squire barked with a wave of his hands. His pale features quickly flushed red with frustration. It sounded like an argument the two had frequently engaged in.

"Unknown variables crept into the equation," the Squire said in a calmer voice. "The problem was not in the calculations. As always, the variables are at fault."

"As always," Elias echoed. "Those damn variables."

"Yes, as much as it grieves me I have been forced to put it out of my mind and move on. Too many hours have been wasted on what is beyond my reach. The situation remains that I have two hundred acres of wilting corn that will not produce anything near what I have promised.

"My Chief Magi here tells me I must abandon half of my crop and concentrate on what we can produce. Even then, the yield may be less than half of what was anticipated."

"Better than nothing at all," Elias ventured.

The Squire shrugged his shoulders, his enthusiasm deflated by the realities he faced. Like so many idealists who have seen their lofty dreams dashed by an uncooperative world, he tread on the dark precipice of resignation. Elias could see it creep into his features, dim the brightness of his eyes. Yet there was something else there.

"There's more, isn't there?" Elias suggested. "There's more at stake here than the displeasure of the King."

A sad looked passed from the Squire to Eustace. He turned his back to the men, facing the high wall of books behind them.

"The King wouldn't pay for all the expenses of the Commission,"

Montford told them. "All of my personal fortune is behind this as well. Of course, the King gets paid back first. So, if we harvest less than half of our projections then I lose. I lose a lot."

Elias had no answer for the Squire. He hated seeing the proud man brought so pitifully low. There was a sense of some lost nobility in what he did, defying the decay of a dead world. The Squire stood against the awful entropy that seemed to have taken over everyone else. Alone, he would face the march of doom and carve out some place of life amidst the Blight.

Except he was failing too. Even this last, great flash of human ingenuity stood no chance against the flood that had swept all things away. It made the very notion of hope seem ridiculous.

A part of Elias wished he could save the Squire, to lift him out of his despair and bolster his hopes. But that part of him was dying too, the part that cared enough to try and fight the passing away of the world, that part of him that echoed the Squire's passionate plea. And like the Squire, that dream of what could be never quite stood up to the cold fact of what was.

"You can't afford to let me stay, but you can't afford to let me go," Elias summed up what he figured was on the Squire's mind.

The Squire nodded and turned around to face him. Elias could hardly bear the look of pleading on his face, could hardly watch the last flicker of hope fix itself on him.

"If you think you could help, then we will find room for you and your guard, as well as the woman and her son," the Squire offered. "I'm afraid we can't afford to board the other man traveling with you. Even if I wanted to. As it is, he did not leave a favorable impression on me."

"Yeah, he has that effect on people," Elias muttered, his mind beginning to drift elsewhere.

"He is not essential to us," Bannus chimed in for the first time. "We traveled together for convenience, nothing more."

The Squire nodded, relieved. For him, the matter had been settled. Thoran would be cast out into the wild while the others would enjoy the relative refuge of the palace.

Looking back, Elias couldn't figure out why he said what he did next. Certainly, he shared the Squire's disdain of Thoran. From the outset, the stranger had unsettled him.

That he unsettled Bannus too was hardly reward enough. In the long run, Elias would rather deal with the gruff and thickheaded

Bannus than the incessant sarcasm of Thoran; that and the dark visions of storm that often mirrored in the stranger's eyes.

Perhaps Elias felt a small surge of pity for Thoran, alone and wondering in the wilds. That loneliness was something the two men shared. But he also knew his pity for the man was a small thing. What really pushed him was that he just didn't feel right about letting Thoran go. As much as he didn't like the man, to abandon him reeked of wrongness. He passed it off as loyalty and pushed the debate out of his mind. The very thought of being bound to Thoran in even the most tenuous way sickened Elias.

"He stays with us," Elias heard himself say. "If I stay, so does he."

Bannus glared at Elias but didn't object. The Squire shook his head and held up his hands in helplessness.

"There's just no way," he protested.

"He can work," Elias suggested. "In the fields or with the guards."

"We don't have the rations. Especially for full grown men."

"I'll make up what he eats in extra produce."

The Squire thought on this for a moment then opened his mouth to speak. Before he could say anything, the library door opened and Dragis returned.

"Your seeds," he said, dumping a handful of dried corn into Elias's hand.

Elias turned the kernels over with his fingers. Reaching into them, he immediately felt a telltale flicker.

"These are magically enhanced," Elias said, holding up the fistful of seeds.

"Aren't they all?" The Squire asked.

"No, these have a custom trace on them," Elias clarified. "These were made special."

"Of course they were," Squire said with a touch of indignation. "I thought it best to have the seed enhanced for this particular soil. I assumed it would give us better results."

"Not a bad idea, but it makes the seed trickier to work with."

"Can you write up a schematic?" Eustace asked. "Hell, would that even help?"

"I really don't do schematics," Elias said as he put down the handful of seed and picked up the withered stalk of corn.

Gathering the roots in his hand, Elias held the stalk up so that it pointed towards the ceiling. Tendrils of the spidery tubers tickled his hands. He drew himself into the plant through the roots, feeling the places of power sleeping in the crop. Carefully, like a priest unfolding an ancient scroll, Elias unfolded the trembling life.

"What I do, is evocation," he said.

Stirred by an unseen wind, the stalk of corn shivered. Glints of green light sparkled, just so that the eye could barely catch it. A shuffle of withered leaves sounded in the library.

The Squire watched with his mouth open as the stalk filled with green life, all the brown and withered edges smoothing to flawlessness. The stalk grew in Elias's hand, tall and strong, thickening at the base. Shocks of white silk sprung out and fattened into ears. Seconds later, the silk browned and shriveled.

Elias reached out and pulled off a healthy ear of corn. He tossed it to the Squire who immediately tore into it, his face breaking into a wide grin as he caressed the white kernels draped in locks of silk.

"Can...can you do this to all my corn?" he asked, almost bursting with glee.

"One stalk is different from two hundred acres," Elias explained. "Takes more time. You want the harvest to come in at once. Obviously, you want to grow them a little at a time. But I could definitely help."

"Why does it have to come in together?" the Squire asked. "Can't we just grow the stalks one at a time like this?"

"I've already told you it doesn't work that way?" Eustace said, sounding more than a little defensive.

"Yes, but why?" The Squire's frustration came out strong.

"Take a bite," Elias offered, pointing to the ear of corn the Squire held.

The Squire pulled the ear close, sniffing the white kernels first. Taking a small bite he chewed experimentally. His face blanched and he spit the half-eaten pieces back into his hand.

"What's wrong with it?" he asked.

"That's what happens if you grow it too fast," Eustace answered. "Something about the way the sugars and protein come together. They take time."

"It's sweet and bitter all at once."

"Besides, you get a lot more yield if you let the magic work over time," Elias added. "Magic isn't supposed to grow the corn. It's supposed to help it along. You do it right, and you get the most."

"What do you think we could get?" the Squire asked tentatively. "How many bushels?"

Elias looked up at the stalk and considered the question. He knew he could provide an outstanding yield. What he didn't know was if he wanted to. Did he want to waste his powers on one more futile attempt to save the world? A part of him, a loud part, knew that the Squire raged at a thunderstorm. The world was dying. Resistance would just prolong the agony.

Marveling at how easy it was to give up, Elias forced himself to consider deeper. Another part of him still cared. That part of him was withering as quickly as the dry and dusty world around him. Withering like the corn he had surreptitiously restored to life.

"You allow room and board for me and all my companions," Elias said as he made his decision. He made certain stress the word, all.

"And I will get you twenty-six thousand bushels."

Chapter Thirteen
Seamus

Many hours later Elias stumbled back to his room. Thoroughly drunk and confused in the vast hallways, he turned down one wrong hall, then another, until a servant gently led him to his rooms. For the second time, Elias collapsed on the bed without undressing.

After Elias had assured the Squire that his guarantee was no empty bluster, Montford responded with gregarious enthusiasm. He brandished the decanter and poured more whiskey. This time, filling glasses for Bannus and Dragis.

"To Elias!" he cried out in toast.

The men clinked their glasses together and downed the whiskey. The Squire quickly refilled them all.

"To the Interior Land Commission," Elias said, raising his glass.

Squire smiled and nodded. Once again, the glasses went up in toast.

This happened several more times before the drinking slowed down. They toasted the King, the Prince, the Hope of Magic, and even to the restoration of the world. By the time they toasted this last one, Elias felt warm enough to actually believe it. The others excused themselves after toasting the land. The Squire put a hand on Elias to stay him.

"One more drink with me," the Squire insisted. He filled their glasses and the two of them fell into chairs beside the empty hearth.

The one more drink quickly turned into three. They talked for many hours, covering any and every subject, sometimes switching so quickly it defied sense. At every empty glass, Elias tried to leave. Every time he was stayed by the Squire's insistence on one more.

Only when the Squire fell asleep in his chair was Elias finally able to get free. He carefully plucked Montford's half empty glass from his hands and tried to pour the contents back into the decanter. Most dribbled down the side of the glass, or missed altogether by Elias's swaying hands.

Cursing, the magi slammed down the glass and stumbled his way back to his room. Once in bed, Elias couldn't sleep. He had passed that point of intoxication that made the room spin every time he closed his eyes. He felt the bed drop out from under him, the walls fall away. He tumbled head over heels into a featureless, black sky.

With a groan, Elias picked himself up and searched to fix his eyes on something stationary. The room was too dark. It spun along with the whirling of his head. Soft light spilled in from the balcony window. He locked his eyes on the pale light until his head leveled.

It took the better part of an hour for his head to spin itself out. Bit by bit, in the clumsiest magic he had ever cast, Elias slowly helped his body process the glut of alcohol in his blood. Exhausted, he pulled the covers back this time and crawled into the soft sheets that swallowed him up in comfort. He was asleep in seconds.

* * *

Thunder woke him up.

A flash of lightning, a boom that shook the walls, and Elias started out of bed. His head clear in warning, Elias walked to the balcony and looked out.

Nothing.

The walls of the estate were gone. The guardhouse, the stable, the wagons; all gone. A flat and empty land stretched out under the windows as far as he could see in the moonlight.

A solitary figure stirred in the expanse. Elias leaned forward, his eyes drawn to the movement. Somehow, he knew what it was despite the distance.

A sparrowhawk.

The little bird lifted up and flew to the rail of the balcony. All the feathers and flesh had been stripped from the head. The bare skull cocked to the side and fixed an eyeless gaze at Elias.

"Seamus!" the sparrowhawk squawked at Elias.

Elias recoiled. The name stabbed into his heart and suffused a feeling of numb dread through his limbs. He fell back through the balcony door and turned to flee.

Lightning flashed.

Elias stood in the library. Darkness filled the room. A flicker of light from the storm outside and then darkness fell again.

Panic swept through Elias. He tried to remember, but couldn't. How did he get here? Who was he? Who was Seamus?

A figure sat motionless in the giant library chair. Only then did Elias remember the Squire. Did he fall asleep alongside the Squire? Maybe he only dreamt of returning to his room.

Something wasn't right about the Squire. Elias couldn't figure it out. The darkness hid too much. Something about the awkward way the Squire sat in his chair disturbed him. He was propped up unnaturally, his head drooped to one side.

"Montford?" Elias called out softly. "Montford, is that you?"

Elias crept toward the sleeping figure. Alarming panic continued to clang in his head. That uneasy feeling of dread settled into him, a certainty that something awful was about to happen.

"Montford," Elias called out a little louder.

Lightning flashed.

For one instant of illumination Elias could make out every detail of the Squire's prone figure. His back was arched and his hands gripped the arms of the chair. Out of his open mouth a torrent of sand spilled out onto his lap where his black pants had faded to grey. His skin was dry and shriveled, as white as chalk in the flare of the storm.

Elias recoiled into darkness again.

Lightning flashed.

Firelight appeared around him. Twelve individual bursts of flame formed a circle in the blackness around him. Twelve torches.

Elias tried to rise but found his hands and legs bound fast. He fell back onto the cold slab of rough stone. Above him, a domed ceiling rose high in the distance. But even in the dim light he could make out the cryptic and sibylline figures carved into the stone. Symbols of power. Vast power.

"Where is the tamarisk tree?" a voice boomed out of the darkness. "Where is the tree?"

He didn't know the answer, but he wanted to. A desire, unquenchable, tugged at his lips, begged him to answer the voice. But he didn't know. And he was scared because he didn't know.

Elias lifted his head and saw a circle of robed figures around him. Black hoods hid their faces in shadow. A menacing silence emanated from them, terror that needed no expression.

"Where is the tree?" a voice boomed out again, the sound echoing in the vast reaches of the chamber. "Where is the tamarisk tree?"

Elias heard himself laugh, heard it even as he tried to stop the sound from coming out of his mouth. He mocked the robed figures, called them fools, dared them to find the tree.

"Elias," a softer voice said. "Elias, I love you."

One of the robed figures leaned forward so that the darkness of the hood hovered in front of Elias's eyes.

"I love you, Elias," the figure said in Gregory's precise baritone.

Hands reached up to pull the hood away. Kyrie smiled devilishly down at him and leaned in for a kiss.

Lightning flashed.

Cold, wet steel felt slick beneath his fingers. He gripped the twisted bars of metal in front of him. A wind blew in with the torrent of rain that slashed at him through the bars. The cage swayed in the wind.

The sharp taste of blood filled Elias' mouth. He spat, sending a red drop onto the muddy ground just a foot beneath him. The crimson spittle bubbled in the rain and washed away.

A figure stood in the rain. Naked and arms apart it walked through the deluge and through the forest of hanging cages, just like the one Elias found himself in. The figure strode casually toward him, oblivious of the storm.

Elias recognized the smile on Thoran's face. With arms outstretched he stopped in front of Elias's cage. The coldness of steel filled the magi's bones.

"Father," Thoran croaked as blood spilled out of his mouth.

Lightning flashed.

* * *

Sleep did not touch Thoran that night. He required very little. In fact, the worst part about traveling with others were the long hours pretending to sleep. Even though he took the longest and most frequent watches of the night, he couldn't take them all. That would invite questions Thoran didn't want to answer.

It had been a long time since he had enjoyed a night. For weeks he had laid still every night, pretending to sleep. Keeping his eyes closed, unmoving for hours at a time felt like pure torture. And the tedium of it all was almost unbearable.

Having his own room that night almost made Thoran giddy. He paced around the space, out to the balcony, rifled through the mostly empty desk. For several hours he crept around with his ear to the floor and wall, searching for hidden passages. Beside the fireplace he could tell a hidden chamber waited behind the walls, but he couldn't find any way to access it.

As soon as Elias fell asleep Thoran knew it. The hour was late, extremely late. The rest of the palace most certainly slept as well. The hour belonged to him.

Casual and cautious at the same time, Thoran stole from his room and out into the empty, marbled hallway. His feet lightly touched the bare stone as they walked toward Elias's room. He could feel the magi on the other side of the door.

One hand on the door and the sensation deepened, images of strange dreams dimly raced through Thoran's mind, along with the feelings of panic that went along with it. Thoran smiled, taking morbid pleasure in Elias's discomfort.

Leaving the magi to his nightmares, Thoran continued down the hallway. He worked his way back to the interior passages, up the small wooden staircase used by servants, into the hidden veins of the palace.

Frequently, he would place his ear to a door and listen for sounds within. Most were quiet. Once, he heard the soft moans of suppressed pleasure, followed by the light laughter of two female voices.

After wandering through the servant quarters, he moved to the main area of the palace. He found the Squire snoring blissfully in his library chair. Thoran blew out the lantern and left him alone in the quiet dark.

All through the palace he wandered that night. He wandered, for that was his nature. Too many hours had been wasted feigning sleep. Tonight he was free. He would give reign to that impulse that drove him more insistently than hunger or exhaustion or even thirst. He was a creature made to wander. So he traced the vast hallways of the palace, into areas unused and untread. Coils of tension bred by nights of stillness slowly unwound, granting him peace. If what he felt could be called peace. For him, he knew there would be no peace until... He shook his head, refusing to think of that day.

Only one other figure passed him that night. An old man shuffled down the hallway in one of the deserted areas of the palace. Puffs of dust kicked up in the drag his feet. Thoran drew into the shadow of an alcove.

The old man was oblivious to Thoran as he trudged by. He muttered some nonsense to himself, pulling at the night blue robes of the priesthood that he wore. On every hem a circle with a cross inside was stitched onto the dark cloth – a priest of Gaia. The tottering fool who pulled at his tangled, gray beard was a priest of the goddess of the earth.

Once the old man passed, the palace was Thoran's again. He gave in to that one, mad impulse that drove him. After a time, he paid no heed to where his steps took him. His feet moved with a will of their own until light began to appear on the horizon and the servants stirred to prepare the palace for the coming day.

There was a dawn that waited for him too. Its name was Elias. His wandering would be at an end, driven by that other impulse that nagged and bit at him. The impulse that called him to his death.

Chapter Fourteen
The Interior Food Commission

"There he is, our hero," Eustace greeted loudly as Elias stumbled into the palace courtyard early the following morning.

"And doesn't he look heroic? Like he has just been eaten by a pack of wolves with the stomach flu and crapped out in his whites."

A weak smile managed to find its way across Elias's face. He took the reins offered by Eustace and pulled himself up the thin, but serviceable horse. The other magi patted him amicably on the back.

"How long did you and the Squire stay up?" he asked.

"Way too late," Elias said, shaking his head. "Feels like I fell asleep about ten minutes ago."

"You know, I have some blue angel if you want," Eustace offered. "No shame in using it. We all need it from time to time."

"Already took care of that," Elias said. "Just tired, that's all."

A strange and measured look crossed Eustace's face. He smiled wryly and shrugged his shoulders.

"Of course, the great Elias Whitsun wouldn't need to use potion like a normal magi. He just wiggles his fingers and it's done."

"I don't remember you being the jealous type," Elias said.

"Not usually. But when it comes to walking in your shadow we're all the jealous type. Shall we?"

Eustace prodded his horse into a slow walk. Elias followed, unbothered by the other man's envy. It was something he had long grown accustomed to. Others always seemed to expect an excessive show of modesty to somehow balance out his talent. He had tried that, and found it did little to allay the spite of the lesser able. As long as he didn't make a spectacle of himself, people could keep their envy mostly in check. From time to time, though, he figured it would come out.

The men rode out of the larger courtyard gate facing west. Immediately, they turned north, passing by the courtyard walls. When they moved out of the shadows, the heat of the morning struck them with full force.

"Don't think I'll ever get used to that sun," Elias muttered.

Eustace shrugged his shoulders and Elias didn't immediately press him for conversation. Up ahead, another walled enclosure loomed. It was a massive structure, running up the distant hill before disappearing from sight.

"Those are the palace gardens," Eustace said, pointing towards the wall. "We'll come back around to them on our way back. I want to get us out to the corn first."

They steered west and followed the trail that snaked in between the rise of two hills. Hard-packed and brown earth rose up on either side.

"We put the cornfields behind these hills," Eustace said as the pass rose up then back into the folds of earth. "It offers at least a bit of protection. Makes it impossible to make out the fields from a distance."

They rode through a bend in the trail that took them in between a gap in the dusty hills. As they turned their horses, a valley opened up, revealing a field of green that veritably screamed out against the backdrop of brown and featureless sand. Memory stirred in Elias as he looked down at the vast expanse of living crops. Even from this distance he could tell they struggled, but they still managed to remind him of a younger, happier world where sights like this were the norm.

"As you can see, the lowland fields make us a little vulnerable," Eustace said, pointing out the strategically inferior position the valley occupied. "But this is an old riverbed. The soil is somewhat healthier. We figured it was hidden enough to risk, a place this big and fertile."

Elias nodded as he looked over the valley, making his own assessment. Green fields sprawled through the dried up riverbed. The one in front of him was circular and gently graded, so that the center was its lowest point, just as the Squire described.

Small buildings dotted the valley. The ones he could make out looked hastily thrown up, made of mismatched planks of wood and filled in with globs of black pitch.

"There are guard houses throughout the fields," Eustace said, pointing out the ramshackle buildings. "We have the guards divided into three divisions. Thirty-six in all. One division takes the palace area along with the walled garden, another surveys the fields. One is at rest. They all rotate throughout the day."

"No guard towers?" Elias asked.

"We thought about towers on the hills." Eustace explained. "But we figured our best defense was secrecy. A visible guard tower would just announce to anyone that walks by that something worth stealing was close.

"We put the money in horses instead. We only have a dozen down there, but they're ready to go at a moment's notice. We figure speed is more important than brute force. Besides, twelve mounted men could probably repel anything that comes this far out."

As the two rode down into the valley, Elias noted how quiet it was for such a large operation. A horseman passed by on patrol, nodding a quick salute to Eustace. Someone knelt down on the edge of the field, repairing some of the cloth that covered the ground.

Reaching out to the desolate corn, Elias balked at his earlier optimism. Twenty-six thousand bushels? The corn was alive but dying fast. And it wasn't the state of the crop that bothered him, it was the scope. To bring all of the corn to harvest at the same time wasn't like making one stalk bear fruit. All two hundred acres had to be brought along at the same pace and kept alive and growing so they could be harvested within a brief period of time. It wasn't so much a matter of power as being able to extend oneself over a large area.

"It's a lot of corn," Elias finally said as he and Eustace stopped in front of one of the ramshackle houses.

The pitiful structure looked even worse up close. Giant gaps stood out between the slats of dark and splintered wood that even the tar couldn't fill. Yet so much was thrown on it that it dripped down the walls. The whole structure listed uneasily to one side, like a ship that had taken on too much water. Elias vowed to himself not to take a single step inside unless his life depended on it.

"It's not too much for you, is it?" Eustace chided, but there was genuine worry behind his playful tone.

"Hard to be everywhere at once," Elias shrugged. "Twenty-six thousand bushels may be optimistic, but I don't see why we can't get close, especially with some help."

"Ah yes, the help," Eustace said. He let out a sharp, shrill whistle.

"Boys! Get your asses out here!" he yelled.

"I make it a point never to go into the shipwreck," Eustace explained.

"The shipwreck?"

"Yeah. It's what the damn thing looks like. Held together with tar and rusty nails. Got to be a total fool to go in there."

As if on cue, three figures stumbled out of the shack. They squinted into the sun, trying to adjust their sight to the sudden brightness.

"That's right my little babies," Eustace teased as he slid off his horse. "Come on, time to make another failed attempt at earning your keep.

"Elias, here is your army of trained magi."

Looking at the three teenage boys in front of him, Elias could immediately see why the corn was in such miserable shape. That they were too young was obvious. Two of them had that awkward, lanky figure of underdeveloped manhood. In fact, they almost could have been twins, sharing pale skin and thick, black hair. Only their faces gave them away. One was pinched and angular, the other open and full.

The third boy was shorter than the rest, almost unnaturally so. But he had an intelligent glint to his eye and seemed more comfortable in his body than his taller companions.

At first glance, Elias could see age wasn't the main issue with the boys. What they lacked was either training or raw power. Incompetency was the issue. It was as clear as if it were written on their faces.

As he looked over the boys, Elias searched for that telltale sign that marked a competent magi. It was a certain bearing he wanted to see, a carriage that most non-magi saw as arrogance. The way a magi walked, the way he held his head, even in the way he spoke indicated he was a man who dealt with great power. But even this was on the surface. What he really wanted to see was how they looked at the world around them.

A magi appraised the world differently. You could see it on their faces. They looked beneath the surface, their gaze peering below what the rest of the world could see. It made most people uncomfortable, to have the gaze of a magi resting upon them, their eyes seeming to plumb the depths of the soul. Even highborn nobility thought it haughtiness. But it wasn't arrogance at all. A magi saw what others could not, and that reality played out in every glance of the eyes and motion of the body.

Looking at the three boys squinting up at him, Elias could tell they possessed very little of that vision. The two taller ones hunched over, a slightly confused look on their faces. The shorter one fared a little better. Elias could see depth in those eyes, the way they stared back at his a little longer before dropping to examine the dust at his feet.

Eustace walked over to stand behind the boys.

"These two we call the twins," he said, patting the two taller boys on the shoulder. A puff of dust flew up from the tattered, black robes, faded almost to gray.

"They're not actually related. I swear, though, they look more like each other every day.

"This one is Hap," he indicated the boy with angular features. "And this is Reynauld."

"Over here," Eustace stood behind the shorter boy. "Is Phistus. He doesn't look like much but he's got more talent than he knows. Plus, his pecker is so long that he has to roll it up like a bandage to keep it from dragging on the ground."

The two taller boys, the twins, snickered at Eustace's comment. Phistus turned a deep shade of crimson and dropped his head even lower.

"Thank you for that very useful bit of information," Elias replied.

"Just trying to be thorough," Eustace said with a grin.

"So, where were your boys trained?" Elias asked.

"Latrea," they all mumbled.

"You look a little young to be graduated already. How long did you train?"

Two of the boys said four years. Only Hap noted that he was at the Enclave for five.

Elias turned to Eustace, a look of deep consternation drawing his eyebrows together.

"What the hell are they doing out here?" he asked.

Eustace held up his hands in helplessness. "I was supposed to get fully trained Peregrinators. This is what they gave me."

"I guess the Latrine Enclave is living up to its name," Elias suggested.

Neither of the boys seemed to bristle at the insult.

"It's happening everywhere," Eustace explained. "Everyone is desperate for magi, so they put them out quick, hoping they'll learn on the job."

* * *

The two men rode by the vast acreage of corn. Eustace explained the layout. Two hundred acres divided into three fields, graded like a bowl and covered with the Montford cloth. Drains at the bottom diverted flash rain water to a reservoir, in which the excess water was stored.

Eustace stopped and lifted some cloth to show the irrigation ditches beneath. Water brought by wagons from the reservoir and nearby well was poured into the ditches for more regular watering.

The stalks of corn were still green, just knee-high, brown and withered at the edges and overall looking too thin. Eustace picked at a piece of the black cloth that covered the ground beneath the corn. A four foot tear peeled back the cloth to expose the dusty ground beneath.

"Got to get someone out here to fix this," he said and remounted his horse.

"So you see, the flash rain and water problem are handled all at once," Eustace said as he pointed out the reservoir that stood just outside the cornfields.

"That just leaves us with the magic problem."

"The magic problem," Elias nodded and followed Eustace up the rise of the hill.

The two men headed back towards the palace. On the way they passed both Bannus and Thoran out in the fields of knee-high corn. Thoran carried two buckets of water balanced on the ends of a shoulder yoke. The weight didn't seem to bother him at all. He smiled up at Elias as he passed by, even winking one of his storm blue eyes.

"Your friend is housed out in the field barracks," Eustace told him. "Hope you don't mind. Montford wanted him out of the palace."

"Can't say I blame you," Elias answered. "I don't care for him much myself."

"Why did you want them to stay then?" Elias asked. "Squire would love to get rid of him."

Elias couldn't even answer to himself why he fought for Thoran to stay with them. He turned to watch the retreating figure carry water down the edge of the cornfield. As if sensing Elias' stare, Thoran turned around and met the magi's gaze. Jerking the horse's reign, Elias move forward again, fearing the sound of thunder that came with the man's eyes.

"Guess I just got used to him being around," Elias gave by way of answer, knowing full well how hollow it sounded.

Bannus passed by, close behind Thoran. He only spared Elias and Eustace a brief glance. His eyes were fixed on Thoran, intent on keeping the stranger in sight.

Passing by the acres of corn, Eustace guided them over the hills and up to the gates of the massive enclosure just north of the palace. Elias peered up at the stone walls, only fifteen feet high, but still impressive for the great length.

"How big is this?" Elias asked.

"There's forty acres enclosed in these walls," Eustace told him.

"That's a big garden," Elias noted. "Even for a prince."

"Wasn't a garden originally," Eustace said as they passed through the open gates and into the sprawling interior of the walls.

More of the vibrant green struck Elias as he drank in the sight. It burst all around him, filling his vision everywhere he looked, pushing at that deep awareness as his power sensed the life that filled the place. Directly in front of him lay carefully planted squares of broadleaf plants. To each side were more containing short bushes, vines, stalks. He saw rows of beans, stakes of tomato plant, squash, musk melon, okra, peas, beds of lettuce, garlic, onion and some that were unfamiliar to him altogether.

"Montreux used to be renowned for their white wines," Eustace said as the two men paused and looked over the vast sprawl of gardens. "One of the old princes thought it was due to the grape variety that he cultivated here, so he built the walls to prevent someone from stealing them. It was only later that they discovered it was the soil that gave the wine its particular taste."

"So this was all a vineyard," Elias said, even as he noticed vines still growing off in the western half of the walled garden.

"Yeah, we still have a good fifteen acres of the grapes growing. It was one of the main selling points of the project. The whole court would trample each other for another taste of Montreux."

Eustace gestured off to the eastern boundary and turned his horse in that direction.

"The vegetable gardens take up the middle section," Eustace explained as Elias rode behind him. "Those hives you see behind us run most of the way along the north wall. And over on this eastern half we have our fruit trees and bushes. Blueberry, blackberry, peach, strawberry, figs, lemons, limes and oranges."

"What do you do with all these fruits and vegetables?" Elias asked. "Can't store them that long. What is it? A three-day journey to the coast?"

"Fermentation," Eustace said over his shoulders. "We've been harvesting pretty frequently. In the southeast corner over there you can see the old wine house. We'll make the wine there, of course, but until then we brine the vegetables, jam the fruit. Fruits and vegetables are harvested every two weeks. By then, the earlier batch is finished. The Squire takes the barrels to King Aethus' castle just outside of Iachs. Comes back with new barrels full of saltwater."

Elias nodded, impressed with the efficiency of it all. More impressive was the Squire's planning. He seemed to possess a mind that could contain vast, complex and interrelated information. Elias couldn't help but like the man.

As the two men rode toward the eastern edge of the gardens, Elias took in the sights of, and the feel of, the place. The garden plots were laid out the same meticulous organization that reflected in everything the Squire did. A long section of tomato plants passed them by, giving way to thorny blackberry bushes.

The plants here, in contrast to the corn, fared much better. Either more time was committed to this place, or more talented magic directed its growth.

Elias drew up as they came to a grove of peach trees. The rough branches opened up like gnarled hands, displaying proper cultivation. Small, pale fruits bunched thickly among the vibrant, green leaves.

A laugh sounded from nearby. The sound startled Elias, striking him as familiar and foreign all at once. He slid off his horse just as Silas ran into view, his feet kicking up clouds of orange dust.

"I'm over here now," he yelled out, ducking behind a peach tree.

"You won't get away this time," he heard Kyrie yell out in the closing distance.

A smile crept over Elias's lips, marveling at the transformation of the boy in just one day. Perhaps it was the comfortable, safe bed, or the abundant food that brought about the change. Or maybe just being in a garden, surrounded by green life, stirred up the dormant energy that always wanted to burst forth.

Whatever the reason, Elias couldn't help but feel happy at what he saw. Silas breathed heavily as he crouched behind the tree. A trickle of sweat ran down the red dust that covered his cheek. He looked up at Elias and placed a finger to his lips.

"I'm getting closer," Kyrie called out as she burst out from a row of trees and faced Elias.

She too, looked happy. A smile spread across her face as she stepped into the row. It fell as soon as her eyes met Elias.

She stopped and put her hands on her hips as she caught her breath. Like Silas, she had changed much in the course of a night. The simple, blue dress she wore helped. But the dress alone didn't account for the glow that suffused her features.

"It's you," she said, exasperated, though not as thoroughly as usual.

"It's me," Elias echoed.

"All right, Silas, break time. Our game is interrupted."

"Ha!" Silas yelled as he jumped out. "You were this close."

"Oh, this close," Kyrie clinched her fist and said in mock frustration.

"I want to play," Eustace said, stepping towards Kyrie. "I bet you could find me."

"But who would want to?" Kyrie shot back.

"The lady is witty as well as beautiful. Just my type."

"Don't be too flattered," Elias said. "Every woman is his type."

Kyrie curled her lip to snarl at Elias, but he could see there was the slightest hint of a smile that played with the corners of her mouth. Perhaps she hated him a little less today.

"Hey Silas," Elias turn from the others and beckoned the boy over to one of the trees.

He reached out to caress one of the small, green fruits. The fine fuzz of down played under his fingers. He could feel the life trembling beneath it. His hand moved over to another of the fruits, searching for one that had grown on the tree long enough to give him good taste.

"You know, I had an uncle that loved peaches," the magi said as he reached for his lumen and plunged it into the heart of the tree. He traced it up the trunk and to the branch that held the peach beneath his fingers.

"He used to say that God could have made a fruit better than a peach, he just didn't."

Silas opened his mouth to respond but left it open as he watched the peach grow, then take on a rich, red and orange color. Elias plucked the ripe fruit from the branch and held it out to the boy.

By now, being used to Elias's gifts, the boy readily took the fruit. As he bit into it Elias couldn't help but smile again. The boy's eyes widened as the peach hit his tongue and orange juice ran down his chin.

"Mom, you have to try this," he turned to his mother and said with a full mouth.

"I'll get another," Kyrie answered, obviously enjoying the sight as much as Elias.

The boy didn't argue. He opened his mouth to bite into the fruit again. The mouth paused, and his brow furrowed. He looked up at Elias.

"Who is God?" he asked.

Elias tried to respond, but anything he could think to say froze in his mouth. The question stunned him. Something about the way the boy asked it made the magi uncomfortable. He felt an immediate loss as to how to answer, as if it were something he was supposed to know but had forgotten. He looked back and forth to the other adults who looked equally as confused as he.

"I'd appreciate it if you wouldn't ripen the fruit early," a voice cracked from behind them, relieving Elias of having to answer.

They all turned to regard a stooped figure in a black robe standing nearby. The hood was pulled down low, obscuring most of his features.

"Ah, there you are," Eustace said, extending his arm toward the slight man. "May I introduce to you the youngest old man you will ever meet. This is my assistant magician, Anton."

The face under the hood looked up to scowl at the grinning Eustace. Elias couldn't guess the man's age, but he looked to have some heavy years upon him. A long and hooked nose stuck out of the shadows of his hood. The rest of the face was decidedly thin, with dark eyes bulging out of his sunken eye sockets. Wisps of thin, blonde hair crept out from under the black cowl.

"We shouldn't be ripening fruit early," Anton chided, ignoring the playful jest. "I've worked hard in here, you know."

"Anton, this is Elias Whitsun and his friends," Eustace said, also ignoring the other man's criticism.

The eyebrows of the hooded man arched only a slight amount. Otherwise, he gave no indication he knew the name or reputation.

"Then you should know better," Anton turned to berate Elias.

"It won't hurt a thing," Elias said, somewhat amused by Anton's petulance.

"Maybe this work doesn't come as easy to others as it does to you," Anton shot back. He turned to retreat back towards the far edge of the garden.

"I work very hard in here, you know," he muttered over his shoulder.

"Now that you mention it, we should discuss how we will allocate our efforts," Eustace called. "Elias is joining us. We need to talk strategy."

"I thought we couldn't feed any more mouths," Anton remarked without turning around.

"We had to make an exception. The Commission is failing."

"What's there to discuss?" Anton asked, still with his back to the others. "I take care of these gardens."

"The gardens are already well-established," Elias jumped in. "The boys should be able to handle fruit production. We need you out with the corn."

"But I've worked very hard out here," Anton said, his voice climbing to a whine.

"I've noticed that," Elias said. "But I also notice there is some wasted effort in here."

This time, Anton did turn around. He fixed Elias with a incredulous stare that looked sinister on the thin face.

"What do you mean?" he asked.

"I notice some flowers over by the southern wall," Elias pointed out.

"What of it?"

"It's a waste of effort. We've got corn that's barely growing out there. We can hardly afford to expend energy on flowers. It's pointless."

"Flowers aren't pointless," Anton argued. His eyes moved away from Elias and searched the other faces.

"Here, they're no good," Elias said.

"Perhaps, the lady would beg to differ," Anton responded with a flick of his wrist. A white flower appeared in his hand. He stepped forward with a bow and presented it to Kyrie.

With a hesitant hand Kyrie took the flower. She inclined her head in thanks and brought the blossom to her nose.

Eustace stifled a laugh into his hands. The assistant magi stiffened and whipped around, retreating back into the peach groves.

"None of this will matter unless we get the corn in," Eustace said. "You know that."

Anton turned his head so that his sharp profile stuck out of his cowl. His thin lips bent into a frown.

"As you say," he answered, and shuffled off into the shadows of the garden.

"Charming guy," Elias observed once Anton had passed from sight.

"Yeah, I haven't gotten a read on him yet," Eustace remarked. "Not exactly a people person, but he's my best magician."

Elias nodded. "He's certainly the most competent of the bunch."

"Just surly."

"How old is he?" Elias asked.

"You might not believe me, but he's just twenty," he answered.

"Looks forty," Elias said and shook his head, feeling a surge of pity for the man. He found it easier to hold back his visceral dislike knowing the man was so young.

"Is it an illness?" Kyrie asked, twirling the flower thoughtfully in her fingers. She brought it up to let it touch the end of her nose.

Eustace shrugged. "He won't talk about it. He won't let me search him either. If it was something magic could fix he would've learned how to at the Enclave."

Something tugged at Elias's mind while he nodded his head absently. He should know. He should remember. A cloud passed over his mind, drowning out the sounds of the garden. Thunder sounded distantly.

"He probably just doesn't like you," Kyrie spoke up, stirring Elias back to the garden. "Have you ever thought of that?"

"What's not to like?" Eustace asked. A playful smile danced across his face.

"It might be the stink of the world's death that clings to you," Kyrie sneered. Elias stood amazed at how quickly she could switch on the scathing spite.

Eustace seemed unperturbed. If anything, Kyrie's anger made him more interested.

"Is that what that smell is?" he jabbed back. "I thought I just forgot to bathe."

Chapter Fifteen
The Ossir

Later that day, as the sun set, Elias took dinner with Eustace on his wide, stone balcony. Orange and purple hues filled the western sky, bathing the desert sands beneath them in a mix of crimson light. A breeze came over the sands, not as hot as the rest of the day. It fell on Elias's dusty face, thick with the salt of dried sweat, and it almost brought relief. Distant images of an older, more abruptly vibrant world flashed in the sunset and echoed on the wind. It was just beautiful enough to make the magi ache.

One of the female servants brought the plates out along with a bowl of water and a rag to wash their hands and faces. As she leaned in she looked Elias over with an appraising smile, containing more boldness than servants usually had. Elias noted how attractive she must have been as a younger girl, with bright blue eyes and blond hair. Both were subdued by the signs of age; wrinkles forming around the edge of her eyes and gray coming in on her hair.

"Don't forget desert," Eustace said as the servant straightened and turned to leave.

"What desert?" She stopped to ask, hands on her hips. "There's no desert."

"I guess you'll have to do then," Eustace answered with a knowing look.

The serving girl rolled her eyes and turned away.

"Seriously," Eustace added to her retreating figure. "You make life sweet, you know."

The woman responded with a dismissive brush of her hand and walked out. Elias could see where the boldness came from. Clearly, at Montreux, social roles were flexible, at least where Eustace was involved.

"She'll be back," Eustace assured as he watched the door to his chambers close. "She's crazy about me."

"You haven't changed much," Elias observed with a wry smile. He remembered Eustace's reputation as a lecher from his days at the Enclave.

"Why deprive the women of the world?"

Elias chuckled and turned his attention to his plate. He picked up a green bean and crunched it with appreciation. As he savored the taste he tried to remember the last time he had eaten something so fresh.

"Hard to believe that used to be common," Eustace remarked, noting Elias's enjoyment.

Elias nodded thoughtfully as he chewed. Eustace reached over with a dusty bottle and poured a generous helping of a light, red wine, almost pink in color.

"From Laimark," he said, holding up the bottle.

"You eat like this every day?" Elias asked. He took a big sip of the wine, savoring the light, sweet flavor, and the cool texture on his tongue.

Eustace shrugged. "We apportion a certain number of the fresh harvest for our own consumption. So that big garden out there is more than just a selling point for the commission. It's what we use to feed ourselves while we're here."

"What about the wine?" Elias asked. "Does the Prince know you're in his stash?"

"I doubt the Prince is ever coming back," Eustace answered, taking his own big sip. "I assume he meant to come back at one point. Otherwise, he wouldn't have left so much good stuff behind. If he does come back we've already noted how some parts of the palace have been occupied by squatters and looters. I guess some made their way down to the wine cellar."

"How unfortunate for the Prince," Elias remarked.

"How unfortunate, indeed."

"However," Eustace continued. "I keep telling myself the supply will run out one day and I should scale back on what I drink. But I always seem to postpone that until tomorrow. Then again, tomorrow grows more uncertain every day. There's a good chance we won't be here tomorrow, or at least the day will find us worse off than we are now. So we might as well drink what we can today."

"That seems to be the general mood," Elias said, unaware of the dismal tone Eustace had taken.

"This wine is from Laimark, you know," Eustace said.

"Yeah. I think you mentioned that," Elias pointed out.

"I'm from Laimark too. Do you know where that is?"

Elias looked over at Eustace, searching his own fractured mind for old geography. The man sitting across from him had a distinctly southern look about him. The dark, curly hair, the black mustache and stubble on his face, the bronze skin and large, full lips reminded Elias of a people he should know.

"Somewhere in the Southern Kingdoms," Elias guessed. "A small place if I remember."

"Oh, it's small all right," Eustace laughed. "It doesn't even exist anymore. The land is still there, though nothing like I remember. The olive groves are gone, the vineyards, all the whitewashed houses are faded. The plazas famous for her festivals are gone. And the women... ahh, brown and lovely, hot blooded. And the dirtiest talkers you'll ever meet. Never in public, mind you. But get them behind closed doors and the things that come out of the mouths. You might not believe this, but Laimark prostitutes were known for being able to get a guy off just by talking to him. No lie. It was a special talent of theirs."

"I can see their influence in your life."

Eustace raised his glass as if Elias had complemented him. "We are a passionate people and I'm proud of it."

"Are there many of you left?" Elias asked.

Eustace frowned into his glass. Brooding clouds passed over his eyes.

"The place has been churned up by the so-called princes, fighting over a pile of sand. We are a passionate people. We like to make war as well as love. We'll fight even when there's nothing left to fight for. Even when our fabled war bands only number a dozen people strong. Pathetic really. But it's who we are.

"Hurts to remember, though. Remember how things used to be."

"Hurts worse not to remember," Elias huffed. "Believe me."

Eustace sat back and narrowed his eyes at Elias. The sun had gone down completely and cast dark over the balcony. Somewhere below, he could hear the guards laughing.

"That's right," Eustace said. "I heard something about that. You had an accident or something."

"Something like that," Elias said. He stood up and walked to the stone rail of the balcony and leaned on it. Stars began to light up the dark skies, familiar constellations rising in faithfulness. Mixed laughter rose up again from below, louder than before. He heard Eustace shift behind him.

"Couldn't recover it?" Eustace asked.

Elias shook his head.

"Think I heard something about that too. Of course, it's hard to separate fact from rumor."

"I'm not sure I know the difference either."

Heat lightning flashed somewhere in the distance. Memories

flashed at the edge of Elias's mind. Storm. Lightning. Steel beneath his hands. The taste of blood in his mouth as water poured down his face.

"According to some, you lost your memory in a magic battle with Gregor. Others say you were dabbling in forbidden magic and opened a portal to Hell."

Elias laughed and emptied his glass in a big gulp. He twirled the stem in his fingers and watched distant torchlight reflecting off the silver.

"My favorite theory is the one where I go mad reading a tome in High Lorian and wake up with no memory."

"I like that one too," Eustace agreed.

"I doubt any of those are true. Though I can't say what happened."

"How bad is it?" Eustace asked. Silence stretched out, thick and heavy as the heat of the day. Even the laughter below had suddenly quieted.

"Ten year gap," Elias answered. "Total loss. Absolute Memory Eradication."

"Never heard of that," Eustace remarked. "Doesn't even sound possible."

"No one thought it could happen until it happened to me. I'm the only known case."

"What is it?"

"A missing room," Elias said.

Eustace coughed, choking on his wine.

"How does a room go missing?" he asked, incredulity thick in his voice, bordering on mockery. "That's not possible. You would have to... I don't know, remove part of the mind for that to happen."

Elias shrugged. "It's what happened."

The sound of a chair hitting the floor sounded as Eustace jumped up. He stepped up to Elias and leaned one hand on the rail.

"You can't remove a part of the mind," he argued. "It's just not possible. Even if you remove part of the brain it won't take away a part of the mind. What you're talking about... Elias. How could you believe such a ridiculous idea?"

Elias shook his head. "Do you think I wouldn't know? I've seen for myself. Gregor's seen. Artherus has seen."

"You had to mingle with that one?" Eustace asked. A shudder passed through him at the mention of the Grand Inquisitor. A reputation of particular cruelty and terror stayed attached to his name.

Elias nodded with a grim expression on his face. He held up his empty cup which Eustace readily filled. As the mild wine ran down his throat he wished for something stronger. Something that would burn.

The sound of laughter rose again. This time the noise sounded high and feminine and came from the room behind them. The blonde servant girl stepped out onto the balcony, followed by two other girls. These were both dark-haired and younger than the blonde.

"I guess we're having dessert after all," Eustace said as he leered at the girls.

"We just came for the booze," the blonde said shaking the empty bottle of wine.

"You want to help me find some more wine?" Eustace asked the other magi.

"Shouldn't we save the supply?" Elias asked in return.

"We'll start saving tomorrow."

* * *

The sound of their steps echoed unnaturally as Elias and Eustace walked the halls of the nearly empty palace. Darkness peered all over, seemingly untouched by the glowing crystal Eustace held in his hands. A small circle of light surrounded them, ending abruptly in the abandoned night just outside their reach.

Strange and spectral phantoms stretched out and fell away at their approach, cast by dusty furniture and carved figures silently decorating the marble. Portraits of Montreux's ancient lords fell under the passing shadows, casting imperious frowns at the two interlopers who violated the sacred and lofty halls.

"The place is much too big for us," Eustace said, almost apologetically. His voice bounced off the marble floors and empty passages. "Of course, we keep the staff to a bare minimum."

They passed by a long tapestry that seem to go on forever. Lordly men on a hunt stretched down for at least thirty steps. A beleaguered stag huddled beneath the circle of brandished spears in the final frame, while pale faced and long-necked women looked on with docile stares.

After passing the molding tapestry, the two men took their circle of light to a broad landing. Above them, on the north end of the wall, the ceiling curved up in glass panes, allowing starlight to filter into the palace.

A sound rose up from the stone stairway. A human voice, low and mumbling, bouncing off the cavernous stairway. It sounded vast and distant, almost godlike. At first, Elias couldn't make out the words. A shadowed figure passed up the stairs and the sound drew closer.

"Enim corpit viscis no haben te lausus est conite algur arescis me ulmen tu."

The old tongue sounded through the echoes. Words Elias hadn't heard in decades fell through the empty halls. They stirred memories of an old world in him, one that shouldn't have been distant, but could have been dead for centuries.

A hunched figure, dressed in shadows came up the grand staircase and turned down the hall toward the magi. Eustace said nothing. He stopped talking and stood aside as the figure approached.

As he drew closer, Elias could make out the features of a shuffling old man. His dark, blue robes hung loosely over his thin frame. The circle with intersecting lines – a sign of Gaia – decorated the hem of his robe. A long, tangled mass of gray hair sprouted from his head, matching the voluminous beard. Thick aromas of incense wafted from him as he passed by the circle of light. His eyes stayed fixed firmly ahead, wide-eyed and glassy, staring intently at something only he could see in the distance.

"Epaltum gesit invidaric veldum restus carintalis te urbum du lumdare," he muttered, moving his arms out in front of him as if he were swimming.

The old man passed by the magi without giving them the slightest glance or look of acknowledgment. It was as if he occupied another world in which he was the only occupant. The sounds of his muttering trailed behind him, echoing off the marble.

"Barbadios is a lot more with it in the daytime," Eustace said.

"Is he a priest?" Elias asked, fascinated by the man as if he had seen a relic.

"The Squire is very devoted to Gaia," Eustace explained. "He's fairly eclectic, if you hadn't noticed. Very forward thinking and innovative but also dedicated to the old ways."

Is that what has become of our once proud culture, Elias asked himself as he watched the old priest amble away. The faithful led by doddering old men? The keeping of strange and eccentric minds? Have we become a piece of history already?

"Can't be that effective as a priest," Elias observed, giving a generous assessment of the old Barbadios.

"Like I said, he's better in the day," Eustace said. "Suffers from Twilight Madness. While the sun's out he's fine. As soon as it gets dark, he becomes another person."

They left the mutterings of the strange man behind them and moved down the steps. On the ground level, the two magi crossed deeper into the palace until they came to a wooden door recessed into a stone arch. Eustace pulled a key from a leather strap around his neck.

"Only a few of us get access to the cellars," Eustace explained as he fumbled the key in and turned the lock.

"Trusted men like yourself?" Elias asked.

"Of course," Eustace responded as he stepped down into the dark stairwell. "Not just anyone would be able to appreciate what we've got down here."

A dry and musty smell rose up from the dark stairs. Elias followed the circle of light down, cool air enveloping him as he stepped deeper. By the time his boots hit the flagstone at the bottom, the temperature had dropped to a deep chill.

"Well, this is what we got," Eustace said, indicating the rows of racked wine and dusty bottles that stretched the entire area of the vast cellar. On the far wall he could make out stacks of oak barrels. Most of the wine racks were still full.

"Looks like you got a pretty good stash," Elias remarked, not seeing any empty spots in front of him.

"I always start at the back," Eustace told him as he guided Elias down the aisle between the two long rows of wine racks.

"There's a good mix in here. I don't think there's any organization to it. A lot of the newer ones are in the back with real old ones mixed in. Reds, whites, plum wines, meads, some rice wines even. Not crazy about those. Gave me a terrible hangover. Although, it could have been that I drank two bottles of it by myself. Still, can't hardly think about it. Kinda have to pick through it but I'm getting less picky as time goes by."

As Eustace guided the other magi through the aisles, Elias began to notice the empty slots. The attrition seemed considerable in some places. Towards the back, an entire row stood empty and bereft of bottles. Elias turned down one aisle and began to pick through the remaining bottles in the row.

"One time in my life I fancied myself somewhat of an aficionado. Being from Laimark, I thought I possessed a natural pallet. But we always think we're naturals at everything. It didn't take long to discover I had no taste for complexity. I would swish wine around my mouth for hours trying to taste pepper, mushrooms, or a hint of coriander. All I could taste was wine. I think they make up a lot of that crap. Made more sense just to drink what tasted good to me. Let the lords sniff out coriander."

Elias had lost track of what Eustace was saying. Something tugged at him nearby. It was like hooks inside his mind grabbing at him from the far wall, beyond, pulling at him, softly but insistently.

"Do you feel that?" Elias asked, nodding his head towards the wall where the small barrels were stacked up.

Eustace shook his head as he held a dusty bottle up to the light crystal. He squinted his eyes, trying to discern something in the dark and cloudy glass.

"I don't touch the rum," Eustace remarked. "Every once in a while the Prince sends for a cask. I haven't gotten desperate enough to dig into that stash."

Elias stepped out into the aisle and approached the far wall. The little casks of rum were stacked up as high as the domed ceiling. He reached his hand out and sent his lumen searching. It flared in his mind immediately.

Curiosity consuming him now, Elias began pulling down the casks. Long shadows stretched out in front of him as Eustace looked out from the racks.

"Seriously, Elias, we can't touch those."

"There's something back here. You can't feel that?"

Eustace stood there watching him for a moment. Seeing that Elias was undeterred he set the glowing crystal on a cask and began to help. A stone wall appeared behind the rows of barrels, and as they cleared more a corner of a doorway peaked out.

"Did you know there was a room back there?" Elias asked, feeling the surge of power grow the closer they got to the door.

"I never came down here looking for anything but wine," Eustace explained with a shrug.

In a few moments, they had the oaken door cleared away. Sigils had been written across its surface in iron bands. An iron lock sealed the door, also guarded in sigils. There was no lock for a key. A solid square of metal, thick by appearance and invulnerable to tampering, stood out where a lock would go.

"Sealed pretty tight," Eustace remarked, nodding at the iron designs on the door. "And if I'm not mistaken, that's a fire ward. No way we get through that without blowing ourselves up."

A smile crept across Elias's face as he traced the iron bands that formed the sigil on the door. As Eustace said, the fire ward kept it from being forced open. Only the right combination of magic would disarm it, and that didn't even take into consideration the lock. It was enough to deter any magical attempt to break in.

Elias closed his eyes and reached for his lumen. The power beyond the door, whatever had grabbed his attention, pulled at him insistently. Whatever lay beyond was strong.

"What are you doing?" Eustace asked, taking a step back. A nervous quiver crept into his voice. "Elias, don't be stupid."

"Relax," Elias answered him. "We'll be fine."

"Burned to a crisp is more like it. Dammit, Elias, you're going to destroy the rum too."

"Iron wasn't the best choice in warding," Elias said, ignoring the other magi's protests. "If they had used gold, there would be nothing we could do. But iron..."

To finish the thought Elias ran his hands along the sigils written in iron bands. The metal turned orange beneath his fingers. It darkened to a brown, then flaked, peeling in long strips of now brittle metal. At last, Elias brushed his hand across the wooden surface, wiping away the last of the sigils. He wiped the rust from his hands then bent over to the lock.

"Bring the light over here," he instructed Eustace.

The other magi didn't respond at first. He regarded Elias with a mix of distrust and fear. Moving his eyes over the door, then at the pile of rust on the flagstones, he began to understand. He sighed and stepped back up to the door and held the light out for Elias.

"Where did you learn that?" he asked, his voice still a bit shaky.

"Marconus," Elias answered, not looking up from his inspection of the lock.

"The necromancer?" Eustace asked. The light began to tremble in his hands. "Did Gregor know?"

Elias touched the lock gingerly with one finger. The thickness of the metal posed more problems than the bands, but the iron would still give way. He felt the energy of decay within, pushed at it, pushed at it again, fed into it, accelerated it. An orange stain appeared on the surface. Then the stain spread and bloomed.

"He's the one who introduced us," Elias answered.

Like the iron bands, the lock grew dusty with light orange rust, then darkened before flaking and peeling up the surface. Elias held on, pushing until the flakes began the flutter down and settle on to the floor.

"Would you like to do the honors?" Elias asked, stepping back.

"Will I explode?" Eustace asked. His mouth had gone dry and his voice cracked when he spoke.

"If so, we both will."

Eustace shrugged and kicked his foot out towards the door. The lock shattered in a cloud of rust and the door flew open. Darkness yawned beyond, swallowing up the small light from the crystal.

As Eustace stepped forward and held the light up, the other magi stood beside him. Sparkles of light glittered off hundreds of smooth and polished surfaces. Colors cascaded against the wall in kaleidoscope shapes.

"We need to cover this back up," Eustace whispered. Elias could discern fear in the magi's otherwise unflappable demeanor.

"The Prince probably doesn't even know it's here," Elias remarked, stepping past Eustace and into the treasure room.

"There's a fortune in here. The Prince will be beyond pissed if this is touched."

"Why would he leave this?" Elias asked, gesturing with his arms out wide. The chamber was small but full. Plates of gold and silver, bowls, orbs, scepters, piles of coin, stood tightly but neatly packed in. Jewels from necklaces, rings or crowns flashed as he moved his eyes over the horde.

"Probably a stash for safekeeping," Eustace answered. He still hadn't stepped inside the chamber. "You saw it was locked, and hidden behind the barrels as well. Come on, Elias. The Prince probably has this as an emergency cache. We can't touch it."

Elias shook his head. "That door was old. I could tell. It was warded but the lock rusted easily. This has been here for a while."

"Still. Were not taking any of this stuff."

"It's not treasure I'm interested in," Elias said. The pull on his lumen grew even stronger as he stepped further into the chamber. He could feel the pull precisely now. At the back of the chamber, where a large cabinet stood in the corner. Elias stepped over a stack of silver coins to move towards it. His heel grazed the top, sending the pile tumbling to the floor with the sound of little bells.

The pull grew into a physical sensation as Elias stood in front of the cabinet. It jerked his hand forward as he moved it over the small drawers, growing stronger as he waved his palm over the doors on the bottom. He opened one of the doors and reached inside and pulled out a bundle wrapped in cloth.

The smile across Elias's face was irresistible now. He was giddy with excitement, already knowing what lay under the cloth. Eustace had knotted his brow as he looked on. Then his eyes went wide with recognition when Elias pulled the cloth back and revealed the blue orb beneath. By his expression, Elias could tell that Eustace finally felt the pull of the powerful artifact.

"What did we promise?" Elias asked, holding the blue orb up triumphantly. "Twenty-six thousand bushels? I bet we can get thirty thousand."

Chapter Sixteen
Some Conversations

The Squire was almost beside himself when Elias explained what they had found in the wine cellar. He tugged at his mustache so hard Elias thought it might rip clear off his face.

"It concentrates magical power," Elias explained, holding the blue, crystal orb out to the Squire.

Montford took it gingerly from the magi. Turning it over in his hands he stared into the clear, blue depths, as if he could understand its properties just by looking at it.

"What's it called again?" the Squire asked.

"An ossir."

"Ossir," the Squire repeated reverently, enjoying how the word felt in his mouth.

"And how does it work?"

"No one really knows for sure," Elias admitted. "Like most magical items, there is a bit of guesswork and a whole lot of mystery involved."

The Squire shook his head and frowned, as if the very idea of something unknown was repugnant to him.

"What do you know?" he insisted.

"It uses what is known as free energy," Elias explained. "Every place is full of it: the earth, the air, water, even people. It used to be called wild magic. A lot of people use it without even knowing it. But what an ossir does is focus the free energy, or wild magic, a certain place possesses. An able magi can connect his lumen to the ossir, thereby magnifying his own powers."

"Incredible," the Squire whispered in awe. "Why would anyone leave something so powerful behind?"

"It's only good here. Ossir's are made particular to a place. It's connected to the energy that flows out of this location. I'm not sure where the center is, probably not hard to find. But the further you get from the center the weaker the ossir gets."

"What's the range?" The Squire asked, looking up from his inspection of the orb.

"Depends on the ossir," Elias told him. "Most are effective within five miles of its nexus."

The Squire smiled broadly, his eyes lighting up with excitement. "Plenty of room for us."

He didn't even remember to ask how they had found the ossir in the first place.

Life quickly fell into a routine at Montreux. It was something else the Squire dutifully enforced. Everyone must know their place. The Commission must run with the accuracy of a clock and the kind of efficiency that tolerated no wasted motion.

"Everything must be precise," he told Elias many times over the next weeks. "That's the only way we can control the variables."

Every morning Elias would rise early and meet the young magicians in the garden. He looked over their progress from the previous day and set them to work again. The place wasn't flourishing as much as when Anton worked it, but it produced well enough.

After the garden inspection, Elias met Eustace and Anton in the cornfields. Despite his reluctance, Anton proved a capable magi. Elias would work with the ossir, his power allowing him the greatest range. At times, he would share the artifact so the others wouldn't think he was hoarding all the power. At night, he allowed Anton to take it so he could tend his flowers.

Sometimes, during the day, Elias would pass Thoran. He usually didn't notice when anyone passed nearby as he worked. Holding the ossir outstretched in his hand, he focused most of his attention on the flows of power as he walked among the corn. He could feel people pass by, but never noticed them.

Thoran was the only exception. Anytime the bothersome man walked by, Elias felt the tug at his mind, much like how the ossir pulled at him in the cellar. He would look up without thinking and see Thoran standing among the corn, fixing him with an expression of mild amusement in his pale, blue eyes. More than once, Elias heard thunder sounding somewhere in the vacant spaces of his mind.

At least twice a day he would see Kyrie as well. The first visit took place after breakfast. Just before he would set out to the garden, she would find him.

"We are probably leaving today," she would tell him, her arms crossed and an icy stare fixed at him. Elias would usually nod and say nothing.

"Just wanted to make sure you won't be coming after us," she explained. "That we're settled."

"We're settled," Elias would agree.

Later that night, she would find him again. This time, Kyrie would inform him of their intention to stay one more night.

"We couldn't get our stuff together," she would tell him. "I couldn't find Silas all day," or, "I think another day of rest would do us good."

Silas, for his part, always made sure he found Elias several times during the course of the day. He would walk beside the magi as Elias worked the corn. Sometimes he would ask questions, sometimes he would talk. Other times he said nothing, walking beside Elias as if he simply enjoyed the magi's presence.

"I wonder what makes the corn grow." he wondered aloud one day when the corn was up to Elias's shoulders.

Unlike before, the stalks were strong and green. Little tufts of silk had begun to appear. Looking down at Silas, Elias could see a similar transformation in the boy. The pale features of his face had filled in with color and substance. The eyes didn't look quite as empty and suspicious as before. He seemed lighter somehow, unburdened, excited and full of wonder. He seemed much like a little boy should.

"Is it magic? How did they grow corn before people knew how to use magic?"

"Hold on," Elias answered with a smile. "One question at a time."

Something triggered on the edge of his awareness. A flaw, a dying spot in the nearby stalk of corn arrested his attention. Elias concentrated his lumen, drawing power from the ossir and filling the dead area. It quickly filled again with life, allowing nutrition and energy back into the stalk.

"It's not magic, but life that makes the corn grow," Elias said, allowing a bit of his attention to drift back to the boy.

"There's a great power that flows throughout the whole of heaven and earth, through all the worlds. It moves everything, fills everything, directs everything. Out of this one power there are four distinct forces. One of these is called the Vion, the power of life. This is what gives all things life. Some refer to it as vital essence. But all living things: plants, animals, insects, even people; we are all alive and have life because of the Vion. It animates us, gives us energy. It also makes the corn grow."

"So why do we need magic?" the boy asked. His arms were spread out wide, brushing the corn as he walked beside Elias. "Why doesn't the corn grow by itself?"

"Well it does," Elias answered. "I mean, it can. Magic doesn't make anything grow, the Vion does. All magic does is open up the power of the Vion, release it, give it a push so to speak. Sometimes, it directs the Vion in one direction or another."

"My mom says that magic ruined everything," the boy said nonchalantly. "She says plants won't grow anymore because of magic."

The sun felt hotter on Elias all of a sudden. "That's not exactly right," he tried to argue gently. "Magic didn't cause the plants not to grow anymore."

"Then how come we can't grow corn without magic?" he asked. "How come the corn can't just grow by itself?"

Elias opened his mouth to offer a defense on behalf of magic, but that argument died before a word came out. How could he explain something to a boy that he didn't understand himself? He decided on the truth instead.

"I don't know," he answered. "I don't know why we can't grow corn without magic. Something happened, Silas. I just don't know what."

The boy didn't push his argument. He walked beside Elias for a moment longer. Then, as if overcome by a stronger impulse, tore off running through the corn.

* * *

After a long day in the fields, Elias would retreat for a rag bath. Only a small portion of water was allowed for bathing. Just enough to wet a cloth and wipe off the dust. Even then, the bowl of dirty water was returned to a special reservoir that would be recycled for the crops.

The bath would be followed by a small meal, usually taken alone and consisting of bread and a portion of the garden's fruit and vegetables. Sometime after his bath or during his meal, Kyrie would find him to deliver whatever reason she had concocted as to why they wouldn't be leaving that night. After that, Kyrie would then be pressed upon by Eustace to have dinner with him, which she always refused. She and Silas would entertain themselves in the library, perusing the huge collection of books, or in night walks about the palace grounds.

After Elias' brief, and somewhat awkward, and very regular interaction with Kyrie, he would seek some distraction for the night. When the Squire was at the palace, this meant chess. Usually, they played in the Squire's room, but on some occasions they went to the balcony. On even rarer occasions he would hand Elias a cigar or a glass of the dwindling bourbon.

The two men would talk as they played, sometimes becoming so engrossed in the conversation that the pieces of the board would lie untouched. The topics ranged as wide as the Squire's interest, which seemed to have no end or order. Clearly enjoying a man of equal intellect, the Squire kept Elias up many nights with his boundless energy.

One thing remained constant in their talks. Elias and Montford never discussed the grim reality of the dwindling world. They stuck to the unspoken rules of their ritual. Life became regular, predictable, molded into a routine.

* * *

Life followed this model at Montreux, except one night when it didn't. Without warning, two of the regular routines were broken. And as is common with any system, one little change can end up having drastic and far-reaching consequences.

These two changes happened on the same night, about a week before the harvest was due. Elias and his company had been there thirty-five days. They had integrated themselves quickly into the life there, so much so that the original members did not consider them refugees any longer. Silas especially, being the only child present, quickly gained the affections of the others.

As time grew near, the corn growing high, it's stalks thick and roots bulging through the Montford cloth, the excitement took over all the people of the Commission. The guards scanned the horizon with growing caution, as if the darkening silk on the corn would draw marauders by smell alone. Montford stayed on constantly, forgoing any trips to the coast. He surveyed the lands all day, treading over the same area twice in several hours. At night he was given to increased pacing.

Perhaps it was the energy that gripped the place that led to the change. It was like a new season coming on. The fields of green corn, the earthy smell of life on the nearby wind, anticipation of success gripped the whole Commission. With accomplishment so near, perhaps the Squire let his guard down and allowed some of his darker concerns to come bubbling up to the surface.

"What's happening to the world?" the Squire asked without warning.

They sat on the Squire's balcony while unusually cool wind blew in from the west. Darkness had fallen fully over the day. Over the horizon a waxing gibbous moon began to show itself.

The Squire had been staring at the chess pieces without saying a word. Elias watched nervously as he noticed his rook left in a vulnerable position. But the Squire did not go after it. He stroked his mustache as he stared at the board, then looked over the balcony into the night.

"It's your move," Elias reminded him, noticing for the first time the Squire's pensive mood.

"What's happening to the world?" he had asked then.

Elias was unsure how to answer. Obviously, with Montford, he would not be able to dodge the question. And as the Squire turned his searching and somewhat sad eyes up at Elias, he knew he would not be able to get away with anything other than the truth.

"I don't know," Elias answered, hoping the Squire would not probe the issue, though knowing full well he would.

"Is it something we've done?" the Squire asked, turning his gaze out again towards the night where in the distance his corn flared life in an otherwise barren land.

"You mean magic?" Elias asked him, assuming Montford would finger the usual suspect.

"Bah!" the Squire exclaimed with a wave of his hand. His face grimaced at the suggestion. "A bunch of populist garbage!"

"How can you be so certain?" Elias asked, reversing his normal role.

"It doesn't make any sense for magic to be responsible," Squire argued, turning back to Elias. His native energy had returned now that he was engaged again.

"If magic were responsible for the Blight then only the fields that had magic used on them would be affected. But that's not what happened. Everything was affected, the whole land. Forests that had never been altered by magic withered away. Uninhabitable swaps dried up. Farms that tried to operate without magic had the same problem as those that used magic. No, it doesn't make sense Elias. Not at all. If magic destroyed the land then the Blight wouldn't have become systemic. We would only see destruction on those lands used intensively for magical crop cultivation."

Elias shrugged. "I guess."

"You don't think magic is responsible, do you?" the Squire asked.

"Normally, I would say no. Like you, I believe the Blight looks bigger than magic. Then again..." Elias let the thought trail off, unwilling to finish it.

"Then again? What?" the Squire prodded. He leaned across the table and took on a sober expression. He looked old all of a sudden, the carrier of many years and burdens.

"Magic used to be easier," Elias finished.

"What do you mean? I didn't realize magic had grown more difficult."

"Magic itself hasn't grown more difficult," Elias began to explain. He picked up the ivory king from the board and felt the carved surface beneath his thumb.

"It's... It's the world that doesn't respond the same. It used to react with a touch. If I wanted a flower to bloom I would just brush it with power, and it would leap, like it couldn't wait to open up. Now, it's all different. You have to coax the flower to blossom. It resists, fights back even. It used to not be like this. It's not the magic that has gotten harder. Life has become more resistant to it."

"How would that kill everything?" the Squire asked, indicating the darkness beyond the balcony that hid a world reduced to dust. "Why would trees that have stood for hundreds of years dry up and die if the world grows resistant to magic? That doesn't explain anything."

"I know," Elias agreed. "Whatever it is, the problem is, like you said, systemic. The very life that magic manipulates isn't as strong as it used to be. It just doesn't have the same potency. It's the things that magic touches - the Vion and all the other forces - aren't as strong as they used to be."

The Squire's eyes went wide as he suddenly understood what Elias implied. "What are you saying?" he asked in shock and dismay. "Are you saying... Elias? Are you saying the world is dying?"

Words dried up in Elias's throat. The look of desperate agony, lostness on the Squire's wide and tired eyes withered his response before he could answer.

"I couldn't begin to guess at that," he managed to get out.

"Is that what you think, though?" the Squire pressed. "You think the world is dying? I mean, really dying?"

"I don't know," Elias shrugged. "It feels that way sometimes. And it gets worse the more time that goes by. I always fear that one day... One day I'll reach out and the earth won't respond anymore. I'll ask the flower to bloom and it won't answer. There won't be anything there, and no matter how hard I try there won't be anything to touch or to grow. Then I know the earth will be dead."

The dark and silence of the night bled on to the balcony. Held at bay no longer by the Squire's boundless energy, the dead that infected the rest of the barren world took over Montreux. The Squire dropped his head into his hands.

"It just doesn't make sense," he hissed into his hands. "Makes...no...sense."

"This could just be my irrational fear speaking," Elias offered by way of small comfort. "The world still responds."

Elias didn't express what lurked deeper in his heart. He didn't dare tell the Squire that he could feel the world dying. He didn't say that he didn't even need magic to know it. Even without reaching with his lumen Elias could feel the vitality of the world slipping away.

"What's the point of this, then?" the Squire asked. He stood up and walked to the edge of the balcony, his shoulders slumped in resignation. "Is there any point to this at all?"

"What choice do we have?" Elias suggested. It pained him to see the Squire so defeated. At that moment, he realized how much he relied on Montford's energy. There had also been a resurgence in Elias during his time at Montreux. And if the Squire fell to despair, Elias might as well.

The Squire straightened suddenly, as if Elias' words had strengthened him.

"Defiance to the end," the Squire turned around and said. "You know, you're right. We will be defiant to the end. Spit in the face of coming darkness."

He paused as if weighing the words, testing them out in his mind, testing them against his collapsing worldview.

"Fight to the end," he said one more time then strode decisively from the balcony.

* * *

The usual pattern of the night broke for Kyrie as well. Perhaps it was the heat of an unusually hot day, or that Silas played harder than usual. Whatever the reason, when Kyrie went to their rooms to get him for their time together, she found him fast asleep.

At that moment, he looked so peaceful to her, all traces of concern and his usual seriousness evaporated from his face. She couldn't bear to wake him. Regret welled in her, as it had hundreds of times before, for stealing his childhood. She reached out a hand to trace a finger across his cheek. He was such a somber child. The changes that had taken place at Montreux had been good for him.

Then a different guilt struck her, as it always did. How many people died each day as she wiled away her time in luxury? She grimaced at the painful stab of emotion that tore at her heart. The hand that so lovingly stroked the cheek of her sleeping child now gripped itself into an angry fist, bunching up a handful of Silas's hair.

The boy groaned and stirred in his sleep. Kyrie gasped and drew back, appalled at what she had done. How quickly the violence could overtake her. It even frightened her sometimes. But as she thought about it, her ire only increased. This wasn't her fault, after all. It was nobles and magicians, the destroyers of the world. It was their fault she was angry, their fault Silas couldn't have a normal childhood. In fact, she and her son should leave this very minute, she decided.

She looked down again at her sleeping child, and her heart softened. She had never seen him so happy, so peaceful, so childlike. A heavy sigh drew out of her as the mother triumphed over the widow.

One more night, she decided. They could always leave tomorrow. She turned from the room and out into the empty halls of Montreux to find something to do with her night.

* * *

Eustace was as shocked as anyone when Kyrie knocked on his door that night. She looked as ravishing as ever, especially as the days of more regular eating had filled her figure out. He noticed with growing eagerness how the green dress not only blended with her emerald eyes, but seemed more snug in the chest than the last time he saw her in it.

"I've already had supper," he said when she asked to dine with him. "But I'm sure I can fit in a little more for a good cause.

"Tell you what, there's a place I'd love to show you. It's a place no girl should leave Montreux without seeing."

"If it was anyone else promising that I wouldn't be so afraid to ask," she replied.

"Oh, the wit of a beautiful woman," Eustace gushed. "But no, this place is safe. I promise you won't regret it."

"I'm sure many a girl has heard that line before."

Still, when Eustace gave her directions to the observatory, she agreed to meet him there while he went to get them food.

He tore through the palace to the larder, afraid that if he hesitated too long then Kyrie might change her mind and he would never get the opportunity again. Grabbing some wine, along with cheese and olives, and a desperate gamble in taking some of the Squire's chocolate, Eustace hurried back upstairs and towards the eastern, more deserted, part of the palace.

Unlike most of the unused palace, the route to the observatory was well-lit. Candle and torchlight led the way through the empty rooms, past the furniture covered in white and ghostly cloth and the stately fixtures of marble and bronze.

He couldn't help but smile as he reached the winding staircase. Perhaps destiny was working for him today, Eustace thought. The stone steps circled the tower, seemingly in an endless spiral until they opened up into the wide chamber called the Star Room. Eustace stopped sharp as he flew up the last stair, his breath almost catching, despite him being winded from the climb.

Kyrie turned at his approach and smiled. For a moment, Eustace could only stare, drinking in the sight. She waited in the middle of the large chamber, standing beside the table. One of her hands perched on the back of a chair, as if she had stopped just before pulling it back. The mixture of moon and starlight bled in from the glass panes of the domed ceiling that soared above. The glow of the small lantern on the table blended with the blue light from outside. Neither shined too bright, but suffused the room in a soft glow. Circling the room, small candles reflected the silver constellations inlaid in the blue stone of the floor. It seemed to Eustace a perfect mix of mood and shadow. And the centerpiece of it all was Kyrie, looking as if the entire scene was painted to display her unique beauty.

"Did you set this up?" Kyrie asked with a laugh, her hand indicating the romantic stage of the Star Room.

"I don't know what you're talking about." Eustace shrugged. His feet finally found their motion again, though a part of him didn't want to disturb the enchantment of the scene.

"This place. How did you know I was going to eat with you tonight?"

"Don't I always ask you to eat with me?"

"I always say no," Kyrie reminded him.

Eustace set the food and wine out on the table. He pulled out two glasses of crystal and filled them both up.

"I keep it set up this way every night just in case you would one day take me up on the offer," Eustace said as he pulled out Kyrie's chair for her to sit.

"Really? That might be the most pitifully desperate thing I've ever heard in my life," Kyrie told him, even managing to put a pitying tone to her voice.

Eustace grimaced as if wounded, sliding into his own chair. "In that case," he said, "The Squire likes to come up here, so he orders the servants to keep the way lit, as well as the space."

"Can't say I blame him," Kyrie said, tilting her head back and marveling at the view of the night sky. It seemed they stood on the very edge of heaven, the stars leaning so close to them, it might be possible to reach out and grab one.

Eustace and Kyrie talked playfully as they ate and drank through the first bottle of wine. Eustace would flirt with Kyrie, filling the light conversation with as much innuendo as it could hold. Just as playfully, Kyrie would shut him down, insulting and spurning his every advance.

When Kyrie had finished eating, Eustace produced a small, wooden box and placed it on the table in front of her.

"Open it," he instructed.

Kyrie lifted the lid, revealing a pair of porcelain dancers, holding one another mid-step. They stood on a circle of gold recessed into the box. She looked back up at Eustace.

"Pretty. What is it?" she asked.

"It's a music box," Eustace told her. "It plays music."

Kyrie shook her head and shut the box. "Let's not ruin the night with your magic tricks," she said.

"Not everything is magic," Eustace told her as he opened the box again. "This one just winds up."

He smiled at her as he took hold of the key on the side of the box and cranked it. Soft music played as the dancers turned at last. The sound came out like bells, playing a tune that evoked an image of little feet tracing innocent steps along a nursery floor.

Eustace stood and offered his hand to Kyrie. She accepted without hesitation and allowed herself to be escorted away from the table. Thinking of destiny again, he placed his hand gently on her side as she reached out for his shoulder. They clasped their free hands and began a simple dance.

Soft light sparkled off of the lapis floor as they danced. Their feet moved over the blue stone, tracing the figures of stars and planets inlaid in silver. It made Eustace feel as if he were dancing on the stars. And Kyrie moved so effortlessly beneath his lead, revealing an expertise in dance rarely found outside of court life.

"So what are you and your son doing out there?" Eustace eventually asked, and noting later that was when the conversation turned serious. "Wandering around the wasted interior? Why don't you go to the coast or something?"

"There's a lot of work to be done," Kyrie answered.

"What work?" Eustace asked with a snort. "People in the interior move from village to village until they get a passport to a coastal city."

"Justice needs to be done," Kyrie glared at Eustace and answered. Her eyes felt especially harsh in the moonlight.

Eustace spun Kyrie around then pulled her close, holding her tightly with an arm around her waist. She let out a grunt but didn't resist.

"Most of you people involved in the revolution business are a lot more secretive," he said. "You're kind of mouthy for a woman who works in illegal activity."

"Ha!" Kyrie scoffed. "It's illegal to want to live?" She spun out his arms with an expert grace, putting an arms distance between them again.

"In this day and age it is. Especially if it involves pissing off the Enclaves," Eustace remarked with all seriousness. He pulled her back towards him again and they resumed their original position. "One word and both you and your boy would get thrown into prison. You would be hung immediately."

"We have resources," Kyrie said, her face growing as cold as the starlight that filtered through the glass ceiling.

"Who is this we?"

Kyrie stopped and jerked her hand away. "Thank you for the wine," she said and turned to leave.

"No, don't." Eustace reached out and grabbed her arm. "Please. Stay. I didn't mean to pry."

"All the same, I think maybe I am too mouthy," Kyrie responded. She pulled Eustace's fingers away and walked from the room.

"I know Haytham is still alive," Eustace called after her, hoping to stall the departure.

It had the desired effect. Just over the stairway, Eustace saw her silhouette pause. The figure turned towards him, or away - he couldn't make out any of her features.

"Haytham was slaughtered at Covenant," Kyrie said from the darkness.

"Not so," Eustace answered. "I know he's alive and so do you. I know you used to work for him. I know that you stick to the interior because the powers you wish to overthrow are weakest out here, or in most cases nonexistent. I know you work on gathering resources for Haytham and his people as you wait for... a better opportunity."

"What else do you know?" the shadowy figure of Kyrie asked. There was a tremor in her voice.

"I know the story of a young girl, a nobleman's daughter. It was said she fell in love with a musician and ran off with him. Her father, so incensed, threatened to throw her dowry into the sea, but found that it was already gone. The two disappeared, only to reemerge in Covenant a few years later, just before the Wheat Rebellion. It was said the young girl's dowry was used to fund the uprising."

"I've heard the story," Kyrie's icy reply came back.

"Have you?"

"Yes," Kyrie answered. "Except in the version I heard it was an actor she ran off with."

"An actor, then."

"What do you want?"

"I want to help," Eustace said, almost pleading. "Please, come back. Sit down."

A pause from the shadowed figure, then she moved again. Kyrie stepped back first into the starlight, then into the candle light. Her face remained smooth and unreadable. She sat down stiffly and Eustace poured her a glass from the second bottle of wine.

"We're not all alike, you know," Eustace said as he filled his own glass and sat down.

"Minor variations in character, perhaps," Kyrie agreed. "Not that it amounts to anything."

"You're wrong there. Some of us are very different. Some of us are sympathetic to your cause. We want things to change too. We want them to change fundamentally. We really do. We've even reached out to some of your leaders. But they won't talk with us."

"You have to forgive us if we're a little skeptical," Kyrie answered. "There were a lot of magi at Covenant. None of them were on our side."

"I know, I know," Eustace said, leaning across the table. "We were very few then, and none of us realized the gravity of the situation.

Since Covenant our numbers have grown. We've learned a lot since then. Much has changed."

"Why don't you do anything, then? Why is it we only hear rumors about you? Where's the action?"

"We are, we're doing a lot," Eustace insisted.

"What are you doing?" Kyrie hissed. She threw her hands out. "I don't see you doing anything except being Montford's lapdog."

"Just because you don't see it doesn't mean we're inactive. If the Enclaves knew who we were the reaction would be swift and permanent."

"We risk just as much."

"Yes, but you are not as much a threat as we are," Eustace pointed out. "Do you realize how dangerous we are just by existing? We promote a different kind of magic, a different power structure, a different relationship to the people and the land. Do you realize what that would mean? Do you realize what that would do to our present power structure?"

"When will you act?" Kyrie asked. "How long will you linger in the shadows and talk about what you will do while others risk their lives?"

"The time has to be right," Eustace said. He lazily picked up an olive and sucked off the salty brine before pushing it into his mouth.

"These decisions are not made by me."

"What do you want from me then?" Kyrie asked him. Her distrust wavered just enough so that she sipped at her wine.

Fate, Eustace thought to himself. It wasn't there to help land him a woman tonight, that much he could tell. Clearly, fate had other things in mind, things larger than Eustace's amusement. This was an opportunity they all had been looking for.

"We want to help," Eustace told her. "And you know we can. But you have to trust us."

"Prove that we can," Kyrie said, leaning across the table.

"How?"

"Tell us about yourselves," Kyrie suggested. "What you call yourselves? What is it you do?"

Eustace found that his answer choked up in his throat. Caution screamed out at him. Could he really trust her? Did he even have a right to expose his brothers to threat? Was this his decision to make?

He pushed the concern out of his mind. Nothing would ever change if they stood still.

"The Restoration of Aeryon," Eustace answered for her.

"What does that mean?" Kyrie immediately followed up. "What is Aeryon?"

"Something out of magical lore. It's an old place. It was important to magic long before the Enclaves came into existence."

"What do you do? How are you making a difference?"

"We're trying to restore the world," Eustace answered.

"How?"

"New ways of looking at magic. Or rather old ways in a new light. Trying to figure out what went wrong and what we can do about it. But not approaching it in the conventional way. Approaching the problem differently."

"Do you admit that magic is what caused the Blight?"

"Of course it is," Eustace bluntly answered. "I think that's kind of obvious, isn't it?"

Eustace could see tears forming in Kyrie's eyes. The candlelight glittered off their glassy surface. She wiped them quickly away and looked down.

"I didn't think I would ever hear a magi admit it," she said, emotion edging her voice.

Eustace marveled at the impact of his admission. Something about it triggered emotion in her. Was it validation? Was it relief at finding an ally in the right place? Was it a sense that, perhaps, what she worked so hard for, sacrificed so much for, was finally beginning to make a difference?

"It's not just magic," Eustace said when Kyrie had gathered herself. "It's bigger than magic. But yes, magic played a huge role in this. But we're determined to fix it."

"I've heard you call each other bird names," Kyrie said, looking up again at Eustace. "To keep yourself secret."

Eustace nodded, amazed at how much she knew. "The birds were sacred in Aeryon. They were seen as messengers of heaven, holy even. Some were considered more sacred than others. We have adopted those names to keep the brotherhood secret, especially in communication with each other. Secret names, that's all. But it also honors what we want to do. The heritage we wish to reclaim. The heritage and tradition that should be magic."

"So what's your secret name?" Kyrie asked. "The Horny Duck?"

Eustace chuckled at the joke. The intrusion of humor was welcome, restoring a lightness to the conversation that had grown altogether dreadful.

"That, I cannot tell you," Eustace said. "For my own safety, and for yours."

"Who is your leader, then?" Kyrie asked. "Who's calling the shots among the Restoration of Aeryon?"

"I wouldn't tell you that if I knew," Eustace answered. "He approaches us through intermediaries and we report, when necessary, through the same channels. Most of the membership is kept a secret except for those directly above me, and those I direct."

"How many do you direct?" Kyrie asked.

"About a half a dozen. They report to me and I send what they give back up the chain."

"Doesn't sound very efficient," Kyrie observed.

"It's not," Eustace admitted with a shrug. He leaned back again in his chair took a big swallow of his wine. "But at the moment, it's required."

"How much progress have you made? How close are you to finding a solution?"

Eustace rubbed his temples and groaned. Anytime that subject came up it elicited the same reaction in him. Frustration. Dashed hopes. The crippling disappointment of being so close. These emotions tore him to pieces when he thought about their lost progress.

"We were close," he told Kyrie. "Very close it seemed. Then...something happened. It all fell to pieces."

"What happened?"

"Some key members were seized by the Enclave. Anjibar mostly, and Gregor were behind it. Most of our progress was lost. Some of us were found out and hunted down. We had to go deeper into hiding."

"How many were found out?" Kyrie asked. Her voice had softened with sympathy.

"About a dozen all told," Eustace answered. "Some were killed, most of them are still in prison. And one of them...well one was the hardest loss of them all. He was on the verge, it was said. He had figured it out. Just when it seemed like it was all going to come to fruition, Gregor caught wind of it somehow. He wiped out everything we had done."

Eustace grimaced and banged his hand on the table, feeling the frustration all over again. A soft hand reached out to take hold of his. He looked up and saw a tenderness that had always been missing from Kyrie's features.

"I'll put a message in," she told Eustace. "We'll see where it goes from there."

She patted his hand again, then stood to leave. Eustace made no move to stop her. But she stopped on her own and turned back toward him.

"I only do this out of necessity," she said. "Because it will help our cause. For the record, I still hate you and your whole kind."

Kyrie left Eustace alone in the observatory. He stayed there long after her scent dissipated through the cavernous room. Watching the dwindling candlelight he finished his wine alone.

The frustration that had been stoked in Eustace was not so easily drowned. So he stayed up, drinking, and cursing Gregor for all that he had destroyed. He cursed him for the good magi killed and for those still in prison. He cursed him for the progress that had been knocked away by a sweep of his powerful hand.

But Eustace's most powerful curses were for what Gregor had done to the one. The one who held the secret. The one who had brought them so close - had brought the world so close - to restored life. That one had been the recipient of Gregor's most potent and awful torture, his most gratuitous display of wrath.

Eustace's most vehement curses were for what Gregor had done to Elias Whitsun.

Chapter Seventeen
Storms

Five days before the anticipated harvest, the Flash Rain fell. As always, it appeared without warning, only giving hints to those of magical sensitivity. Even then, the warning was slight.

It came at the end of the day. Elias stood in the corn that had grown a foot above his head, the dusk lighting the sky to the west. The stalks were thick, sprouting deep, green leaves and topped with fat kernels and withering silk. He felt lost in the maze of corn. But the sensation pleased him. Even hot and covered in brown dust, sweat trickling down his face forming tracks of mud – it pleased him to be surrounded by so much green. He could almost forget the barren desolation of the hills that surrounded him. Even the dust that stung the corners of his eyes and crunched beneath his teeth couldn't destroy the illusion. It felt too good to be true.

Elias walked more briskly than usual. He held the ossir in his left hand. A faint, blue glow shimmered in the smooth crystal. A brief smile played across his face. In the corn around him he heard other people moving and talking, the lightness of anticipation clear in their voices.

Without warning, the ossir began to brighten. The change was slight at first, barely noticeable. Elias had time only to look at it curiously when it blazed with a sudden flare.

Blue light exploded from the ossir. The orb warmed in his hands, covering the corn in an azure glare. Elias turned to shield his eyes from the sudden brightness.

Then he felt it.

An immense power gathered over his head with a speed and intensity that ripped fear through the magi. He almost fell to his knees, stumbling as his lumen was struck with the infusion of sudden power.

"Flash!" he screamed out, just as the sun darkened and black clouds formed from the empty sky, blotting out the red streaks of sunset.

The skies opened up and rain fell. In thick, pouring sheets it flooded. Gray streaked before Elias's eyes. He felt water pooling around his feet. Streaks of rain blinded him so that he could see nothing but the ossir blazing and dancing off the wall of falling water.

Panic replaced fear as he saw the world washed in grey. The corn, he thought. How can the corn withstand this? In his mind he saw all of his work washed away in a few minutes of rain.

The corn swayed and bowed beneath the power of the torrent. The sound of rain striking the green stalks screamed like a thousand voices rising up at once. The water rose to his ankles, then to his calves.

But the corn held.

A current pulled at Elias's legs. He looked down to see the water, guided by the gentle grade, flowing over the Montford Cloth. The cornfield had been turned into a large river. Elias watched the corn sway with growing panic, waiting for the inevitable snap of stalks as the water tore away all his effort.

Then, as quickly as it had begun, the rain stopped. The clouds dissipated, folding in as quickly as they had appeared. The grey retreated, allowing the soft light of sunset to return. As the rain stopped the glow from the ossir faded with it, then fell dark.

Elias looked around, water dripping from his face. Deep, panting breaths tore through him as panic still raged in his veins. He spun, looking all around him, not believing what his eyes saw.

The corn had held.

Someone yelled nearby, not a sound of fear or pain. It was a yell of triumph. Another one echoed in the distance, then another. Soon the field was filled up with jubilant cries of victory. Elias heard his own voice crying out too. No words, just a sound of surging joy. The Interior Food Commission had faced the worst the blighted world could throw at them. And they had survived.

Elias' yell turned to a laugh. He lifted the ossir high and let the joy flow unobstructed from them. He turned, reveling in the sensation.

He jumped back as a face glared at him from the corn.

Thoran stood, still as deadwood, an unreadable expression on his face. Something like hate flashed across his features. Then it disappeared as quickly as the rain.

"Thoran," Elias said as his smile faltered. "Are you trying to discover new ways to be weird?"

"I have to talk to you," Thoran said, ignoring the jab.

"Okay," Elias relaxed a bit though still on his guard. "Let's talk."

Thoran looked around. They were alone in the corn, though voices could be heard near and far.

"Not here. Tonight," Thoran insisted.

"What about?" Elias asked.

"It's important," Thoran said. "Tonight, among the grapevines.

Right after the second watch begins."

He turned and disappeared into the stalks. The sound of cheers faded in the distance. Water dripped from the long corn leaves. At his feet, Elias saw the water as it dissipated, leaving large drops on the cloth. Elias tried to smile again, but Thoran had managed to dampen his mood. He lit the ossir again and continued his work on the field. He was so distracted, so lost in his thoughts, he walked right by the hulking shape of Bannus, hidden in the high stalks of corn.

* * *

Later that evening, under the full dark of night, Eustace had a similar encounter with Thoran. He walking out onto his balcony, pausing only for a brief look at the stars overhead and collapsed into his chair. He hadn't even bothered to bathe yet. Exhaustion wouldn't allow him. He rubbed his dust-covered face and groaned, when he felt a presence nearby.

Thoran stood only a few feet away, staring intently at him. Eustace wanted to start in alarm, but forced himself to be still, unwilling to give Thoran the satisfaction.

"I assume you have some good reason for entering my quarters uninvited," Eustace challenged the strange and silent man.

"I do," Thoran said with a nod.

"Well, spit it out then," Eustace demanded irritably.

Thoran leaned forward. A slight smile played over his lips.

"I know who you work for," he said.

"Of course you do," Eustace replied. "You work for the same man, for now. Though I dare hope once the harvest is done we won't have the privilege any longer."

Eustace closed his eyes and turned from Thoran. Inside his chest, his heart thumped wildly. He knew full well what Thoran implied.

"They call you the Kingfisher," Thoran said quietly.

The words entered Eustace like a dagger in his gut. His eyes shot open and he leapt to his feet. Reaching within, he grabbed hold of his lumen, ready to use it in any way to destroy the man before him.

"Who sent you?" he hotly demanded.

"The same people that sent you," Thoran replied, his smile broadened. It was as if he enjoyed watching Eustace suffer.

"Prove it," Eustace hissed. "Prove it or I will not hesitate to destroy you."

Thoran laughed but held up his hands in a conciliatory gesture.

"I work for the Restoration of Aeryon," he told Eustace. "I know you are called the Kingfisher. I know you report to the one called the Gray Owl, though I don't know his identity. I do, however, know who the Golden Eagle is."

"You lie," Eustace tried to yell, but it only came out as a whisper. How could this filthy cretin know who the Eagle was? Hardly anyone knew that.

Thoran shrugged, unperturbed. "I also know that Elias was called Sparrowhawk, was he not? Although he doesn't remember that. Part of the lost years."

"Go on," Eustace urged, his heart racing faster by the second. Sweat beaded down his forehead and wet his palms out of fear and the effort of holding onto his lumen.

"I know your precious Sparrowhawk was the key to everything," Thoran continued. "Elias was on the verge of being able to end the Blight when Gregor got wind of it and brought it all to an end. I even know he was betrayed by the one called Skylark."

"You lie!" Eustace did yell this time. His hands itched to pummel Thoran. "Rion is dead! Gregor saw to that!"

"Rion lives at an estate just outside Anjibar," Thoran contended. "He had hoped to live like a king, but Gregor has him more a prisoner."

Eustace's head spun. It was almost too much to take at once. Thoran, an agent of the Restoration. One of their own he believed had been martyred was not only alive, but a traitor on top of it.

"What is it you want?" he asked. "What are you doing here? What do you want from me?"

"For now, just listen," Thoran instructed. "It's time to put the Sparrowhawk back in play."

"I don't think he can help us now," Eustace said with a shake of his head. "Whatever Gregor did to him ruined him for good. Those memories - whatever plan he had in his head is gone."

"Gregor didn't take his memories," Thoran insisted. "Elias did that himself. And we have to help him find them again."

"How?" Eustace asked, his voice barely a whisper, wondering how many such revelations he could bear at once.

"I couldn't begin to guess that. What I know is that we have to put him back in play. I'm going to try to do that tonight. If it doesn't work I may need your help to encourage him. "

"Are you going to tell him everything?"

"Hardly," Thoran huffed. "I still don't know what condition he's in. Gregor might not have taken his memories, but he did some awful things to Elias under captivity. I'm not sure what he would do if he learned everything at once. He's not the same person he was."

Eustace nodded his agreement. He too had noticed the marked change in Elias. He was but a shell of his former self. Maybe he had been an arrogant ass at times, but he was, at the best of times, a wonder to behold. The apathetic and world-weary man who worked with him for the Commission may still be a talented magi, but nothing like the real Elias, the Elias Eustace remembered. It had been Elias who made them all believe. It was his fire that really fueled them. His fire that still fueled them.

Eustace shook his head, the memory too painful for him.

"What do you want me to do?" Eustace asked, turning away from Thoran and resting his arms on the balcony.

"For now, just listen," Thoran reiterated. "I meet with him tonight in the grapevine just as the second watch begins. Hide yourself there and listen to what I tell him. It's something you need to hear also."

"Then what?"

"Hopefully he will be convinced to search for what is lost," Thoran said. "He's the only one that can put the pieces back together."

"Are you certain he can do it?" Eustace asked. After finally getting used to the disappointment of losing everything he had fought for, he didn't know if he dared hope again.

"He can," Thoran answered. "He has to. He's the only hope we have."

There came no other words. Eustace heard the soft rustle of clothes. Then he felt himself alone on the balcony in the stillness of the night.

* * *

Complaining of exhaustion, a highly believable possibility, Elias excused himself from the nightly chess game with the Squire. Montford didn't even look up from the board as the magi slid out of his chair, leaving his opponent to brood over the ivory pieces alone.

Halfway down the stairs of the dark and empty palace, Elias stopped. He turned to go back up and continue the game, or to bed, or anywhere but the grapevines to meet with Thoran. He stood, undecided, not sure what he would do. The idea of talking with Thoran filled him with an uncomfortable dread. Like being stuck in a room with someone of overbearing affection, the man elicited that same feeling of suffocation in Elias.

But it was more than that. Something about Thoran made him feel like Elias' personal gadfly. He felt goaded by the man, crowded out of his equilibrium. He felt too much would be asked of him, expected of him. Those thunder-blue eyes, they searched his soul and stirred something, hidden deep and complete.

A sound echoed through the marble walls. The now familiar figure of Barbadios, at first an unformed shadow, came ambling up the stairs. As he climbed into view, his unfocused eyes passed over Elias, neither noticing nor seeing the magi. Rhythms of ancient Vascan fell from his tongue while the priest waved his arms in rituals only he could see.

Elias watched Barbadios pass him by and seemed to forget the decision he had made seconds before. Continuing on his way he passed through the empty halls and out into the yard behind the palace.

Only a single guard passed by outside. The night was mostly his as Elias took towards the south end of the garden. The heavy, wooden gates opened with the squeal of its hinges.

Once inside, Elias inhaled the deep fragrance of fresh flowers. It suffocated the night air. A blue light glowed off towards Elias' right. In it he could see strange shadows cast off a robed figure along the south wall.

As Elias approached the mixed aroma of flowers grew more intense. Honeysuckle and jasmine jumbled with the scent of roses and gardenia. It made his head swim with its intensity.

Anton didn't regard Elias as he stepped near. A small pause in his movements was the only indication he gave that he knew he was no longer alone.

"This is my private time," Anton said sourly.

Elias felt the unwelcome sting. The small man shifted so his back was to him.

"I beg your pardon?"

"My work is done," Anton said. "I have done what is required of me. I didn't cheat the Squire. This is my private time."

"I was just seeing what you are up to," Elias clarified.

"I know you don't approve," Anton said stiffly. He continued his slow ministration to the flowers.

"It's not that I don't approve. I just don't see the point," Elias said.

"It's a waste of energy. Flowers don't do us any good. People are starving all over the world. What good are flowers?"

Anton paused again. He seemed to be regarding his own thoughts, then turned to face the elder magi.

"People need beautiful things as much as they need food," he said.

Elias smirked at the comment and scoffed.

"Beauty doesn't keep people alive," he told Anton.

"No," Anton replied softly. "But it makes them want to stay alive."

The younger magi returned to his work. Soft chant mixed with the blue light of the ossir. Blossoms and the sweet aroma of beauty took flight on the night air again.

A laugh died on Elias's tongue. He wanted to say that that was the stupidest thing he had ever heard. He wanted to mock Anton for a fool and starry-eyed romantic.

For some reason, the laugh wouldn't come. Whatever mockery wanted to erupt from Elias's cynicism, it could not find its way out. With no answer he shuffled away awkwardly, making his way toward the grapevines.

It was the fourth row of vines that Elias peered down that revealed a shadow waiting. He didn't have to be told who it was. Even if Elias didn't recognize the broad shoulders of Thoran, or the way he was able to hold himself unnaturally still, he would've known. He would've known without using his magic.

Irritation flared in Elias, and that emotional claustrophobia that comes when we feel a person is too close, that they tread too deeply into our intimate selves. Without even speaking, Elias felt suffocated by the man. There was a connection between them, and he hated it. He couldn't explain it either, so he hated Thoran all the more.

"You've come," Thoran said as Elias approached. From the sound Elias could tell he faced him.

Elias shrugged. "I did. What's so important you had to meet me in secret?"

"What, no small talk?" the shadow teased.

"Out with it."

The shadow that was Thoran cocked his head. Elias didn't have to see in the dark to know that Thoran grinned at him. That stupid, smug grin.

Thoran shifted so the moonlight fell on his face. There was no smile there. A more sober look than Elias had ever seen on him fixed upon Thoran's face. His mouth set firmly and his brows pressed in together.

Reaching for a pouch at his side, Thoran offered it to the magi. The smell of oil and leather wafted up as Elias took it in his hands. Thoran nodded for him to look inside. Elias loosened the strings and dumped the contents into his hand.

A dozen large, dried seeds filled the magi's palm. He could still make out their faded green color.

"Beans?" he looked up at Thoran to ask. "Is this your idea of a joke?"

"Not at all," Thoran said, his voice a whisper. Anticipation edged his words.

"What do you want me to do with them?" Elias asked.

"Touch them."

"I am," Elias said, holding seeds.

"You know what I mean," Thoran hissed.

It was Elias's turn to smile. He had never gotten the best of Thoran. The strange man looked perturbed, nervous even, knocked off his usual pedestal of smugness.

Whatever joy Elias took in the small victory failed the moment he touched the seeds. Almost absently, he opened his lumen and grazed the dried beans in his palm. At first, he felt their age, almost too old to be vital. Then, deeper, and his eyes widened in shock.

"Where did you get these?" he asked, his voice a breathless whisper.

Elias's hand shook as he plunged deeper into the seed. An alarming suggestion, an impossible one thundered in his mind. Power emanated in the seeds, latent and hidden, but impossible to miss. It was like nothing he had ever felt before. Or something he had not felt since...since when?

He looked up at Thoran, to ask again where the seeds came from. Lightning flashed before his eyes. Thunder shook him, deep into the core his bones. Rain pelted him, thick and heavy rain. It ran down his face, in his eyes, and filled his mouth.

Elias reached out to take hold of the world. It spun and slipped from him. Cold, iron bars were all his hands could find. He tried to speak but blood filled his mouth, choking out his words.

Lightning flashed.

He grabbed the iron bars in front of him. Elias looked around, surrounded by them. A wind blew sheets of rain in his face and his cage swayed, the iron chain groaning overhead, singing with the howl of the storm. A cry came tearing out of his mouth, lost in the ravaging weather and the forest of empty cages that surrounded him. All of them were empty except for his.

Lightning flashed.

Warm soil replaced the cold metal in his hands. Blue light faded into his sight. A stuttering and coughing breath rushed into Elias's lungs and labored out again. He still gripped the seeds in one hand, their latent power thrummed insistently. His other dug into the ground.

Thoran's shadow moved over him.

"What are they?" he asked.

"Where did you get these?" Elias managed to ask, rising from his knees. His hand shook even more now. The vision had never hit him so hard.

"Tell me what they are and I'll tell you where I got them."

He didn't want to say what they were. Not only did it seem impossible, but they had triggered that waking nightmare in him, so strong that for a moment it seemed real. It seemed so real that the taste of blood still tainted his mouth.

The fierce gaze of Thoran's eyes met his own as Elias looked at him. There was something grim and prophetic in those features. Also something immovable.

"They're seeds," Elias gasped. "Real seeds."

Words from an old teacher at the Enclave, Master Lumos, came back to him. He had lectured them one day about seed potency. It was the first time Elias heard anything remotely related to the world dying. As the green and fertile earth shriveled into dry and dusty wasteland, those words, the first hints that something had gone wrong, came frequently back to mind. Now, holding those seeds in his hand, real seeds, the lecture reverberated in his mind again.

"Seed potency is everything," Master Lumos told them as he paced the front of the classroom. Large diagrams of seed parts and schematas of their inner workings covered the wall behind him as he lectured.

"Without seed potency, magic is useless. As magi, we do not add any power or strength to the vion already within the seed. It must reside there already. What we do is unlock it.

"It is very important that you always work with a viable sample. You will be saving yourselves wasted work and effort. For example, seed harvested from a crop that has been subject to intense, magical enhancement will display a slightly lower level potency than the original seed. This is most likely due to a shortened growing period that may have interrupted essential vion entering the sample. Of course, this only means that the harvested seed be enhanced to retain full strength, but it must be something you are always aware of. Second generation seed is always less potent than the first."

Elias didn't ask the obvious question, and no one else seemed to think of it. If the second generation of seed was weaker, what would happen years down the road? Despite being assured later on, when he did ask, that a little extra work on the seed would restore any potency that was lost, Elias felt the first stir of foreboding about the world during that lecture. And that foreboding had been fulfilled with awful reckoning. Seed that had once been vital and potent barely responded to the touch of magic. Seeds had lost their power.

The seeds he held now were different. Power leapt out of them. As soon as his lumen grazed the inside germ, Elias could feel the bolts of vital energy that sent shivers of ecstasy through his body. He hadn't felt this much power in seeds in a very long time. There was only one explanation for such potency.

"These are original," Elias continued. "Untampered by magic. These are real seeds."

Thoran only nodded, his stare still fixed on Elias. The magi forced himself to meet the stare, to push away the thunder that still rumbled in the distance of his mind.

"Tell me," Elias said. "Tell me where these came from."

"I don't know where they came from," Thoran said.

"To Hell with your lies," Elias hissed. He balled up the fist that held the seeds and shook it inches from Thoran's face.

"Tell me where these came from or I will incinerate you where you stand."

"I can't tell you where they came from because I don't know. I can only tell you where I got them."

"Where did you get them, then?" Elias asked through clenched teeth.

"You gave them to me." Thoran answered.

The revelation should have staggered Elias. But he had been knocked down too much that night already. He was surprised to feel a trickle of relief begin to fill him.

"So I do know you," Elias said, reveling in the rare moment when his present connected with a lost memory. "Back in Hiram's Well, you said we had never met."

"I lied," Thoran bluntly stated.

"Why?"

"Why?" Thoran asked back, a tone of condescension in his voice. "Do you realize what's at stake here?"

"Yes, I do," Elias said, holding up the seeds. "The yield from this small bit of seed could probably equal the yield of at least an acre of conventional seed, maybe even two. Do you realize what we could do with this?"

Thoran threw his head back and laughed. It was a hollow sound, falling dead among the silent vines heavy with late fruit.

"That's exactly why I lied to you," Thoran snapped at the magi. "Give me the seeds back. You don't deserve them."

Elias's hand jerked back. Thoran didn't make any move towards him.

"You'll do the same thing to those seeds that you did to all the others," Thoran flatly accused. "In two years they'll be as worthless as the ones we already have."

"What else are we supposed to do with seeds? Just carry them around in our pouch, for who only knows how long? They're worthless then. Worse already than the seeds we have."

"These were meant for something more," Thoran insisted. "You gave them to me for a greater purpose."

"Whatever that grand purpose is, it's long forgotten," Elias said. "Forgotten with all the rest of those years of my life. They're gone and they're not coming back. Just like this world. The Blight is our only reality now. It will not pass. This is not a phase. The old world is not coming back. Today is about survival and nothing more."

"That's not why you gave me the seeds," Thoran repeated.

"Why did I give them to you then? If not to bring back an old world?"

"These were to plant a new world," Thoran told him. "To restore all that was lost."

"Then I was an idiot," Elias said with a sardonic smile. He shook the fistful of seeds. "I was young and stupid. This pitiful bunch of seeds isn't enough to bring us a new world. A teardrop in a hurricane, that's what these are."

"There are more," Thoran said.

The grin fell off of Elias's face. He tried to read the other man's features. It was an impossible feat in good light. In the full shadow of night it wasn't even worth trying.

"Where?" Elias asked.

Thoran held up his empty hands. "Only you know that."

"Then they're as good as lost."

"You can find them."

"How, Thoran? How?" Elias felt his anger rising, fueled by the years of frustration, a feeling of being incomplete, of walking around with a piece of himself missing – an ache so deep that it had filled him with a loneliness that never went away.

"It's gone, nothing left up here," he said, jabbing his temple with his finger. "It's all gone. I've looked. I've tried. Gregor has tried. The whole cursed Enclave of Anjibar has tried. It's lost forever. I'm trying to move on. I'm trying. But this..."

Opening his hand Elias let the seeds fall to the ground. They clattered in the dust at his feet.

"This is futility. And if I try to follow it, I will go mad. I'm barely hanging on as it is. I can't go chasing cries in the dark. I won't do it."

Elias turned and stormed down the row of vines. Thunder began to sound in the back of his skull. He shoved it away.

"There's a tree," Thoran called out.

Elias ignored him. Nothing, he told himself, would make him turn back.

"A tamarisk tree," Thoran said.

A cloud of dust rose up as Elias's feet skidded in the dirt. The move was involuntary. It was as if his feet had stopped of their own accord.

"What did you say?" Elias asked, rooted to the spot, his feet heavy as millstones.

"A tamarisk tree," Thoran repeated.

The word reverberated through Elias's mind, striking the core deep within him. He almost remembered something. It hovered, right on the edge of consciousness.

Slowly, he turned around. Thoran was stooped on the ground, picking up the dropped seeds.

"There's a tamarisk tree," he said as he gathered up the small kernels. "I don't know where exactly. Somewhere to the south. It shades the entrance to a barrow. An old one, vast and deep. At least that's what you told me. Inside are seeds, thousands of them. Seeds of all sorts from the world before the Blight. They're waiting. You're supposed to return and use them to start a new world, to bring life back."

Thoran walked over to Elias and took his hand. He pressed the seeds back into Elias's palm.

"You are going to make all things new."

For a moment, Elias felt complete. That sense of alienation, of being partial, fled when Thoran spoke of the tree. And in holding the seeds in his hands again, it was like being found.

"How can I?" Elias gasped, gripping the seeds again, reveling in the warmth of life that spread from them into his body. "I don't remember."

"We piece it back together," Thoran said. "We retrace where you went, where you journeyed. We follow your own steps and we will find the tree. And when we find the tree you will know what to do."

"How do you know?" Elias asked, disbelieving. He didn't want to reach out and take hold of that hope again.

"You told me," Thoran answered. "You gave me the seeds, told me to find you when it was safe again. I was to tell you about the tree and then...well, then we will find it."

"I told you to do this?"

Thoran nodded.

Elias looked down at the seeds in his hands. They were real seeds, that much was true. Specimens such as these had long gone extinct. It seemed to verify everything Thoran said. It was almost as if Elias had known what was going to happen to him and made preparations for it.

The thought was almost too much to take in. How could he possibly have known his memory would vanish? How could he have possibly prepared for something like that?

But there, in his hands, he held what seemed like proof. Seeds, real seeds lay in his grasp. And a tree, the very mention of which made him feel complete. Did that mean he had to believe?

That belief meant he had to trust Thoran when every other instinct within him screamed at him to be wary of the man. It would mean retracing all his steps and trying to piece together ten years of lost memory. And even if that worked and he found the tree, what then? He was going to save the world? Or would he just be back to where he was five years ago? With the same thing happening again? And what about Bannus and Gregor? Surely the Enclave wouldn't let him go chasing his old memories.

The enormity of what Thoran suggested came crashing down on Elias all at once. He looked around the gardens. So much had been built there. So much promise grew within their walls. So much was being done there. But the seeds? Thoran wanted to chase phantoms fifteen years old. What existed in the garden was real. What the Squire was doing was real.

That old malaise came reaching out to Elias again, growing from within like a vine, curling around his mind, his heart. Thoran wanted to wander the wasteland, while here, he had a garden. Thoran wanted to chase old dreams that Elias had conceived as a younger and more foolish man. The world wasn't going to get saved, Elias decided. It didn't want to get saved. Who was he anyway to think that he could do it? It all seemed like...like too much trouble. It was hunting down old memories and trees. The seeds were nothing but relics of the past. The world was different now. The world was not going to be saved by ancient grandeur.

Elias handed the seeds back to Thoran.

"I'll think about it," he said.

Thoran cocked his head at Elias as if not believing what he had just heard.

"Think about it?" he echoed incredulously. "The world is dying, Elias. What is there to think about?"

"Look around you," Elias said, stretching his arms out. "This isn't death. This is life. What we're doing here is working."

"The Interior Food Commission?" Thoran spat. "You think this is going to do anything? This is like sneezing into a thunderstorm."

"It's better than chasing after trees that probably aren't even there, even if we could find it."

"What's happened to you?" Thoran asked. "What have they done to you? The Elias I knew never was so apathetic as you. Do you even care anymore?"

Elias tried to look as if the criticism didn't sting, though it cut him deeply. It hurt even more considering he didn't really know what kind of man he had been. It felt as if he were betraying himself.

"You know nothing about me," Elias countered, turning to leave.

"You're a shell of the man you used to be," Thoran called out to Elias's retreating figure. "Just a shadow. You've changed, Elias."

"People are supposed to change," Elias muttered under his breath. He dared not ask himself if the change was for the better.

Alone for the moment, Thoran watched Elias disappear into the rows of vines. He looked down at the seeds in his hands and put them back into the pouch.

A rustling sound came from beside him and Eustace stepped out of hiding to stand beside Thoran. They both gazed at the empty spot where Elias had stood.

"See what I mean?" Thoran asked.

"We'll have to convince him," Eustace answered.

"How?"

"Let's wait for the harvest. I'll talk to him then."

"We're running out of time," Thoran said before leaving in the same direction as Elias.

Now it was Eustace that was left to contemplate these things alone. I will convince him, he told himself. He thought back to his hometown, to the memory of olive groves and wine festivals and the sun-darkened women of the coast. It was that memory that kept him going no matter how bad it got.

"We will have it again," he told himself, and he too abandoned the grapevines.

The only figure left was unseen by all the men that night. Twenty feet from where Elias and Thoran had argued, Bannus carefully rose from the thick leaves and fruit heavy vines, hardly making a sound.

Chapter Eighteen
Failed Experiments and New Intelligence

Gregor was displeased. The sensation came so infrequently that the Lord Prefect hardly had any idea how to cope with it. He was, without question, the most powerful man in the world. Disappointment came rarely.

The smell of burning wheat filled his dark workshop, reminding him of his failure. He walked over to the stone table to smother the few burning embers that remained. After pressing the hem of his robe down on the smoldering pile of wheat, he lifted it again only to find the embers still wafting smoke. He pressed down again, harder this time, leaning on the small stone surface to smother all traces of the fire.

Once again, smoke rose up from the remains. Gregor cried out and swept the remains away, scattering the smoldering seeds over the floor. The two slaves flinched at the outburst, as they should, in Gregor's opinion, and hurried to clean up the mess.

"Leave it!" he yelled, feeling a little bit better having yelled at someone.

There was no threat of further burning. The floor where the smoking wheat lay scattered was made of black marble, while the walls, carved out of dark rock couldn't possibly burn. He had done much worse here, he remembered. The shelves carved into the side of the cavern held all manner of instruments, their purpose impossible to determine, even by the most educated magi. The opposite side of the chamber held the glass vials of both liquid and powder, herb and strange apothic. Deeper still, in the part of the chamber unlit by the few torches and oil lamps, hid the door that led even further down. The results of many of Gregor's most ambitious experiments lay safely locked away down that corridor.

Gregor fell into a chair by his desk and looked over the record of his latest work. He sighed and turned back to the stone table. Perched above it, a halo of thin, jagged needles wrapped in fine copper snarled at him as from the mouth of a metal beast. Something had gone wrong, that much was too obvious. Moments ago, that device – an iron ring protruding dozens of the thin needles – did nothing but burn his wheat.

A quick look over his notes brought on fresh frustration. He slammed the book shut and pinched the bridge of his nose. A wave of his hand brought one of the slaves over to fill his wineglass.

"No! No!" he growled. "Get me something else. A beer. Get a beer for me."

"Lord," the slave said with a deep bow. "The barrels have been depleted."

"Is there none left?" Gregory asked.

"Why yes, but you asked that the other set of barrels be..."

"Beer," Gregory said, less than a yell but quite emphatic.

The slave scurried off to fetch Gregor's refreshment. He signaled to the other to bring his secretary, Albinus, to the chamber.

For the few moments he had alone, Gregor stewed over his problem. Except it wasn't just his problem. It was the world's problem. If he failed, then inevitably the world failed. That weight, massive beyond belief, had been placed on his shoulders. But it was a burden he was willing to bear.

The thought secretly pleased him, though Gregor would never admit this. Before any sense of self-satisfaction could emerge from his secret heart Gregor smothered it and weighted it down in suffocating admonitions of duty and reminders of the burden that had been thrust upon him.

The slave delivering his beer appeared first. Gregor took the mug without a glance and drank deeply. He frowned over the warmth of the drink and how the froth bubbled too thickly on the top. He decided to push these matters aside and clumped them together with the general misfortunes of the day.

A shuffle of feet over the black marble told Gregor the other slave had returned with Albinus. The secretary nodded his head in deference as the slaves took their place against the wall.

"How are the experiments today?" the secretary asked as he glanced around the room.

Gregor waved away the question, knowing full well the secretary could tell exactly how the experiments had fared that day.

"Never mind that," Gregor said, managing to keep the growl out of his voice. "I need some good news today. What of the intelligence reports?"

"There is much to report, your Grace," the secretary replied as he opened up the hefty book that he kept under his arm.

True to his name, Albinus sported a mane of hair so white it practically glowed. It contrasted sharply with his black robes, and seemed to leave his thin face his least memorable aspect.

"As you know there has been no full intelligence briefing for some time, as your Grace has no doubt been consumed with much more important matters."

Gregor thought he heard an admonishment in Albinus's tone, but he chose to ignore it.

"Reports from the north stand in our favor," the secretary began looking over the pages of his book. "Stefano and the Raulian forces have won a decisive battle on the Northern Reaches. They laid siege to Tolven as of two days ago and the city seems ready to sue for terms. Raulia should be a coastal kingdom by the end of the week."

Gregor nodded, pleased for the first time that day. He waved for Albinus to continue.

"Food riots have begun again in Iskar. The first two were put down with moderate casualties. A third still rages in the peasant quarter, though the city militia has contained it. The captain has refused to kill any more citizens. He was to meet with the mayor and refused. Now, it seems the Duke has intervened and sources say he comes with an army to do what the militia captain would not. We are paying close attention to that situation.

"Count Saban has acknowledged one of his bastards and threatens to disinherit his other children. Of course, they have filed a complaint with the courts. There are at least two seaside estates in question.

"The Southern Princes are on the verge of war again..."

A sharp laugh from Gregor interrupted the report.

"I didn't realize they ever stopped."

"Of course," Albinus agreed. He flipped a few pages, glancing through them with a disappointed frown.

"Aurek has been abandoned," he continued. "It was the furthest inland city still occupied by Celicia. With the food riots, King Aethus thought their resources stretched too thin."

"Aurek? That's only ten miles in."

"Yes, well it seems two separate food trains have been sacked twice in the last month, and the yield on the local lands have dropped well below sustenance level. With four of their town magicians murdered, as you know..."

Gregor waved him on impatiently.

"Lady Vania died two nights ago. Lord Vania already has announced his intention to begin courting immediately.

"The summer fishing reports show a decreased yield again. It is suspected that boats will begin to go as far as three leagues this fall.

Grain yields are also suspected to be worse. Northern production has suffered the most. The great ducal farms are doing much worse than they report. One informant even claims that they hardly work above subsistence. But such an exaggerated report can hardly be believed."

"Enough of the blather," Gregor said, slamming his mug down and wiping the froth from his mouth. He reached forward and poured a glass of wine for himself, gulping half of it down before the slave could hurry forward.

"Real news," Gregor demanded. "Give me some real news."

"There isn't much of that to report," Albinus said, his tone dropping conspiratorially. He closed the large book he had been reading from and pulled a thin, small volume from inside his robes.

"Well, what is it?"

"Word has come from Bannus," Albinus said with hesitation.

Those words caused Gregor to sit up. For a moment, he forgot the failures of the day.

"He and Elias remain with Squire Montford at Montreux. The two pilgrims are there, as well as the other vagrant that joined them along the way. The harvest will begin soon, reportedly quite successful."

A scream sounded from the dark corners of the chambers, from somewhere behind the door on the far wall, the one that was ominously locked with thick bands of steel. The sound came out like a garbled screen, something half man, half animal. The slaves jerked their heads in the direction of the sound, blood draining from their faces. Albinus and Gregor seemed not to notice.

"What else?" Gregor prompted.

"There is...other news," Albinus said, looking briefly over at the terrified slaves.

"Let's hear it then," the impatience became evident in Gregor's tone.

Albinus glanced over at the slaves again. "It came by way of the...voxis." He emphasized the last word.

The cry came again from the depths of the chamber. It lingered long and agonizing, dying away in gasps. One of the slaves trembled visibly while the other held his eyes tightly shut.

"Fine, go on then!" Gregor growled, dismissing the slaves.

Relieved, they hurried from the chamber. When Gregor and Albinus were alone the secretary opened the thin book in his hand.

"Interesting developments concerning Elias. Bannus was able to observe a conversation between Elias and the stranger named Thoran who began traveling with them after they left Hiram's Well. According to Bannus, this Thoran claims to be in possession of real seeds."

"What does he mean by that?" Gregor asked.

"The claim is that the seeds have been untouched by magic," Albinus clarified. "The kind of seeds used from before the application of magic in agriculture."

Gregor felt his heart quicken. Excitement seeped through his body.

"Impossible," Gregor said out loud. "No seed could've stayed viable that long, and no one has been using the original strains for decades."

"I thought the very same thing," Albinus agreed. "Apparently, the genuineness was confirmed by Elias. He didn't believe it either until he touched them."

Gregor leapt out of his seat and began to pace the dark workshop. The energy that had gripped him would not permit him to be still. This was exactly what Gregor needed.

"Go on," he prompted, his mind racing with possibilities.

"This Thoran then claimed that the seeds were given to him by Elias himself, which of course Elias didn't remember. He claims that the seeds were supposed to be some kind of clue. Thoran said that Elias was to take them and find a tamarisk tree, and there they would find other seeds and..."

Albinus paused, hesitant to finish the thought.

"And what?"

"If Elias were to find the tree he would uncover, or rediscover, the key to ending the Blight."

The pacing stopped abruptly as if Gregor had stepped into a wall. He looked up at Albinus in disbelief.

"It's what we've suspected for a while," Albinus said, answering Gregor's unspoken skepticism.

Gregor nodded. "Yes, but this is all more incredible than we thought possible. If Elias instructed this Thoran to find him, give him seeds, then tell him about this tree, then it sounds as if..."

The thought trailed off of Gregor's lips. It was too bizarre to consider.

"Then Elias knew he would be losing his memory," Albinus finished.

The chair creaked as Gregor dropped into it again. He put his head down, gripping the temples with both hands.

For years he had tried to figure out what Elias had done. It seemed impossible then, and impossible still now. He had searched for those memories. The inquisitors had searched. Every power of magic had been employed to no avail. He had researched and read every book on memory and magic associated with it. He had even consulted known practitioners of forbidden magic. The memories were gone. Even more, a part of his mind was gone.

But this was worse. If what Albinus reported were true, then not only did Elias cause the memory loss, he anticipated it happening. That Elias was responsible Gregor long knew to be true. It had to be a magic he was unaware of, forbidden perhaps. It could even be a magic that Elias himself had discovered. Who knew what Elias was capable of. That kind of potential haunted Gregor's nightmares.

"What do we know about this Thoran?" Gregor asked, his mind going into many directions at once.

"Nothing," Albinus shrugged. "He's not associated with any of the other Enclaves, nor on the list of known rebels."

"He could be using an alias," Gregor got up from the chair and paced again. "We need to find out who he is. I want every available agent on this. No, make that all of the agents."

"All of them?" Albinus asked in horror.

"Nothing else matters," Gregor said, spinning on his secretary. "This is our top intelligence priority right now. Do you understand? I don't care who is marrying who or what these idiot dukes are up to. This is of prime importance. I want to know who this Thoran is. Get his description out to our people. Start asking around in...what was that place? Hiram's Well. Find out everything you can about him. Anyone not looking into Thoran will be looking for this tamarisk tree."

"Understood, my Lord."

"Good. Tell Bannus to keep observing for now. Don't let those seeds, or Elias, out of his reach. If Thoran leaves with them and without Elias, tell Bannus to kill him and take the seeds. As long as the two of them, and the seeds are together, just observe until further instructions."

Leaning back in his chair Gregor tried to bring order to his thoughts. It had been a shock of news and mostly unexpected. But Gregor always believed that as long as your information was good and you had some time to plan, then you could always bend it to your advantage. He had no doubt this time it would be true again.

Information was treasure, and today he had been delivered a gem.

He looked up and saw Albinus still rooted in the same spot.

"What are you waiting for?" he asked.

Albinus coughed. "There's more, your Grace."

"Go ahead."

"Well... It seems this Thoran was in communication with another magi that night. They may have been working together on this."

"And..." Gregor prompted, waiting for the boulder of another revelation to drop.

"Eustace Vanni, of Laimark."

Gregor sighed and nodded his head. It wasn't as bad as he feared. Eustace had been considered a person of suspicion once, and later taken off the list.

"Is he a part of the Restoration?" Gregor asked.

"I think we should at least list him as a person of suspicion."

"Very well," Gregor decided. "We will decide what to do with him later. For now, we watch this Thoran and look for an opportunity to get the seeds.

"Oh, and contact Prince Stefano. Tell him I need a company of men and his best commander. It's time for him to repay a debt."

Chapter Nineteen
The Harvest

True to predictions, Barbadios was more intelligible by day. The difference was so stark Elias couldn't help but marvel. He saw almost no semblance to the muttering fool who wandered the palace at night.

The Squire insisted everyone gather at the temple after breakfast. Elias had declared the night before that the corn was ready.

"We must do all things properly," Montford had insisted, his eyes aglow with excitement. "The harvest must begin as it should. We must thank Gaia for the success."

The sudden show of piety startled Elias. He knew Montford to be an eclectic man, and had known about his devotion. Still, when it showed like that it surprised him. He bit back the retort on the tip of his tongue, that it was he who had been sweating in the heat and the dust these past weeks, not Gaia.

He said nothing until later that night. Their evening chessboard lay forgotten and half played. Montford had indulged a glass of rare bourbon for them in celebration, but promised to hold back. Both men leaned back in their chairs, enjoying the night and the cool air on the balcony.

"So, you really do believe in all this stuff about the gods?" Elias finally asked, trying to keep the ridicule out of his voice.

The Squire arched an eyebrow at the magi. "You don't?" he asked in return.

"As long as I don't think about it I do," Elias said with a shrug. "They tell us there are gods. I guess people have always believed in them. The idea is always there, in the back of my mind. But then when I think about it, it all seems ridiculous. Never seen a god, never encountered one. I don't know. Maybe it's all made up."

"Why were the gods invented in the first place, then?" Montford asked. "If they aren't real, why even dream up the idea?"

"Ignorance," Elias offered. "Or maybe some power-play. You know, the temples used to be quite influential. Before magic, they had all the explanations for how things worked, wielded all sorts of power. Maybe that's why people invented the gods, to keep others in order, legitimize the rule of kings and princes, that sort of thing."

The Squire leaned forward and stared intently at Elias. He hovered so close the magi could smell the oak scents of bourbon on his breath. In such moments, the intelligence in Montford's eyes blazed with something bordering on ferocity.

"So what you're saying," he began. "Is that there was a time when no one believed in gods, then a person or persons stood up and said, there are invisible creatures out there who rule the world, and they speak to me. They have put me in charge and expect us to worship them. Now, you have to do what I say no matter how idiotic it may sound. Is that what you are suggesting?"

"When you say it like that it sounds ridiculous."

"Then how was it?"

"I don't know," Elias said, feeling defensive for reasons he could not guess. "I'm just saying the idea sounds incredible sometimes. Is that why you believe in the gods? Because their invention is too far-fetched to conceive of happening?"

"That's not why I believe," the Squire answered, leaning back in his chair. "Just pointing out that either the gods really do exist, or people once were so stupid and gullible that they would fall for anything."

"Then why do you believe?" Elias asked.

As he stared into the night, the Squire's face took on a distant and wistful look.

"That's not a conversation for this night," he said. "Ask me again after the harvest."

* * *

So harvest day found them kneeling on the stone floor of the circular temple. All but the guards were present, gathered in the dim, morning light. The pillars holding up the dome cast long shadows from the rising sun. Only natural light entered the holy space, fire being forbidden in the temples of Gaia.

Barbadios, dressed in long, green robes recited the rites of harvest. Circling the apple tree that stood in the middle of the temple, he spoke first the ancient words of the Vascan Rite, and then turned to address the kneeling congregation.

"For this abundance, we give you thanks," the priest intoned.

"Gaia, we thank thee," the congregation responded together.

"For the life that awakens our eyes."

"Gaia we thank thee."

"For the breath of our lungs."

"Gaia we thank thee."

"For the generations of our loins."

"Gaia we thank thee."

"For seedtime and harvest."

"Gaia we thank thee."

"For fields and flocks."

"Gaia we thank thee."

The words fell out half-mumbled from Elias's mouth. His attention stood riveted upon the apple tree, full of white blossoms. It couldn't help but remind him of his conversation with Thoran. The seeds, the tamarisk tree, the knowledge of the world's restoration, the fact that they had known each other before, that Elias had even planned for his own memory loss – all these brought back the distant rumblings of thunder, the feel of rain, and the taste of blood in his mouth.

He turned from the apple tree to shake the thoughts away. Instead, his eyes met Thoran's. His gaze no longer seemed smug. Now, there was accusation in his eyes, and an anger that bordered on hatred.

Elias turned his attention back to Barbadios. The old priest had opened the barrel of ceveris and dipped his hands into the black liquid. Lifting his hands to his mouth he drank. Once again, he dipped into the barrel, this time sprinkling the liquid along the roots of the tree.

"For this harvest, we thank thee, Gaia, most generous and giving of all the Children of Heaven. From your bosom we are fed."

Montford followed the priest. He too drank from the barrel, then sprinkled another handful along the roots of the tree, mumbling something Elias could not hear. The other members of the congregation stood and took their turn at the drink offering. He watched Kyrie and Silas make their obligations, the boy reaching out to touch the tree. Anton lingered after his offering, admiring the perfect blossoms he had most likely formed. Thoran watched the ale drip from his fingers before absently sprinkling some along the roots of the tree.

After most of the people had taken their turn, Elias figured he had to do the same as well. Walking uncertainly up to the center of the temple he dipped his hand into the barrel. The ceveris tasted rich and malty, combined with the sourness of the live yeast necessary to make the drink holy, a living thing to the goddess who gave life. The next handful Elias sprinkled along the roots.

"Well, I guess we should thank you," Elias said, too quiet to be heard by any one else. "And if you want to tell me how much beer it would take to bring the whole land back to life I would be happy to make it."

He looked up at the sky as he spoke. The fading stars of night peering through the circular opening of the dome. A thought struck him as he turned back to his seat that sent a jolt of fear through his body. If there were gods up there, he thought to himself, there was a good chance that they really didn't like people at all. Given the present situation, this seemed more likely than he wanted to consider.

* * *

Everyone participated in the harvest. The guards were scaled down to the bare minimum, and the rest were put to work in the fields. As one was cleared, those guards joined the harvest in the next field. Wagons were piled with ears of corn and pushed into the walled gardens where even fewer guards would be able to efficiently watch over them.

Elias couldn't remember working so hard in his life. Row after row, he broke off ears of corn and threw them into the wagons, then moved to the next. After each row another one waited. Row upon endless row of corn until Elias thought he would see it for the rest of his life.

That night, he slept deep and dreamless, still dirty from the quick bath he had taken before collapsing into bed. The next day he didn't even bathe before exhaustion overtook him, every muscle in his body more sore than the next.

By the third morning, almost all the corn had been harvested. At first, Elias was thankful he wasn't assigned to the fields that day. But by midmorning, after hours of picking beans Elias longed for the upright work of the cornfields.

That day the Squire let everyone off of work early. Most of the work had been finished, he said, and he wanted everyone rested for the harvest celebration they would have the following day. Exhaustion made everyone glad of the respite, and Elias shuffled off to his bed after a short meal and a splash of cold water.

The extra sleep certainly seemed to help. Spirits were high the next morning as the garden was harvested and the last wagons of corn were pushed in behind the walls already bursting with full carts.

The Squire called all the workers together except for a few guards to meet in the walled courtyard outside the palace. As they entered, the sights of celebration greeted them. Long tables had been laid out, unadorned with food as of yet. White bolts of cloth hung suspended from the palace, stretching out above the courtyard. Servants set the last torches in place while another group pulled vats of white grapes from the wagons. Standing out among the dull, brown dust that made up the courtyard grounds, the place beamed with latent joy.

But none of these things brought the broad smiles to the tired worker's faces. This joy was elicited because the Squire stood next to the long, marble pool that had been the Prince's goldfish pond. Empty ever since Elias had been at Montreux, it now glistened with clear, inviting water.

"Good workers of the Interior Food Commission," the Squire began, emotion rich in his voice. "I call you friends now. Friends, this endeavor has succeeded beyond what I thought possible. I knew it could be good, the data told me it could. For a moment though..."

He stopped and dropped his head. A hand moved up to his mouth to stifle the emotion that threatened to break out. When he looked up, his eyes glistened like the pool behind him.

"For a moment, it looked like it might fail," the Squire managed to continue. "But Gaia is good, and she sent us help. Elias, thank you. Everyone, thank you. This wouldn't have happened without all of you."

The Squire breathed deep, overcome again. He opened his mouth, but nothing came out. A laugh escaped his lips, then he tried again.

"Thirty-six thousand bushels!" he yelled out, abandoning all show of ceremony. "Thirty-six thousand!"

At first, no one could respond. Most knew the initial projections, but few had been made privy to the new estimates since the ossir was discovered.

"Thirty-six thousand!" the Squire cried out again.

A cheer rose up from the workers. People hugged one another, laughing. A few hands reached out and touched Elias. Some of the women even wrapped their arms around him.

"Thirty-six thousand!" the Squire yelled out again with a laugh. "For that, my friends, we will celebrate!"

Then, fully clothed, the Squire dove into the pool. Another cheer rose up and everyone followed, piling into the clear and cool water.

Instantly, the people were lost in the joy of celebration. They splashed and dove, and lay back on the water. Silas pinched his nose and dipped under, laughing as he came up for air again. The men pulled their shirts off, and some of the women followed suit. Kyrie laughed and covered Silas's eyes, though he didn't seem to notice why.

Elias swam to the far end of the pool, as alone as he could get from the splashing celebration. He flipped over on his back, floating, letting the cool water roll over him, seep into him, draw away the incessant heat that burned and burned without respite or mercy.

Above, the clear, blue sky passed by his drifting eyes. Muted sounds of laughter came in through the water. The stillness took over as Elias drew in a breath and held it, until he could feel his heart pounding inside of him. He smiled, not able to remember when he had felt so happy.

* * *

As the sun set, the torches were lit and the feast laid out in the courtyard. All the people of Montreux, bathed and dressed in their finest, came with smiles and light hearts. The Squire had few words this time, only enough to offer the table set before them. There would be no formal meal. All were invited to simply take as they pleased.

Beneath the torchlight they ate their fill. Squash and beans, loaves of warm bread with honey filled ample plates. Slices of tomato, fresh melon, peppers, fruit jams were taken on second helpings. Bottles of young, white wine passed around, filling eager glasses, until the people grew mellow and glassy eyed.

Elias watched one group sing, while another danced clumsily to the impromptu music. The orange torchlight cast a soft glow upon them, enveloping them in intimacy. One of the girls swayed as her head lolled from side to side.

He looked across the courtyard at Kyrie. She and Silas had stepped into the vat of white grapes, the last harvest of the vines. Barefoot, they laughed as they crushed the grapes. Silas jumped, sending a spray of juice up into his own face.

"No jumping," Kyrie chided with a smile. "Step. Just step. You can't rush the grapes."

She lifted the hem of her white skirt, almost nothing more than a shift, exposing her legs up to the thigh. A strap fell off her sun-browned shoulders. Either she didn't notice or she didn't care to lift it back in place.

Elias stared as every high step exposed more of her smooth and tanned legs. He stood transfixed upon her every motion and gesture, each movement an expression of hidden magic, an enchantment only the beautiful possess.

As if feeling his eyes upon her, she looked up and met Elias's gaze. In a rare moment, her look held no contempt. Instead, she stuck her tongue out and turned away from them.

"So this is where the view is the best," Eustace said as he came to stand by Elias.

The magi nodded in the direction of Kyrie. The other strap had fallen off her shoulders now, exposing her back to the men.

"Almost makes up for the waspish personality," Elias said.

"Oh, it more than makes up for it. Actually, it makes her personality pleasant and congenial, almost winsome."

Before Elias could answer an arm fell over his shoulder. A happily inebriated Montford appeared between he and Eustace, an arm draped around each.

"My boys, my boys," he said with a mild slur. "The best magi in the whole land. I swear by heaven and earth it's true. You're the best. You boys made this happen. It was all you."

"No, not at all," Eustace answered for them both. "You put this together. This was your baby. Yours. We just executed."

Montford smiled and turned to Elias as if to confirm what the other said. Elias nodded his agreement.

"It's true," he said.

"Aha! You give me too much honor!" the Squire gushed. "That's what makes you so great. All that talent and willing to share your glory with others.

"We can do great things with this, my boys. Great things. This is just the beginning. Thirty-six thousand bushels. The King will be very happy. We can double the next commission. Make it better. Fix our mistakes. Set up others, have them going constantly. We can fill the interior with farms again. There is no limit! None! We can feed the world! Of course, we can get rich as kings in the process. But oh, think of the good we will do."

The Squire slapped each of their shoulders and stumbled off.

"My boys! My boys!" he cried out as he made his way to the food table.

"You know it won't work," Eustace said as soon as the Squire was out of earshot. "You have to know that."

"It worked this time," Elias pointed out.

Eustace barked out a short laugh. "It took a miracle to pull it off. If you hadn't wandered up here I would've had sixteen thousand shriveled bushels of corn probably not even suitable for animal feed."

"Yeah, but with the right magicians and the planning more realistic..."

"Why are you fooling yourself?" Eustace interrupted. "How much longer are you going to do that?"

The comment stabbed into Elias, chilling his warm mood. Weighty thoughts of the world in destruction and the cries of starving anguish wrapped their leaden chains around Elias's thoughts. He gulped down the taut, young wine in hopes of washing them away.

"What choice do we have?" Elias asked in return. "The Squire has something good going here. Better than anything else I've seen. At least he's trying."

"He's not the only one trying," Eustace said through gritted teeth. "He's just the only one you seem to want to help. Others are trying too. Trying to fix the problem. Not just trying to stall the inevitable."

"What are you getting at?" Elias asked, though he knew exactly what Eustace meant.

"I know about the tree," Eustace said.

"I don't know what Thoran told you. But I'm not your savior."

"Before you lost your memory..." Eustace began.

Elias shot his hand up to stop him. "Stop it," he said. "I don't want to hear it."

"You don't want to hear what I have to say?"

"I don't care," Elias snapped. "It doesn't matter. Whatever it is, it doesn't matter. Besides, you're ruining the party."

Elias stormed off in search of something to bring his pleasant mood back.

"You used to care," Eustace called his retreating figure. "You still do. Down deep in there, somewhere, I know you still do. You have to let yourself be human again."

The words piled on him even as Elias tried to shrug them off. He didn't care, he told himself. He didn't want to care. Why was it so damn difficult to just let things go? Just let the world rot itself like it was doing?

The sound of splashing water sounded in the dark part of the courtyard where Elias fumed. Kyrie sat by the pool. With her white skirt pulled up, she gently washed her legs. Scooping up handfuls of water she drew them up their length, cleaning off the crushed grape and juice. She seemed to luxuriate in the motion, running her hand slowly, almost sensually, down her outstretched legs and up back to the thigh.

How different she was from him in all ways. Her ceaseless energy compared to his chronic apathy. Her passion and his malaise. Her conviction and his doubt.

"This is the second time tonight I've caught you staring at me," Kyrie said, not looking up from the attention she lavished upon herself.

Elias moved beside her and squatted down to look her in the eyes. The fire that blazed there was muted then, bearing a softness in their green depths. Elias was not foolish enough to believe it had been put away far.

"How do you do it?" he asked.

"Do what?"

"How do you care all the time? How do you muster the energy to fight day after day? It's a pointless battle. How do you keep doing it?"

Kyrie must have noted something different in his tone, for she did not appear offended or ready to fight. She leaned forward and rested her arms on her knees.

"How do you not?" she asked in return. "To care is...it's human. It's what we're supposed to do. People are supposed to care. They're supposed to fight for what is right. They're supposed to find a better way to live. They're supposed to stand up to injustice and evil.

"I'm just being human. What I want to know is how you don't care. How do you shut that off when the whole world is dying around you? When people are starving? How do you pretend like everything is okay?"

"I don't think everything is okay," Elias hotly responded. "I don't pretend like it's okay. I just... I don't know what to do. I don't know what can be done."

Kyrie leaned forward even further. A hand reached out and touched his cheek. The gesture was soft, though without sensuality. It was the touch of a mother.

"You have to care first," she said. "Once you care, then you will know what to do."

"How do I care?" he asked with sincerity. Sadness overwhelmed him as he spoke the words, afraid of their truth. "How do I learn to care?"

"I can't teach you that," Kyrie said, then stood up and left him.

For a moment, he didn't notice she was gone. Dark thoughts enveloped him in a morbid silence. Perhaps he was unable to feel. Perhaps whatever memories he lost took his humanity as well.

Then, he thought of what Eustace had said to him, that he didn't allow himself to care. He knew this was closer to the truth. It wasn't that he was unable to care. He didn't want to care.

"Hey Elias," a small voice called out.

Silas hurried over to where Elias still squatted by the pool. He grinned with excitement and pulled out something wrapped in cloth.

"Look at this," he said, pulling the cloth aside revealing the ossir.

"Where did you get that?" Elias asked.

"Eustace gave it to me. One of the magi was playing with it, making the corn pop. It was funny. It looked like little pieces of cloud."

"Why did he give it to you?"

"He told me to put it away."

"Well you better put it away," Elias said, looking over the boy's shoulder for Kyrie. "You know how mad your mother would be if she saw you with that?"

The boy didn't seem to hear a word Elias said. He stared transfixed at the clear, blue crystal. A tentative finger reached out to touch it.

"Why does it do this when I touch it?" Silas asked.

Just under his finger, where his skin made contact with the blue stone, a pulse of light glowed. It was dim, even in the dark. But the response from the ossir was unmistakable. Silas lifted his finger and the glow disappeared. He replaced the finger and the point of light returned. He slid his finger over the ossir and the light followed beneath.

"Am I doing magic?" he asked, excitement rich in his voice.

Elias didn't answer, dared not answer. The boy wasn't performing magic, but the fact that the ossir responded to his touch was a clear sign that he was able. Kyrie would be furious if she found out.

"Seriously, put it down," Elias chided. "Your mother's going to kill you if she sees. And me too."

"Make it light up," Silas said. "Like you do in the fields. Make it full of blue light."

"If I do it will you put it down?"

Silas nodded and the grin spread across his face. That sort of enthusiasm Elias found impossible to resist.

"Promise?"

"Promise."

The infectious smile spread to Elias's face as well as he reached for his lumen. Without laying his hands on the instrument he pushed his lumen into the ossir and it responded with the glow, much stronger than the one created by Silas's touch. It flared and filled the entire stone.

The grin on Silas' face grew even bigger. He held the glowing stone up as if wielding it. Light bathed his face, complementing the wonder that shone from it.

With his lumen touching the ossir, Elias felt his senses come alive, multiply with the power. He felt every living thing in the courtyard, the glow of life among the happy people, concentrated and pure. Beyond the courtyard he could feel the emptiness of the wasted land beyond, devoid of the life that had once thrived there. He could even feel the life in the walled garden beyond. The concentrated hum of the harvest loomed the largest in his heightened sense. But he felt the smaller concentrations of life there as well, from the steady pulse of the vines to the hum of the bees that stirred in their hives.

"Silas!" Kyrie cried out, anger and fear all at once in her voice.

Elias felt his heart drop as he saw Kyrie, still with shock and horror, glaring at them. All the muted passion of the earlier evening blazed to full fire now. Silas jumped at the sound of his mother's voice.

"What are you doing?!" Kyrie screamed. "Put that damn thing down!"

"Mom, I'm not doing anything wrong," the boy complained. "It's beautiful. Just look at it."

"It's of the things that killed your father!" she screamed. "How could you touch it? It's the tool of murder!"

"Just give it to me, Silas," Elias said, stretching his hand out for the ossir.

"You!" Kyrie whirled on the magi. "How dare you?! How dare you infect my son with your filth?!"

"He already had it," Elias argued, stepping back from Kyrie's fury. The ossir still glowed, bathing her in harsh, blue light.

"I don't care! You don't touch him! Stay away from my son! I will not let you infect him!"

Elias brought his hands up in defense when he felt a stab through his lumen. Still attached to the ossir, his magical sense blazed with the added power. Alarm screamed out. Wrongness flowed through the blue stone, snaking into Elias. It was like a warning being cried out from a great distance.

"Stop!" he yelled to Kyrie.

"I will not stop!" she yelled back, unaware of his intent. "I will not stop until you and all your kind rot in the barrows of history!"

The warning increased in intensity. A thousand dim, but insistent cries pulled at him. Needle points pierced his heightened sense. But it all fell and jumbled in a mass of confusion. Voice after voice cried out, one on top of another, cascading and falling and hammering at his head all at once. He closed his eyes and put his head down, trying to concentrate and shut out the fury of Kyrie as the buzz of noise continued to bear down on him.

"I will not stop!" he heard her continue to scream at him. "Listen to me! I will not stop!"

It struck him all at once, and Elias felt his blood go cold.

"Move!" he yelled at Kyrie, pushing her aside.

Elias ran towards the rest of the party, waving his arms in desperate warning.

"Montford! Montford!" he yelled out.

The Squire turned with bleary eyes towards the magi. The mellow features of his face hardened into sudden wariness.

"The bees!" Elias screamed. "The bees are swarming! We're under attack!"

Elias jabbed a finger to the north, where the harvest lay behind the walled gardens. Every head turned to look.

It was then that they saw the flickering, orange glow against the sky.

Chapter Twenty
The Battle of the Garden

The Third Division of the Commission Guards ran in front of Elias and the others as they all raced toward the gardens. Montford flew with deceptive speed, carried by desperation and fear. Bannus and Thoran quickly outpaced the magi and Montford, coming in on the heels of the guard. Behind Elias, it sounded as if the entire Commission ran to the alarm.

Elias cursed his drunkenness as they drew near. The orange flames rose higher into the night as they ran. He tried to reach out with his lumen. He could feel the flames raging, feel them as if they flicked inside of him, though he could exert no power over them. Every drop of alcohol he had consumed that night battled against his own will, slid control of his lumen away each time he tried to take hold of it.

The walls of the garden rose up as they approached, blocking out the orange light. A boom sounded as the guard crashed into the doors. The wooden gate buckled but did not give.

Montford cried out as soon as he perceived the doors were still locked.

"What the hell is going on?" he screamed out to no one in particular. He pushed the guards out of the way and threw himself futilely against the heavy, wooden gates.

"Open, damn you!" he screamed as he pounded the doors. "Open!"

Elias shouldered through the quickly gathering crowd and pushed himself beside the Squire. Reaching out his hand he closed his eyes and touched the door. Even intoxicated, what he needed to do here he could manage half conscious.

Deep into the door he thrust his lumen. Then, into the fabric of the wood itself. He pulled at the strands and fibers of wood. His lumen slipped away. He breathed deep and grasped again, forcing himself to slow down even as he felt the fire grow on the other side of the door.

Slowly, he pulled at the strands of the wood until he found what he was looking for – a dark energy that loomed deep inside every living thing. He dove into it, stirred it, woke it up. The dark energy flowed out. Elias took hold of it. No subtlety or control was needed. He let go and pushed the darkness through the wood, releasing all the pockets of decay within.

The door crackled like the sound of parchment being crunched into a ball. It shuddered as the soldiers watched the wood grow dark and flakes peel away. A large pop sounded as a fissure appeared in the door, rending a crack from the top corner to the bottom. Long, gaping fissures grew across the surface. One of the guards, perceiving what Elias had done, kicked the door, breaking it open into a pile of rotten splinters.

The soldiers burst in, pushing the unexhausted Elias to the ground. The magi landed on his hands and knees, struggling to catch his breath. A pair of hands took hold of his shoulders and lifted him up as others pushed past. Elias turned his head to see Thoran gently holding him.

"Go," he said, pushing the man away. "Help the others."

Thoran nodded and released Elias. The magi swayed as a wave of dizziness took over, but managed to keep his feet. The rest of the body streamed past, heading to the far end of the garden where a great blaze lit up the night in a fury of flame.

Elias stumbled forward as his head cleared, not believing what he saw. At first there was only fire, burning on the far side by the vineyards, where the piles of wagons heavy with corn lay packed tightly together. As he neared, he saw dark shapes outlined against the flame. Sounds came roaring in over the fire, sounds of dozens of human cries, some in agony, some in joy. A shadow lifted its arms in triumph, spread wide against the fire. It crumbled to the ground as another shadow, bearing a sword slashed into it.

Sounds of fighting faded into his ears as Elias drew closer. A wave of weakness hit him, and he fell against one of the carts. Smells of fresh corn hit his nostrils, mixing with the tang of smoke that swirled in the night air.

"Push back the carts!" he heard the Squire yell over the tumult. "The carts! Push the carts away!"

Dark shadows set into motion. They converged on the carts pushing them away from the fire. They came toward Elias, women pushing past, eyes wide with fear as Elias stumbled forward.

A billow of smoke came down over his face, obscuring what limited vision he had. He coughed as acrid smoke forced its way into his lungs and stung his eyes to tears. Sounds of women screaming filled the air around him. Just beneath the screams, echoes of war trailed by. Men howled in agony and glee. Steel rang out. And the fire raged, roaring above all the other sounds of chaos.

Chaos. It swirled around him like the rolls of dark smoke. It tore at his lumen, screaming at him from a thousand directions at once, striking deeper than any human voice.

Chaos. Elias needed to make some sort of order out of it. He gripped the edge of a cart, pulling himself on top. Walking over the piles of corn stacked tightly together, he made his way through the smoke. Another cloud blew into his face. He stopped to retch, and covered his mouth with the hem of his sleeve. He knelt down to crawl over the corn, towards the raging fire and swirls of human chaos.

At the edge of the carts a successful breach had been made between them and the corn that was being consumed by flame. Elias stopped and rose unsteadily to his feet. Horror washed over him as his jaw dropped open and his knees weakened again, threatening to drop him back down.

Before him, the fire raged. Carts piled high, filled with ripe corn, fed the blaze. Dark figures tore at the vineyards, ripping up the thick vines and tossing them on the fire. More pulled at the unburned carts full of corn and led them to the flames.

Elias couldn't make sense of what he saw. The dark shapes that streaked by were unfamiliar. Men and women, dressed in robes of black ran past him, grabbing, tearing as they howled, laying hold of anything they could to throw up on the flames. A guard hacked at one of the figures as it ran by. He collapsed soundlessly as the sword rose and fell in quick succession. Three more burst out of the dark and leapt upon the guard, tearing him to the ground.

Out in front of the carts another guard held off five of the black clad figures. He swung his sword in wide arcs, desperately trying to hold them off.

Spots of resistance were meager and few. For every sword that worked to stem the flow of madness, there seemed to be ten of the robed madmen howling and tearing up, and consigning to the flames.

A voice rose up chanting out above the sound of fire. The words sounded familiar and foreign all at once. Elias turned to the sound and his horror doubled.

Beside the fire, atop an overturned cart, Barbadios stood with his arms wide. His robes had been pulled down to his waist, revealing a wasted torso. Thin arms reached out, stretching as far as they could go. The marks of madness stood out on the strained face as the priest howled undecipherable words. They crackled in the night air, shrill as the scream of the zealot. The entire right side of his body and face swelled red and angry from the heat. Blisters bubbled up and burst on his skin, the pus sizzling in the heat. Barbadios raged on without noticing.

Elias looked down at the carving on the priest's ragged chest. A crescent moon bled and ran fresh streams of crimson. Understanding pounded into Elias with renewed terror.

The Prophets of Thanatos.

Shaking himself out of shock, Elias reached for his lumen. He thrust it into the fire, seeking to draw all the force and energy from it.

Something pushed at him. Another force filling the fire fought back his touch. Elias pushed harder. The fire resisted, immune to the touch of his lumen. Another force struck his, pushing him out of the fire completely.

"There's other magi there!" a voice called out. Elias turned to see Eustace and the three younger magi standing by the carts.

"There's magi, feeding the fire!" he said, discerning what Elias had tried to do.

"You can't push through?!" Elias asked, already knowing the answer.

Eustace shook his head, tapping his temple. He was as drunk as Elias, though neither man could feel the effect. Both only felt the energy of fear raging through their veins.

Through the flames, Elias could see three of the black robed figures standing still in concentration. The pulse of magic flowed out of them, their power feeding the flames and keeping out the weakened strength of the other magi.

"Form up!" Lieutenant Omar screamed as he ran into the fray.

The First Division poured into the garden, adding their strength to the desperate struggle.

The reinforcements brought courage to the defenders. Responding to command, they fought with renewed energy, hacking out of the closing circle of attackers and joining the freshly arrived soldiers. They closed in together in a tight half circle keeping away fresh attacks from the unburned corn.

"Can you keep the fire at bay?" Elias yelled out to Eustace. "Just keep it from spreading."

"How long?" Eustace yelled back.

"Hopefully just a few minutes!"

"What are you going to do?"

"Sober up," Elias said as he closed his eyes and reached again for his lumen.

Searching through his own body he could easily see the effects of the wine. All the energy within him slogged through it, mired in the intoxicating effects. All aspects of his body and mind slowed, especially the movement of his lumen.

Slowly, deliberately, ignoring the cries of the battle around him and the heat of the nearby fire, Elias found the alcohol circulating through his blood, soaking into his organs. He pulled at it, separated it, commanded his cells to push it out.

The process picked up speed as Elias focused. He could feel his mind clear, strength return to his muscles. Cold sensations went through him as the wine pulled out of his cells.

Nausea rose up as Elias's body did in minutes what normally took hours. He felt new effects on his beleaguered system. It would extract a price for speed.

The sick feeling began deep in his bowels as the forced out alcohol took the only route it could. Cold sweat broke out over his entire body, mingled with hot sweat. His limbs trembled, suddenly cold despite the blazing fire nearby. The nausea rose up stronger, infiltrated the pit of his stomach, rising up bile and rejected fluid.

Elias opened his eyes, losing control of his lumen. He opened his mouth and retched, falling onto his knees. Vomit spewed from his mouth, spilling half digested food and acid and wine over the corn and through his fingers. He heaved again, his mouth and nose burning as he threw up more.

Just as quickly as it began, it was over. The nausea dissipated and his limbs eased their tremble. Sounds of harried battle came ringing back into his ears. A honeybee buzzed in front of his eyes, lost in the churn of chaos.

Elias wiped his mouth and stood on shaky feet. The soldiers had tightened their line of defense around the corn. The black robed attackers still raged over the garden, but they began to gather at the line of soldiers, ready for a surge. Elias could see the guards were too few. Even with the reinforcements, they would be overwhelmed. The garden would be lost and all that they worked for destroyed in madness and fire.

"Elias!" someone screamed nearby.

Silas ran into the light, just behind the line of soldiers. His mother reached for him, fear stretching her features in contortions of terror.

"Silas!" she yelled, taking hold of his shirt.

"Elias!" Silas cried out again.

The boy broke out of his mother's hold and surged toward Elias.

He thrust his hand out and a gleam of blue reflected off the firelight, arcing toward the magi.

Elias threw out his hand and caught the ossir as it fell towards him. He reached for his lumen and the stone exploded in blue light.

This time, when he pushed into the fire, there was no resistance. Elias thrust away the other presence – all of them – with a mighty sweep of power. The magi on the far side of the fire recoiled and cried out as their own lumen was forcefully ejected from the fire. One fell to his knees, clutching the sides of his head.

The fire belonged to Elias.

He could feel the fire intimately, as if it were part of his own body. He knew every flame and spark. He could feel the heat roil through him like thousands of threads, rising and swirling. The threads belonged to him, responded to his touch and thought.

The chaos of the garden faded to a whisper. For Elias, there was only the fire. Men fought below him in a silent struggle, drowned out by the cry and call of the flame.

Taking hold of the threads of flame, Elias didn't try to extinguish the fire. Instead, he drew them around. Thread by thread he pulled them around, flame circling flame, fire rotating around the burning pyre.

Twists appeared in the blaze. One flame licked around in a circle. Then another, instead of forking up, wrapped around the others.

Elias still held the fire. He twisted the threads of heat. More flame circled, stretching around to spiral up, stretching out the whole fire before sending sparks up into the night.

The spirals pulled at each other, gained momentum as Elias held the glowing ossir out in front of him. The fire rose, twisting in a pillar of flame. He stretched the threads up higher, tighter, circling again and again upon itself.

Barbadios was one of the first to notice. Perhaps because he was the closest, or because his entire right side had flared to angry, red blisters. He felt the sudden loss of heat, like cold on his burned skin. Beside him, the fire had withdrawn. No longer did it blaze wild and chaotic. The fire had morphed into a twisting pillar of flame.

The attackers at the back of the crowd stopped next, followed by those who pushed at the front lines. The soldiers dared a quick glance, and found themselves unable to turn away. The women and the other workers froze where they were. Montford went to stand by the Eustace, his mouth agape in wonder. Kyrie pulled at Silas and folded him into her arms. Only a few of the attackers had not stopped to watch, still plundering and pulling at the garden.

Other than them, every eye fixed upon Elias. He stood up on the piles of corn, arms outstretched, holding the ossir aloft, bathed in its blinding light.

Before him, a giant pillar of fire rose up, twisting like a maelstrom of flame. Heat sucked up from the garden in an arid wind, pulling at the people who watched in amazement.

Barbadios broke out of the spell. Pointing a bony finger at the torrent of twisting fire, he spat ancient curses.

"In tolles met collum enscipe! Grim sollus! Et vonosce riscum majeste Thanatos! Thanatos majeste!" The old priest hurled the forgotten tongue at the fire.

The fire answered.

A burst from the pillar sent a ball of fire at the priest. With bare arms still outstretched, he exploded in flame. His screams rose up, imprecations unintelligible. The outstretched hands reached to the sky. His burning body sank to its knees, skin bubbling to black and melting off the bone. Still flaming, the bare skeleton toppled and shattered charring pieces of bone.

The crowd still watched, transfixed, as three more balls of fire shot out from the pillar, each one striking a Magi of Thanatos. They burned as quickly as Barbadios. Screams rose up from their immolation, arms flailing helplessly.

Another ball of fire shot out, striking another of the black clad figures. Then, two more hissed through the air, finding their mark.

Realization dawned on the attackers, understanding that the fire had somehow turned against them. Some began to peel off and run. Balls of fire flew out and struck them down. One after another, the flaming missiles flew out of the pillar, destroying a figure in black. They followed in quick succession, each one finding a mark. Orange flame streaked across the garden, too fast to follow, too numerous to count.

Screams of fighting gave way to screams of pain. Burning bodies writhed for only seconds before falling still, even as the fire ate them up. Everywhere bodies burned, like watch fires on a cold night. The smoke of burning flesh rolled out of the flame, it's awful stench drawing the soldiers back.

Still, Elias stood, wrapped in the ecstasy of his magic. The pillar grew higher and higher, sending showers of bright spark into the sky.

The crowd backed away, afraid of the living fire and the wide eyes and rictus grin of the magi, cast in eerie, blue light.

Distantly, Elias heard someone call his name. But the flames drowned it out and pushed it aside. He was the fire. It's roar was his. It's heat was his.

He heard his name again. Hands took hold of his shoulders. A face loomed in front of his eyes.

In the blue light, even with eyes wide in fear, she was still beautiful. She mouthed his name but Elias heard nothing. A hand reached out and touched his cheek.

"Elias, it's over," he heard Kyrie tell him.

With a final burst, the fire roared into a ball and flew up into the night sky. Tongues of fire spread out then crackled away into darkness.

The light of the ossir winked out just as the fire died. The blue stone rolled from the magi's hand and he collapsed onto the piles of corn.

Chapter Twenty-One

Darkness, vivid and incorporeal wrapped around him. He sat in a place of no horizon, of no feature. No landmarks or trees or hills, or even sand.

There was only dark. Quiet and total night.

He sat in a cage, suspended above the darkness. There was no storm this time. No rain. No blood. No thunder.

His head was bowed, hands folded in his lap. The cage swayed by a dark wind. Slow. Methodical.

The quiet felt welcome, kind. The darkness folded over him as a mercy. Relief from the sensation.

He didn't want to feel. Not now. He wanted quiet. And dark.

He welcomed the oblivion. He thanked it. And sat, with hands folded and head bowed.

Chapter Twenty-Two
The Morning After

The taste of ash lingered thick as Elias slowly came back to consciousness. A harsh glare of late morning light struck him, filling his head with pain. A groan came out involuntarily as he tried to roll over. Weakness stifled his every move.

It took a few tries to collect the strength, but he managed to heave off the bed. The floor shifted at first, then steadied. Elias held his arms up, and breathed deep, trying to collect his balance.

Memories came irregularly from the night before. The attack, the fire, the ossir – all crept back to his mind. The magic... He shook his head at what he had done. That much power could have burned him out.

The palace halls were quiet as he stepped out of his room. A call brought only echoes in response. He stumbled down to the stairs, tender at first, but feeling better with each step.

By the time he reached the gardens, Elias felt capable, though still weak. He hobbled to the gates, which lay in dry tatters among the sand. Looking at the crumbled door, it felt like it happened a lifetime ago.

The gardens looked worse in daylight. Cartloads of the salvaged corn had been pushed into a protective circle. But the rest of the garden was ravaged, either with marks of fire, or the torn remnants of vines and bushes, or the trash of wanton and pointless destruction.

On the far end, a black mound still smoldered as people moved around, working to clean up the mess. The movements were slow, uninspired, weighed down by exhaustion and the disappointment of loss.

As Elias walked, a woman stopped gathering together a scatter of broken wood. Another man, picking up pieces of a shattered cart, noticed him walking by and also stopped his work. They watched Elias walked by, their expression somber and unreadable.

The further he walked into the garden, the more that reaction followed. As he passed by, people stopped their work to stare at the magi. Eventually, people came in from the further points of the garden, until a row formed on either side of him, creating an aisle of silent, watching faces.

The Squire waited at the far end, next to the smoking pile of embers. He turned to face the magi, and Elias felt a pain deeper than what tortured his body.

All the light that perpetually animated the Squire's face had vanished. The eyes looked haggard and empty, circled with dark rings. The muscles of his face hung slack, adding another twenty years to his appearance. The weight of despair seemed to pull at him, body and soul, as if the act of living had become a burden.

"My friend," the Squire said as Elias approached.

Before the magi could respond, Montford stepped forward and took him into an embrace. Elias wanted to weep, but only weakly returned the gesture, feeling too awkward with all eyes on him.

"We've lost it all," the Squire moaned, his voice almost breaking into a sob. "Oh, Elias, it's all lost."

"How much is left?" Elias asked, pulling out of the Squire's embrace. He gestured over to the many wagons of corn still remaining. "There's still a lot we saved."

"Twenty thousand bushels," the Squire said with a shrug.

"Where does that leave the Commission?"

"Finished," the Squire said, choking back the words.

"Twenty thousand? The Prince should get his money back with that. What with the wine. The preserves."

"It's over, Elias," the Squire said emphatically, gaining control of his voice. "He'll break even. Even I'll break even. But you don't understand, too much was lost. The Montford Cloth, they ripped most of that to shreds. Most of the bushes were destroyed. Fifteen of the Prince's soldiers are dead. But even that is replaceable to him. It's the vines. Elias, most of the vines were destroyed. The Montreux vine might be gone for good. He will not forgive that. No, Elias, the Commission is over. Despite our best efforts, we failed."

Over the course of the morning, Elias was able to piece together what the rest had figured out. Barbadios was a traitor. Either his twilight madness was feigned or a part of his service to Thanatos. He kept in contact with the Prophets that Elias and the others had fled from, and at the most opportune moment, they struck. They dealt out death to the dark god that craved it.

The priest was able to get into the gardens, then open the north gate for the Prophets to stream through. They surprised the guards and slaughtered them. The one that survived the initial attack recounted the swift and rapid nature of the assault. All told, fifteen guards had been killed and seven commission workers. Five had been women.

One of the magi died in the attack. Anton's body was found

skewered through, pinned to the vines of white jasmine. He died with arms outstretched, as if defending the flowers.

Elias walked through the ruins of the garden. Memory of what once was, and thoughts of what would never be, filled his heart with sorrow. Most of the grounds had been cleaned up. But what was left seemed worse than a ravaged garden. Now, it was mostly empty, as barren and desolate as the rest of the world.

He poked a pile of black ash with his foot. By the vaguely human shape, Elias could tell it had been one of the Prophets. Nothing was left of him now but scorched sand, ash and bits of black bone.

Turning from the ash, Elias let his dark thoughts carry him. The world, it seemed, was dying in more ways than one. Why any living person would worship death with such wild devotion defied sense. Or perhaps, it defied sense only in a living world. As theirs faded and wilted and turned to sand and dust, it almost seemed that death made more sense than life.

He walked towards the east of the garden, which had survived somewhat untouched. Most of the trees still stood, though untended they would not last long. Many of the bushes had been ripped up, but they would meet the same fate as the trees. Further up, Elias reached the wall of the garden, where Anton's small collection of flowers had been so lovingly nurtured.

He stared at the flowers, dazzling in their display of color. Anton's words came back to haunt him. Beauty, the young magi had said, was what made life worth living. It reminded people why life was worth fighting for.

The white jasmine that Anton had died upon was in full bloom. Hundreds of the little blossoms covered the vines like dots of snow. Their scent rose up on a hot and dry wind. But the smell of jasmine transformed it to a gentle breeze, mitigating its harshness.

Anton's words made perfect sense now to Elias. Beauty could change the world. Or at least, change how men perceived it. Maybe he was right to fight to keep beauty in the world. Maybe it was even more important to hang on to what was beautiful as the world grew uglier. It could even be, that what was beautiful was more important than what was necessary.

Red streaks among the white flowers caught Elias's attention. He peered closer, noticing how many of the blooms had been spilled with blood. Whether Anton was right or wrong, he believed in it strongly enough to give his own life.

"Could I do the same?" Elias whispered to himself as he reached out to stroke one of the stained flowers. He was afraid to answer that question.

"Doesn't make any sense, does it?" Eustace asked as he drew up beside Elias.

"You were right," Elias said. "This is never going to work. Not with people out there who would do this. Not in a world gone mad. We can't put this world back together."

"It wouldn't have worked anyway," Eustace answered him. "The Prophets just hastened this along. The Commission could've slowed it down. But you're right. We can't fix the world."

Elias nodded, understanding at last. Finally breaking through the shields of apathy, a deep and settled conviction took over where the day before had dwelt a comfortable resignation. If Anton could die to defend a handful of flowers, cannot he, Elias, live to bring hope to a battered and dying world?

"What do I do?" he asked, ready with all sincerity for any answer.

Eustace surprised him by placing in his hands a pouch of seeds. Elias didn't have to ask what they were or how he had gotten them.

"Find the tree," Eustace said.

"How?"

"As much as I hate to tell you this, you might have to trust Thoran. But only as much as you absolutely have to. He seems to be the only one that has any idea what's going on. So, I guess you have to retrace your steps. Go where you went before."

Elias nodded and gripped the bag of seeds. "The last thing I remember," he said. "Was traveling with Lord Mobray. We were just outside Dubres. I could see the mesas in the distance."

"I guess you go to Dubres," Eustace said.

"Will you come with me?" Elias asked.

Eustace shook his head. "There are some things I have to take care of here. Give me a few days and I'll meet you there."

The two men stared at the little flower garden, filled with the blooms of white jasmine. Elias gripped the pouch of seeds, weighing it in his hands as if he were weighing his own destiny. It felt right to finally assume that responsibility, made him feel more complete. Perhaps that was what he had been missing the whole time.

As he turned to leave, Eustace spoke again.

"Take Kyrie with you."

Elias stopped and shook his head. "Why would I do that?"

"She can help," Eustace answered him. "She has contacts we might need. She can help in ways we can't."

"I prefer to do this alone," Elias said.

"You already tried that. Maybe this time, maybe this way, it will work out better."

Elias considered what Eustace proposed. He had little fight in him at the moment, but still didn't want to give in completely to the idea. Then he remembered how she had found food for them at the abandoned post, how much more able she was at enduring the deprivations of the interior. Perhaps she could be of help. Maybe with her things would turn out differently.

"I'll ask her," he agreed. "We'll take it from there."

This time, when Elias left, Eustace watched in silence. He turned back to the flowers, scenes from the night before replaying involuntarily in his mind. The weight of their dilemma, the world's dilemma, seemed so large, and they so small. And all their hopes rested on the broken mind of a single magi who was just beginning to learn how to hope.

Chapter Twenty-Three
Farewells

It was Eustace who convinced Kyrie to go along with Elias. She had initially rebuffed the invitation in a way that left no room for doubt. She would rather dry up in the wasteland, she told Elias, than take a single step with him in paradise.

"Kyrie, you need to go with him," Eustace argued, almost pled with the woman.

He had caught up with her early the next morning. She and Silas were hurrying out the front door of the palace, just as the sun was rising. Early morning light poured through the open door. She hesitated on the threshold, looking out to the dry land that waited for her, past the empty fountain in the courtyard, then again into the dark coolness of the empty palace.

"Kyrie, wait!" Eustace called out, running down the stairs.

"I don't want to go with him," she simply stated when Eustace stood beside her in the doorway. Light from the rising sun cast long shadows of them across the marble floor of the palace foyer.

"I can't stand to be near him," she added.

"You can't hate him that much," Eustace said. "Sometimes I could swear you even like him."

"How could I feel anything for a man who feels nothing himself?" Kyrie asked with a shake of her head. "Besides, I have work to do. I've wasted enough time here pretending things were different."

She turned to leave but Eustace took hold of her arms.

"Kyrie, you can run around raiding food trains and making speeches about inbred nobles or you can really make a difference?"

"How?" she hissed back at him. "How is Elias going to make a difference? He doesn't even care about the world."

"Do you remember that magi I told you about?" Eustace asked, staring intently into her. The soft colors of dawn spread over her face, casting her features in an almost surreal glow. It made Eustace wish he was the one who should travel with her to Dubres.

"The one who could end the Blight?"

"It was Elias," Eustace said. "He was on the verge of figuring it all out. He may have even figured it out."

Understanding dawned on Kyrie's face. Her hand quickly flew up to her mouth.

"His memory," she whispered. "It's there, isn't it? Somewhere in his lost memory. It can't be. Does he have the answer, Eustace? The real answer? Not some cooked up pack of lies from the Enclaves?"

Eustace nodded, releasing his grip on Kyrie's arms. He told her then about Thoran and the seeds, about the tamarisk tree. He explained how Elias had to retrace his steps, shape his memory of those lost years. What he didn't have to say was that the fate of the world depended on it.

"What can I do?" Kyrie asked when Eustace was finished. "This is all about magic. Besides, he has Thoran and Bannus to help him."

"Bannus is a spy for the Enclave," Thoran told her. "And Thoran can't be trusted. Kyrie, Elias needs a friend. He needs someone that is on his side. He needs someone to..." Eustace struggled for the words.

"He needs someone to keep him from getting lost."

"How can I keep him from getting lost?" Kyrie laughed. "He can make it to Dubres without me."

"That's not what I mean," Eustace said. He looked out at the rising sun, so full of promise except for that it rose over a wasted world.

"He needs someone to help him find his way. He's lost now. Kyrie, oh, I wish you could have seen him as he was before. Now, he's just... he's lost. He needs someone to help him, someone to help him find his way again."

By late morning it had been decided. Kyrie and her son stood again in the palace foyer, this time with Elias and Thoran. Eustace and the Squire stood opposite the unlikely group, saying their farewells.

"Where's Bannus?" Eustace asked, noticing the absence of the burly guard.

"Said he had something Gregor wanted him to do," Elias answered with a shrug. "We're not waiting for him. If he wants to find us, then... I guess we'll deal with him then."

A conviction edged Elias's voice that Eustace had not heard in a long time. For a moment, he sounded like his old self. The moment passed quickly as the magi turned to say his goodbyes to the Squire. Defeat crept back into his features, a weariness that seemed incapable of dealing with the burdens of life.

"I wish I had a position for you," the Squire said as he clasped Elias' hands. "I promise, though, it won't take long. You can come with me now. We'll make it to the coast before you know it, and once the King gets over his rage I'm sure he will find a place for you."

Elias looked to Eustace, then felt for the pouch that hung from his belt. The gesture seemed to reassure him of what his purpose was now.

"I have some business of my own," Elias answered. "Long overdue business."

"I will certainly miss you my friend," the Squire said.

He handed Elias a dark, velvet bag. The magi took it and felt what was inside through the cloth. He did not open it.

"Drink sparingly and think of me," Montford told him. "Dream of days when we can drink it freely again."

Elias nodded and put the gift in his pack. They all exchanged a final farewell. All except for Thoran. He stood by the door, pointedly ignored by Montford. Eustace stole him a single glance as the group made their way out of the door. A chill ran through his body when their eyes met. A part of him wanted to throttle the man where he stood. Too much depended on him, though. Too much of their hope was wrapped up in the enigma of who he was. That made Eustace hate him all the more.

Silas' small hand waving goodbye was the last they saw of them. The palace door boomed shut and Montford and Eustace were left in the shade of the foyer. They silently regarded the closed door for a moment, both feeling that Elias' exit was somehow the official end of their project.

"Well, that's that," the Squire said.

He turned to Eustace. "We're leaving within the hour to deliver the corn. Finish up what we have here and meet me in Capecia. I should be there in about five days."

It was the last Eustace ever saw of the Squire.

* * *

As soon as Eustace said his farewells, he hurried to his own quarters. On the way, he grabbed one of the few remaining servants and told her to send Lieutenant Omar to his room immediately.

The lieutenant arrived soon after. The magi had just enough time to grab ink and paper when a soft knock sounded at his door.

"Enter," Eustace said as he found a pen and situated himself at the desk.

He heard Omar enter and come stand beside him. Eustace's hand trembled as he held the quill. It seemed unbelievable what he was about to write. He had waited so long to either write or hear these words, and now that the time had come, he wasn't sure it was even real.

"I need you to take a message for me," Eustace said to Omar. "To Osengar."

"It'll have to wait," Omar sighed. "There's still much to do here, and the Squire expects me to catch up with them by tomorrow afternoon."

"It can't wait," Eustace said, turning to the lieutenant.

Immediately, he regretted what had to be done. The look on Omar's face appeared more haggard than most. Not only had he fought at the garden, but he also stayed up that night to guard while many of the others slept. His face was pale and his eyes bloodshot and weary. Still, more would be asked of him. More had to be asked.

"I'm sorry to ask this of you," he said. He was sincere in every word. "But I must. This is for the Gray Owl. He must receive it as soon as possible. This isn't ordinary intelligence. It's about everything we've worked for."

Omar nodded, a grim expression on his face. By all appearances he seemed to anticipate what lay ahead.

"I'll go see a horse is ready immediately," he replied. He turned to go, even heavier than when he entered.

Alone again, Eustace steadied his hand and began to write out his message. He made it quick and to the point, carefully crafted in the script developed by the other members of the Restoration. Anyone else who looked at it saw nothing but a meaningless series of dots and lines.

Just as he finished, the door opened again and heavy steps approached the desk.

"That was fast," Eustace remarked.

Hardly were the words out of his mouth when a thick hand fell across his neck. Eustace felt himself lifted out of the chair and thrown across the room. Breath violently forced itself out as he made contact with the wall and crumbled to the floor.

Tears swam in his eyes. He opened his mouth to breathe but nothing would come into his lungs. Grasping at the air he flailed his hands for some sort of purchase.

The hands grabbed him again, tightening around his neck. They lifted him from the floor, suspending him in the air.

Eustace pulled in a desperate gasp of air. It came in ragged through the grip on his neck. He pulled at the hands, unyielding as stone.

With the one breath his vision cleared. Eustace looked down at the thick arm holding him. He knew who it was even before he saw the face. Bannus glared up, hateful and triumphant.

"Only one message is going out today," Bannus growled. "This one is from Gregor."

Bannus thrust his sword into Eustace. The magi felt cold steel enter. At first, the sensation was pure and painless. Then, agony exploded in his gut as the blood drained from his body and spilled onto the floor.

"This is what happens to traitors," Bannus snarled, twisting the blade in. "And this is what will happen to your Restoration, one by one. Most of all, this is what will happen to Elias, once we are done with him."

Bannus jerked the sword out and let Eustace fall to the floor. The magi bore all of this in silence. But when the guard stooped down and tore the parchment from his hand, he gave a strangled cry.

"What is this stupid gibberish supposed to be?" Bannus asked, holding the paper. "Never mind. Gregor will figure it out."

The soldier leaned in and leered at the dying Eustace.

"He always figures everything out," he said. "You should've known that by now. Maybe then you would have been on the winning side."

* * *

With a detachment he didn't think possible, Eustace observed how time slowed down when you died. With his quickly fading strength he took hold of his lumen and held onto the energy within him. He could feel the flow of his life failing, slowing down, drop by drop, eking out of his body. And there was something else there too, another energy, cold and dark. This power rose as his life faded.

Eustace thought of home. Images came to him of the warm sun reflecting off the white walls, sparkling off the ocean water as fishing boats drifted by. He heard his family laughing around a table full of bread and dates, olives and the pink wine they were known for. He saw the women of Laimark, so dark and lovely, full of the passion that drove men to wild ecstasy. He saw one in particular, the one whose eyes always made him dizzy and whose voice sent thrills down his spine.

With a poignant ache he remembered his mother. He could feel her soft hands, smell the warm scent of her hair. He remembered how she used to call him, little minnow. Most of all he remembered how she told him, constantly told him, God was always at work in the world.

"He may hide sometimes, but he is always there, working at the fate of the world. We only get glimpses, and we call it destiny. But never forget, little minnow, it is God."

Eustace smiled and thought of the sliver of light that had woken him up those many mornings ago. So much had happened since then. And just as he was beginning to believe destiny might finally be working for good, he found himself laying in a pool of his own blood, barely hanging on to life.

Maybe destiny had one more trick, he thought to himself. Then, he waited. He couldn't tell for how long. All of his power pushed into that one act of holding on to the fading heat of his life.

Finally, footsteps, and a cry from Omar. The lieutenant rushed to Eustace and took him up in his arms.

"No, no," he gasped. "What happened? Who did this to you?"

Yes, Eustace thought. One more trick. At least one more for me.

"The message," he managed to whisper. "You must deliver the message."

"Of course. Of course. Where is it?"

Eustace leaned in and whispered into Omar's ear. Twice he spoke the short message, then pulled back to look into the lieutenant's eyes.

"Can you remember?" he asked.

"I will," Omar said.

Eustace reached out and grabbed the sides of his head and pulled him close to look intently into his eyes. "You must deliver this," he said with his fading strength. "Promise me you will deliver this."

"It will be done," Omar promised.

Peace settled over Eustace. He smiled and leaned back, releasing his lumen. The last heat of his life faded from him as that dark and cold power crept up his limbs.

Omar cried out to Eustace, shook him. He demanded to know who had done this to him.

Eustace couldn't hear him. The sound of ocean waves breaking on the beach was too loud.

Third Interlude
Seeds of Hope and War

All things must grow from seeds. And from seeds all things grow. Every tree, no matter how great, begins as a seed. Every life, in one way or another starts its journey as a seed. A seed is but a body of potential. It is not a thing in itself, but the beginning of a thing. There is no guarantee that at the start, whatever grows, will reach its full potential. It may flounder and die, or it may flourish and become the greatest of all its kind. No one knows, not even the seed itself, what will be, nor what latent power lies within.

Ideas begin with seeds. They start as the hint of a thought, a peek behind the curtain of inspiration. All great philosophies and sciences have begun in such a way.

Movements also have their seeds. A discontent, an injustice, a hungering for freedom, a thirst for greater life – these are the beginnings of revolution. They take root, nourish, grow and bear fruit. From their harvests come the toppling of kings and empires.

So it is with all things. They begin small, vessels of only potential. Then they grow, in hope and war, and come to full blossom and give life or wreak fury upon the land.

Such were the seeds carried by Elias. Not only did he carry the pouch of seeds as they struggled over the wasteland. Within, he carried the potential for wonders of which he was unaware. Kyrie bore the seeds of revolution. Her son fostered a different type, a potential unmatched by any other because of his youth. His was a seed of a new tomorrow. Bannus carried within him a darker seed, one born of murder. Thoran held something altogether mysterious and unknown.

But it was Elias who carried the seeds of hope. He passed over a dune and squinted out over the vast sands that separated him from his goal. A native apathy began to rise up, and like weeds choke out what had just begun to grow in him. Then he remembered a young magi, stretched out upon his flowers, giving his life for something beautiful. And the memory gave nourishment to his hope. He traveled on, undaunted by the miles that lay ahead.

Further west, Squire Montford neared the coast, followed by wagons loaded with corn. Another sort of seed took root in him. Wondering again where his trusted lieutenant had gone, dark roots took hold of his heart. He felt all alone, abandoned even by those who he trusted most. Now, a broken man, in spirit if not in body, the blossoms of his former self began to wither.

Further north, in the dark towers of Anjibar, Gregor, Lord Prefect and most powerful man in the world, began to lay the seeds of war. He wrote letters to all the kings and princes whose ear he held, warning them of something dangerous that had been uncovered. Peter Illich, the Archon of Dubres, was most certainly involved, and considerations should begin at once to move against him. Only to a trusted few did Gregor reveal the true secret – that real seeds had been found.

Like dried wildflowers scattered on the wind, rumor and truth mingled together to plant vagrant ideas in the fertile soil of man's imagination. Word spread, slowly at first, like tiny roots branching out in search of water. Then, as the ideas took hold, it spread faster and faster every day.

Ladies at court whispered to each other that relics of the ancient Evani had been discovered. Fishermen talking over their catch at seaside wharfs spoke of a new seed, developed to end the Blight. In other places, kings received reports of a seed that destroyed the land, while peasants begging for food got wind of a new crop that could feed a whole city on one vine.

Above a cobblers workshop, as men in dark robes gathered at night by firelight, rumors gave way to seeds of death. One man, known in another life as Loren Fulham, believed to be dead by the world, received his own word of the seeds that Elias carried.

"My dark King," one of the robed followers said as he bowed to the shirtless figure nibbling at a raw liver.

"Word has come, dark one, of a magi that carries seeds of pure life. He goes to Dubres, and it is said he will replant the world."

Al-Azuhr smiled, not daunted by this report at all. For just such a tiding was he waiting for.

"My friends," he said, wiping blood from his chin. "I have waited for this sign. The last battle is upon us."

And in the north, within the white towers of Osengar, another seed was about to be planted. A horseman approached the city, flying madly in a cloud of dust. He flew through the open gates, clattering over the cobbled streets. People going about their business had little warning before having to leap out of the way lest the hastening animal bear down on them. A quick look at the horse could tell the animal had been driven hard. Foam flew from its mouth, and blood seeped from its nostrils.

Still, the animal looked better than his rider. Bedraggled and hardly upright, the rider held on to the reigns, guiding the horse to the city center, toward the Enclave of Osengar.

Pulling to a stop in the courtyard, Omar fell from the horse and stumbled forward. A guard tried to apprehend him, but Omar had words that made the guards melt away. These words of authority, and the deathly look on Omar's face brought him deep into the Enclave unopposed.

Iannus Ordan, the Lord Prefect of Osengar jumped when the doors of his study flew open. His secretary came hurrying in with a bedraggled and dust-matted man behind him.

"My lord," he said apologetically. "There is an urgent message."

Iannus looked to the haggard messenger. Through the dust and exhaustion on the man's sunken face, he was astonished to recognize Omar.

"Leave us," Iannus commanded with an impatient wave.

As soon as the doors closed, leaving Omar and Iannus alone, the lieutenant collapsed onto one knee. The Lord Prefect felt seeds of fear growing within him.

"What desperate message is this?" the Prefect asked.

"It's for the Gray Owl, from the Kingfisher."

"How does the Kingfisher fare?" Iannus asked, his voice shaking.

"The Kingfisher is dead," the words choked out of Omar. "Murdered the day he sent me to you."

Fear grew to full dread. If Eustace had been killed, then their entire branch of the Restoration could be at an end.

"What is the message?" the Prefect dared to ask.

It was only one sentence. But in those few words the seeds of fear that had rooted in Iannus were pulled up and in their place, a hope was planted that he had waited five long years to nourish.

"The Sparrowhawk has returned."

www.ingramcontent.com/pod-product-compliance
Lightning Source LLC
Chambersburg PA
CBHW032138270626
47172CB00008B/234